Between Lies And Revenge

Hannah D Sharpe

Cover Illustration © Nat Mack
Distributed by Simon & Schuster

ISBN: 978-1-998076-50-5
Ebook: 978-1-998076-52-9

FIC031010 FICTION / Thrillers / Crime
FIC030000 FICTION / Thrillers / Suspense
FIC044000 FICTION / Women

#BetweenLiesAndRevenge

Follow Rising Action on our socials!
Twitter: @RAPubCollective
Instagram: @risingactionpublishingco
Tiktok: @risingactionpublishingco

To my husband, for always encouraging and believing in me, supporting my endeavors, and never letting me give up, even when I thought everything else in life needed me more.

The women hustling are not the enemy. They are only a vessel, molded and shaped, manipulated and abused, by the man who created MLMs to make money off of someone else's dreams.

Between Lies And Revenge

Before

You may not miss me, but I miss you. Every single day. You were my best friend. My protector. I was supposed to protect you in return. I was supposed to put my love for you first.

Instead, I killed you.

Elle

Sunday, August 28th

People don't come back from the dead. I know that better than most. Death is a theft of life that can't be found, forgotten, or forgiven.

Stolen jewelry, though, can be. For twenty years, I've been determined to find mine and I've refused to forgive or forget.

In all my searching, I didn't expect it to be hidden in plain sight, in a neighborhood skirting an expansive country club across the city from our rental home. I came here after the boxing gym to burn off my pent-up boredom with a reasonably-paced run and strong imagination. The thud of my feet on the pavement creates a rhythmic beat in tune with my plans for all the ways I could steal from these rich-ass people ... if it wouldn't mean breaking a vow.

As I come to an abrupt halt on the sidewalk, I realize I'm no longer imagining.

It's not stealing if it's already mine.

I can't take back what's mine, not here, not with all these impeccably-dressed people milling about, their children yards away at the play area. So many seemingly innocent eyes pretending *not* to watch me, the outsider. Several gazes and glares slam into me as I turn to face the crowd surrounding several tables with gold tablecloths and health products on display. Their expressions are a mix of weariness and dislike—my free running disrupting them from purchasing their optimal health.

Most of my onlookers return to their shopping when I bend over and plant my hands on my knees, gasping for air. I must look like I'm on the verge of a medical emergency, and they would rather pretend that I'm not here than feign concern and help.

Lucky for me, I'm not struggling to breathe due to the run, asthma, or a bee sting.

I bow my head, trying desperately to pull in air, and I close my eyes. Open. Blink, blink, blink. Slowly, I lift my head and look back in the direction of where I saw the brunette, hoping I'm right, and hoping I'm wrong. My gaze roams the crowd until I find her again, at a different table, picking up and examining a large canister of protein powder.

I could be wrong because ...

That emerald and diamond bracelet with the stones interlaced in delicate white and yellow gold ...

Those elegant gold rope earrings, each with a large sapphire in the basket attached to the post ...

That show-stopping ring with tiny pebbles of emeralds surrounding the sapphire setting ...

They all could be replicas.

I've found look alike pieces before, and while I haven't seen anyone with more than one, it's not impossible.

Except ...

The emerald cross dangling from a simple gold chain at the brunette's collarbone—that's not a fake. It doesn't have doppelgangers.

My muscles twitch as I refrain from plowing through the crowd to place the brunette in a choke hold and taking back what's mine when her unconscious body folds to the ground.

Instead, I watch as a woman with dyed blonde hair and sunken cheeks comes to the brunette's side and takes her arm, leaning in to whisper something to her.

"Erin, we'll be back," the brunette calls through the crowd, and sets down the large canister.

Someone in my periphery waves at them as the bottle-blonde and the brunette pivot and head across the unnaturally manicured lawn toward a building tucked under several sprawling trees.

I wait long enough to give them a head start before I set my feet in motion, returning to my jog. I follow the sidewalk around the bend toward the facilities, then push the door open to the women's restroom. It's pristine—nothing like what we commoners have at public parks. Glancing for feet first, I walk past the two occupied stalls, then step inside the one at the end and lock the door, pretending to use the toilet.

"Clara's tired lately. She asked to decrease her hours. I think we'll have to find a new nanny. Maybe someone who's younger, who doesn't have her own family yet," one of them says. The way she speaks is like nails on a chalkboard, all haughty and whining with almost audible eye rolls.

"Oh, that's too bad. Did she say she wanted more family time?" the other woman asks, clearly not too bothered by the bathroom conversation.

"God knows. I didn't ask. But why take the risk of hiring some other nanny with kids," the first says. "Of course, I can't have a nanny that's too attractive, either. I wouldn't want Billy's eyes wandering."

"Billy's so in love with you, I doubt—"

"Please! It only takes one slip. But you're right, Billy *is* obsessed with me."

This woman's a bitch. If it's the brunette, I may strangle her after all, but something tells me it's the blonde who appears to focus on reshaping and changing her body rather than dressing up what she's been given.

There's a noisy flush, and the second woman shouts over it, "You want me to wait?"

"I'll be out in a sec," the first says, not answering the question.

I flush my unused toilet, partly deciding to trust my instincts on which woman the brunette might be, and partly because I want the slowpoke with a superiority complex to stress about how much longer she's in the bathroom compared to others.

The brunette is washing her hands when I step out. I give her a pursed-lip smile as I lean over the sink next to hers, then glance at the bottom of the mirror to examine her. She finishes washing her hands, then stands next to the towel dispenser when she's done drying.

I step away from my sink and take two paper towels before looking her in the eyes.

"Sorry," she says, shuffling a half step away.

"You're fine," I say to her with my warmest smile and nod.

The other woman's toilet flushes, queuing me to make a move.

As the blonde steps out of her stall and heads toward us, I pivot toward the door, then stop in my tracks and turn back.

"Those pieces—your jewelry—are stunning," I say, pointing a finger and moving it in a circle to complement her pairing.

"Thank you," she says, her cheeks growing pink.

The blonde shakes water from her hands and turns around. With her back to the counter, she yanks several towels free and looks between her friend and me. She elevates her left arm to face level and gently pats the two-carat rock on her ring finger, and then her wrist, which sports a glistening tennis bracelet.

"Mrs. Bradley—such an old soul—loves her *antiques*," she says with a chuckle, accenting the last word with her lofty disdain.

The brunette's cheeks morph from pink to fiery red.

"Can I ask, where did you get them?" I address the brunette, making a point to keep my gaze off her friend.

"Excuse me," the blonde says, moving until she's almost between us, then tosses her wadded towels on the counter rather than the trashcan. "Why do you need to know?"

Even an idiot could discern the question as an accusation. I immediately interpret every assumption she's making about me. Some would be correct. I could react in kind, but I need to utilize my pawns wisely to remain in play.

"They're very inspiring," I say, sticking close to the truth. "There are so many jewelry makers these days—so much competition. Only a few craft something so unique."

The brunette opens her mouth but doesn't say anything because the blonde steps between us, demanding my attention and halting any conversation that could have been.

"So what?" the blonde chastises. "Are you one of *those* jewelry makers?"

"Something like that," I say, making sure my tone contrasts hers.

"Steal your ideas off someone else," the blonde says, then grabs the other woman's arm and yanks her toward the door. "Let's go, Olivia."

The brunette gives me a sympathetic look as she passes me. When the door slams between us, I allow the grin that I've been suppressing.

People may not come back from the dead, but the things stolen along with their lives ... that's an entirely different story.

Olivia

Tuesday, September 20th

T he fan in Sarah's office oscillates until a gust comes through the door and hits the side of my face, causing my curls to flutter, again. I wrap my sweater tighter and huff. My boss' need to run a fan at the worst times is a constant reminder of all the things that I can't control, and how I've failed at making something of my own.

This was a dreamy job once. I spent a few years engrossed in my position as Sarah's assistant, finding joy in coordinating conferences and thriving in the organized chaos. It became my world after I'd dropped out of my post-grad program when I couldn't handle being on campus with happy people who hadn't been through terrible things. When Sarah gave me this job fourteen years ago, she saved me.

I wish that the reason I remain in this position was out of loyalty to her or because of the fulfillment I get from the work. Then, perhaps, gatherings with friends would be easier, without the social divide becoming more prevalent as time goes on. None of my friends need to work anymore—if they ever had to—and many choose not to, instead taking up proud titles such as 'housewife' and 'country club member.'

The truth is that this job lost its luster long ago.

I can tolerate it, usually. Today, I can't complete a single task. I can't focus on anything but the subtle twisting and pricking happening under my pelvic bone. It's not the familiar cramping I've come to dread, or a constrictive barbed-wire pain that would indicate the return of endometriosis. This could be it. The sign that I'm finally going to succeed at something.

Butterflies in my belly take flight as I imagine a moment of confirmation when I'm unable to control my glee. My phone vibrates on my worn desk, momentarily expanding my thoughts to sharing the news with Camden.

I pick up my phone, tapping the text icon. My stomach drops, killing the butterflies.

Larry's texted with an invasive reminder.

> *It's that time of the month again. See you Saturday afternoon. Bring cash … 700 will do.*

I take a slow breath in through my nose, but it does nothing to slow the uptick of my heartbeat. As I do, my phone vibrates again. I wince as I glance at it and am relieved it's not a follow-up text from Larry, who is the epitome of an absent father, except in moments like these. Instead, it's Erin, letting me know that I can come by to pick up the NewLife order I placed weeks ago at her *informational* in the park, where she said that we should experience the benefits of the sun while simultaneously telling us that our bodies can't absorb enough natural elements to fulfill our nutritional needs. At least I've already managed to pay the hefty price tag—the money portion, anyway.

Still, my surroundings close in, and I stare up at my computer screen, trying to calm the pulsing that's moved to my head.

"Olivia, did you hear me?" Sarah calls, mild annoyance in her tone.

"Sorry, I was reading an email," I lie, standing and moving around my desk.

As I rest my shoulder on her doorframe, the fan pans in my direction, sending my blood pressure up a notch. I focus on her to keep from showing my internal reaction. She's pretty, with her peppered hair framing her face and bulky purple glasses.

"Have you heard back from all the prospective booth renters for the real estate conference?" Sarah asks, tapping her pen against her desk.

"I gave them until end of day tomorrow," I answer, straightening my shoulders. With my aggravation growing, I almost believe the confidence is my own.

"It should have been today," she mumbles in her normal passive-aggressive tone.

"We decided on end of week," I say, firm but professional. This isn't the first time that she's moved a deadline on me.

If I had my own business—the dream that led me through school when I was young and hopeful—I wouldn't have to put up with a boss who exerts her dominance by undermining my work and messing with my strictly scheduled timeframes.

She glares at me from above her glasses, her hands not leaving her keyboard.

"Also, there are no new posts on our socials today."

If only people knew this company wasn't so perfect. Instead, what I deliver on all the social channels is the impression of an impeccable business, with well-lit images of moments that appear serene, laced with "candid" moments of the "happy family" team she so desperately wants to convey.

A sharp pain erupts through my pelvic floor, and my chest tightens in fear.

"I'll take care of it," I snap. "I always do."

I turn abruptly and grab my new-to-me Chanel purse from the corner of my desk, and slip its thin strap over my shoulder.

"I'm taking a break," I say with renewed niceness.

As I head out of the office and down the long hall, a warm fluid leaks into my panties.

My thoughts scatter, searching for an explanation that's anything other than the obvious.

Not again.

I rush into the bathroom and lock myself in a stall, lowering onto the cool porcelain as my body temperature rises. I don't inspect my damp underwear. I don't have to.

My throat constricts as stinging starts behind my eyes. I won't get to celebrate or tell Camden I'm pregnant. My body didn't prove me wrong. The possibility of no longer failing is gone.

A familiar ache grabs my chest, breaking my heart and stealing my breath. A sob escapes my lips, echoing off the metal walls etched with profanities and testaments of love.

Elle

Tuesday, September 20th

E mbossed lettering sprawled across the faux shiplap wall to my right announces *Love is patient, love is kind.* Fucking people. They love to love and are compelled to plaster its sentiments everywhere.

So many horrible quotes exist because of one fact. People in love are blind.

It's the first of three things that I can always count on.

It's how I remain hidden in this baby boutique, my target just outside. Her blonde friend—so self-infatuated—gave up her safety and her full name because she wanted to be the object of my affection.

Olivia Bradley has worked at Conference Accomplished—the number one conference planning company within one hundred miles of Leesburg, Virginia—for longer than most people live in one place. With the office located downtown, it's convenient for her to cross the street every weekday and stand outside the sprawling window I am peering through, taking in the nursery display.

She's obsessed with this store, yet in three weeks, she hasn't been inside once. Instead, each day, she sidesteps until she's in front of the door, then promptly leaves. From the precision in her repetition, I doubt she's *ever* been inside.

It's allowed me an unlikely sanctuary where I watch, wait, and process my observations. I am developing a plan to befriend her so that I can learn how she acquired so many originals and if that means that she has the entire collection, including the antique jewelry box.

"Winter pieces arrive in a few weeks," the owner says behind me.

"Thank you," I say, mindlessly flipping through the tiny outfits with adult-sized prices.

I squint past the streaks on the glass and catch sight of her.

There *she* is. Olivia Bradley.

She makes her way from her employer's office building and stands in front of the window.

Her eyes are pale brown in the late afternoon sun, but they darken with longing and tears as her gaze travels across the tiny outfits and bassinet propped up on display. She threads her fingers around the gold chain of her necklace, finding the emerald cross.

The object she uses to console her holds my memories of a time when I had hope for a future free to love, and free of lies.

That was before I recognized love for what it truly is: manipulation and entrapment.

Olivia does her usual sidestep to the door, but this time, she reaches for the handle.

I suck in a sharp breath. If she comes in here, she'll recognize me, and I'll be caught in the lie that I've told the shop owner—stuck pretending to be pregnant for the foreseeable future.

Her hand just hovers with space between her fingers and the door.

I audibly exhale when she lets her hand drop.

Again, her fingers go to the cross. *My cross.* The one stolen from my neck while I slept. The one I've searched for diligently for nearly twenty years ...

Love is not patient or kind, but the people who fall victim to it, like her—like me—are fucking blind.

After Olivia drives off in her shimmering white Lexus, I leave the baby boutique with no intention of *ever* going back in. I open the heavy glass door at my next destination, then cross the vacant lobby to the elevator. Pressing the up button, I drum the toe of my tennis shoe against the travertine.

I'm acutely aware of my close call and dread my advantages yet to come.

When the doors open, I step in and press three. A man enters the lobby, his hand lifted in a request to hold the elevator. I push the close doors button instead.

My nerves pulsate with the vibrations of the elevator's gears. When I step out, my head is pounding, but I ignore it and move toward the door that reads *Dr. Marcellus.*

The last time I saw a psychologist, I was in prison. Before that, I was mandated by the state. None of it helped me. The system only helps itself.

My face scrunches with the bad taste of regret as I grasp the doorknob. I can't bow out now—Zane knows that I'm coming here. He's not just eager to get rid of my nightmares, he's fucking desperate. Unfortunately, they're as much a part of me as the deaths that they represent. No amount of intervention will cure me unless this Dr. Marcellus shits magical unicorn dust that would make the nightmares stop.

The middle-aged admin assistant doesn't look up at me when I enter.

"I'd like to make an appointment," I say, as sweet as artificial sugar.

"You can call the appointment line." Her snarky tone is incredibly inappropriate.

"I'd rather not," I say, my falsetto in tune with a desperate woman begging for acceptance.

I'm not willing to lose the spot I've commandeered with proper reconnaissance and bribery. The lady who was kind enough to give up her prime slot contacted me an hour ago to let me know that she's moved her appointments, and I promptly sent her the second half of my generous gift.

The solitaire game on the assistant's screen reflects on her smudged glasses. I drum my index fingers on the counter, causing her to sigh, exasperated that I'm taking her from her *job*.

"I'd like Thursday afternoons, at four p.m., if that's possible."

"Thursdays are full," she says, not looking up as she clicks and drags her mouse around.

"Could you double-check?"

More clicking.

I lean on the counter, hoping it'll piss her off and cause her to bring her eyes up from her fucking game.

When a thrumming sound erupts from the computer speaker, indicating that her electronic cards are restacking, she huffs and squints as she reads something on her screen.

"Well, aren't you lucky," she says with condescension. "Someone moved their appointments. So, Thursday ... at four o'clock ... is open." Finally, she looks up, her expression curious.

"Oh wow! Timing's everything, I guess," I say cheerily. "I'll take it."

She shoves a clipboard with a stack of papers across the counter, hitting my arm.

"Fill these out," she says, her hand returning to the mouse and her attention to the game.

I swipe one of her fancy gel pens and cross the floor, sitting in the same seat that I saw Olivia in last week when I peered through the narrow window by the door.

Of all the frauds in this building, she had to lead me here ... not that I'd expect any less. Her rituals, obsessions, and anxious tics make her the perfect mark for those who want to *help*.

I rummage through my bag, then pop a piece of nonexistent gum in my mouth and smack on air. I hunch over the clipboard in my lap, reading each word multiple times, adding taps and clicks of the pen between each chomp of fake gum. Through my lashes I watch the admin assistant's muscles grow tenser with each smack, click, tap.

When I finally finish my paperwork, I come back to the counter and ease the clipboard toward her until she looks up, jaw clenched.

"Finally made it through, did you?"

"All that medical jargon gets the best of me," I say, beaming.

She hands me an appointment card. "See you Thursday."

"I look forward to it." I glance at the nameplate in front of her as I slip the gel pen behind my ear. "Thanks so much for your help, Laura."

I can count on my ability to read situations and people, then insert myself into their lives. Typically, I play a role that's favorable, but I fucking love it when opportunities like this come along where I can fester under someone's skin. Usually, I'm equal parts Sherlock and Hannibal, but right now, I'm straight-up, badass Amy Schumer, in *any* role she's ever played.

My hand runs over the counter as I turn to go, sliding her nameplate into my bag. She won't be needing it here. I'll see to that.

When I step outside again, I hover by the doors of the building. A group of women deep in gossip pass, unaware of the man behind them, his eyes glued to their legging-wrapped asses.

The creep pulls his eyes away long enough to examine me, and I wink playfully at him. He reciprocates with a smug, come-hither look like he's gifting me the opportunity of a lifetime.

I monitor him as he continues at an ogling distance behind the oblivious women. He stops when he reaches the bar on the corner.

I stroll down the sidewalk, then follow him inside, and sit on the barstool next to him.

"Can I buy you a drink?" he asks, leaning close to me.

"Sure," I say, lifting a finger in the air and calling, "Jameson sour."

The bartender pours with quick tilts of the bottles, then sets it on a cocktail napkin with a thud. The man examines me with newfound respect burning in his eyes, but not in the way that women want. It's more like he has an unstable desire to hump the lady who's bold enough to drink whiskey.

His yellowing teeth are unavoidable when he flashes his disturbing smile.

"What's a girl like you doing in a place like this?" he asks in a tone that he no doubt deems sensual.

"Looking for a man like you," I say, answering his horrible pick-up line the way he dreamed I would as I twist my red hair around my finger.

I'm in a horrible mood. This better be quick, otherwise I'll lose my shit.

"Why don't you head to the restroom? Clear it out for us," I suggest.

"Kinky. My kind of seductress." He wiggles his thick eyebrows.

Sleazebag.

I lift my hand and slide it down his back as he leaves, lingering over the curve of his ass.

He clomps to the back, yanks open the door to the men's room, then turns back with a sneer across his ugly face. The curl of his grimy finger is meant to beckon me.

I down my drink.

As the bathroom door bangs to a close behind him, I pull a twenty from his wallet and slap it on the glistening black counter before walking back out the front door, his wallet tucked in my coat pocket.

God, I fucking hate Leesburg, with its well-maintained historical buildings. Each one is unique, with a variety of colors, façades, and intricately designed signs that extend over the wide brick sidewalks. Normal people meander from shop to shop, arms linked, relishing downtown's quaint perfection.

To all of them, this place brings joy—it isn't tarnished with memories of death.

Moving every year has its disadvantages, but I never thought that one of them would be landing me here—again. With six months left on our lease, time may not be on my side when it comes to getting my stolen shit back, but it's in full support of pushing through this year of hell so we can leave and never look back.

I walk quickly, resisting the urge to stop and pet a puppy. I only pause at a trash can in front of a boarded-up shop—odd for this area, where every other storefront is gleaming and attractive.

It takes two seconds to remove the cash from the wallet and drop the revolting leather into the bin. As I slip the cash into my pocket, I take the final steps to my car.

As soon as the engine turns over, I pull away from the curb. The man I've stolen from has likely come out of the bathroom to figure out why I haven't joined him. He may have even noticed his missing wallet already.

A mile up the road, there's a familiar man holding a faded cardboard sign next to a stoplight, his adorable pooch by his side. The man's clothes are weathered, his hair matted. I pull to the side and hold out the fifty-four dollars I acquired from my con. He takes it with a nod. I hand his dog a chew bone as he shoves the money into his front pocket.

"Bless you, Miss Elle," he mumbles, patting his dog on the head.

He may be religious, but in his current state, abandoned by his country after his loyal service, I doubt that he respects any higher power that would leave him this way. One thing he can count on is me giving him a few bucks when I pass.

"Almost forgot," I say, reaching into my bag.

I hand him Laura's nameplate and both of us grin.

"Laura loves it," he says, patting the dog as she sniffs the cheap, gold-coloured metal.

Despite my reservations about his sentiments, I understand him. It's hard living on the street. It's even harder to come back from it—once you've faltered, it's all people see—but everyone fails. Success is only a construct, how well we cover up our worst failures with our best lies.

Olivia

Tuesday, September 20th

I stumble through the front door in a haze, kicking off my Jimmy Choos. On the way to the kitchen, I stop, turning toward a noise coming from the hall.

Camden's moving down the corridor, his dog Bella close behind, probably on their way from his office since every other room in that corridor is vacant. I don't focus my gaze on him, though. I'm too distracted by the door across from our vast den—leading to the room with light yellow walls and a collection of onesies, cute animal prints, and various things that I once thought we couldn't live without.

But what I really can't live without is a baby. A family of my own.

"You pick up dinner?" Camden asks, suddenly in front of me.

My face scrunches as I try to work out what he means. Bella groans as she lays on the massive area rug in our main living room.

"I asked you to pick up dumplings..."

"Oh, sorry," I say, pulling my hands behind my back to scrape my thumbs along my nails.

"Camden, I ... I want to try IVF," I mumble the request.

"We're taking a break from fertility treatments," he says, shaking his head.

We weren't, but he doesn't know that. I moved forward with two more rounds of medicated cycles and trigger injections with him think-

25

ing I'd been initiating sex for enjoyment, not managing well-timed and efficient intercourse.

"But I—"

"Babe, we agreed we'd focus on *just* us for now," he says, his tone too sharp for his soft smile.

Unable to resist his gravitational pull, I choose to trust the smile and get lost in his pale blue eyes for a moment.

"You okay?" he asks, grazing his thumb along my chin.

I can't tell him that I'm crushed from my period arriving and marking the loss of hope. This was the last round of a more simplistic approach. *A good stopping point to reevaluate and consider other options*, as Dr. Foltz put it.

Instinctively, I bring my hands together in front of me. My thumb catches on a piece of rough acrylic on the middle finger of the opposite hand.

Camden reaches for me, stopping the destruction of my nails. I relax, knowing he's on my side, but he stiffens, tightening his grasp on my right wrist.

"Where did you get that bracelet?" he asks, staring at the gold cuff decorated with rubies.

His question pierces through me, hitting the sore space in my chest that's been beaten by failure—mixing disappointment with my carelessness.

I have a rule—the jewelry I've taken from the basement is fair game if I take it off before I see Camden. He doesn't need to know that I've been pilfering—no, borrowing—from the things that he and his Uncle Jared leave down there. Besides the box I found this bracelet—and the other items—in have been down there for years, untouched and unloved. Their sparkle is fading with dust and neglect.

Camden's reaction is disconcerting and I question whether the jewelry is something more than a forgotten collection from Jared's storage unit purchases.

"I—" The single syllable trails because I'm at a loss and suddenly terrified I was wrong. Maybe the box doesn't hold someone's menial possessions—maybe they're his.

As fast as the thought comes, the pressure of his hand on my wrist has me dismissing it. My brain only went there because I'm still reeling from the repercussions of taking something of his from the basement a year ago. It was for the nursery, as a surprise. The surprise was all mine, though, because I met a new side of Camden. He didn't hit me. He never would. He would grab my wrist, sure, but he'd never leave a bruise. He doesn't have to—there are things far worse.

Panic rises in my throat when I'm unable to break from his grasp. I glance toward the front door, looking for an escape. Instead, I find an answer with my Jimmy Choos discarded haphazardly in front of it.

"I picked it up at an estate sale," I explain, as I imagine one of the mansions I've recently been to, filled with high-profile artwork and an extensive wardrobe of designer clothing. "I think it was the one in the Montressor neighborhood a few months back. I went there to check out the furniture. For the den."

"Hmm ..." Camden nods, his forehead still wrinkled. He doesn't get why I go to estate sales in extravagant neighborhoods outside our own community. He only knows I return with second-hand items ... like my Jimmy Choos.

"I found this bracelet there, with other pieces," I say, continuing my charade. "I got them for a great bundled price. They all looked so fancy and expensive that I couldn't pass up the deal."

Annoyed by my own rambling, I press my lips together to keep from spewing nonsense or revealing something that I shouldn't.

My heart thumps as the wrinkles fade from his expression.

"It's nice," he says, dropping his gaze and my wrist. "It looks real. Familiar, even. Must be a great fake." The cadence when he says *fake* is a slap to my ego. I had never said it wasn't real, not that I'd know—but neither would he. When he proposed, he had needed *my* help shopping for an engagement ring since he'd never stepped foot in a jewelry store before.

"Would you order something?" he asks, changing the subject too quickly and causing a lag in my comprehension. "For dinner ..."

"Dumplings?" I ask as he takes a step back and looks down the hall.

"Whatever, I just need to get back to work," he says.

"Camden?" I say quietly, rubbing my wrist and wishing his hand was still there. At least we'd be together.

I swallow to ease my sore throat and stamp away the doubts of the speech I'd prepared. "About IVF—"

"Babe, I don't want to try anymore." His words are quiet but firm.

"I want to give it a shot," I croak.

"We don't have the money," he says, his shoulders stiffening.

We don't have the money. Translation: I don't have the money. I never will.

His money is elusive; his paydays come in waves. Even when his tech contracts bring large influxes in his earnings, he keeps tabs on it. When we got married, my personal checking became our joint account. We never did add his name, but he watches it with hawk eyes as if it's his credit—his reputation.

"I could take out a loan ..."

"No loans," he says, his voice growing louder.

"The fertility clinic has finance options—I could pick up a part-time job to pay for it."

"No." He doesn't have to yell for his response to be deafening. "Let me know when the food arrives," he says with a nonchalance that has me questioning whether I've imagined our entire interaction.

He's already halfway down the hall when I compose a response. "Okay," I whisper, but I'm the only one to hear it as Bella trots past me to catch up to him.

I move into the kitchen as I unlock my phone to order food. I lean on the marble countertop and mindlessly scroll through Instagram instead. The immaculate women doting over their children are too much, so I open Messenger.

From Sadie: *Hey Hun! I'm so excited to reconnect with you after all these years! I've been catching up on your profile and have an opportunity I think you would be perfect for ...*

My shoulders tighten. I can't afford another *friend*.

I switch to the Facebook app and look through the notifications. Carly posted in her group about a promotion her direct sales company is having and how she's working toward the next goal. And Erin has added me to three—no, four—interest groups because she thinks I'd be a great fit on her team.

The pressure compounds on my chest, and I lock my phone, needing relief. I quickly unlock it when I realize that I've forgotten the food. I navigate to the Uber Eats app and find a place with dumplings that doesn't have an exponential delivery charge for prime delivery time.

When the order is placed, I stare at the tracking screen, wishing this day was over. I strum my nails across the white marble, the *thud-thud-thud-thud* of my acrylics becoming background noise as I try to come up with a solution. One where I get pregnant. One where I can proceed with IVF. One where I can make the house a home and stop feeling so alone.

A notification populates across the top of my screen. Another post has been made in Carly's Facebook group—she's closer to her goal, but not there yet.

These women who surround me, who constantly reach out, have been there for me when Camden couldn't. They give me hope and positivity and a distraction from the void I've created in my marriage. It's unfair of me to feel dread when seeing their persistent messaging or irritation when they blindly add me to another Facebook group. The least I can do is support them after all they've done for me.

I follow the link on Facebook to Carly's *rank-up* promotion and scroll through the products. All with hefty price tags.

My chest tightens with a fresh wave of grief. I set my phone down and then make fists. The pressure of the acrylic nails on my palms gives me clarity. Tonight, I went too far. I need to respect Camden's right to choose. I messed up because I was focused on my own selfish desires.

Heading across the wide planks of the open living space to our bedroom, I don't stop until the cool travertine of our ensuite chills my bare feet. I pull the light blue craft box out from under my sink, then collect everything I've been using for my conception journey and shove it inside.

Something borrowed, something blue ... but in the years since our wedding, it's become my True-Blue, storing various objects of importance. It'll protect these things until Camden's ready.

Before I can overthink, I tuck it under my arm and head across the house. I stop in front of the last two doors. To the left is Camden's office, to the right, the door to the stairs leading to the basement.

Through his office wall, I hear Camden speaking. "Ninety thousand ... yeah ... you in?"

My curiosity is piqued. I wish that I could hear the person on the other end of his gaming headset. Whatever gaming tech he's been working on has possessed almost all his time. Glancing at the box cradled under my arm, I remind myself that his job has deadlines, and our marriage does not.

I open the door to my right and descend the stairs to the finished basement, then step inside the vast room we use as storage space.

The only thing I can't hide in True-Blue is my debt. I told Camden that the medicated fertility regimens would be covered by my lousy insurance and kept him from the details that he'd punish me for, like the cost of the continued treatments, and the way I've paid.

I weave through the locked, red-lidded black bins that safeguard proprietary gaming equipment, coming to a stop in front of the shelf on the back wall. It's packed with Camden's possessions and some of Jared's valuable finds. I try to find space among them. I don't bother looking at the far bottom corner where I've obtained the jewelry, not wanting to implicate myself. Now, I've lied and gotten away with it. And, because Camden encourages me to store things elsewhere—this space is his.

I finally find a spot next to a worn cardboard box where True-Blue might fit. Maybe it'll even catch Camden's attention—nudge him in my direction when he sees that I've stored everything with care. I use this as a reminder. Shelving this doesn't mean that I lose hope. I take a deep breath, close my eyes, and visualize two pink lines.

It's only happened once, but the image is sharp in my mind. The grimy tan tiles of a drugstore bathroom. Nausea rising from my stomach to my throat faster than I could ease it.

My eyes sting beneath their lids, staying in the memory.

I'm jarred back to my surroundings by the doorbell chiming overhead.

I try to shove True-Blue into the questionable space next to the worn cardboard box. It doesn't fit. I try shifting and pushing, but it's no use. It must be a sign.

I yank True-Blue from its wedged spot. A binder slides from atop the worn cardboard box and topples to my feet, landing open on a page of baseball cards. Letters that were stashed inside scatter across the floor. I scramble to pick them up as the doorbell chimes again. Bella barks. I shove the letters into the binder and return it to the spot it came from. With True-Blue tucked under my arm, I dart from the room and up the stairs.

When I reach the landing, I call, "Food!" He can come and get it for himself. I'm too busy being selfish.

Elle

Thursday, September 22nd

Doctor Marcellus is a swindler. She's covered up her dingy walls with gold and maroon floral wallpaper and infused the musty air with lavender and vanilla to create a ruse meant to whisper, *confess your sins to me.*

Unlike her, I'm aware that creating an alluring lie is like crafting an expensive piece of jewelry. When finished, the light must strike it perfectly from all angles, flaws undetectable, entrancing the beholder. Her office does none of these.

She's also spent the better part of an hour trying to poke holes in my marriage, which makes her a fraud with little imagination. Unfortunately for her, my husband is the closest thing there is to a fucking saint.

I bounce my knees. Gulp.

"My husband's gone so much for work," I say with a meek staccato. "I miss him, you know?"

I do miss him. His extraordinary body pressed against mine, the taste of bourbon on his lips. The way he insists we play chess instead of watching TV. I even miss his uncanny ability to notice a speck of dust or frame that's slightly askew.

Glimpsing the one-carat diamond on her left ring finger, I ask, "Do you ever worry your husband, or wife ..." I widen my eyes as I let my words trail off. After a beat, I pull my mouth into a quivering pout and whine, "I love him so much, and he loves me, but ..."

She sets her notebook down and opens her arms. "This is a safe space."

It's all I can do to keep from laughing. Safe isn't the word I'd use to describe it. They let me in, so it's not that safe.

I nod. "I keep thinking that ... maybe he's cheating."

Squeezing my eyes tight, I conjure tears with simple memories—my family, blood stains, alarms from hospital monitors ...

I'm technically here for nightmares, but depression and anxiety are easier to portray, especially since Dr. Marcellus dug for this dirt. Real or not, this is what she gets.

I never intended to talk to her about my real problems, even though I *could* be anxious and depressed from my horrific dreams, lack of sleep, and Zane's insistence that we move annually to keep my Boogey Man away.

Dr. Marcellus glances at her watch. "The fear of infidelity. Shall we explore this more next Thursday?"

"I'd like to explore it now," I say. "We have some time left."

She's not going to cut me short. Thief. I want to be here less than she does, but this is my game, not hers. Her gaze flits to the clock on the wall that I'm blatantly staring at.

"Alright," she sighs.

"Sometimes I wonder if he has a different life," I whimper like a scorned, helpless woman from a Lifetime movie.

"What do you mean, a different life?" she asks, intrigued.

I hunch my shoulders and draw my legs together as I descend deeper into my unraveling. "What if he has another family somewhere, and he just says that it's his job that keeps him away?" The thought is hilarious. Zane loves me too much, and there's no way he could stand the messy hell that it would create.

"Do you really believe that?" Dr. Marcellus asks, analyzing my sanity.

"Lately, yes. There's no reason that I couldn't go with him," I say, tapping my finger and thumb to portray nervous movements. "Still, he never invites me, and when I ask, he says no."

Her eyes show concern. To her, I'm hopeless.

"How does that make you feel?"

Fuck this generic dynamic.

"It makes me feel helpless."

"Do you do anything to alleviate your perceived loss of control?"

I'm ready for this shit to be over, but I refrain from checking the clock. I want to take more of her time since she wanted to deprive me of it before. "I go to a boxing gym. Yoga helps sometimes." I do like to punch things. Slow stretches and meditation, not so much.

There's a knock on the door, and then it cracks open.

It's the new admin assistant, not the jaded hag I got fired.

"Dr. Marcellus," she says. "Your five o'clock is asking if you're running behind."

Her blue eyes glisten with both a fear of repercussion and a hope of recognition. I know that expression too well. It's one that I used to bear, unintentionally.

Dr. Marcellus holds up a finger. "Megan, I'm in the middle of a session."

Annoyance pricks up my neck. I abruptly stand and sling my bag over my shoulder.

"We can pick this up next week," I say, crossing the worn gray carpet toward the door.

"Oh, alright then," Dr. Marcellus stammers.

I pause briefly to glance at a shelf full of pictures. I must have imagined the flash, because I don't see a source.

When the door closes behind me, I straighten my shoulders and nod with a kind smile to the assistant. She's shorter now, behind the elevated counter of the reception desk, and disappointment is written on her face.

I lean on the counter, lowering my head so I can speak candidly.

"Don't let the doctor treat you like that. You deserve better."

"Thank you," Megan says. Her cheeks flush as she nods, like a child who is unsure which adult to believe.

I turn to go, my gaze landing on the woman who has been waiting while I manipulated time. Her long brown hair is perfectly curled and swept back, drawing attention to her silver-rimmed glasses and diamond earrings.

Her fine jewelry collection is impressive, complete with a massive rock on her left ring finger. I bet her husband fixes his guilt with expensive gifts. That would explain her ongoing need to show up here.

It's not the extravagant pieces that draw my attention. As always, she's wearing my gold and emerald cross. She also wears a bracelet—a cuff with a sapphire and ruby on each side. It's another piece from my great-grandmother's collection.

She looks absently toward me. I turn toward the door, then glance back. I pause.

"Do we know each other?" I ask her casually.

"Uh, I'm not sure," she says, looking at me thoughtfully.

I scrunch my face, squint toward her, as if trying to place where I know her from.

"Oh!" I point at her neck. "The cross ... that's it. I saw you not too long ago. I asked about your impressive antique jewelry collection."

She looks at me, taking in my appearance. Today I'm wearing my best jeans and a dress top. I adorned them with some faux diamonds I've been working on. It's the perfect fishing attire.

"At a park," I add to conclude this part of our introduction.

Her expression shifts as it clicks, and she melds her memory with the woman standing in front of her.

"Oh, yes." She smiles. "That's right."

I extend my hand. "I'm Elle."

She takes it, shaking gently. "I'm Olivia. Maybe it's cliché, complimenting you like you did me, but wow! Your diamonds are stunning."

"Thank you," I say, genuinely delighted.

It's an excellent introduction—natural and informative.

Olivia

Thursday, September 22nd

The clock on the wall ticks louder than usual. Today, it echoes a lecture.

Tell the truth. Tell the truth.

"Are you sure there's nothing bothering you?" Dr. Marcellus asks for the second time in thirty minutes.

I straighten my shoulders and immediately regret it. Curling them back down, I slouch into my palms, elbows balanced on my knees, doing my best to avoid my destructive picking now that my manicures are spaced further apart.

"I've been lying to Camden," I confess, the weight of my secret momentarily lifting to allow me a breath. It quickly settles back onto my shoulders. Some secrets must be kept.

She allows her silence to communicate for her.

"I paid for two additional rounds of medicated cycles. He said that he wanted to stop trying, but I wasn't ready. I was just so hyper-focused."

"Hyper-focused," she repeats. "Because of your ADHD?"

I nod as a wave of sadness washes over me. She passed right over the bits that I feel most.

"Do you feel like you're losing control?" Dr. Marcellus asks.

"Lately? Yes," I say, trying to recenter myself on my overwhelming mental health needs.

"Can you elaborate?"

"It's hard to focus, at work, at home—at all, really. And I've been shopping more. I opened another credit card last month. It wasn't easy, either. Several companies rejected me first due to my debt-to-income ratio. I have four cards now. The debt is overwhelming, but I can't stop. Camden doesn't know about any of it. He can't know. I feel so guilty, and the more guilty I feel, the more that I buy." I pause, processing the information as she does.

Camden's Uncle Jared taught him at a young age to avoid debt. Camden lives by this rule as if it's gospel and expects me to as well since we're inextricably linked. He paid cash for our house and our cars. To seal up my fate if he finds out, the high-dollar businesses he contracts with, they like people working for them who have impeccable histories. Any one of them could pull his credit report at any time.

"I think ..." I say slowly. "I'm trying to fill a void."

It grows larger with each passing month and every failed cycle. And with Camden seeming more distant by the day. It doesn't help that the compounding debt is drowning me, yet I keep swimming into deeper waters. It's affecting my attention, my ability to be present, and my sleep. I toss and turn, worried that I'll dream about the debt. What if I sleep talk and Camden hears? Despite how analytical he is, he somehow believes that dreams have clout.

Dr. Marcellus' lips pull together, and she taps her pen to her pad of paper. She begins talking about the different ways to treat my ADHD, including referring me to someone who can start me on stimulants again, but I can't focus on her words. I've heard it all before, and I'm not going back on meds when I haven't given up hope on becoming pregnant. It could happen naturally. Other people with endometriosis and polycystic ovaries have managed. I just need to decrease stress, starting with what's surrounding my marriage.

My throat aches as I swallow. I can't believe it's taken me so long to figure it out.

I've been convinced that our marriage was sinking because of me. I thought it was our lack of a child.

I know now it *is* my fault. He's been telling me the reason all along. All he wants is me.

I haven't been focusing on him—on us—like I should have been.

I can fix it. I'll start by picking up a gift for him on the way home.

The bright lights of a well-lit jewelry store drew me inside as if screaming for my attention.

I move slowly from one case to the next, admiring the shimmering items. My Burberry cardigan and Chanel purse give the impression that I belong here, masking my discomfort from being surrounded by a thousand tiny things that I can't afford. I stop at the case full of men's watches—a good option that can be obtained at a reasonable price.

A twenty-something woman behind the counter comes over.

"Is there something I can help you with?"

"Yes." I nod and point to a navy-faced Citizen watch with rose gold numbering.

"Ah, the Atomic Timekeeping series. An excellent choice," she says, smoothing her already perfect suit.

She unlocks the glass cabinet and carefully pulls it out, setting the watch on a black felt pad in front of me.

I pick it up and run it over my fingers, admiring how it shines. I discreetly flip the tiny tag and glance at the price.

There's a familiar tug of guilt and uncertainty as I try to determine whether I want to spend the money or if I simply don't want to waste this lady's time.

"I'll take it," I say, the tug in my chest turning into a constriction that tightens with each deafening thud of my heart.

She takes the watch and my American Express from me and disappears behind a large cash register. I force my eyes to move casually across the case in front of me, hoping that I don't appear too nervous. The last thing that I want is to draw attention to myself as a potential risk, or worse, a thief.

"Olivia?"

I spin toward the familiar voice. My eyes betray me, widening at the sight of Camden's uncle. When I smile, it's a beat too late.

"Jared," I sing. "What are you doing here?"

It's all I can do to not glance toward the lady who's ringing up my purchase.

"Just browsing," Jared says.

His words sound relaxed, but his body language says otherwise. His gaze doesn't shift to the cases on either side of us—it stays trained on me, just as his frame stays squarely fixed on my location. It's like I'm his beacon ... I'm the thing he's browsing for.

I let out a nervous chuckle.

"Mrs. Bradley? I'm ready for you," the saleswoman says in a too-bubbly voice.

My legs tremble as I take the steps toward the register, offering an apologetic smile to Jared then to the woman.

I rush to sign the warranty agreement and the merchant receipt. She moves at a snail's pace, placing the watch in a box, then wrapping it in tissue paper before sliding it into a sleek gift bag. When she finally holds the fabric straps out to me, I snatch it and offer a quick thank you.

"So, how have you been?" I ask Jared, who's watching me with a curious expression. "It's been a while. We should have dinner at our place soon."

He glances at the bag, then at the Amex between my fingers.

The air seems thin as I curl the card up into my hand. Camden and Jared are incredibly close. Jared knows all the rules set out for me because what's mine is Camden's.

"Dinner would be good."

I swallow. "Great. I'll figure out a time and let you know."

Until two years ago, Jared would come to our place for dinner every Sunday, but that tapered off. Was it because of me? Jared and Camden still get together, but not with me. I was relieved when the small family dinners stopped because I always felt awkward, and I had other things that I wanted to do. Maybe that is another thing I've failed at. Perhaps it was my job to keep the family dinners going—to ensure that I remained part of the family.

"Sounds good," he says, patting me on the shoulder. "Happy anniversary."

I must look absurd as my face scrunches against my will.

"Anniversary?" I whisper, my voice cracking at the end.

He nods to my glossy bag. "The gift for Camden. It must be coming up, right?"

I nod. We got married in spring. Jared was there. If this is a test, I can't say Christmas, either, because we both know Camden's stance on the holiday.

"I like to be prepared," I force the words from my rapidly drying mouth. So much for expressing my timeless love to Camden—I'll have to hold onto this until our anniversary.

BETWEEN LIES AND REVENGE

I leave the bag in my car and dash across the street to get take-out from Camden's favorite Italian restaurant. I can't help but feel Jared's eyes on me. He's always watching, always looking out for Camden's well-being.

43

Elle

Thursday, September 29th

I lean against the brick wall of the alley that's cool from the shade. I'm watching and waiting. I cross one arm over my body and prop the other against it, my hand to my face, taking a deep inhale, then letting it escape through the O of my lips.

Olivia seemed distracted today. I'd expected more dialogue this week, but she barely acknowledged me.

I was off my game, too. Dr. Marcellus asked too many questions with extreme specificity. It threw me after last week's overly generic dialogue. It was like she'd been studying my mind. The way she pried about my past, implied it was checkered, asked about my parents, my hobbies. She almost had me second guessing what lies I'd told or if I'd accidentally signed a consent for her to obtain records from the social workers while I was in the foster system.

Or from the psychologist in juvie.

Almost.

At least Olivia will be in a better place after blurting out her confessions in a room she believes is made for storing secrets.

A woman's voice comes from around the corner, so I drop my invisible cigarette and grind the pavement with my toes. I peer out of the alley, scanning the sidewalk around the corner.

I see her, but she's not alone. So much for bumping into her. I slip back into hiding and listen intently. The man speaking to her has a gruff, condescending tone. My shoulders tighten in response.

"Listen," he says sharply, demanding her attention. "I know you've been spending too much. I'd hate for Camden to find out."

"I don't know what you're—"

"Don't play dumb, Olivia. You know that he keeps his credit clean. And you're running around charging on numerous credit cards."

There's a pause. Everything is still.

"Pay them off and close them. Today," the man barks.

"I don't have the money," she says, her voice shaking.

The thud of one of them grabbing the other reverberates in my mind. My skin tingles and my heart picks up as I ready myself to pounce on him.

"Take this," he whisper-shouts. "Pay *them* off. You'll pay *me* back."

"Jared, I—"

"I'll have some work for you in the meantime. Consider it interest payments," he says firmly. "And not a word to our Cammy boy."

Heavy footsteps thud in my direction, and I glance at him from the alley. He's tall and bulky, with a salt and pepper mop on his head. His gaze meets mine, and for a second, recognition burns in my brain. There's recognition in his eyes.

His gaze flits away, and he storms down the sidewalk. I look at the wall across from me, searching for understanding. His eyes resemble those of every man who has mistreated me over the years. The hollowness. The hatred. He's not familiar to me, but his type is.

Sucking in a steadying breath, I come out of hiding and head in Olivia's direction. I come to a stop in front of a misfit boarded-up shop.

I'm too late. She's already gone.

Olivia

Thursday, September 29th

The pinks and oranges of the sunset are disintegrating into a darkening blue by the time I pull up in front of the house.

I left downtown in a hurry, but promptly needed to pull over to vomit. To process. To manage my thoughts well enough to drive. By the time I was on the road again, most banks were closed, even the one with later hours where I keep a secret checking account for managing expenses that no one else knows about.

Thirty-thousand dollars ...

It runs on repeat through my head, and still, I can't quite process it. Jared just handed me thirty thousand in cash like it was nothing more than a few bucks to him. All this time, I've been accumulating debt that's so overwhelming for someone like me—paying one credit card with the other, moving and shifting so I can keep up appearances—while he can pay outright for anything he wants.

How did he know about my credit card debt? It can't have been just from the watch purchase last week with my AmEx. He couldn't have deduced that I'd need this much cash to pay it all off. Could he? Was it just a lucky guess?

It's odd, him wanting me to do his accounting in return. What kind of family charges interest, aside from mine?

I turn the car off, and listen to the engine click and pop as it cools. When I'm certain that Camden isn't coming out to greet me like he used to, I step out of the car and open the back door. Where does one keep bundles of cash during transport? I had no idea, so I hid it on the floor of the back seat.

Slipping the money under my shirt, I wish I'd found a different secondhand purse than the Chanel. Not even one of the three bundles bound by rubber bands fit inside. If I was still using my Kate Spade, it wouldn't be a problem, but all the other women upgraded to higher-end purses.

I open the trunk, then with one hand, I hug the money to my torso while I pull the grocery totes from the back of the cargo space. Inside the totes are the various products I've collected this week. A new skincare regimen, several pieces of clothing, a shampoo that promises shiny locks. The NewLife protein powder and vitamins I couldn't bring myself to pick up last week.

All the things I've been planning to sneak inside when the time was right ...

I tuck one bundle of cash into each of the three totes, hiding them under the existing contents. Suddenly, I'm not so concerned about disguising the products as groceries as much as I am about the ridiculously priced items hiding my money.

As I close the tailgate, I nervously glance behind me at the cul-de-sac. Someone is watching me from a car across the street.

My heart picks up, but as my eyes adjust, I realize that there's nobody in the car. At least, I don't think that there is.

Regardless, I hustle inside, locking the door behind me. I hold the bags away from my body to prevent them from rubbing against me and causing unnecessary attention.

When I reach my personal walk-in, I push the door until it's almost closed, acutely aware of the squeak of the hinges.

I rush to the bottom drawer at the back of the closet, where I have hidden other purchases, then empty the products inside. Since I'm still alone—I always am—I grab a scarf from a hook and wrap it around the money, then shove it to the back of a drawer.

It's not enough to have it hidden, so I stand guard.

I text Camden from across the house.

> I'm not feeling well. Going to take a shower and g to bed early

He doesn't come to check on me, and for once, I don't care. I lie awake for hours, staring at the shadows on the dark ceiling. Sometime after midnight, Camden finally comes in. I pretend to be asleep, but there's no chance of drifting off.

Thirty-thousand dollars ...

Pay off the debt. That's what I've been tasked with. But it's there, available, and the banks won't know what I'm supposed to do with it. The banks ... they don't need to know at all.

Besides, my debts reach beyond the banks. And so do my desires.

I have only ever stolen once, an iPod. The theft was meticulously planned, complete with reconnaissance, risk versus reward, calculation of financial losses, and excellent execution. It also got me what I'd planned—a spot at the popular table with the rich high schoolers who gauged worth by expensive things. The newest, top-of-the-line, MP3 gadget did the trick.

I never got caught.

I was willing to do whatever it took to fit in and to finally be accepted, but that desire is menial compared to others.

Thirty-thousand dollars ... that could pay for IVF.

While I've never been comfortable around Jared, he's not scary. I deal with far worse. The elite circles are brutal. My guilt over failing to provide Camden with a child for two years has nearly killed me.

It was our dream to have a family and fill this home with love and joy. Camden says that he wants to focus on just us, and I get it. Having your heart broken every month is excruciating, but with a baby, we'd be whole again.

Camden would forgive the credit cards. I doubt anyone's checking his credit scores these days. He has an impeccable reputation. That's worth far more than a clean credit report.

Maybe with a baby, Larry would finally ease up and be more of a father.

As for Jared—I need to pay him back regardless. Who cares what I use it for? Especially if he doesn't know. If no one knows.

Thirty-thousand dollars ... it will *pay for IVF.*

Before

A Juvenile Delinquent

A hand presses firmly on my shoulder, forcing me to the ground. I don't fight; there's no point. This way, I get to lay my cheek onto the warm concrete instead of having my skull shoved into it.

The cool touch of metal on my wrist is followed by a click of a cuff locking into place. As the cop yanks my other wrist behind my back, he says something to me ... my rights, maybe.

I watch CSI and Cops—so many ideas have come to me watching great criminals—and terrible ones—so I'm sure he's rambling about a court-appointed lawyer.

I can't process the words as the officer shouts them. They're too much for my brain, maybe because of the ringing in my ears from when they burst into our hideout or from the shots Sam fired to warn us that they were coming. It might be because I can't go thirty seconds without thinking, Travis is gone. Travis is dead.

My heart thuds against the concrete. Focus. Sam. He's lucky he didn't hit anyone. Helps he wasn't aiming, but warning shots are almost as stupid. I search for him, my gaze darting around the small warehouse, but I don't see him. I only see some of the other dealers.

The cop yanks twice on the cuffs around my wrists and then steps into my view. He doesn't glance back as he goes to help a cop who's struggling to cuff the guy with massive forearms. Corey? Or is it Tommy? I don't fucking know, and I don't care, just like the man who cuffed my wrists didn't care about me, a freckle-faced teenaged girl who weighs one hundred and ten pounds on a bad day.

Travis would care.

I'm no threat to the cop, just like Corey, or Tommy, or whatever, isn't a threat to me. I'm dating the guy in charge, or I'm dating the guy who tells us what to do, once he gets instructions from a drug lord or some shit like that.

I lift my head slightly and turn it, then rest my other cheek on the ground.

There he is. Sam has three officers surrounding him. If they didn't know that he was the head of our little pot operation already, they do now. How did they know about us? We were careful. And come on ... I know marijuana is illegal, and selling to minors is some sort of criminal offense ... but don't they have better things to do? Worse gangs to bust? We're small potatoes.

Sam stares at me, blood dripping from his nose and onto the ground. One of the three cops surrounding him has her gun pointed at his head.

Hot tears sting my eyes. I'm so glad that Travis isn't here. The authorities told me that they think he's dead. That was yesterday.

My throat constricts.

At least he's not here. Prison would have killed him. He was meant for college, to become some snooty businessman, or lawyer, or something—where he could skate around this momentary blip and get back onto the straight and narrow.

Sam mouths, You. His stare burns through me. You did this.

No. He can't think that. I must have read his lips wrong.

I try shaking my head, but the concrete stops me.

A couple of weeks ago, everything was fine. I'd almost gotten Travis and myself out of the gang's grasp. I'd made enough money with my side hustle to buy us out and walk away. It was time. I sensed a shift in power. Sam was acting like an uptight squirrel.

One night, I took Sam the money I'd been saving. He had always told me to give him a heads-up—because that's what a girl does for her boyfriend. That night, I acted like a good little girlfriend, too. I smoked pot and drank, just like he asked. Being buzzed helps me tolerate him lately anyway, but I wanted to keep my wits about me. Apparently, I misjudged, because I was smashed by the time I got home. I don't remember telling Sam that Travis and I were done, but the money I'd taken with me as our getting-out deposit was gone the next day, just like my brother—and our inheritance. The only thing left was some of Travis' blood on the carpet and a massive mess of an apartment.

I hadn't heard a thing. No thuds, no calls for help ... nothing had disturbed my slumber.

I'm only sixteen. My parents are dead. My brother is missing ... no, dead. That's what happens to people who love me.

I deserve to be locked up. At least in juvie, I won't be able to hurt anyone.

Elle

Saturday, October 1st

This musty old barn smells like money and memories. I can't stop searching sales like these because a part of me is possessed by them—keeping *his* memory alive. It was a relief when Zane started joining me because it keeps me grounded in the present.

When he comes with me, I don't get caught in a loop, thinking, *Travis is gone. Travis is dead.* The memories don't threaten to collapse the world around me. They don't push me back in time, leaving me with childish thoughts that he could still be alive. They never found his body.

Zane loves numbers. He collects and analyzes data for work and for fun. He no longer needs to repeat the statistics for me. His presence reminds me of the numbers he's engrained in my memory.

Just under 825,000 people were reported missing that year.

Most were found—alive, or dead.

About 10,000 people remain missing for longer than a year.

On average, 4,400 unidentified bodies are recovered annually.

Even if I could reconcile my past—and in some ways I am—I wouldn't stop digging through other people's trash. It's a habit and how I find treasure. Plus, there are other considerations—my own data.

Twelve years ago, Travis was presumed dead—officially—by the Social Security Administration. However, the police had suspected it from the beginning. For seven years, they waited for validation while I agonized over it.

Seventeen years ago, I met Ricardo and Eddy. They took me in and gave me a second chance, a job, the education I was craving, and the love that I didn't deserve.

Fourteen years ago, I met Zane. And nearly eleven years ago, we were wed, sealing the incredible thing between us in a way words never could.

I meander alongside Zane by the front of the barn. Its massive doors are open, creating the illusion of an indoor-outdoor setting. The sunbeams enhance the recently cleaned furniture and illuminate the still-hovering clouds of dust and dirt. It masks the value of the piece.

Zane stops in front of a mid-century dresser. That's my queue. He gives my hand a quick double squeeze before releasing it. The tired floorboards groan under my step as I move past the entrance—past the people fawning over antique furniture. Away from the woman running this estate sale.

As I move deeper into the barn, I run my fingers over the faded covers of books stacked haphazardly on shelves and ignore the houseware displayed on plywood tables. I pass racks of clothing eaten by moths and reeking of absorbed body odor.

A shelf next to worn dresses has random knickknacks and old board games. A small wooden box is tucked next to a checkerboard. *Idiots.* They can't tell the difference between chess and checkers. I lift the hatch and touch the pieces inside. They're beautifully carved; one player set is a light oak, the other a dark cherry.

Wooden box in hand, I move into the deepest, dustiest depths. Tucked back in the far corner, surrounded by cobwebs, I find wilting cardboard boxes scattered around a weathered folding table.

Jackpot. I peek inside them until I find what I'm looking for in an aged shoebox big enough for cowboy boots.

Jewelry.

A twinge of desire sends me searching for my heirlooms, though I'm not surprised when I don't find any. Someone else already has ... I can only hope that she didn't discard the felt-lined wooden box that they were once kept in.

I check my surroundings for lurkers, then extract my loupe from my pocket. I flick the LED light on and start inspecting the pieces. The box may be falling apart, but the gemstones will outlast my lifetime.

Almost all of these are real, forgotten by the stupid fuck who left them here to rot.

I pick out the pieces that are made of glass and artificial gems, tuck the wooden box with the chess pieces under the rest, and place the fake jewelry on top.

When I'm certain that none of the other boxes contain treasures, I peek around the corner by the board game shelf before heading back toward the front. As I pass the books, a weathered orange spine lingers in the corner of my vision. I free it from its prison as I proceed.

I wait for a solid two minutes at the makeshift register, before interrupting the attendant engaged in conversation with a couple of other women.

"How about thirty bucks for this box of costume jewelry?"

She turns toward me with disinterest.

"Can I see inside?" she asks, reaching for the box.

My jaw tightens. Nobody trusts anymore. It's fucking aggravating.

I hand her the box, and she glances inside.

"Fifty," she says.

"I have forty, cash," I say, as if I come to these sales unprepared.

"Fine," she huffs, shoving the box back into my arms.

I'd suggest the copy of *Catcher in the Rye* be part of the deal, but she's back to her conversation, ironically about some jewelry that she has on display with a flashy Cross Avenue sign. It looks more appealing than the stuff I've commandeered, but its value is far less. I shove the cash into the woman's still outstretched hand, not bothering to stow the book away like a common thief.

The crowd surrounding the old-ass furniture has grown. If only they knew what real value was. As I walk past Zane, I run my fingers along his spine. Thank god he's not a trend-following zombie. His infatuation with antique furniture goes way back. He'd never smear expensive paint all over history like the others here.

"Be there in a minute," he says, pulling me in for a quick kiss.

At the end of the long gravel drive, I start the car before removing the wooden box with chess pieces from the shoebox. I tuck it inside the center console under the napkins, then admire the jewelry for a moment.

Some of the pieces can be sold online. A simple clean up, some antique hashtags, and I'll have people clambering on eBay to buy them well above their actual worth. People are convinced that history means increased value, even when there's no significance.

The rest will be my project. Salvage the stones. Assess and melt the metals. Refurbish, reuse, recreate. Unlike furniture that'll always look old, when it comes to jewelry, when metals are buffed and reshaped, stones removed, new etchings applied, and placed in a new setting ... that shit is cash—pure fucking gold.

I place the box in the backseat, then watch Zane through the windshield. He's marveling at the furniture with the rest of the flock. I'll never get it, his obsession—I love how it contrasts with his fastidious cleanliness.

"Sorry," he says when he finally climbs into the passenger seat.

"You know I don't mind waiting, Love."

He sighs, staring longingly back at the furniture. "There were some great pieces, but they couldn't handle regular moves."

"Love, there's no reason to keep running. My past—it's not chasing us," I say, reaching across the console and squeezing his hand.

I served my time for the drug crimes that I committed. Nobody else needs to know about the other crimes, not even Zane. Travis did, but he took my secrets to his grave. Those who once wished me dead, to pay for my sins, haven't shown signs of searching for me for almost a decade.

"It's not worth the risk," he says, looking at me now. "No piece of furniture, no house needing repair, no amount of money ... nothing would ever be worth risking you."

This isn't an argument worth having. I say everything I need to by throwing the car in reverse and whipping out of the gravel drive.

"That box looks like it's gone through hell," Zane says, helping with the change of topic.

"It's not the box, Love."

"Looks like a big find," he says with a grin.

I cherish his enthusiasm, even if he doesn't know exactly what I'll do with it all. The dirty pieces will wait for me to have time, an empty house, and a glass of whiskey. Only then will they reach their full potential. That's only for the real gems.

I have much bigger plans for the fake stones. With all the laws they may help me break—Zane can never know. The only person I've told is dead.

Over the last nineteen years, I've written 2,273 letters to Travis—a dead man. He was the last one to know the real me. While I love ferociously, I'm not willing to reveal my truths.

Because far more than statistics and data, I can rely on my instincts. And they tell me that there are only three things that I can count on.

One, people in love are blind.

Two, I am ingrained with a keen sense of people—reading them, fitting in with them, manipulating them ...

Three, the people who know the real me wind up dead.

Olivia

Saturday, October 8th

The doorbell chimes for a second time as I rush from the laundry room. Bella's whining and pacing in the entry; for once, she's not shut in the office with her favorite human. She probably became too restless, considering how many hours Camden's been locked in there without a break.

I pause at our grand front door with its high gloss finish. It's a perfect mockery of my life. With a deep breath, I smooth my clothes, then pull the door open, a smile plastered on my face.

"Charlie," I exclaim, trying not to let my bewilderment reach my face.

If Bella hadn't been out here revealing my presence and hers, I could have pretended that I wasn't home and told Camden it was a salesman.

My nerves fire as I glance over my shoulder to examine the vast foyer behind me. I didn't invite her over, but I'll be blamed.

"I was in the neighborhood visiting Annaliese and thought I'd stop by," she says, sliding past me to let herself in. "Besides, it's been ages since you've had me over."

"I'm glad you're here," I say with feigned sincerity.

Bella wags her tail and nuzzles her nose into Charlie's hand. Charlie pulls away, scrunching her nose.

"Your place looks ... the same," she says as she moves past the entry and into our main living room.

My neck pricks. Was her disgust directed toward Bella, my house, or both?

"Would you like something to drink?" I ask, hoping she'll decline.

I don't want her to stay, and Camden doesn't like guests unless it's his uncle.

"Nothing for me." She waves away my offer and sets her tote-sized Louis Vuitton on the coffee table, then settles into the sofa. "I can't stay long. I need to run some errands before I see you again in a couple of hours."

Precisely why you shouldn't be here, I think with such ferocity that I fear she'll read my mind. We're supposed to meet to get last-minute essentials for the Glamorous Kitchen party she's hosting tomorrow. There's no reason for her to be here—and she's ruining my plans.

I take a meditative breath and sit.

"So, what's up?" I ask, ready to move this along.

"I wanted you to be one of the first to know," she says, bouncing in her seat.

My heart quickens. Is she pregnant? She'll have a third child, and I don't have to compete. Old habits ... I contacted the fertility clinic this week. I've paid in advance, leaving me with just enough money left over to take care of some other business. The scheduler will be reaching out any day to give me dates when I can get started.

Charlie flashes her whitened teeth and digs into her bag, pulling out a long microfiber cloth.

"As you know, I'm always crafting. In August, I had this brilliant idea. And ..." she trails off, allowing for a silent drumroll, "I've decided to start my own business, making jewelry."

She unrolls the cloth on the cushion between us, revealing an array of unimpressive handmade jewelry. Her eyes dazzle as she grabs a pair of earrings and holds them up.

"These are my favorite. Don't you just love them?"

I nod. "You're so talented."

"I know," she squeals. "Which pieces would you like?"

My lips press together as I focus on the options she has, hoping that I can get away with only a couple of pieces. The pressure on my chest reminds me that aside from getting IVF, everything's the same—I still have debt.

"Those earrings," I say with pretend enthusiasm as I point to the pair still in her hand, then pick up a bracelet. "And this."

"Annaliese bought five items," she says when I shift away from her collection.

My jaw defies me, tightening at her unspoken threat. This is how it goes. If I buy only two pieces from Charlie, who is my *best* friend, I'll be the next subject of gossip. Charlie wouldn't need to complain to the others. She'd only have to say I bought two items, and they'd compare—do the math. It would be like wildfire with murmurs and whispers just out of my earshot, glares and smirks cast my way.

I can't afford to play the game of numbers. It's a masterful competition of who outbuys who. If I don't play, I can't ascend the rungs of the social ladder I've been determined to climb since high school. If I make one wrong move, my grasp will slip—leaving me broken on the floor.

I'll be ostracized by the women who give me community, who make me feel less alone. My grasp's been loosening, and soon, I'll be unable to afford even my own rung on the ladder. The richer I appear, the further I'm extended financially. My friends may be playing, too, but our obstacles are not the same. I had to start from square one. The fertility treatments send me back three spaces each time—my lousy insurance unwilling to pay, and Camden unaware of the costs. The secret I pay to keep is becoming more expensive, and I've added additional, more costly, debts.

I grab four more pieces from her haphazard collection without paying attention to my selections, then stand—preventing this from carrying on—and walk to my purse.

"You take cards?" I ask, doing the mental math of available credit on each.

"Not yet. If everything goes well, I will. I'm going to debut my business at my Glorious Kitchen party tomorrow! Won't that be great?"

My stomach drops. "Cash only then."

I peer at the secret stash in the side pocket of my Kate Spade wallet. It's the money I've withdrawn during grocery store visits—pilfering the cash under the illusion of increased food prices—combined with the small amount remaining from Jared's loan. I need all of this. Today. There's no time to covertly accumulate more.

"How much do I owe you?"

"Fifty a piece. That's the best friend introductory price," she says, tilting her chin up with a conceited smile. "Tomorrow, they'll be sixty-five."

"Three hundred," I say, the words coming out in a pained croak.

I swallow, trying to soothe my rapidly drying throat.

"Yes, please," she says, pride plastered on her face. "You sure you don't want any others at this rate?"

"I would, but I don't have enough cash," I answer, carefully removing only the three hundred I need while keeping the rest hidden.

She opens her mouth, probably to suggest Venmo or something else that's too convenient.

Before she can speak, I blurt, "Plus, you need all your inventory tomorrow, to start strong and promote your brand."

Bella gets to her feet and heads toward the hall behind me.

"Charlie?" Camden says.

I jump at the sound of his voice. He comes off confused, but I don't need to turn around to know it's a disguise.

My heart flutters as I swivel to face Camden. Bella's already at his side, begging for attention, but he ignores her, rubbing the back of his head instead—his tell that he's annoyed.

"Cam!" Charlie rises, gliding across the floor to where he stands. She touches his cheek, then gives him a delicate hug.

A buzzing starts in my ears. She's lingering. When she steps back, I'm simultaneously struck with relief and self-loathing. Jealousy is not becoming. Camden loves me. Charlie is my best friend, and she's married to Camden's best friend.

"I stopped by to show off my latest creations to Olivia," she coos.

His gaze is on the money in my hand. Too many twenties.

I hold it out to her. "I'm so glad you did."

Camden intercepts, taking the cash from me before Charlie can. His lips move as he silently counts.

"Three hundred dollars?" he snaps, glaring at the items I'm holding. "Isn't that a bit steep?"

"Oh, come on, Cam," Charlie elbows him. "You know I'm worth it."

The odd words sting. *You know I'm worth it.* As if she's a name brand.

He shoves the money in her hand, and she flashes her toothy grin at my husband.

"I better get going," she says, turning to retrieve her purse.

Camden and I watch, unmoving from our positions, as she lets herself out.

"Tell Billy I say hey," Camden calls after her.

She nods, and before she closes the door, she says, "Oh, Olivia. Don't forget to wear your new pieces to the party tomorrow."

We stare at the door in silence for several seconds before I feel Camden's gaze shift to me.

"I told you to watch the spending this week," Camden says, glaring at my new possessions.

"I know. It's Charlie, though. I had to."

"You didn't," he says sharply.

A jolt of guilt ripples through my chest. This is what keeping up is like in a sea of rich housewives.

"I need to get going," I say, glancing at my smartwatch and ignoring the shake in my hand.

I clamber to get my boots on. As I reach for a sweater, Camden runs his fingers down my arms and then turns me toward him.

"Sorry," he says, bowing his head.

"No, I'm sorry. I shouldn't—"

He presses his lips to mine, melting my worries away. It shuts out the thoughts of him handing Charlie money, of her too affectionate hug, at the familiarity in his eyes when he looks at her.

"I thought you were meeting Charlie," he says as he steps back. "But clearly not."

She shouldn't have stopped by. I rub my chipped thumbnail behind my back.

"I am ... I need to run some errands first," I say, then desperately change the subject. "I forgot to ask you ... a couple of weeks ago I was in the basement—putting away the fertility things—and I knocked over an album of baseball cards. Some letters fell out."

"Letters?" He scrunches his face in confusion.

"Yeah. Addressed to a Travis?"

His puzzled expression deepens, then smooths. "Probably some left-over stuff from one of Uncle Jared's storage units." He shrugs, one side of his mouth pulling up in amusement.

"Do you think someone misses them? Maybe we could return them somehow."

"If it meant something, the people would have paid for their locker," he says, squeezing my arm gently, then turning toward the hall. "Will you get takeout on your way home?"

"Sure," I say, watching him disappear around the corner.

So much for saving money.

When I'm in my car, I send Larry a text,

> *Running a few minutes late*

His response is less than parental.

> *Time costs money, Olivia. Tick-tock.*

Elle

Saturday, October 8th

I focus on Zane across the table, trying to block out the compounding noise of this restaurant. It's not full, but the people here are too loud.

The deal was, if I lost our chess game, we'd go out for lunch before he left for the airport. I took it easy on him today since he hadn't won in a while and seemed to really want to try the food here.

"You sure you don't want any of these fries?" Zane asks.

I blink slowly, purposefully.

"This will do," I say, bringing a glass of sangria to my lips. I suppress the urge to grimace from the excessive amount of sugar, but it beats straight wine.

"Come on." He pats my shin with his foot under the table.

"I'll eat later."

There's no telling what grease they use to fry their potatoes, and with the food they serve here, there's exposure to animal products even if the grease is plant-based.

He shoves a handful of fries in his mouth, ignoring the disgust radiating from my side of the booth. I bring my drink to my lips and don't set it down until there's only ice left.

"How long will you be gone?" I ask, hating that we're spending valuable goodbye time here.

"At least a week, but not sure."

BETWEEN LIES AND REVENGE

I love how he answers me every time I ask this question, despite us both knowing there's never a set number of days.

My gaze shifts over Zane's right shoulder to the door opening at the entrance.

A pang of anticipation mixes with the alcohol in my otherwise empty stomach.

Olivia is here.

I slouch in my booth and retrieve the menu that's still sitting next to me. I hold it in such a way that I can watch her while hiding myself. I don't need to look like a stalker—we were here first.

She's meeting an older man on the opposite side of the room. His beard is scraggly, his hair disheveled. He's not the man I saw from the alley, either. Interesting.

"What are you doing?" Zane asks with a chuckle.

"Deciding whether I want another drink," I say, pulling my eyes away from the couple briefly to look at the man of my dreams.

When my eyes return to Olivia, she's in a heated discussion with her companion. Clearly aggravated, she reaches into her tiny pink purse, seems to fight with it even, before managing to extract an obnoxious floral wallet. She takes a stack of cash from it, slamming the bills onto the table, then she stands, and starts to leave.

She halts when the older man calls after her, "You've already been so generous, but perhaps a little more—"

"What you have is all I've got today," she says loud enough for those paying attention. She then turns in a huff and storms out of the lounge as quickly as she came.

An exhilarating thrum courses through my veins. Olivia's keeping secrets.

"My head hurts," I say, setting the menu down. "I don't need another drink."

"I should get on the road, anyway," Zane says halfheartedly.

He stands, dropping cash on the table, then reaches for my hand, pulling me from the booth. As we exit, I slide my hand into Zane's back pocket and squeeze his ass.

"We should have fucked in a bathroom stall," I say, disappointed in a missed opportunity.

He laughs and throws his arm over my shoulder. As he presses his lips to my temple, he whispers, "You're perfect, even if your chess game isn't."

"That reminds me," I say, as if I could forget. "I got you something."

Opening the back hatch of my car, I reach in and remove the gift bag I hid. He takes it from me, pulling out the wooden box. He unlatches the lid and admires the carved chess pieces inside.

"These are ..." he says, holding a bishop in front of him.

"Amazing?" I help.

"Yeah. And awesome. And cool. And ... thank you."

"There's no matching board," I say, grabbing the folded paper I had by the gift bag, then close the tailgate and step back on the curb. "But I was thinking you could take them with you when you travel, and we can play long distance. I drew you a board."

I hold out the folded paper, and he opens it, looking at the squares I painstakingly measured to make sure they are perfectly symmetrical.

"You *are* an artist," he says, grinning.

"It's a bunch of squares," I say, shrugging off the hours that it took me because I wouldn't want him to get subconsciously stressed by inaccuracies.

He wraps his arms around me, resting them on my shoulders.

"They're perfect," he whispers into my hair. "Just like you."

From the corner of my eye, I spot a brunette. I glance across the street and see Olivia coming out of an office supply store.

I kiss Zane affectionately, then send him on his way. He has a flight to catch, and I have a brunette to follow.

Olivia

Saturday, October 8th

Charlie and I grab our orders from the barista and find a table near the window of the busy coffee shop. Caffeine is the only way I'll manage the rest of this day after the chaos that Charlie caused. But we've found her perfectly perfect—incredibly expensive—decorations.

She's topping off her bragging by talking incessantly about her children.

We settle for a small metal table in a crowded corner, and I wipe the crumbs from its surface. She finally takes a breath.

"So, what about you? Are you guys going to try IVF?" She drums excitedly on the table. "You and Camden have never taken so long to decide anything. A whirlwind romance, a short engagement, a home purchased immediately afterward, but no babies. I know *you* want them. What's the deal?"

My pulse quickens. I never should have told her about the fertility treatments or my hopes in general. That was before. I shift my eyes to my paper cup and take a sip, burning my tongue.

"Hot," I say with a gasp. "I'm going to grab a water."

The long line is a reprieve, but I'll need to return to Charlie, who doesn't forget a thing. This new secret is already challenging me.

Larry even had some snide comments about how easily and quickly I gave him more money. I'm never surprised when he demands money between monthly installments, but it's always a struggle to come up with it when he does.

A wave of nausea hits my gut, making the water more a necessity than a distraction tactic.

I try to forget about Larry, about IVF, because allowing my anxiety to spiral won't help when I return to Charlie, who is smiling at me from across the packed room as if she knows something.

The memories I keep locked away don't need to be released to remind me; maybe she does.

"Olivia?" a sweet voice asks from behind me.

I spin around, facing the redhead in jeans and a long-sleeve crop top who's speaking to me. It takes me a moment to place her. Elle, the woman from Dr. Marcellus' office.

"Hi, Elle. What a surprise!" I announce loud enough for Charlie to hear.

If I play this right, I may be able to skirt Charlie's questions. She wouldn't dare push the subject in front of a stranger.

"A timely coincidence," she says, swiping some hair from her cheek. "I'm glad I bumped into you. I should have gotten your number Thursday, but I felt so silly asking. My husband and I are new to the area, and I'd wanted—this is funny—to grab coffee with you."

"Well, then. It *is* an excellently timed coincidence," I tell her.

She peeks around me. I follow her gaze to the now-open register.

"A water, please," I say to the young man behind the counter, then turn to Elle. "What are you getting?"

She waves her hand at me, "No, that's—"

"I insist." I really do. I need her to owe me—to save me from Charlie.

"Americano, please, black."

As we move out of line to wait for our drinks, I respond to Charlie's curious eyes with a smile and a wave.

"I'm here with a friend," I say to Elle. "You should join us."

"I wouldn't want to impose." Elle shifts between her feet.

"We'd be happy to have you, if you'd like. No time like the present to have our coffee date."

"Okay, if you don't mind," she says, her shoulders relaxing. "It's harder to make friends these days."

There's something intriguing about Elle. She doesn't seem to hide behind a mask like the rest of my friends.

"Not if you know the right person," I say, grabbing my water and her coffee from the counter.

I hand the coffee to Elle, then retrieve a vacant chair and slide it to our table for her.

"How's your tongue?" Charlie prods.

She doesn't want to know how my tongue is, not really. I speak fluent Charlie.

"This is Elle." I lift my hand to present her as she sits down elegantly between us. "She's new to town. I thought she could use some company."

A hint of a glare flashes across Charlie's eyes before shifting to a large grin to greet our new acquaintance.

"Nice to meet you, Elle," Charlie says.

"We actually met, sort of," Elle tells her.

Charlie just stares at her with a blank expression, aside from her fake smile. It is odd. It took me a minute to recognize Elle when I first talked to her at Dr. Marcellus' office, but I still recalled meeting her, and Charlie never forgets a thing.

"You know, it was probably someone else," Elle says, making a wiping motion in the air. "It's nice to meet you."

"Don't sweat it," Charlie responds. "Do you like kitchenware?"

As Charlie jumps right in, the ideal host for any direct sales associate, I lean back against my chair, satisfied.

Elle

Saturday, October 8th

"I'll see you at my party?" Charlie calls after me as she heads to her Land Rover.

She flaunts the vehicle, complete with a pat on the hood, before climbing in.

My insides scream in annoyance. Rich bitch. To think I avoided swiping the cash wadded up in the little front pocket of her purse.

"I'll be there," I say, wiggling my fingers in the air.

"You don't have to come," Olivia whispers next to me.

"Nonsense, I want to." I try not to grit my teeth. "She's quite the character."

"Charlie?" She shrugs. "She grows on you."

"You two are close?" I need the scoop in case I need to beat out this woman for Olivia's time.

"Yeah, she's my best friend." She waves at Charlie as she pulls out of the parking lot, deliberately avoiding eye contact with me. "We've known each other since high school. Camden and I used to go out with her and Billy all the time. Double dates, before ..."

I wait, but she doesn't finish the thought.

"Children?" I nudge.

She turns to face me.

"Yeah," she says, leaving something unspoken. "You really don't have to go—"

"Nonsense," I protest. "It'll be a blast."

"Okay, well, if you change your mind, you can just let me know. Not a big deal." Olivia turns her keys in her hand and then retrieves her phone from her purse. "What's your number? I'll text mine to you."

It's painfully obvious how casual she was trying to be, as if she'd ever join me in bailing on a dumb-as-hell housewife gathering.

I reach my hand out, and she immediately places her phone in my palm, a new contact at the ready.

When I've finished, I give the phone back. Her gaze darts over her screen. She taps and scrolls. Her forehead wrinkles.

"Something important?" I ask. I don't have all day.

"Not really. One of my friends, she just ..." Her thought trails as she looks up.

I give her a concerned look and ask, "Everything okay?"

"Oh, yeah. She just wants me to participate in her newest downline's launch party." She rolls her eyes. "She added me to the group without waiting for my permission. She's asking me to engage in the posts and wants me to make a purchase so others attending are less likely to hesitate when they see the prices."

She pauses and takes a long, slow breath. I allow her the space, giving her the opposite of the chaos surrounding her.

"Sorry, I'm rambling," she says.

"No, you aren't." I shake my head. "I don't do social media, so I'm sorry, I don't quite understand."

"No, I'm sorry! I shouldn't have assumed." She puts her hand on her forehead and laughs. It's a nervous sound. "Okay, so, most MLM representatives sell products through social media. My friends—many of them—are big leaders for these companies. They like to have parties in person for content creation and motivation for their teams. It's how we socialize these days. They build teams online through social media channels. When people sign up under them, my friends help them launch their new businesses online. Most of the people in their downlines only promote their businesses on social media. Facebook groups, mostly, but some have gotten creative."

"MLM's?" I ask, finally getting a word in. Then, because I'm irritated, I add, "You mean, those pyramid scheme companies?"

"They aren't pyramid schemes," she protests, but it's negated by her nervously picking her nails.

Still, she keeps talking. "It's short for Multi-Level Marketing. Essentially, people can join and start their own business. They can choose to only sell products or also build a team. It gives them flexibility and control on how much time and effort they put in; and likewise, how much they earn."

"So ... you also sell things for one of these companies?" I ask, needing her to say no because I don't want to be stuck in hell for the foreseeable future.

"Oh, no," she says. "I just go to the parties, help them out, things like that. Like I'm helping Charlie with the Glorious Kitchen party she's hosting."

"Then Charlie," I say, knowing I should tread lightly but can't be bothered. "She's part of one of these companies."

"No." She chuckles. "One of our other friends sells Glorious Kitchen. Charlie is hosting, which means she throws a party, invites friends, and based on total sales, and some other factors like additional parties booked or people signing up to sell the products at her event, she gets rewarded. If it's successful, she'll get a ton of free products. And knowing Charlie ..."

"It'll be successful," I add, as if she needs me to finish her sentence.

"Yeah. Her new business—she's launching it tomorrow at her party—it'll probably turn to gold too."

I tilt my head in a question.

"Don't ask," Olivia says. "But it's not with an MLM."

"Okay, to clarify, these companies—the MLMs—have complete sales teams that aren't employed by them," I say, because I need to firmly understand this world. I'm not going in blind tomorrow, but I'm going in because I need to solidify my *friendship* with Olivia.

"Correct," she says excitedly. "They aren't employees. Once they invest in a starter kit, they become business owners."

I bring my hands together, forming a triangle.

"When they start out," I say, tapping my thumbs together at the base, "they're down here."

"Yes," Olivia says with a nod.

"And when they build a big enough team, and those teams build teams—like your friends," I say, tapping my fingers at the triangle's peak, "they reach this level."

She nods again, her smile disappearing.

I shove my now unoccupied hands in my pockets. I'm ready to leave, but after that enrapturing conversation, I need to lay down more flattery.

"Thank you for explaining it to me. You're really a great friend, helping them all out," I say.

"They'd do it for me," she says, blushing.

"Thank you for inviting me to have coffee with you," I say, changing the subject and batting my lashes. "You didn't have to do that."

Flirting is a necessary element of developing friendships. Anyone who says otherwise is an idiot. We don't just flirt to fuck. We flirt when we want something and when we want others to want something from us. We even flirt to recover from situations that are less than ideal.

"I'm glad you joined us," Olivia says. "And I'm glad to get to know you—to make a new friend."

I take in her genuine smile and my emerald cross on her neck.

"Friend. I like that," I say, grinning. "Hey, since we've been talking about businesses, I was wondering if you could help me with mine."

She opens her mouth to speak, but I put my hands up in protest.

"Not like anything you do for your other friends. In fact, it's more of me helping you," I say, making sure I sound desperate like her friends undoubtedly do. "I'd like to clean your jewelry for you. It's been tough to get myself reestablished after we moved, and the stores in the area haven't been wanting to contract me for appraisals, so I've been in a bit of a slump."

"That's how you knew my pieces were unique," she says, not answering the question.

"Yes, exactly. So, what do you say?"

I see the hesitation in her eyes, which gives me relief. She shouldn't hand jewelry—my jewelry—over to just anyone.

"Not today," I add quickly. "Trust takes time, and I'm boldly asking for you to give me yours. I was thinking, if you were up for it, you could pick me up tomorrow for the party. I don't know my way around anyway, and my GPS has been on the fritz. If, after the party, you'd like to see my machinery and license, I'll give you a quick tour of my home office. Then, if you decide to help me out, when you're ready, I'll clean your pieces for you. If you like my work, you could tell your friends."

"Then I'd know where you live," Olivia says, then laughs at her own lame joke.

"Precisely," I say cheerily. "I really need to go. My husband is waiting."

I wish he were, anyway.

"I get that," Olivia says. What she doesn't say, though, tells me there's a story there.

"No pressure on the help—not even on the ride," I add, turning toward my car. "You can text me later and let me know if you're up for it. If not, I'll see you tomorrow, pending the cooperation of my GPS. Again, thank you for today."

As I climb in my car, I call, "I'll talk to you later. Next time, coffee's on me."

She stands in the same spot, waving as I pull away.

She makes wooing her so easy.

Elle

Sunday, October 9th

O livia shows up at my house ten minutes early. It took her only thirty minutes to send me a text agreeing to pick me up.

"I thought we could grab a coffee on the way," she says.

Right ... the get-a-coffee excuse I so conveniently provided her with.

"Coffee sounds great," I say, grabbing a short suede jacket, aware that I can't take a hoodie today.

In the drive-through, I clasp and unclasp my hands as we order our drinks, mimicking Olivia's anxiety.

As we wait for our coffee, Olivia stares into the distance. I follow her gaze and see a billboard of a baby. It's one of those anti-choice pieces of propaganda shit that prey on poor women who are too hormonal to think of a time when an abortion could be necessary.

"Don't worry," I say softly. "That baby is still alive."

Bad joke. I know it immediately. Still, I stifle a laugh.

"Huh?" she says, turning to study me.

"The poster ... you were looking at it?" I point in its direction.

"Oh, yeah. I know. I was just ... lost in thought," she says, taking her foot off the brake to bring the car to the window.

She watches the baristas through the glass until one of them slides it open.

"You really like your coffee black like that?" she asks, handing me my hot paper cup, her attempt to change the subject.

"I do," I answer.

I could tell her why I don't order extravagant beverages packed with dairy, but I don't want to. Besides, nobody likes a vegan, and I need to be liked right now. Following up with a statement about how I don't like any of the artificial crap they offer won't win me brownie points either.

"So, what's this chef product being sold today?"

"Glorious Kitchen?" Olivia giggles. "It's a company that sells kitchenware, mostly. It's a bit expensive, but it's quality. You'll like it."

Her chipper certainty makes me want to proclaim that I won't, but I bite my tongue.

"I'm sure that I will."

Olivia turns the radio on, and I fidget and drum my foot to the beat, pretending to be nervous.

When we're stopped at a red light, Olivia keeps her eyes fixed forward, not moving them to the young man on the corner holding a *Need Help* sign. I take a banana and a five-dollar bill from my bag, then roll the window down and hand both to him.

Olivia's nervous energy fills the car, only easing when I roll the window back up. I ignore her. She has no idea what it's like to be the person needing help.

She lets out a sigh of relief as she pulls from the light and turns a corner. To hide my disgust at her reaction, I stare into the side mirror. There's a black car behind us, much like the one that was behind us before the Starbucks drive-through.

My muscles twitch in anticipation of an altercation.

I'm being followed, because nobody's following the basic housewife to my left. Olivia pulls into a neighborhood and the car continues down the main road.

Not following us. Not after me.

"Charlie lives in this neighborhood?" I ask as we pull into a development with massive homes.

"A bit further up here, yeah."

"What does she do?" I ask, genuinely curious.

"Funny thing." Olivia chuckles. "Charlie is debuting her new business today. She and you may have something in common. She's getting into the jewelry business."

"Very cool," I say more monotone than I should.

Charlie and I have nothing in common, not even our professions.

When we arrive at our McMansion destination, Olivia jumps into last-minute preparations while Charlie retreats to her room, taking full advantage of her bestie.

I shuffle napkins around, pretending to be helpful, like a guest who doesn't want to leave her only friend's side.

Charlie doesn't rejoin us until the women start to pour in through the front door, chatting loudly and filling the large space with their fake, overly perky presences.

There are more than twenty women circling about, sipping champagne like it's brunch, and daintily eating crackers with various spreads, when Charlie clears her throat and grabs everyone's attention. She introduces Beverly, though I'd be shocked if all of them didn't know one another already.

"Thank you, Charlie, for this wonderful gathering. It's so nice to see all you women here today, coming together to celebrate your sisterhood. I won't keep you all too long, but I'd like to share with you a couple of basics regarding Glorious Kitchen."

She holds the room's attention as she rambles, walking along the display she's set up. She affectionately touches each object, smiling like a proud mother.

"I'd also like to tell you a bit about me. Why shop with me? Well, for those of you who don't know, I'm a mom of three kiddos who are an absolute delight, and my husband, Mike, is so wonderful. He works so hard to support our family, and this is my way of giving back. With your purchases, I get to help pay the utility bills and buy the kids clothes and school supplies. I even get to support more local charities. This year, all three of my kids get to do an extracurricular activity of their choice, thanks to all my loyal customers."

Her eyes glisten, and I try desperately not to laugh. Her false gratitude is sickening.

I hardly care about a woman wanting to help her husband pay the bills, especially when it's a line—nobody here struggles. Neither do the two women to my right, who whisper about Beverly's sales tactics and clothing choice and how they do it far better than her. If she confessed her need to do something for herself, I might be intrigued, and these dumb bitches to the right may shut the fuck up about their *superior* company.

As she finishes her speech, Charlie adds, "Ladies, don't forget to check out my display on the kitchen table. Each piece of jewelry is handcrafted with love, by me."

Charlie searches the room for something, and Olivia jostles nervously next to me, pulling her hair from behind her ears so it drapes around her cheeks. Charlie glares across the room at her, but nobody else notices—or nobody fucking cares.

The women are already making their way to the table, picking up various objects. They scan a barcode on the table to place their orders.

Olivia weaves through the crowd, picking up scattered napkins and paper plates, mothering all these grown-ass women who should be taking care of their own trash. One woman stops her, gives her a big hug, then lifts her phone above their heads, posing for a selfie. Olivia smiles with her, then slips out of the woman's grasp as soon as the picture is taken.

After tossing her collected trash, Olivia drifts away from the crowd. She sits on a couch on the opposite side of the room by herself. I decide to give her a moment alone and join the rest of the crowd in ogling the items on display. I purchase some plastic organizers and a set of steak knives—investing in my deception—before making my way to Olivia to instigate tedious small talk.

"You have a lot of friends. I saw you taking some selfies."

"Yeah, Lexi. She's big on Instagram." Olivia's words are laced with annoyance. A woman after my own heart.

"I used to post things all the time," Olivia adds, her head dropping. "Back when I thought I had something to say."

She's keeping secrets, but she's not ready to confess them to me—or herself—just yet.

"So, alternately, you go around the room, picking up after them?" I ask in a calm, understanding tone.

"My mom, she was a nanny. Which basically meant she cleaned all the time. I'd help her out on the job, at home." She smiles faintly at her recount. "It's just habit to take care of others, like she's always done."

"My mom cleaned up other's messes as well," I tell her honestly.

"Past tense? Did she retire?" Olivia asks, looking at me.

"Something like that," I say, only comfortable with mild truths. "She owned a small jewelry store with my dad. It wasn't all luxury like it sounds. It was hard work; money was always tight." She nods. At least we have something in common, aside from taste in jewelry.

Charlie comes toward us, and Olivia shifts, her body tightening.

"Olivia," Charlie says, her bravado nauseating and her lurking annoying. "Did you get your order in?"

"I will before I leave." Olivia puts on her dutiful façade, smothered in honey. "Just deciding what else to add first."

"And your party ... have you signed up for one yet?" Charlie sits on the arm of the couch next to her, positioning her towering body to mimic her personality.

"Oh, not yet. I—"

"Have you seen how successful my new jewelry biz is? I'm almost sold out ... you always wanted your own business, to finally put that degree of yours to use, right, Olivia?" Charlie's condescension is grating.

"Someday," Olivia says, keeping her same sweet tone, but her fingers start tapping rapidly on her knee.

"It's tough work, creating a product that people will love. Maybe you should choose something simpler, like joining Glorious Kitchen. You could finally start cooking for Cam. He does love a homecooked meal," Charlie says, her face like stone, but her lips still upturned, putting on a show for the rest of her guests. "If you signed up to be a consultant today, that would help more than the party you're avoiding hosting."

"I—"

Charlie doesn't bother sticking around for whatever Olivia's about to say. She rises and spins on her heels, calling out to the next guest in the crowd. One that needs decidedly less shaming.

Olivia's head falls, and she begins fidgeting with the ring on her finger. It was Travis' favorite.

"That's a beautiful ring," I say, leaning in her direction.

"Thank you." She lifts her hand up between us and admires it.

"Do you mind if I take a look at it?"

"Sure," she finally agrees, sliding it off her finger and placing it in my palm.

"It's gorgeous," I gush. "I didn't tell you this yesterday. Officially, I'm a gemologist. I studied the history of jewelry in college. Antiques are my favorite. So much sentimental value."

My body thrums with excitement. My family ring in my possession.

Carefully, I run it through my fingers, inspecting it for myself and creating an illusion for Olivia.

"This prong is worn." I crinkle my face in concern. "It should be repaired soon, or you'll lose the diamond."

"Really?" Olivia reaches for the ring, and I return it to her. She squints, inspecting it for herself. "I'll have to take it in."

"I could ..." I let the thought trail off, lingering between us.

"You could fix it, when you clean it?"

Friendship at its finest. We can finish each other's sentences.

"If you'd like me to. I have the equipment."

She beams, nodding her agreement.

Elle

Monday, October 10th

Taking a break from my work, including on Olivia's ring—my ring—that she willingly handed over to me, I trudge into the kitchen. I grab a snifter and a wine glass from the cupboard, as my phone chimes obnoxiously.

Some people choose ringtones that they enjoy, signifying their love of the caller. I prefer a tune that makes me want to rip my hair out, so that I'm reminded to answer faster. As it blares, the wine glass slips from my fingers, shattering onto the gray slate tile and warming my chest with delight.

"Hi, Love," I sing into the phone as I place it on speaker and inch around the broken crystal to retrieve a bottle of bourbon.

I splash it into the snifter, and my tongue tingles in anticipation.

"Hey. What're you up to?" Zane asks.

"Wondering where you've been all my life," I say seductively.

"Oh yeah?" He chuckles.

I take a sip of the bourbon and set a half empty bottle of wine by the sink, admiring the label before dumping the dark liquid down the drain. The color is a vivid reminder of the blood bags that hung over my father's stretcher the night he and my mother died.

"It's how I fill my time, but I have you now," I say. "How's Washington State?"

"It's raining and miserable. I bet it would be great in the summer. They have a ton of wineries here. I grabbed a couple of bottles to bring you this time, but if I get called back here, you should come."

I take another swig of the bourbon.

"That sounds great, Love," I say an octave higher than normal.

Ten years of marriage and fourteen years of lies. If I went with him on one business trip, he'd want me to tag along on others. Soon, I'd never get to sneak to New York city or take a break from the burden of this person I've created, but damn, I miss him.

"When are you coming home?"

His tone turns melancholy. "Not sure yet. We're still in the middle of this case."

"Okay then, you want to take this to FaceTime?" I suggest, downing the rest of the bourbon and tiptoeing around the wineglass shards to the bedroom.

Phone sex with video is far better than any audio only call, and I'm needing to stare at Zane's hot as fuck body.

"Hun, it's the middle of the day here. I'm working," he protests.

"So, go to the bathroom. Or your car. Behind a building—I don't care." I pull my shirt over my head and switch to video.

"Hun!" he shouts, but the sound of a door clicking tells me he's followed my direction.

His smile is mischievous when he accepts the FaceTime request. It'll be a cold day in hell when he turns me down.

Travis' dead eyes stare at me. His surroundings are blurry, like he's in water.

"Where are you?" I call to him.

He doesn't answer. He's not breathing.

"Where are you?" I'm crying.

Flies swarm around his body. Buzzing.

"It's your fault," his voice says behind me.

I spin around, fear deep in my bones. Vibrating through me. His skin is ashen.

"No, it wasn't me," I protest.

A cackle ripples through the air. Not him. But him.

"Don't lie. We both know it was," he says, his tone gruff. "You fucking bitch. You had to run away. Had to have money. A home. Had to drag me into it. Now I'm dead."

"Where are you?" I ask again, my words quiet.

"Does it matter?"

"You have the jewelry. The—"

"You think I'm giving them back?" He laughs again.

He backs away, blurring into the space around us. It's darker now. Almost black. But it's now that I notice the two gravestones on either side of him. Mom and Dad.

"You'll never find it. You'll never get the key. You don't deserve it. Not after murdering us." Travis' voice echoes around me.

I sit up in bed, gasping. Drenched in sweat.

"Fuck," I say into the darkness.

Instinctively, I reach to my left. Zane isn't here.

Slipping from the bed, I wrap my arms around myself as I shiver. I move through the dark to the kitchen and pull a pen and notepad from a drawer.

The aching in my chest compels me to write. I shouldn't do this, not that anyone will ever find the letters that I write to him. It's the only thing that keeps him close, makes him feel more alive. I'd never tell the counselor from juvie that she was right, that composing these letters brings me comfort and closure, but they do. We wrote letters to one another excessively as children, from our rooms across the hall. It kept us linked when our parents died, and we were separated in foster care. It helps me carry on in the wake of his death.

Dear Travis,
What are you trying to tell me? I'm fucking tired of these dreams...

The words flow, and the eeriness from the dream fades.

I sign it as I always do.

Miss you with all my heart.
~L

I fold it neatly and go to the office where my lapidary equipment looms in the night. The closet doors slide easily, and I shove the basket of spare blankets to the side before searching for the indent in the floor. When I find it, I wedge my fingers into the crack and grip the carpet until the cover lifts, revealing a small space. I reach inside and extract a shoebox full of letters to my brother. Placing my newest inside, I return it to hiding.

I can't bring myself to get rid of them or to stop writing them. When they pronounced him dead, without a body to confirm it, I'd dream of him walking around somewhere like an amnesiac in a movie. I was a kid. I had high hopes. I guess some things never change.

It's easier to go back to bed after the familiar process. The dreams and the letters are the only things that remind me why things must be as they are, and why I must be the way that I am.

They are another nightmarish reminder that people who know the real me end up dead. I trap her in my letters to the dead and keep the dead alive in my dreams.

I return to bed to wait for sleep, scared to see Travis but desperate for him to come back.

Elle

Thursday, October 13th

I cross the dingy carpet in Dr. Marcellus' office toward the sofa, trying, not successfully, to ignore the competing stenches of lavender and vanilla, that I now permanently associate with this place. Imagining freshly ground coffee, I compose my expression, then turn to face her and sit.

"How are you doing this week?" Dr. Marcellus asks before I'm settled.

"Good." I make myself comfortable, burning time.

"Would you like to elaborate?" she asks.

I'd planned to drag this out and meet Olivia in the lobby, but I'll figure out another way.

"Very good. In fact, I think you've cured me."

Her mouth falls open.

"I think I'll be okay. I don't think I'll need any more sessions."

She eyes me, her body tensing. "Typically, I see my clients for several months. I know it may seem like you're making a turn for the better, but everything has peaks and valleys. The nightmares, the anxiety ... perhaps stick it out a bit longer."

She can't help me. The things that have ruined me can't be undone. She can't bring people back from the dead. Despite attempts by well-meaning *helpers*, I still blame myself for my parents' deaths and for my brother's death. Nothing this woman can say would ever change that.

She can't erase the image of my parents' mangled bodies being extracted from their brand-new car—the car they bought just before our last family trip to fucking Leesburg.

My blood boils.

Right now, I'd like to blame my anger on Zane for bringing me here, for not knowing my morbid connection to this place. I'd like to ignore the unbearable knowledge that they were coming to see me on the opening night of *Little Shop of Horrors* to deliver the blonde wig and form-fitting animal print dress for my role as Audrey. I'd intentionally left them at home because I knew that they had somewhere more pressing to be, but I selfishly wanted them to be at my opening night instead.

Dr. Marcellus can't help me. Nobody should ever try.

Nightmares are my punishment for my parents and for Travis. They trap me in my sleep, just as I was trapped the night that my brother died. I'd only had one drag from Sam's joint and a couple of beers, and yet, I was dead to the world—sound asleep—my emerald cross swiped from my neck, my brother's life stolen.

My head burns from the memory. "I'll come back if things fall apart," I croak.

"I may not have any openings." She lets the statement linger between us.

They obviously don't teach psychologists sales tactics. Anyone with common sense would catch this desperate attempt to keep a client from a mile away.

"I'll take my chances," I say, standing. "I'll save you the rest of your hour. With your schedule so booked, I'm sure that you don't get much rest."

Her mouth falls open for a second time.

I move swiftly to the door but pause at the bookshelf, the red light catching my eye.

"It's unethical, right?" I ask with an intentionally snarky tone.

"What?" she responds, questioning eyes watching me.

Stepping next to the bookshelf, I pull on the seemingly normal frame, a hidden camera in the back.

"Filming your patients without their consent."

Her normally radiant complexion takes on an ashen tone.

"You'll be sending me a refund."

I head out the door and through the waiting room, then down the elevator and out through the lobby for the last time.

I need something to kill time while I wait for my new friend.

Olivia

Thursday, October 13th

I didn't notice Elle until I turned from the window display of Cutie Pie Baby Boutique. Elle's leaning on the brick wall next to the entrance of Dr. Marcellus' building. Even though she's not looking in my direction, I can't stop my cheeks from warming at the idea that she could have seen me in my trance.

When I'm only steps away from her, my nerves prick my skin, and I rush to look at the time on my phone. Text notifications from Jared steal my attention,

> *first payment due this weekend*

and

> *don't disappoint me*

concluded with a third:

> *not a word to our Cammy boy.*

"You're not late," Elle says, snapping me back to thirty seconds ago when I was stressed about making my appointment on time.

She's right; I'm not.

"Why aren't you inside?" I ask, locking my phone without responding since I have no clue what I'd say to him.

"It was my last session," she says it nonchalantly, but I feel like I'm pushed backward by her words.

"Oh," I say quietly, and immediately recognize how pathetic I sound. I've been coming here for so long, and every week, I feel further from ever being okay.

"Dr. Marcellus just isn't the right fit for me. That's all. You know how it is. Sometimes things seem to fit, then one day we wake up and realize we must let it go for something else."

I nod, though clearly, I don't know *how it goes.*

"I have something for you," she continues, reaching in her purse.

She hands me a felt bag. I reach inside and extract the ring, then admire it as I slip it onto my finger.

"That was fast," I say excitedly. "It looks brand new."

"Oh, sorry," she says, shifting. "Sometimes I clean too well."

"You buffed out the marks on the gold too." She's made miracles happen. "It's perfect."

In fact, it shines like it's worth a ton of money now. I can't wait to show it off.

"Thank you so much for doing this," I say, feeling giddy. "You sure I don't owe you anything?"

"Just keep the pieces coming and brag about my work," she says, grinning.

"I can definitely do that," I say, nodding.

"If the rest of your antiques are in the condition that ring was, they're in desperate need of an old-school caretaker like me—before they disintegrate into worthless dust."

I touch the cuff on my wrist, then the long strand of pearls braided with gold hanging past the cross at my collarbone. Suddenly, the pieces feel like the noose of another urgency threatening to take my life.

"They can do that?" I ask, removing the pearls.

"Over time, but don't worry, we'll get them taken care of," Elle says. Still, I hand her the pearls and the cuff.

"Want me to work on the cross, too?" she asks.

I shake my head because I need it for comfort. Instinctively, I reach for it, rubbing it between my thumb and finger.

"Another time, then. I should get going," Elle says, glancing at her watch, then pushing off the wall. "You should, too. Maybe we could grab coffee this weekend? I still owe you."

"Yeah, that sounds great," I answer.

We turn in opposite directions as she heads the way I came, and I go to the door of the building.

"Oh, I almost forgot," Elle says, stopping me. She digs through her purse again as she walks back toward me. "An appraisal. For insurance purposes."

"Thanks," I say, taking the slip from her.

"My pleasure," she says, turning to go again.

She had said that she does appraisals, but I'd never expected this. Elle's gone above and beyond.

"Hey," I call after her—now my turn to hold us up. "I have a bit of an idea for you. For your business."

It isn't fully formed yet, but this ring is gorgeous. Since she told me what she does, I've been mulling over an idea. With my new debt collector knocking, I'm hoping it'll appeal to her, and we can go into business together.

"Oh yeah?" she asks, a smile on her lips.

"I could tell you about it at coffee," I say.

"Perfect. I'll text you. You can bring more jewelry then, too."

I shove through the door into the lobby. It's decorated for Halloween. I lift the appraisal to tuck it into my purse, but a number catches my attention, and time stops.

The ring that's back on my finger ... is worth fifteen thousand dollars.

My heart races and slams against my chest.

This ring isn't technically mine. It's not technically anyone's, since Jared abandoned it in our basement, and Camden believed my fib about buying the bracelet from an estate sale. Nobody seems to care about it or the other pieces in that old jewelry box but me.

It's so clear—so simple. If the jewelry was important, it wouldn't be hidden away, collecting dust instead of memories.

Jared wanted me to clean up my mess so he could protect Camden. Turns out, he's helping me, too, by giving me access to this ring.

My official plan: Give Camden a child. Gain Jared's blessing and fall back in to his good graces. Do the right thing and pay off all my debts. Start fresh.

This ring will set me on my path to redemption.

Obviously, I couldn't give Jared a large sum of money out of the blue, but it's easy enough to spread it out over time as if I were making payments without any more credit card debt.

Without thinking, I step back through the door, beeline for my car, and climb inside. Only once I've searched the internet for nearby places to pawn jewelry do I realize that I should probably call and cancel my appointment with Dr. Marcellus.

I sit outside Second Love, a secondhand jewelry store, for a solid fifteen minutes before I get the courage to go inside. My self-condemnation of what I'm about to do competes with the thrill of possibility. Finally, I grab my keys and my purse and climb out of the car, thinking, *if you don't like your life, change it.*

Still, it feels wrong as I push open the heavy glass door to the shop.

The stale air makes my nose curl. I shake it off before I'm seen as a snob by the middle-aged man on his cellphone behind the counter.

"Can I help you?" He groans, boredom nearly oozing off him.

He doesn't even glance up. I guess he can smell my type—a stark contrast to the mildew in this space—a rich person trying to sell their possessions so they can get out of a bind and remain rich.

He wouldn't be entirely wrong.

"I was hoping to sell an item," I say, intending to sound casual but instead speaking in an octave higher than normal.

He sighs. "It depends on what you got. I don't need any diamond earrings. We've got a case of them right now."

"No, not earrings. A ring." Still too squeaky.

I walk over to the counter, and he glances up before returning to his screen.

I carefully take my appraisal slip from my purse, then remove the ring from my right hand.

"We'll need to take a look at it before we can make an offer." He picks up the ring, his lips curling. "Don't expect our offer to match the appraisal. Those are meant for—"

"Insurance, I know." I nod, wishing it weren't the case. I could use fifteen thousand. If they offer ten—even five—I'll be ecstatic.

"I'll just need to take it back to the office," he mumbles.

"Of course," I say, taking a small step away from the counter and hoping that I look more than willing to cooperate.

He turns and disappears behind a door, leaving me alone in the shop.

My chest tightens. I shove my hands into the pockets of my fall coat, trying to stamp down the nerves.

I make my way around the room, peering into the cabinets. The earrings take up a large section. I can see why they're not buying more.

Expensive watches are lined up next to a slew of different bracelets and cuffs. The rings, likely from failed marriages and proposals, sit in another cabinet. They all have varying indications of age. Some even look brand new.

The door opens, startling me, and the man returns to the counter, setting my ring down.

"So, what did you think?" I ask eagerly.

"Your appraisal is worthless. You can't come in here trying to con us with your pretend appraisals and knockoff jewelry."

The sound of silence echoes in my ears, and my mouth dries.

"No, no. That's not right." The words don't sound like mine. They don't sound like they're coming from me at all.

My cheeks should burn from embarrassment—except that I feel my blood drain from my face first. The shelves and walls inch closer until they encroach enough to strangle me.

Before I faint—or acknowledge what's happening—I grab the ring, shoving it in my pocket.

"We'll take the necklace, though," the man says, pointing to my neck. "Seven hundred."

My forehead wrinkles as my throat constricts.

I open my mouth to speak, but nothing comes out. Is it worth it? My cross. Lost for a minuscule amount. The only antique I own worth any sentiment to me is this piece. This was a gift from Camden when we got married that I'd always planned to pass on to our children. It's family heirloom—the only one he's ever shared and the only one I think either of us has ever had. If my mother died, the only thing she could leave me with is her unpaid debt, just like her mother left her—and I already have enough of my own to last me a lifetime.

I shake my head and then turn to flee from the shop but pause with the clearing of the man's throat.

"The necklace. I'll pay seven-fifty. Final offer. We won't buy it if you leave. No telling how you'll try to con us next."

My heart pounds. This is it. This is the moment I betray Camden so I can make good on my word to his uncle.

It was a foolish decision to come here. I'd been convinced I'd be walking out of here with so much cash. More than seven hundred and fifty, but I need that money. Jared's expecting my first payment. Larry's been harassing me all week, insisting I've come into money with how much I gave him Sunday. I haven't even made the minimum payments on all my credit cards yet.

Sucking in a deep breath to counteract the squeezing on my ribs, I step back to the counter and remove the necklace from my neck.

"Deal," I say.

My knees bounce as I wait for him to count out the cash, then promptly sweep it up, fold it, and shove it in the same pocket as the ring.

Elle's right. Sometimes, we need to let things go for something better.

What good is an heirloom anyway, without children to pass it down to?

Before

A Simple Game

"The key to chess is learning how to read your opponent," Xander says.

I glance across the board at him. His expression is dead serious, with a hint of pride. I twist my face into an expression that hopefully looks more contemplative than amused.

"Deep, right?" he asks, leaning back. His core jerks a bit as he catches himself from falling and glances over his shoulder before looking back at me.

It's only then that I allow the laughter bottled in my chest to escape. On cue, a flock of birds fly overhead, chirping in agreement.

Central Park is beautiful this time of year, caught between spring and summer. It's pushing perfect, and the moment fills me with hope. It's almost enough to confess the lies I've told him, to erase the me that was jaded and start with a fresh version—perhaps the real one.

I think about the wine barrel in my apartment and the contraband it hides, tying me to crimes that he doesn't know about. Nobody alive knows about them. It would be so easy to tell him that I don't like wine, that I love him.

With the way that he'd forgotten his concrete stool didn't have a back, he's taken by me too.

I could tell him that I know how to read people. For me, people aren't complicated textbooks—they're simple picture books that lack nuance. If that's all there is to this game, then I'll be kicking his ass in no time.

"People play this game for money?" I ask.

"Mostly the old men here in the park betting, but yeah, sometimes," Xander says with a grin that I could get lost in.

"I wonder how much I could win in a couple of months." I shouldn't have said it out loud, but the moment has my heart.

"Slow down, tiger." He chuckles. "How much you trying to win?"

It's a casual question. Since I like a little shock and awe ...

"Whatever it'll take to pay off my drug boss boyfriend." I shrug. "Or, at least enough to buy me some time until I figure out how to get him off my back permanently."

A shadow crosses his face.

"Ooh! How much do you think I'd need to hire a hitman? That would solve the problem."

"Police officer," Xander says, pointing to his chest. Then he points at me. "Out on parole."

"I'm not on parole anymore, and you're going private. But, good point. I'll keep my plans a secret," I say, pinching my index finger and thumb together, then sliding them across my closed lips in zipper fashion.

"What's going on?" He leans onto the table, almost knocking his pieces off the board.

Shit. My joke—not really a joke—went too far.

"Sam's getting out soon. He thinks—they all think—that I had something to do with our arrests. Or they think Travis did, and since they can't go after him ..." My throat locks up, and I'm unable to finish whatever thought I may have had.

Xander's muscles tense, and his gaze flits to his right, his left, and in the open space behind me. He looks ... scared.

"They'll get their revenge by coming after you."

I nod, unable to speak.

He reaches across the concrete table to take my hand. I thread my fingers with his.

"This isn't exactly how I'd planned to ask this," he says, clearing his throat.

My heart pounds. I don't like being surprised and this feels like he's going to spring something on me.

"I got a job offer. In D.C. Would you come with me?" he asks.

"Come with you?" I croak, finally clearing my throat. "Leave New York?" He must be high. Me—leave New York?

"I know I can't compete. Not really. You love this city, but I ... love you. I'd turn down this job if it meant being with you. Except ..." Xander says, pulling his hand from mine and shoving it between his legs with his other, his shoulders inching toward his ears. "Except that this might be exactly what I need and what you need. I could keep you safe. You're not safe here. You could be, with me."

My gaze trails down and across the chess board. I'm terrified of Sam, which is something I'd never tell anyone. The look on his face the night of the raid burns in my mind—the tell of a man who knows more about me than he let on. He will kill me. He believes I was interfering in his plans to grow his illegal business. Everything I did was to escape—to get the fuck away from him—not to gain power or revoke his.

My fate was sealed the night that we were all arrested, or perhaps before that. If that wasn't enough, I locked it all in by falling in love with a cop.

I grasp my queen and slide it into position. "Check. Mate."

Elle

Thursday, October 13th

I drive a roundhouse kick into the punching bag, needing it to be enough for my aggression today.

The other women don't like going in the boxing ring with me. They say I don't fight nice. Today, they'd be right. I have no doubt that I could find a man needing an ego boost to box me, thinking he'll win, but I can't bring myself to engage with people.

Olivia consumed all my energy. That woman is a rollercoaster of chaos and emotions, and so untrusting.

She could have let me *clean* the fucking cross.

I bring my gloved hands in front of me, take a slow, deep breath, then adjust my stance. My fist slams against the side of the black sandbag, jarring my muscles and filling me with delight.

Just past my bag, I watch two men take the boxing ring. One of them is going on about getting some hot chick. Dumbass. The two laugh and slap each other's arms as they pull helmets and gloves on. Dumbass nudges his friend, wanting to swap promiscuous details. His friend only congratulates Dumbass on his sexual achievements before taking a corner of the ring.

That voice—

A jolt shoots through me, compelling me to focus on the two men. Dumbass' friend seems familiar. So familiar.

I don't know why I do this to myself, more so now that I've located my inheritance. There's something about a boxing ring that always brings me back—it makes me see ghosts.

Pivoting back to the bag, I slam my other fist into it, trying to pick up momentum, but the satisfaction is gone.

At least I scared Olivia into giving me two more pieces today. With her newfound urgency, I may get this done before time runs out. If I'm lucky enough, I'll be given a bonus, receiving the details of how boring, wealthy Olivia has ended up with my things. She's not a thief or a murderer, but maybe she's unwittingly tied to one.

I step away from the bag since it's lost all soothing elements.

What I need to do is get to New York and check in with my people. Sell some flea market, flipped shit.

Turning to leave, I glance at the boxing ring again. *The man could be his clone.*

Maybe the dead have doppelgangers.

I push open the locker room door and I hear a thud from the boxing ring. One of the men was dropped. My money's on Dumbass' friend. I have no doubt Dumbass is sprawled on the floor, his opponent the victor.

My phone chimes. I smile before looking, knowing it's Zane, but the message warms my entire body. He sent a photo of the wooden chess pieces set on the paper board. He's moved a single white knight from the bottom right of the board.

> *Knight g1 to f3.*

I did lose last time, so he starts. Typically, I'm the white pieces.

I step out of my office and go to our chess table, moving his piece first, then mine, before responding with my own picture and

> *a7 to a5.*

When he responds with his next move within moments, I settle into one of the seats, allowing our game to distract me from another, more pressing matter.

As darkness settles over our rental, Zane pauses the game so that he can eat and get back to work. Returning to my now-dark office, I grab the snifter next to my equipment, take a gulp of watered-down whiskey, and then turn back toward the door to turn on the light. Just before I flip the switch, headlights shine through the blinds.

My heart rate picks up. Zane isn't coming home today. No packages are scheduled for delivery.

Not turning on the office light, I step into the hall and move swiftly to the front door. I bring my eye to the peephole, expecting the black car that's been periodically across the street the last couple of weeks. My fists curl at the thought of the mystery car making its way onto my property. A fight would be in self-defense.

It's not a black sedan. It's Olivia's Lexus.

She's sitting in her idling car. She shouldn't be here. We aren't on drop-by friendship status.

Sliding my slippers on my feet, I step onto the porch and shove my hands into my hoodie pocket. After a minute, she turns the car off and steps out; the headlights illuminate her figure as she approaches.

"Everything okay?" I ask as she climbs the steps, playing the part of a concerned friend.

"Um ... can we go inside?" she counters, pulling her cardigan tight around her torso.

I push the door back open, and she follows me in.

"Wine?" I ask. I don't wait for an answer since she's short on words today. I pour her a glass of red and bourbon for myself.

She's still standing in the entry.

"Sit," I say, with a smirk, setting her drink on the coffee table and lowering onto the couch.

She moves like a snail, finally landing in a position next to me but facing me.

If she thinks I'm going to be her sounding board for whatever drama is happening in her life, she's mistaken.

"What is it?" I nudge, ignoring my instinct to make her leave and avoid whatever this is.

"Listen," she says slowly. She doesn't continue but reaches for the wine glass and takes several gulps.

"You'd have to talk for me to listen," I say, unable to conceal my sarcasm.

"Your appraisal was wrong." She takes another gulp of the putrid wine and lowers it onto the couch.

"No. It's accurate." I sit on the opposite end of the couch, crossing my arms.

"I tried to sell the ring." She sets down her glass. "It's not real."

Anger crawls up my spine and wraps around my skull.

"You tried to sell it?" I snap.

"You knew it wasn't real," she says, her voice cracking. "So what? You lied on the appraisal? Why? To get more business? To befriend me?"

An uncontrolled snigger escapes my lips, spilling into the space between us. She's fucking desperate. Not so rich after all.

"This isn't funny!" Her voice rises an octave, and her knee begins bouncing.

"Don't question my capabilities. The appraisal is accurate. The real piece is worth fifteen."

Her jaw drops. Her knee stops.

"The *real* piece?"

"You need me to repeat it?"

She pulls the ring from her legging pocket and turns it in her fingers. It wasn't the easiest piece to replicate. It isn't a piece engrained in my memory—one I could remake in my sleep—like one of the others I mass-produced in my youth. Hands down, it's easier to sell a fake based on a less expensive piece, not that it ever stopped me from trying and succeeding with my more valuable family heirlooms.

"That's why it looks so new?"

"Great work, Nancy Drew." I down the rest of my whiskey and slam the glass on the coffee table.

Olivia stands abruptly, putting her hands on her hips.

"Give it back." Her demand is less than threatening.

I take a breath and lean against the sofa, my arm draped over the back.

"No."

Olivia

Thursday, October 13th

At first, I was confused, then anger took over as ideas formed in my mind.

"What do you mean, no?" I ask, needing clarification of her refusal to give back the jewelry. My skin pricks along my fingers and up my arms.

"No," she says again. Her cool demeaner is jarring, irritating.

"You're a thief!" I shout at her, like I'm one to judge.

"Some would say that." She laughs, rising to look me straight in the eyes.

She holds my gaze, daring me to continue. I can't find the words, though. Instead, my cheeks burn.

I'm not a fighter. I'm a pleaser. A runner. A follower.

She smirks and spins on her heels, moving back into the kitchen for more bourbon.

"You have no right trying to sell that jewelry. It isn't yours to sell." Her tone is ice, cutting through me.

Pressure builds at the base of my skull. How does she know it's not mine?

"Yes, it is," I protest, but the uncertainty in my tone gives me away.

"Where did you get it?" Elle asks, a knowing humor in her voice.

"They belong to me. I've had them." The urge to preserve my standing is strong, but it's not enough to make my words compelling.

"You're lying."

"I'm not."

I begin to sweat under my cardigan. My heart beats faster with each passing second.

She brings the bottle of wine into the living room and refills my glass. On instinct, I pick it up and take another long sip.

"My husband has a collection of things in our basement," I say, resigned.

"Where did he get them?" Her voice is calm now.

"Honestly," I let out a deep sigh, "I don't know. They've been in our storage space for years. I've always assumed that his uncle got them from a storage locker he bought, but I've never asked, and my husband isn't always forthcoming."

Why am I sharing all of this with her? Am I that desperate for some sort of connection? Or redemption?

"Hmm ..." Elle hums.

"It's not like they're important. They're not like a family heirloom, like the cross he gave me," I say, instinctively reaching for it.

The cross. It's gone. Elle is staring at my hand, resting on my bare neck.

"Olivia," she says, accentuating each syllable. "Where's the cross?"

A hollowness grows inside me.

"I sold it," I mutter. "I had to. The ring was worthless. I had no choice."

"How much?" she urges.

"What?"

"How much did you sell it for?" she demands.

"Seven hundred and fifty. It's all they'd give me."

"Seven-fucking-fifty! You can't be serious!"

Elle's face is tight, and her eyes are like daggers. Unable to withstand her anger, I let my gaze fall, revealing her hands formed into fists.

My phone chirps. Unable to ignore that I've been here too long, I wipe my tears and remove it from my bag. It's Larry.

> *Found your mom's address online. Was thinking I'd pay her a visit. Do some catching up. It's been years. I can't wait to hear her thoughts on your little secret.*

Everything goes cold, then hot. My breathing quickens. My mother can never know. She did everything for me. Her whole life. But her beliefs run deep, which is why I trusted him when I needed help.

I type back frantically.

> *How much?*

"Looks like you've got more than one enemy," Elle chastises.

I jump, remembering where I am.

> *One thousand would keep me away for now.*

My phone slips from my hand, slamming to the area rug at my feet.

"Appears I do," I answer, laughing in frustration.

"Get me the rest of the jewelry from your basement, and I'll be one less," Elle says, sarcasm gone from her tone.

I could sell the other pieces from the basement. I have no obligation to her. But Second Love basically told me never to come back, and I don't know the valuation of antique jewelry like Elle does. I've learned one thing tonight: I'm not the person for selling jewelry—not if I plan to make a profit.

"I'll get you the rest of the jewelry," I say. Reaching down to grab my phone. "If you become my business partner."

Elle

Thursday, October 13th

"**F**uck." I slam my hands against the glass door of Second Love.

"They might have a camera," Olivia says meekly.

"I don't fucking care. I need that necklace, and they're supposed to be open for five more minutes."

Whoever should be here is long gone. I'm wasting time and energy, but my necklace is in there. It better be. No way they sold it in twenty-four hours, not in a drab place like this.

"Why do you care so much? It's not your heirloom. It was my husband's."

Nobody aggravates me more than Olivia. I face her, and she begins picking at her nails.

"Your husband's lying to you."

"That's not—"

"Not true?!" I shout. "Come on, Olivia. You don't believe that."

I storm back to the car, slamming the door. The motor turns over, purring as I seethe. Olivia stands in the headlights, likely uncertain whether she should get back in or find a different way home.

"Hurry up!" I yell through the window. "I have shit to do."

Drip. Drip. Drip.

The rhythm is deafening.

I survey my surroundings, but I don't know where I am.

A basement. It must be. Musty. Mildewy. Damp.

Drip.

"He kept it here," a woman says.

I spin to face her. Olivia.

"Kept what here?"

"The jewelry," she says, touching her neck.

Drip.

Picking her nails.

Drip.

Touching her neck.

Drip.

"Where is it?" I ask. But it's not here. I can't see the box. She has no jewelry on.

"I sold it," she says. Picking her nails. "Don't tell him."

"She lies a lot," Travis says in a cool tone, his words filling the space.

I spin again, looking for him. Searching.

Drip.

"Where are you?" My voice quivers.

Drip.

"She doesn't lie as much as you, though." Travis' voice grows louder. "Nobody could lie as much as you."

"I never lied to you," I cry.

Olivia touches her neck. Her fingers trace her chest, but the cross is nowhere to be found.

"Ah, but you didn't have to lie to me to get me killed. It was all the lying with everyone else. With everything else."

I spin again, but it's useless.

"Where are you?" I beg the darkness to reveal him.

"Poor Zane. He's the only one you have left to hurt. And your lies are catching up with you. You know they are. They're stalking you. Have you told him that he'll die next?"

Travis' laugh is chilling, blood-curdling.

"Tell me, Sis ... what will happen when you have no one left to love? No one left to kill?"

Drip.

Olivia reaches out, touching my arm. Her hand is cold. So cold.

"I'll get them for you. I promise. You just have to help me. Please."

Tears stream down her face.

They match mine.

Drip.

"Travis?" I call to the now-freezing room.

"You have to protect me!" Olivia shouts, fear deep in her brown eyes. "They're coming."

"Who?"

She's yanked from the room.

I spin. Spin. Spin.

But I can't find her. Or Travis.

"Fuck," I pant, sitting up in the dark room.

The covers have fallen to the floor. I cross my arms, trying to warm my cooled skin.

In our small, attached bath, the faucet drips.

Zane. I'm putting him in harm's way.

Olivia

Friday, October 14th

The doorbell chimes a second time as I shift nervously in front of Elle's door. I remove two pieces of jewelry from my coat pocket, and when I hear someone fumbling with the lock, I curl my fingers around them.

Elle opens her front door and steps aside to let me in without a word.

"I brought a couple of pieces," I say, hoping I don't sound nervous as my uncertainty with this whole thing grows.

She hasn't told me why she wants or needs them. It's unnerving how she's so certain of herself. And it makes what little courage I have crumble.

"Great." Elle sticks her hand out.

I pass her a bracelet and a necklace. They were the two items with the fewest, smallest stones. I'm hoping my guess was right, but not too right, because I don't want to look distrustful or like I'm not holding up my end of the bargain, but she has the pearls and cuff I gave her yesterday, and I'm not willing to give up all the goods yet. I need her. As long as I have the pieces in my basement, she'll need me, too.

She scowls. "More would have been better."

"We had a deal."

"You have a deal. I've yet to agree." Elle turns and heads down her hall without waiting for me to reply.

I guess we're past pretending to be friends.

Looking around her living room and kitchen combination, I notice for the first time how quaint her mid-century home is, how pristine. The red oak floors don't have a speck of dirt and appear freshly mopped.

I'm glad she hasn't come to my house, and not just because she's a thief or because of Camden's aversion to company. It's ostentatious compared to hers. The house I had to have. I handpicked everything: the layout, the size, the finishes—it was all me. Camden just agreed and wrote out a check, funded by the inheritance from his father and a chunk of money he'd saved from bonuses from developing video games.

That's when he swore that he'd always take care of me. That's when he promised me the world, when he gave me permission to quit my job and live for each day without the constraints of a pushy boss.

The bills for the house started piling up fast, and the anxiety of not knowing when Camden's next paycheck would come in ate at me. When the threats from the power company started to arrive, I crawled back to Sarah and begged for my job back. The groveling was unnecessary—she needed the help—but she let me do so, reveling in my insecurities.

Elle comes back with a wad of cash. She shoves it into her purse and slings it over her shoulder.

"You look like shit," she says, scanning me.

"I couldn't sleep."

She laughs and flings open the front door.

"Let's go." She flips the lock and taps her foot, waiting for me to leave.

It isn't pleasant sitting next to a person who clearly has disdain for me, especially when I was convinced less than two days ago that we were forming a sincere friendship, not that I know what that's like. Everyone has stipulations and conditions. At least neither of us needs to pretend anymore.

My nerves feel like they're on fire, but I need to get this over with.

"You wanted to get your business out there in front of my friends," I say, then immediately regret it. So much for smooth.

"Is that what I said?" Elle says, chuckling. She doesn't pull her gaze from beyond the steering wheel.

"Well, I was thinking," I continue, as if she hasn't just told me that was a lie, too. "My friends are obsessed with their MLM parties, as you saw. We could do that." None of my pitch makes sense. I have been practicing this in my head nonstop for a week. The only thing that's changed is the ending. I've created an addition that I'm sure will intrigue her.

"Do what?" A shadow crosses over Elle's face. "You're making no sense. If you're suggesting I sell direct sales shit, you're—"

"No," I interrupt her before she can destroy any of my remaining confidence in this spiraling situation. "We could use the same premise. We could have parties, where women bring their jewelry for a cleaning and an appraisal. I have a lot of friends who—"

"Who have a lot of expensive jewelry."

"Exactly." I pull on one of my nails too hard, and it tugs painfully at my skin. "I was thinking that we could go into business together. I don't know anything about jewelry—"

"Obviously," Elle mutters.

I continue, ignoring her, "But I do know women. A lot of them. I know how to schmooze them."

She turns a corner abruptly, and I grasp at the door handle.

Maybe I'm explaining this wrong. I messed up my speech.

"Let me back up. Just like the Glorious Kitchen party we went to, there are a ton of those companies out there, and the women I know are always hosting parties. I swear, it's all these ladies do with their time. Have parties, shop with each other, buy ridiculously-priced products to support one another." I loosen my grip on the door. "If we use that concept, get people together at house parties ... you could clean their jewelry, appraise. In an afternoon, you could make more money than you would waiting at a jewelry store for someone to come to you. I think going to them is key. These women have deep pockets. We could do some sort of reward incentive to make it more appealing, like the MLM companies have."

A smile spreads on my face. They have the money that we need.

"If I do this, you bring me the rest of your basement jewelry?" She cocks her head but doesn't take her eyes off the road.

"Yes." I nod. "We'd split the earnings, fifty-fifty. Since I'd do the coordination, the peopling, and you'd do the work with the jewelry."

She laughs. "You're delusional. I don't care how many people you know. You're never going to make enough to pay off whatever debt have you turning ghost white at random moments, whatever has you going from goody two shoes to working with me."

Pressure builds in my temples. She's right. That's why I've come up with a plan, but as I get ready to speak, my mouth goes dry.

"And how long does this arrangement last?" Elle asks, irritation now thick in her voice. "Twenty years, since you obviously are in a deep pile of shit. Who sells something they think is a family heirloom, anyway?"

"Well," my words crack in my dry throat. "I was thinking that maybe you could make some pieces we could sell. Fake, but say they are real."

It's painful saying it out loud. Illegal. Ridiculous.

She shakes her head as she pulls into a parking spot just in front of Second Love.

She climbs out, leaving me before I could finish. I guess this conversation is over.

Elle bangs on the glass until the same unenthused man who helped me before comes to unlock the door.

He huffs when he sees me, but Elle ignores him.

"This woman sold you a necklace with a cross yesterday," she says, aggravated. "We need to get it back."

He looks at her with a flat expression, then over her shoulder at me, and rolls his eyes.

"Listen, this isn't a pawn shop. She sold it to us." He grumbles, sliding back behind the counter. "The only way to get it now is to buy it."

Elle leans against the counter. "How much?"

"Four grand."

My jaw drops. The man catches sight of my reaction and smirks.

Elle turns her head to stare at me, her expression cold.

"You said you sold it for seven-fifty?" she asks in a dry tone.

I nod, unable to form words. Does she believe me? Probably not.

Turning back to the man, Elle says, "I told her you ripped her off. What kind of a place buys a necklace like that and gets away with paying so little?"

"A deal's a deal," he grunts.

"Can I see it?" she asks. "To confirm that we're talking about the same piece of jewelry, and you know ... make sure you haven't fucked it up."

He grunts in response to her matching his terrible attitude. He turns and goes into the back room, leaving us in silence. Elle shoves her hands into her coat pockets.

When he returns, he sets the necklace in front of her and puts his hand over the cross. Elle extracts the wad of cash from her pocket and sets it on the counter between them. He nods, she nods back, and in seeming to come to an unspoken agreement, he hands her the necklace to consider.

"You didn't even clean it," she chastises.

"So?"

"Fifteen hundred," Elle says, gesturing to the cash.

"Four," he counters.

"Can I speak to your boss?" she says, her tone sickly sweet.

"I am—"

"Bullshit," she says, shutting him down. "I'm not stupid."

He huffs, then turns to the door and knocks. In the few seconds his eyes are off her, Elle extracts something shiny from her pocket and pulls the necklace that's dangling in her other hand into her sleeve.

A big man comes slowly out of the office, somehow looking grumpier than the other. Elle offers the fifteen hundred again and again, but there's no room for negotiation. She sets the necklace down and picks up her cash before heading for the door.

I follow her, my fingers tingling from confusion and uncertainty.

"Come back when you have four grand," the man calls. "But I can't promise it'll be here ..."

"Fucking thieves!" she shouts.

Elle

Friday, October 14th

Olivia follows me out of the nasty used jewelry store like a puppy with her tail between her legs. I don't engage in her sulking. She's a grown-ass woman, for god's sake.

"You stole it," Olivia gasps as we climb back into my car.

"I replaced it," I correct.

Reaching into my sleeve, I extract the necklace and clasp it around my neck.

"No, you stole it."

God. She's fucking incredulous.

"The one they have is technically worth seven-fifty, so it's a fair trade."

I yank the car in reverse and peel out of the parking lot. I'll never be back here. Fucking con artists.

"So, your business plan," I say, redirecting her. "It won't work."

"What do you mean? It's a great plan," she says in the annoying, high-pitched voice she uses when she's trying too hard to show her enthusiasm.

"Selling people jewelry, it's not as easy as you think. People these days question whether it's real, even if it is. If you don't have an established storefront and the jewelry store doesn't appear expensive, your friends, no matter how much they trust you, won't buy it. Let's be real. They don't trust you as much as you think."

She sighs and begins picking at her nails. Her fucking nails. I want to cut her fingers off.

"The cleaning ..." She starts thrumming her nails now, doing her best not to pick. At least she's aware of her disgusting habit. "It'll take too long."

"No shit. I don't have a lifetime," I announce. I don't have six months. Relocate. Restart. Always hide. She's burning my time. And it seems she's fresh out of her own.

"How much would I need to pay you to skip this bullshit and get the pieces from you?" I ask. I'm not paying her for my things, but pretending to humor her will be informative.

Her wheels turn. She's clearly not thought of this idea yet.

"One hundred thousand." She says it like a question.

"Nope," I say. No sense in drawing this out longer.

Her shoulders slump. She thought that blackmail would be easy. She chose the wrong woman to mess with.

"We'll split profits seventy, thirty," I say. "No, sixty me, forty you. I don't want this to drag on forever. We offer to repair some of the pieces, like I did with you."

"And ... you replace them?" Her words are shaky.

"Not exactly. That may be too obvious. Not everyone is as naïve as you are," I say. Not everyone is as fucking dumb when it comes to their prized possessions.

"So then, what, exactly?" Olivia asks.

"I take a stone or two from valuable pieces. It'll add up for us, and it won't be obvious to them."

Her shoulders are erect now.

"We should start soon," she says, eyes shining. "With the holidays coming, it'll be ideal."

"If we're going to do this, I need you to know some things. It's important because you'll need to trust me," I say. My secrets. Just two of the three things I know to be true. The third isn't relevant.

"Okay." Her face loses its glow as she focuses on me.

"People in love are blind. People love their jewelry for so many reasons, which can make them do some odd things. So, just be prepared for that," I say solemnly. "And, conning is an art. If you stick with me, and do what I say, things should go smoothly. I say this because I know how to study people and how to deceive them."

She nods in a slow, rhythmic way, absorbing this information.

"Remember, I'm not conning you anymore. I have nothing to hide," I say, holding up my hands in surrender. "So please, trust me."

"I trust you," Olivia says, but she doesn't sound convinced.

Her uncertainty is expected. Trust takes time, and I just ran my game on her. To be fair, I wouldn't trust me. I always have something to hide.

Her knee starts bouncing. There's something else on her mind.

"What?" I ask, knowing that I'll regret it.

"How will we sell the stones once we get them?" she asks hesitantly.

"Oh, honey." I laugh. "This isn't my first rodeo."

Olivia

Friday, October 14th

Annaliese waves from her yard, where she's watering her plants. I return the enthusiastic gesture.

Despite conspiring with a woman who is quite possibly the worst person in the world to trust, she's instilled hope in me.

I hum as I walk to the porch, my gaze down as I dig for my keys in my old Kate Spade purse—switched this morning for practicality.

"Olivia."

I'm jarred to a stop; the hairs on my arms stand up. I didn't see him before, sitting in the corner of my porch, hidden in shadow.

My heart thrums despite my internal reassurance that everything's okay.

"Hi, Jared," I say, trying to sound calm instead of scared.

"I brought some things for you," he says. "Thought I'd drop in since you're shirking your responsibilities and not at work."

"Things?" I ask, shifting to settle an unease in my bones. How does he know I'm not at work? And *what* responsibilities?

He stands and lifts a filing box from beside the chair.

"I need the books updated by tomorrow. Quarterly taxes are coming up." His gaze travels over me, causing me to shiver. "Your first payment's due."

"I—"

"A thousand would be appropriate since you no longer have other debts," he says, letting the last word trail.

He doesn't know? He can't know.

My hand quivers as I reach into my purse. It's like my muscles aren't following commands from my brain. Or rather, my brain has no commands for my muscles.

Money. I'm getting money.

"I only have four hundred right now," I say, fumbling to extract only four of the seven one-hundred-dollar bills from my purse. "I have utilities coming up."

He pulls the cash from my hand.

"Sunday," he says sharply. He sets the box in front of the door with a thud and steps off the porch.

"I won't have more—"

He holds up his hand. "And the books."

I nod.

"If Camden asks, tell him you're helping out by organizing the shit piling up in my office," he says, patting me on the shoulder. "Remember, not a word about the loan."

I watch him as he descends the steps and climbs into his black Mercedes on the street. I can't believe I missed it before. When he whips around the cul-de-sac too quickly, Annaleise looks up from her gardening with a glare. Her daggers don't shoot toward Jared's car. Instead, they're pointed at me.

Defeated, I push the door open and then hoist the file box into my arms. I resist the urge to look back over my shoulder by kicking the door closed. My boot leaves a scuff on it.

I drop the box in front of the couch, sit down, and remove the lid. The accounting book is on top, so I set it on the coffee table and retrieve a stack of papers.

The ledger fills in as I log expense receipts and incoming payments. The money funneling into his business is extensive. I had no idea that buying the contents of unpaid storage lockers could be so lucrative, nor did I realize how much outbound money was required. One of the most recent invoices Jared's paid, to Sad Rabbit, LLC, is for just over one hundred thousand dollars.

When I go cross-eyed, I stand and stretch my sore back. On autopilot, I go into my closet, change into shorts and running shoes, then cross the house to the room with only a treadmill and free weights inside. It's a poor excuse for a gym, but Camden doesn't work out at home much, and I don't run often these days.

I walk for less than a minute before increasing the speed. Walking won't cut it. I need to run off this jittery anxiety.

My lungs burn as my body adjusts. *Take it easy. Don't overdo it.* That's been my motto. For what? The fertility treatments were as useless as attempts at natural conception.

I click up the speed more to avoid tears because crying doesn't offer solutions. Action does. I'm going to pay off my debts. I'm going to get IVF. I'm going to prove to Camden that I *can* give him a child—and I'm not a failure.

"Fight Song" by Rachel Platten blares through my AirPods. My body floods with endorphins.

I need to keep moving.

My muscles scream in protest, oxygen wicked from them as my lungs fight to keep every breath to themselves. Staring through the window to the street out front, I focus on the tree next to my car.

A Maserati pulls into our drive, and the garage door opens, allowing it access.

My Lexus isn't allowed in the garage. Camden parks his cars there. His babies, filling the stalls and taking up residence where I cannot.

Camden said we couldn't afford IVF, but that thing must have cost three times what IVF does, if not more.

I seethe with anger. However much he paid didn't even pass through our account first. He's been hiding it from me so he could have another car. So that he wouldn't have to waste it on an endeavor that he thinks is futile—like my infertile womb.

My feet thud in time with the rhythm as the Rachel Platten repeats the chorus, ready to conclude the song. I'm going to take my life back. I'm going to prove Camden wrong. I'm going to prove them all wrong.

I climb out of the shower and slip into sweats and a tank. My body feels calm and ready to get things done. My steps are confident, my brain relaxed, or it's possible I'm just worn out, my anger burned out because I don't need help. I'm perfectly capable of providing my own success.

The blood in my veins runs cold as I step around the corner from the main suite. Camden's sitting on the couch, holding a stack of receipts in his hands.

He turns toward me, a flash of fury in his eyes.

"What is this?" he demands.

I scurry over. *Please don't let the receipts be out of order.*

"I'm doing your Uncle Jared a favor," I say, grabbing at the stack in his hand and tugging until he gives in to my request.

Flipping through the stack, I let out a sigh. They're in order.

A half smile crosses my face as relief floods me. I return my gaze to Camden, still frozen in his spot on the couch. His eyes ... they aren't angry anymore.

My heart sinks and my smile dissipates. Is that fear? He's never afraid of anything.

"I thought you were working," I say, trying to find a hint of what's the matter, and aware that he went straight from his newest sportscar to gaming. It's what I expected, but it was confirmed when Bella, who hadn't been bothered to get up since I got home, frolicked with excitement as he came in, following him into his office before he shut the door.

"I was taking a break. I heard the shower; I thought I'd come say hey. Then I saw all of this ..." He sounds defeated. Distant.

"Did I do something wrong?" I sink onto the couch next to him.

"No, you didn't, Babe," he says, fixing his gaze on me.

The darkness is gone from his eyes, but my intuition—my fear of stumbling into something that I shouldn't have—now looms.

He reaches up and runs his hand over my hair, then settles his palm on my cheek. His blue eyes envelope my heart, and despite everything, I'm drenched in my love for him.

His fingers travel to my jaw. He tilts my chin up, drawing me closer to him. His thumb slides across my bottom lip, and a warmth erupts through my body and into my groin.

By the time our mouths meet, I'm defenseless, melting into his arms. Accounting be damned. As he stands and pulls me toward our room, I glance back at the papers he was holding. The invoice on top is the paid invoice to Sad Rabbit, LLC, which triggers a revelation. There's a pattern. It's not a perfect system, but between debits and credits, the accounts periodically equal zero—perfectly.

Olivia

Saturday, October 22nd

The call that I've been waiting for finally comes in. The clinic has set dates for IVF. The calendar in my phone now reads December first, *Gym with Elle*. It's the first in a line of many gym dates, ust in case Camden gets nosey—though it's doubtful.

I allow myself a bit of hope, imagining two pink lines. It conjures the memory of when it happened before, and for once, it doesn't break my heart. I've spent so much time torturing myself over not getting pregnant and keeping secrets that I'd begun to believe I'd ruined my chances when I chose an abortion all those years ago. That's simply not true; it was only the catalyst for discovering the extent of my reproductive issues.

The reframing in my mind helps counteract the heaviness that's refused to leave my chest over doubling my debts. No, more than double, with Larry breathing down my neck so much. Add in the interest that I need to pay because I had to pay Jared instead of the credit card companies.

Despite my urgency to get our endeavors rolling, Elle's demanded that I leave her alone for a solid two weeks while she works on other things. She set a locked box meant for packages on her porch and has given me explicit directions to drop off one item at a time, every other day, from the basement collection.

If she doesn't keep up her end of the bargain, I'll be in deep trouble, but so far, she's proven honorable—as much as she can be—bypassing my little test. On my third visit to her new lock box, I left a standard set of diamond studs. It was a risk, but since I can't go back to Second Love, and they're not buying diamond earrings anyway, I wouldn't be missing much other than the studs, which I rarely wear. An hour after I made the drop, she sent me a picture of the earrings and declared that they weren't hers.

Somehow, Elle's probably the only person I can trust right now. Whether she's a thief is the least of my worries with these demanding men in my life.

"Larry," I say, approaching the man at the bar.

"Well, hello, sweetheart." He spins to face me, a wry grin on his face.

"I've told you not to call me that," I snap. "You lost the privilege a long time ago."

"Don't be like that," he purrs, mocking me.

I slam three bills next to him on the shimmering black counter.

"Three hundred should do," I say.

"Three hundred isn't a thousand, sweetheart."

Chills crawl up my spine just as a fresh wave of anxiety wraps its fingers around me.

"You know that money doesn't grow on trees." I try to sound tough, but it comes out wobbly.

"So then, interest-only payment? That's what this is?"

What's with all these men and their obsession with charging interest?

"I'll get you the money, Larry. Just leave my mom alone."

My secret needs to stay between us, but more than that, he needs to stay out of her life. I worked hard after he left to heal her heart and to show that I wouldn't be a failure like him, until he started reaching out, saying that he wanted to make amends. Until one night at a college party that led to the one decision that I knew would make me a failure in my mother's eyes. Perhaps that's why I waited so long.

The abortion was later than it should have been—I was broke, broken, scared, and so naïve. I didn't know about Planned Parenthood, or other options available to someone like me. Instead, I borrowed money from Larry and took a pill that wasn't enough.

Eventually, I had to go to a hospital, where I had an ultrasound, which confirmed that I'd need a D&C to remove the remaining products of conception. It was then that I learned about my endometriosis. Apparently, it's not visible with imaging unless it's bad.

The doctor removed the endometriosis and remaining tissue in surgery that same day. I remember the disdain in the nurse's voice afterward. I was waking up from the anesthesia but hadn't opened my eyes yet, so I pretended to still be asleep as she spoke to someone else in the room. She said that I was lucky to get pregnant with how much endometriosis they'd found. How was it that people like me, who were so young and pretty, who were carefree and careless, who got pregnant and chased it with an abortion for a contraceptive afterthought. It was never the people who wanted to get pregnant who did.

A scorned nurse kept me from telling anyone else about the abortion. I knew that if I told my mom, she'd be angry and so incredibly hurt. I try not to imagine what it would have been like if I'd chosen differently or if I hadn't been allowed to choose like so many women in the United States today. It's hard to comprehend what it would be like having a fourteen-year-old today. I doubt that I could have managed to care for the child. I had been a broke college student, and my mother wouldn't have been able to help financially or with care. I wonder whether Camden would have dated a single mother, whether he would have married one.

"This only buys so much time," Larry says, slapping his hand on the money. He slides it off the counter then shoves it in his flannel top pocket.

"Time is all I need," I answer, picking at my nails behind my back.

"Not too much, sweetheart."

I cringe at his words, wishing I could erase his voice from my head and him from my life. My heart cracks a little. Some men deserve none of the love, but get it anyway.

As I turn to leave, he says, "I found a dusty, old ultrasound printout. I sure do miss your mom. Would love to show her the tiny bean's picture—from before you had it killed."

My entire body has a jarring sensation, but I don't stop moving—don't acknowledge his words at all—because I can't give him the satisfaction of knowing he's gotten to me.

I can't let him know that despite everything, I'm still a desperate little girl longing for my father's adoration.

Elle

Saturday, October 29th

Another Saturday, another socialite pyramid scheme. Plastering a friendly smile on my face, I take in the crowded room and the people filling it. I can't grasp how these women are entertained weekend after weekend by attending these parties and spending hundreds of dollars on overrated products.

It's odd. No, it's fucked up. They believe in all this shit like it's the gospel. The gospel of collecting crap for obscene amounts of money. They fucking trade one another. One woman sells makeup to her friends, then turns around and spends more money than she's made on candles, dishes, clothing, and God knows what else.

None of them sees the vicious cycle that they're all in—or maybe they do, which makes it far more fucked up.

My wandering gaze falls on an unsuspecting blonde across the room. She's tall, her narrow frame dressed in black leggings and a red crop top, topped off with three-inch stilettos and dazzling accessories. From here, I can tell that her two sets of earrings, two chain necklaces, and four bracelets, are valuable. Not all are diamonds and gold, which is smart—otherwise, she'd be a walking target for theft. The expensive crystals that she mixes in don't do much to help her case.

"Who's that?" I ask, elbowing Olivia until she follows my gaze.

"That's Emily," Olivia says. "She's cohosting with Claudia."

If I were ten years younger and crossed this lady on the streets of New York, I'd consider which pieces I could easily slip off her and disappear with. I consider it now, in this place, but I expect to see these women again. I'm in it for the long game.

"She's a perfect target," I whisper, a smirk crossing my face.

Some of the color drains from Olivia. She audibly gulps before continuing her mission of informing me who everyone here is.

"Camille sells the fitness clothing that Emily's wearing." I look in the direction she's pointing toward a woman who's hovering around a display of workout gear. "She makes a killing with so many women living in leggings and sports bras."

Fitness fucking luxury.

A woman pokes Olivia on the shoulder, and I take her distraction as an opportunity to browse the clothes. Anything for a moment of peace. The mask on my face from the other lady pushing products is drying, and it's irritating.

I run the material of a hot pink sports bra through my fingers, then set it back down.

"It's cute, isn't it?" a woman asks.

I glance up from the table of sports bras to make eye contact with Camille. Great.

"Very cute," I coo.

"If you'd like, I can make a list of item numbers for you so you can easily add them to your shopping cart on your phone."

She poises a silver pen atop a purple notepad, and she hovers in the air.

"Sure," I say. "These two sports bras and that crop sweatshirt."

I point out the items slowly as she writes down the numbers from the tags. She tears the paper from her pad and hands it to me.

"My link is there." She points to her contact information imprinted on the paper. "I'm Camille."

"Elle." I reach out and take her hand, shaking firmly. "I'm Olivia's friend. We're starting our own business cleaning and appraising jewelry."

It's not lost on me that Olivia's inching up behind me. Keeping close tabs.

"Oh wow," Camille says energetically. "Congratulations. You two will love having your own business. It's so rewarding."

"We're very excited," I say, turning to Olivia. "We should see if Camille would like to host a party."

Olivia covers her own face in a fake grin and pulls her shoulders back. "I think Camille would be great. What do you think, Camille? Would you be interested in hosting a party?"

"Maybe," she says, wavering now that she's not the one selling something. "My schedule's pretty busy, though."

"We'll work around you. We could have an event with you. Collaborate like you're doing today," Olivia encourages.

"Jewelry cleaning and fitness clothes together?" Camille asks, clearly uncomfortable.

"Women need extra encouragement to buy their workout clothes and go to the gym. If their jewelry is in tip-top shape, they'll be buying things from you to get into the same shape as their shiny accessories."

Olivia pulls up the calendar on her phone, nailing down a date. No backouts, no excuses.

I fold the list Camille gave to me into a napkin and drop it into the trash as I walk by.

I'll need to go to Target after this—get the same quality at an affordable price.

Olivia

Saturday, October 29th

I make my way through the crowd of women who are sipping champagne and sporting charcoal masks until I find Elle.

"When do we get to take this off?" I ask her, pointing to my own gray face.

Claustrophobia is sneaking in with each passing second, and I need an escape from the mask. From the pretending. From what I'm about to do to all these women.

"I personally like my skin so tight I can barely speak," Elle says, lifting her own plastic champagne flute to her lips.

I turn away from her and search the room for Claudia, Emily, or even Emma, who's selling this product. Giving up, I scoot into the hall bath as another woman steps out. Her face is void of mud and all the foundation that she once had on. She's prettier this way, without it.

The door clicks closed behind me, and I lock it before leaning against the counter. There are creases in the mask where my wrinkle lines break through. When did I get so old? It seems like yesterday I was in my twenties, going out drinking and dancing on a Friday night, then sleeping all day Saturday.

Some expensive-looking disposable towels are neatly fanned on the counter. I grab one and begin the process of removing the heavy coat on my face, being careful not to get any on my blouse or the counter.

It crumbles away, releasing the tension on my skin but not on my nerves.

When it's all off, I peer into the mirror again, twisting my hair around my face and clipping it back. My skin feels firm and vibrant. I'll be buying this charcoal mask.

I toss my towel into the little golden trashcan next to the toilet. Everything is shiny for these women. I can't keep up, yet I can't help wanting my own dazzling waste bin.

I step into the hall, then move slowly toward the stuffy, overfilled room.

"Is it true that she can't have children?" a woman says. Instinctively, I stop in my tracks. "So sad. She clearly wants them, boarding on obsession."

"Mmhmm. Doesn't help that her husband doesn't want them." A familiar voice answers. "If you ask me, he's probably messing around. A hot man like Camden ... so many admirers. I know for a fact that she doesn't give him what he needs."

My blood runs cold and hot all at once. Charlie. She's talking about me behind my back. While she gets in digs at me, I never thought—

"Hey," Elle says, popping into view. "You okay?"

"Yeah." I nod vigorously. "Much better now that my face is free."

Elle's face is clean now, too.

"Do you think we'll be putting makeup on next?" Elle says.

Her curiosity sounds genuine, but I know better.

"Who knows?" I shrug.

"Makeovers aren't my thing," she says, her voice louder. "Hiding behind all those fake layers to get others to accept you is a waste of time. No amount of makeup can cover up a resting bitch face."

She throws a glance over her shoulder, smiling wryly at Charlie.

"I think we've done enough research," I say sheepishly.

"Thank God," she says, straightening her spine. "I thought we'd never leave."

A tornado of embarrassment and gratitude for Elle's admission encircles me. I want so badly to tear off Charlie's head or have some witty response to deflate her story and turn the tables … but I could never confront her. The possible fallout from conflict is worse than the rumors she spreads.

Elle laces her arm in mine and pulls me past Charlie toward the door.

I climb into the passenger seat of Elle's BMW and buckle up, then hug my purse.

Elle slides into the driver's seat.

"That Charlie's a fucking bitch," she says, turning on her car and throwing it in reverse in smooth succession.

My brain bounces between two questions. What have I done wrong? What has Camden done to appear unfaithful? But then, I already know the answer, even if I have no definitive proof.

The memories from Charlie's New Year's Eve party last year hit me. They unfold, forcing me to relive that horrible, disorienting night. Her house was packed with people dressed to the nines, myself included, only everyone else seemed present, while I felt separate from my body, watching everyone and everything as if I were a ghost. Couples were dancing. Charlie's husband, Billy, circulated through the crowd refilling drinks. Camden. With Charlie. Alone—together—at the far end of her long, dimly lit hall. Hidden—almost—in the shadows. Standing too close. Even if I could have reattached to my body, I was too shocked—too uncertain of what I was seeing—to say anything.

The moment is forever seared in my mind, tied with another memory from a month prior, when we were on our second cycle of fertility treatments.

To ensure our success, I'd had a procedure to remove the latest accumulation of endometriosis and confirm that the small cysts on my ovaries weren't a problem. With no impeding endometriosis and negative biopsy results, the only issue was my irregular cycle and delayed ovulation. Camden even had his sperm checked, and his swimmers were in tip-top shape.

This streamlined the plan—produce healthy follicles by taking Letrozole at the beginning of my cycle, monitor with ultrasounds, then induce ovulation with an hCG trigger injection. The rest was simple, thanks to Camden's healthy sperm. There was no need for IUI; we could inseminate the old-fashioned way with three days of sex after trigger. Camden was especially fond of this since he'd struggled with producing a sample and had to go to the sperm bank several times before he could.

I wasn't surprised when the first round didn't work, because Dr. Foltz had warned me it could take multiple rounds—but we could keep at it for as long as I'd like.

With hope carrying me, I'd spent time in the would-be nursery, painting and putting up shelves. The room was scarce, so I went to the basement, first to the far corner where I stored a couple of totes that my mom and stepdad brought me before they moved up the coast. I collected my old teddy, a soft gray sweater, and white booties from my infancy. Unfortunately, everything else was gender specific or displayed my name or face.

I went into Camden's storage room and found a small box labeled *childhood* on the back shelf. Inside were all sorts of trinkets that I could use. Some were blue or said *boy*, but mostly the box held things that would integrate into my design. I thought I'd check the other blank boxes to be sure that I didn't miss anything. I started with the box just below, but it only held a large box filled with an eclectic array of jewelry. That was when I heard Camden overhead, coming home from the gym. I brought the small box to the nursery, using what I could from it.

When I pulled him into the room, floating with the excitement that filled my chest, my plans for a happy surprise quickly disintegrated. He packed up his things with rigid, disturbing movements, then barely spoke to me for weeks. A month later, at Charlie's Christmas Eve Party, I observed his lovestruck grin and gaze of admiration that were once reserved for me fixed on her. His punishment for my disrespect.

Amidst the turmoil of my mind, a faint pleasure arises. Elle defended me.

"Why would she say that shit anyway?" Elle says angrily. "You'd think that with the way she gossips, she'd throw out the side piece's name—or proffer a guess. Unless ..."

I look at her, and she glances my way. She must read my expression like a book because her eyes soften briefly before her jaw tightens, and she returns her focus to the road.

"Fucking Charlie," she says quietly.

"I don't know for sure—"

"What you do know is enough," she says firmly. "And if it extends past Charlie's efforts, then your husband's a fuck—"

"Let's not go there. I don't want to know," I tell her, defeated by the situation.

I lean my head back against the cool headrest and look out the window. My stomach drops as Elle takes a sharp corner like she's still aggravated, but she doesn't push, allowing a quiet to settle in the car.

"Listen," Elle says, interrupting the silence as she veers around another corner. "I could feed you a bunch of bullshit. Tell you she's jealous. Remind you she has a bunch of snotnose children running amuck, pulling shit out of their diapers and smearing it all over her walls, but it won't help. What will help is that knowing it gives you an advantage.

She fucking owes you. She'll be like any other fake-ass woman, trying to make up for her gossip by supporting you. That means supporting your new business—*our* business—in a big way."

"Maybe," I say, not convinced.

I know how competitive Charlie is.

"She probably overheard me pitching our business to someone else. We're going to step on her toes, highlight jewelry that she didn't make," I explain. "I'm about to remind our friends of the jewelry that they'd rather be wearing instead of buying her cheap—"

"You know her cheap-ass shit was derived from you?" Elle asks. "Okay, not you, per se, but you, indirectly. From the day we met."

"I don't think—"

"When did you say she started making jewelry?" she asks.

"August," I say, not sure where she's going.

"After. You. Met. Me. At the country club. In the bathroom."

A warmth grows within me.

"You're right," I say, nodding. "I didn't start this. She did."

"She owes you, after today's bullshit. If she doesn't volunteer her loyalty and support, you'll demand it. Own it, Olivia. Don't let her treat you like shit and get away with it."

I don't answer. She's right, but I can't do that. I've hurt Charlie's feelings. I didn't talk to her about my plans like a good friend would. This is my fault. Even if it isn't, demanding her loyalty would have consequences that I'm not willing to unleash.

Elle

Saturday, October 29th

O livia drops me off in my driveway, and I go straight to my car under the pretense of running errands.

Errands to run. People to follow. Same thing.

I pull out of my drive behind her, but as we move from the side streets and onto the main road, I make a right turn and wait a few beats before flipping a bitch, and pulling back onto the same road, leaving a few cars between us. If she thinks I'm trusting her enough to return all my inheritance of her own accord, she's got another thing coming.

Besides, I'm bored. Zane was home for four days before he had to get on a flight bound for the Midwest.

Finally, Olivia's car pulls into a neighborhood with impressive gardens and lawns. I turn off my headlights before following her in, sure to keep enough distance to eliminate suspicion.

When she pulls into a cul-de-sac, I linger at the corner until her car slips into a driveway.

I flip my headlights on and leave the neighborhood, heading toward the country just beyond her McMansion community. The tranquility of dusk surrounds me as I drive for twenty minutes, then turn around and head back.

When I reach her neighborhood again, I creep in slowly and pull along the curb across from her house, half hidden by a large tree in her front yard. Once I make sure that nobody is watching, I extract my phone and take several pictures of her home, doing my best to capture the sides and front entrance.

As I'm taking a photo, a call from a New York area code flashes across the screen. I ignore it. I'm not answering a telemarketing call. It stops buzzing as the call goes to voicemail. Before I can resume taking photos, another call comes in. The same number.

My muscles tighten. My number is private. The only people who call me from New York are Ricardo, Eddy, and my buyer, Liam. As soon as it goes to voicemail a second time, I turn the phone off and drop it into my console.

I take a moment to inspect the houses surrounding Olivia's. It's just as important to know what the neighbors' routines are.

The hair on the back of my neck stands up as a car pulls up behind me with only its running lights on, its engine idling.

My sympathetic system in full alert, I pull down my visor and its light illuminates my head but not my face. I pretend I'm pulling myself together before starting the car.

It must be a coincidence. A fucking creepy one. But I know that fortuitous events should not be overlooked.

I turn on my car and move around the cul-de-sac. As my headlights gleam off the car, I try to make out the person sitting in the driver's seat. As I get close enough, headlights come at me, and a sportscar whips into Olivia's drive as I pass.

I've missed my opportunity, but that doesn't mean that they've missed theirs.

I take the long way home. Zane isn't there, but I'm not bringing my problems anywhere he sleeps.

Before

Wine and Other Terrible Things

I lay on the worn couch with my flip phone pressed to my ear, contemplating whether the popcorn ceiling above me has always been so off-white, or if it was brighter once. The blasé opinion of my ceiling is only worth my focus because Xander put me on hold. Again.

A crackle comes through the earpiece, alerting me of his return.

"Sorry. It's been busy here today," Xander says, as if I haven't deduced that already.

"It's okay, I'm working on packing," I lie, hoisting myself up to go bang about the kitchen as if I'm doing just that.

"Is the landlord going to cut you some slack?"

I'd told him that I had to stay behind when he left for D.C. because there was nobody to fill my lease, and I couldn't afford to break it. It was a lie of convenience, born from another.

When we met, I let him think that I rented my home. It was easier than explaining I'd afforded it at sixteen because I skipped most of high school to craft and sell counterfeit jewelry as real pieces to rich, naïve, housewives. Like a wine barrel, there are things better left covered.

What I once thought was remorse for not being honest when our fling turned into a relationship is giving me extra time to make this terrifying change.

"Sort of. I found someone to take over the lease—landlord approved. I should be able to come out there in ..." I glance at the calendar on my fridge. Sam's parole hearing is in nine days. Better to be gone before then. "How about next weekend? I can catch the train."

"Really?" Xander's voice pitches up an octave. I imagine him jumping up and clicking his heels, though I know he'd never do that anywhere but in my mind. "Yes! I can't wait to see you." My chest lightens.

"I'll just have my clothes. I've sold nearly everything else," I say, looking around my fully-furnished apartment.

The wine barrel, the ragged couch, and the bed will stay. Everything except me and my clothes, and the wine glass that Xander bought me so I wouldn't have to drink his gifts of wine from juice cups.

I reach for the glass sitting on the counter, where it's been since he was last here—the last time I choked down the red liquid. Sliding it across the counter until it's at the edge, then tipping it precariously with only my middle finger, I imagine it slipping and falling—the illusion of Xander's wine-drinking girlfriend shattering with it.

Why imagine it when I can make it reality? I let it go, and watch as it fractures across the tile floor of the kitchen. I gasp reflexively at the catharsis.

"What was that?" Xander asks, sounding concerned.

"My wine glass ... it broke," I say, entranced by the tiny, glistening shards that would be ideal for melting down and shaping into small balls of crystal that I could craft fake diamonds with. That's all behind me, though. I don't make fake jewelry anymore.

"It's okay," he says. "I'll get you more."

"Oh no, don't do that, it's—"

"I've been collecting different wines that my coworkers have recommended. I can't wait to show you—to see you. Wine glasses are easy," he says with so much warmth. "I can grab some on my way home tonight, or we can go together when you get here if you'd like."

I sigh as the weight that I thought I'd relinquished settles back over me. This is a source of pride for him. No—it's the way that he shows his affection for me.

"Whatever you pick is great. I'll call you tomorrow, Love," I say, letting my heart flood with the emotion of leaving something I love for someone I love—and the sacrifices and lies I'll make to keep both.

Elle

Monday, October 31st

God, this apartment is dirty as hell. Eddy sends his niece to come clean it, but she clearly hasn't been here, because there's dust everywhere.

It's so good to be home, even if it's filthy.

Taking the five steps from my apartment's tiny living room to my dramatically outdated kitchen, I search for any clue that it's been occupied. But it hasn't. Not by a housekeeper—or a dead brother.

If I were smart, I'd get rid of this place, but I can't. It's just like the fucking letters.

If I hadn't kept this place a secret from Zane for all these years, then he'd come up with the money to remodel, and it'd no longer be mine because he would insist that we sell it—New York is unsafe.

I'm not supposed to be here. A marriage vow. For better or for worse, in sickness and health, to never return to New York City ... but some vows are meant to be broken.

Opening my liquor cupboard, I can see that Carmen's been here, not to clean, but to steal my bourbon and vodka. Great. Eddy will be thrilled that I've inadvertently provided alcohol to his niece, who's still a minor. While I don't give a fuck about her age, I respect him too much to help his niece get drunk.

I set my duffle on the old, sage green suede couch and shove my ID and some cash in my jeans' front pocket. One of the first rules for surviving in New York City, or at least surviving and not going broke, is to protect my money. There are too many bastards out there ready to steal a quick buck.

I'd know. I had slipped wallets and wads of cash from the back pockets and purses of unsuspecting benefactors for years.

I put my bag on the inside of my coat, since I can't pack jewelry in my pockets. Not if I want to remain a professional, anyway. Before I reach the door, my phone rings.

I freeze, willing the city to be silent around my apartment.

"Hi, Love," I sing and cringe at the sound.

"Hey," Zane says. "Where you at?"

Shit. He'd better not be home. He's always trying to surprise me with reunions. Surprise me or catch me living another life.

"Just meeting up with a new friend."

I'll need a long-ass fake friend date to cover the time that I'll need to get home, and I haven't taken care of my shit here yet.

"Crap, I was hoping you were at home. I needed a number from my nightstand."

"Sorry, love. I don't think I'll be home anytime soon. There's a night of wine planned," I explain, and decide to solidify this lie with another ... Olivia. "I may have to crash at Olivia's place." I'm definitely crashing at her place. By her place, I mean my place. By myself. With great bourbon, not terrible wine.

"It's okay. The number is on the blue notepad. Should be to the right of the top drawer in my nightstand. If you could just text it to me whenever you get home tomorrow, that would be great," he says.

He's so matter-of-fact. His trust is hot.

"I'm guessing you're not in the mood for FaceTime," I say with snark.

"You're at your friend's, Hun."

He's got me there.

"I'll need you to make time tomorrow then, sir." I bite my lip in anticipation.

He laughs. "I'll make sure to reserve a closet."

I hang up just as a barrage of sirens screams past my window. Thank God for short calls and quick husbands.

A middle-aged woman glares at me as I lean against a glass case full of watches. I lift an eyebrow, flash a one-sided smirk, then cross my arms with an exaggerated air of confidence.

She doesn't know that the display she's standing behind often has Elle original pieces. She clears her throat and begins moving around the case, keeping her gaze locked on me—not my eyes, but my body—but stops short when the door to the back swings open, and the purchasing manager steps out, beckoning me over.

"Hey, Liam," I say, reaching across the counter to shake his hand.

I glance at the woman one more time.

Her obvious disdain for me—a stranger—is thrilling. It's rough for her, watching someone in worn jeans and a baggy hoodie get VIP attention.

"Whatcha got for me?" he asks, his tone casual.

I extract the velvet cloth from my bag and unwrap it, revealing six pieces, all of which have been foraged from my recent estate sale find. The best part is that there are still multiple pieces that can be repurposed and sold from that crumbling barn box.

He's already seen pictures of the pieces here, but he picks them up and inspects each one.

"You know the routine," he says, smiling. "I'll be back."

I nod as he picks up all the pieces and heads through the door to the back room. He'll inspect them, make sure they're real, and return with a number. I'd never try to sell him a fake piece—but procedure is important in an establishment like this. It also means that I get top dollar as the designer.

Wandering around the store is soothing. Jewelry is predictable. The metal, the stones … they are what they are, little tells indicating their true value. It's the people—who buy them, turn them into possessions, assign emotional value to them—who are the liars.

I stop at the cabinet with the one-of-a-kind pieces. A couple are mine, priced well. One is affordable, the other not so much. Another catches my eye, braided gold that unravels only to grasp a yellow teardrop diamond. It's stunning. It's Ricardo's.

"That ring will make someone very happy," Liam says, pulling my attention.

"Yes." I nod. "Yes, it will."

"We're all set. I'll take all six pieces. You want a check, or…?"

I shove my hands into my pockets and glance back at the yellow diamond ring one more time.

"Put it in Ricardo's account this time, will you?"

Liam nods.

"When are you going to get someone special in your life?" I ask him, smirking.

His cheeks redden. "Oh, you know. Someday."

"Hmm." I nod. "Well, you should buy this one. It would make a gorgeous engagement ring."

"If it sits here much longer, I just might, but the holidays are coming."

He turns, inputting numbers into the computer. A receipt is printed out and he hands it to me. "Five is in his account."

"Thanks," I say, taking the paper.

"Next time," he says.

I lift a hand without turning.

He won't buy the ring. I will keep slipping money into Ricardo and Eddy's accounts under the ruse of their consignment agreement with Liam. New York will never sleep.

The familiarity of the jewelry store that saved me is deadened with newness. The faded carpet has been replaced by white tile. The dated wooden cabinets have been professionally painted in navy blue, with new glass in the display cases.

It's a hole in the wall in a not-so-great neighborhood, never visited by the rich. For a long time, Eddy and Ricardo struggled to keep the store open, and the increase in business isn't what they'd always hoped for, but it's a part of them. It's a part of me—the place of my salvation that belongs to the people who believed in my second chance ... believed in me. Seeing the store with a facelift gives me pride and sorrow.

I beam at the man who has aged as gracefully as the shop.

"You came here to get a portable jewelry cleaner?" Eddy asks, scowling.

His condescending tone is comforting. It's the welcome home I needed.

"To NYC? Come on, can you blame me?" I deliver the question with the sass Eddy hates.

"Could have ordered something from Amazon."

I won't tell him that I did. I'll return it if I need to. The excuse to come here and see these two is worth any inconvenience.

He shrugs. "Why would you think we'd have something, anyway?"

He acts like he knows nothing about his husband.

"Ricardo hoards shit like the apocalypse is coming, and everyone will be rushing to care for their fine jewelry." I scan him up and down. "Why are you dressed like a wannabe zombie anyway?"

"The real question is, why aren't you?" He holds both arms out, dragging his index fingers down as he points from my head to my toes.

"Oh, right." I shrug.

"You never used to forget Halloween," he adds, his eyes searching my face.

I'm not the same teenager he once took in. We all grow up.

"Yeah, well, I used to not live in a sleepy town that wants to be a main character in one of your beloved Hallmark movies ... and I used to be fun."

"You also used to be a thief." He puts his hands on his hips and smirks.

"Halloween's the best time to steal shit, too." I step away from him, glancing at the relatively new display cases, stopping at one with a few unique rings. "Are these Ricardo's?"

"They are," Eddy says, puffing up with pride for his husband's creations.

My heart purrs. It's about time that he put his work front and center here and not someplace else where he won't get credit, like with Liam.

"Ricardo!" I shout. I'm not waiting any longer for Eddy to invite him out.

"Elle?" A deep voice comes from behind the faux wall.

When he peeks his head around the corner, I can't help but smile at the fatherly love radiating from his rosy cheeks. I loved my father immensely, but Ricardo filled the massive hole that he left behind.

"You have to stop eating all those cheeseburgers," I say to Ricardo as he steps out of his hiding place.

I try to frown through my growing delight at being here with these two in my favorite place on earth. He lifts the counter flap by Eddy, patting his shoulder as he squeezes through the small opening. I move forward and wrap my arms around his middle, my hands not touching behind him.

"Seriously. Eddy needs you around."

He pats my head, letting me go from his bear hug.

He steals a glance at Eddy. "Nah, he'd be fine without me."

"I need a portable jewelry cleaner to take to different houses," I tell Ricardo.

"I've got one if you don't mind it being older."

"You know I prefer the older equipment. Technologically advanced stuff in this field is a waste." I recite this detail just as I've heard Ricardo say it a million times.

He places his hand on my shoulder. "I've taught you well."

Eddy sighs heavily behind him. "You two are obnoxious. You'd save so much time if you advanced with society."

To hell with that. Nothing beats the feel of the metal and stones in my hands. There's something intimate and powerful about knowing how to do every aspect of this job by hand when so many jewelry "experts" need technology to do the work for them.

Besides, saving money has always been the name of Eddy and Ricardo's game—and mine. The less you spend—the more you swindle—the more lucrative business is. Ricardo may be the expert lapidary, but Eddy has all the hidden knowledge for taking advantage of customers, like the jewelry cleaner recipe he taught me when I first came to them, fresh out of juvie and hunting for a real job.

"You have a recommendation for jewelry cleaner jars?" I ask Eddy.

"I'll send you a link."

"Thank you!" I grin at him and bat my lashes. "Unless you'd like to make some for me ... package them up nicely like you used to."

"It'll take time." He crosses his arms in a huff like I'm putting him out.

I know that I'm not. He loves being needed.

I miss our banter, the ease of being with these two, and the comfort of this store. It's my home.

"I'll pay you a cut, and you'd have an excuse to come see the mid-century modern that Zane has us living in. It'd be right up your alley."

His head falls forward. So much drama. "We can come out in a couple of weeks."

"Make it this weekend?"

"Fine," he says, a smile playing at the corner of his lips.

"Thank you!" I say, then blow him a kiss. "Just tell me how much to sell it for."

"Why? You'll just sell it for more."

"Exactly."

Eddy steps around the counter and rests his head against Ricardo's shoulder. The two would have made excellent parents. If only I'd met them before being arrested ...

I wrap the pair in a quick hug, then turn to go. "Can I pick up the cleaning equipment tomorrow morning on my way out?"

"I'll get it ready," Ricardo answers.

"Great," I say, pivoting and heading for the door. "Oh, Eddy. Your niece stole my alcohol."

"Shit." He shakes his head. "She's never going to make it to her twenty-first birthday at this rate."

"Don't be dramatic. She'll get there, she'll just be drunk by the time she does."

"Get out." He shoos me toward the door. "You better go straight home. Zane would be pissed if he knew you were here. Again."

"What do you mean, again?" I bring my finger to my pursed lips.

As I pull the glass door open and step through it, Eddy shouts, "Secrets never keep!"

"Oh, but they do." I blow him a kiss and enter the night, illuminated by streetlights.

My coat pulled tight, I take in the array of adults wearing costumes. A trio of witches pass by. They are familiar, from a childhood that I need to forget. The witches continue, arms linked, doing a weird as fuck side-to-side stride. My gaze falls on a man with a black hood pulled over his head. He's walking directly behind me. His head drops and he recedes a couple feet when I stare.

Facing forward again, I speed up. People in New York have no personal space. Nobody's following me. He isn't following me.

When I slip into my apartment building, I make sure that the door locks behind me before ascending the stairs to my floor.

Elle

Tuesday, November 1st

I'm not sending Carmen any money for housekeeping this month. Next month, she'll be cleaning to replace the alcohol that she stole.

It's past midnight by the time my cleaning frenzy reaches the living room. The bourbon and lemon-scented bleach cleaner made sure that I kept a low profile. Somewhere between scrubbing the bathroom and the kitchen, I was drunk as a skunk with the music cranked up louder than it should have been, but in New York on Halloween, I'm the least of this city's worries.

Ready to give up on the cleaning for the night, I set my supplies on my homemade table. The plywood top, propped on the wine barrel, is a bit worn, but it's still mine, and I love it.

Stumbling to the tiny bedroom, I collapse on the old mattress in the wobbly iron frame. If my eyes were open, I'd see a plume of dust from my not-so-graceful landing. A cough escapes from my lungs, but I don't care enough to get up and try to change the sheets. Instead, I let the dirty musk send me off into an alcohol-induced sleep.

I wake early to a pounding on a door. I lay in the dark, still as can be.

It's not my door. It couldn't have been. All the other occupants here probably think an old man died in this apartment fifteen years ago. None of them would suspect that a thirty-something married woman owns it as a hiding place from the rest of the world.

The pounding comes again. My muscles tighten. It sure as hell sounds like my door, but I don't get up. I'm not answering it. Whoever's out there can fuck off. It better be a belligerent partygoer who thinks that he's found the apartment of his long-lost love.

After twenty minutes, I'm still awake. A tingling hum through my veins keeps stirring me more toward sober and further from sleep.

I slip off my bed and tip-toe to the door, peering through the eye hole. I see the two poorly painted gray doors across the way and the faded maroon carpet in the circular obscured portal, but that's it.

Great, put me back in my home, in the city I love the most, and I become a paranoid wreck. I grab a towel from the closet, shake it out a bit to make sure nothing's made a home in my linens, and head for the shower. Time to flush the rest of the alcohol from my pores, then head back to Leesburg.

Before leaving the apartment, I set a new bottle on the counter with a note:

Cheers. And don't fucking steal from me again.

Elle

Thursday, November 3rd

The house grows darker around me as I squint in the bright light shining over my equipment. Earlier, I had to close the blackout blinds left behind by the last tenant. But I don't want anyone creeping at my windows or catching a glimpse at what I'm doing.

My eyes squint as I take in the edge of the emerald under my microscope. My hands are a bit shaky. I should eat.

I let out a self-satisfied sigh and set down the tweezers that I've been using to hold the green gem for too long now.

I prefer the dark, but I turn on a dim reading lamp before heading to the kitchen. The glow from the fridge is threatening, almost deterring me from the teriyaki-smothered tofu leftovers I saved last night.

As I wait for the food to warm up in the microwave, I reach into the glass cupboard and slowly slide a wine glass to the edge until it tilts and drops. I casually step out of the way as it hits the counter on the way to the floor.

When the food is reheated, I carry the hot plate to the couch, then cuddle up with a blanket and a book.

I'm halfway through my leftovers when lights come through the living room curtains. I'm bombarded with thoughts of the pounding on my New York apartment door and tense when there are faint thuds on the porch.

My blood runs cold. Zane's right. We do have to keep moving. I need to keep him safe from whoever has been stalking me.

Without adjusting the volume on the TV, I slip off the couch and tiptoe to the front door, freezing as the handle turns. I grab a vase and lift it, ready to pounce on the man darkening my entry, but I hesitate, unsure of the intruder.

He grabs my wrist and pushes me against the wall, lifting me as he does. He wrenches the vase from my hands, lowering it on the side table. His lips press against mine, and my body erupts with the warmth and tingling of desire. I wrap my legs around his waist, feeling his erection form between my thighs. He slides his hands under my shirt, running his fingers along my back. I thread my fingers into the black ringlets atop his head.

"Welcome home," I whisper into his ear before biting it.

"God, I missed you," Zane groans into my neck, kissing it as he does.

To reciprocate his sentiments, I hug his neck, pulling his head to my chest.

"If we had a dog, it would protect me from men attacking me at night," I say, daring him to argue.

"Nice try." He chuckles, his breath on my neck now. "How many men do you have arriving like this with their own key?" The warmth of his lips steals my patience as he works his way to my ear. "Why are you so paranoid suddenly?" he whispers.

Because I'm always on edge after being in New York.

"It was worth a shot," I say, then gasp as he runs his thumb across my nipple.

He eases my feet to the floor, then turns to close the front door that he left wide open. I wrap my arms around him, my chest pressed to his back, and slide my hands into the front of his jeans.

He leans against me and moans with satisfaction.

When he can't stand the tease anymore, he spins, squats, and lifts me over his shoulder.

He bumps into the chess table as he tries to regain balance.

"Hard to carry me when you're ... hard." I laugh.

He slaps my ass with his free hand.

"Looks like I'm not the only clumsy one," he says as he carries me past the kitchen.

The wine glass. Shit.

He pushes our bedroom door open and lowers me to the bed, lying next to me.

"Why is it that you only ever drop wine glasses?" he asks, his eyes fixed on mine, his pupils dilated.

"The crystal's slippery." I shrug. "Would you believe me if I told you that it's because I love how you'll rush out to buy me more?"

He runs his palm over my cheek, brushing hair from my face.

"I'd believe anything you say."

My heart squeezes as I consider his words. Then he trails a finger down the center of my stomach, and all my thoughts are lost to his touch.

Elle

Sunday, November 6th

The sauce hits the hot pan on my stove with a quiet sizzling and popping that gradually progresses in volume. I mix it into the already-cooked Impossible Ground Beef, then add a bit of tomato paste and seasoning.

"Smells amazing in here," Zane says, slipping an arm around my waist and sniffing the spiced steam coming from the stove in front of me. Setting the wooden spoon down, I then grab the tongs and ruffle the noodles boiling in the large pot next to the pan.

"God, you're hot," Zane whispers into my hair.

I turn toward him, and as our tongues lock, he leans me back, dangerously close to the gas flames behind me.

"I'll be hotter if you catch me on fire," I say with fierceness and shove him back.

"Shit, sorry."

He's too kind. Every year that we're married, his caring nature gets worse. It's smothering and infatuating.

"Go sweep for the millionth time or something," I harass, slapping his hip with a hand towel.

"I'm not that bad," he calls, already inspecting the floor and reaching for the broom and dustpan. Not that bad, my ass.

He's running the broom along floors already clean enough to eat off when the doorbell rings. He mutters under his breath and collects a pile of microscopic dirt onto the dustpan. God, he's anal.

I turn the burners off in a huff and stomp to the door, hoping the vibrations from my heels will send him into a tizzy.

"I wish you wouldn't wear those in the house—"

Before he can finish his thought, I fling the door open and greet Ricardo and Eddy with an animated gesture of open arms.

"Hey!" I say loudly. "Welcome to Pleasantville."

"It's definitely straight out of a movie," Eddy agrees, his nose up-turned.

Eddy loves New York as much as I do, but he has Zane's back in keeping me away. Protecting me. Just like an overbearing parent.

"It's nice," Ricardo rumbles, stepping in and grunting as he bends over to remove his shoes.

"Oh, don't worry about that, Ricardo." I point to his feet, then wave my hand in an upward motion until he straightens his spine.

"You sure?" he asks, glancing at Zane, who's putting his cleaning tools away.

"Most definitely," I answer, following Ricardo's gaze to Zane.

Zane glares at me, then greets our uneasy guests.

"Thanks for coming, you two." He shakes Ricardo's hand, then gives Eddy a side hug.

"I've got some stuff in our car for Elle, if you could," Eddy directs Zane.

Eddy barks orders to see Zane scramble at his demands, to see how far Zane would go for me. And, as always, he does as Eddy asks, grabbing the keys dangling from Eddy's grip and heading to their trunk.

As Zane's unloading the four boxes of the heavy, handcrafted jewelry cleaner, Eddy leans over and whispers, "Now don't leave that stuff in a hot car. Or a cold one."

"I won't," I respond quietly.

"Can I get you two a drink?" Zane asks, setting down the last box on the neat stack he's made against the entry wall.

"You got any of that aged bourbon?" Ricardo inches across the floor, not daring to remove his shoes but doing his best not to knock dirt free from his soles.

Zane removes a couple of snifters from the cupboard and nods to Eddy. "And what can I get you?"

"I'll have some of that bourbon, too," he says, flashing me a wry grin. "You too, Elle?"

"Not for me, you know that." I slap his back. "And not for you either, since my husband, here, brought home some fantastic red blends from the Pacific Northwest. Can't have you missing out."

I slip around him and sidle up next to my man. After all these years, Zane still hasn't caught on to Eddy's attempts to out my alcohol preference.

I force a couple of gulps of my wine down as I finish up the meal prep, placing the Italian-style food onto the table. As I'm about to take a seat with the men, a knock comes from the front door.

Odd.

I open the door to find Olivia. Shit.

My scalp tingles. I don't want to do this. Too many lies to balance.

She holds too many of my secrets.

"Hey, come on in." I step aside, letting her pass. "You just caught us sitting down for dinner, if you'd like to join ..."

"Oh, I'm so sorry, I didn't mean—" She starts to back up.

"Nonsense," I proclaim. "Olivia, this is my husband, Zane, and our old friends Ricardo and Eddy."

"Old friends?" Eddy grumbles. "Who you calling old? And friendly?"

I point each of them out slowly so she can absorb the introductions properly. I won't be repeating myself.

"Eddy is definitely old and not so friendly."

"Nice to meet you." Her words are timid but polite. Good. She continues to know her place.

"These two taught me everything I know about gemology."

Eddy scoffs, and Ricardo muffles a chuckle.

I lean into her to hug as if we're girlfriends. As I do, I whisper, "Don't you say a fucking thing."

"She already knew what she was doing when she found us," Ricardo says from behind me.

"They're being humble." I link my arm with hers and drag her forward, shoving her into the seat at the end of the table. "They also brought our cleaning products ... I'll grab you a plate."

"So, they know about our business?" Olivia questions, her tone cautious.

"Elle and I share everything," Zane says, flashing his gorgeous smile at me.

I take another swig of the red, wishing it were bourbon.

"Oh, so you know that—"

"That we're about to take wicked advantage of rich women by breaking into the market in a new, fresh way?" I interject. "That we're bringing jewelry cleaning and appraisals to them rather than waiting for them to come to us? Yeah ... he knows."

Eddy takes me in. He's clearly suspicious, but he says nothing. I prep her plate while everyone sits at the table, stealing awkward glances between strangers.

"We have eight parties booked before Christmas," Olivia chatters. I linger in the kitchen longer than I need to, enjoying Olivia's nervous energy. She deserves all that stress, dropping in like this without warning. Finally, I sit down.

Olivia moans in delight, taking a bite of spaghetti, the tension easing from her frame. "I need to know what you've done to season this beef," she says after shoveling a couple more bites.

Eddy cackles. "This isn't beef, sweetie."

Olivia's eyes flash up from her plate, staring at him.

"What is it?" she asks, with a dumbfounded expression.

"It's not dog, if that's what you're thinking," I say, sarcasm thick.

"Fake meat," Eddy says, spearing a bite and shoving it into his trap. He removes the fork from his mouth, clean as a whistle, and stabs it in the air at me. "This one's a diehard vegan."

Great. I'm so glad that Eddy finally got to out me to someone.

Olivia's gaze lands on me, shock deep in her brown eyes.

"I guess that makes sense," she says slowly, allowing her revelation to sink in.

"I guess it does." I lean back in my chair, lifting the wine glass to my lips to take a slow sip.

The silence between us is entertaining but not uncomfortable—for me, at least. I hate the labels that people slap on me, but if she's going to be hanging around, it's better that she knows before she shows up bearing gifts of chicken sandwiches and cheese boards.

"So," she begins, then searches the ceiling for her next words. "How long have you been ... vegan?"

Long enough that you won't convert me back.

"Too fucking long." Ricardo slips up, and laughter erupts from the three men. "You should have seen us trying to feed her when she was younger. Almost impossible, this one."

A laugh jumps from my lips.

"Don't worry," I say, touching her arm gently. "I won't rub off on you."

She hunches her shoulders and stares at her plate, then daintily takes another bite.

Olivia may think that I'm a wildcard she can adjust to. In some instances, this is true. She expects me to be unexpected, but she can't know how unexpected I truly can be. That's intentional.

There's no way she can anticipate what's coming next.

Olivia

Sunday, November 13th

Washing dishes by hand isn't my favorite chore, but it's preferable to leaving them in the dishwasher for a week while I try to fill it with the limited dishes we dirty in this house.

The door to the garage rumbles open, startling me.

I rinse the plate that's decidedly well-washed and grab the next as Camden's heavy steps come down the hall toward me.

"Babe, I'm going to take a shower and get some rest. Okay?" Camden says, coming around the large peninsula and opening the fridge behind me.

I'm surprised when he wraps his arms around me. I set down the plate in my hands and lock my fingers with his, hoping that he doesn't notice how wrinkled and raisin-like they've become from washing only a few dishes.

"Alright." I lean into him, eager for his embrace and willing to ignore the stench of his sweat. "How was the gym?"

Camden's been working more than usual, and needing to do so outside his glorified home office. He's been excited about some new game that his team's been building, but despite the buzz around the soon-to-be-announced product, there are dark circles under his beautiful blue eyes.

"It was good." He leans down and kisses my cheek, sending electricity through my body.

Despite all my efforts to distract myself from my fertility, or lack thereof, I can't help but be in tune with my cycle. And if I'm correct, pending my cycle irregularities, I'm near ovulation.

Turning to face him, I place my hands on his cheeks and pull him into a kiss. He brings my hips to him, and relief washes over me. Take that, Charlie—he has desire for *me*, not some bimbo.

He bends down, cupping my butt, then thighs, and lifts me until my legs are locked tightly on his waist. He carries me into the bedroom.

If I didn't know better, I'd think I was floating.

He pulls my clothes off, giving little care as to whether they might be damaged in the process. I do the same to him, sliding my hands along his body.

"I missed you," I gasp as he kisses my neck and slips his hands around my breasts.

"I was only gone for the day." He moves his eyes from my chest, taking in my longing gaze.

I fumble for the best thing to say. "We just haven't spent a lot of time together recently."

"In that case," he says, sliding his finger over my nipple, "I've missed the hell out of you."

In one quick swoop, he slides his boxers off, then pauses, gazing into my eyes. "Sorry I've been AWOL."

My heart aches with all my love for him. "I'm glad you're here now."

We fall into the sheets as he slides into me, and despite our desperation for one another, my body aches in protest—a not-so-kind reminder of the endometriosis—my secret scars—that have stolen my chance at motherhood.

There are more bruises on him than normal. I try to ignore them as I watch him head into the bathroom, naked still, ready for his shower. He's a gamer, not a professional boxer, but sometimes, with the way he dedicates himself to his boxing gym, I wonder if he wishes that he were.

I climb out of bed and pull my clothes back on when it's clear that he's in the shower, and I'm alone. I return to the kitchen, zoning out as I perform the mundane task of completing the dishes. I'd trade the pristine space for trip hazard toys and messes of applesauce and Cheerios—I'd trade anything, and I am. I'm trading my soul, my sanity, and my clean record.

The blaring of chimes and bells startles me. Camden's ringtone is aggressive. I'll never get used to it. I try to ignore it, but with every vibration, my curiosity is piqued until I glance across the counter at it. White letters display the name *Libby* on the screen, with a local number sprawled out below it.

Libby? I want to believe it's someone on his team, but my aching heart tells me that it's not. I'm losing him. Charlie was right. Our occasional sex doesn't guarantee his commitment. Not anymore.

"That my phone?" Camden calls from our bedroom

I hustle back to my work, washing an already clean dish, fearful that I've been caught. Caught doing what? Glancing at my husband's phone is hardly a crime.

"Yeah!" I shout as his feet thud across our floor, moving toward his device. He picks up the phone and runs his fingers through his wet hair.

"A teammate," he confesses without prompt.

My chest grows tighter, though I'm not sure if it's the innocent protest he's just given to my internal dialogue or if it's the idea of a girl named Libby on his team—demanding his attention.

Stop. I need to stop. He's married to me. He's clearly attracted to me.

"Next Saturday," I say, breaking the awkwardness between us that's probably only noticeable to me. "I'll be with the girls again, but maybe afterward we can go on a date ..."

He looks up, his phone still aglow.

"Do I need to start keeping tabs on you?" He grins at me, then returns to his phone, typing vigorously on the screen.

A twist in my gut pushes me to defend my plans, especially since the obligations are now my own. My business. There's no getting out of this, not that I'd want to, but I can't bring myself to share my new venture.

Guilt and jealousy spring to life at the thought that Elle shares things with her husband, but she can't share everything, not with how she regulated what information I could share with him.

"There'll be more events coming up with the girls since it's close to the holidays," I continue.

"Huh?" He scrunches his eyebrows.

"Just until Christmas, then it won't be so busy."

He's not listening, though. He's wandering toward the hallway, probably on his way to play a game. "Sounds good, Babe. Just don't spend too much ... I'm going to get some work done."

My stomach continues to clench and twist.

"What about the date?" I squeak.

He doesn't hear me.

I stare after him as he moves down the hall and disappears into his office, shutting the door with a thud. Instinctively, I put my hands under the still-running faucet. The steam should have been a warning; instead, I jump back as the scalding water strikes my palms.

"Ouch!" I shout, slamming the handle in aggravation. Annoyed by my inability to focus, I grab a sweater and step onto the front porch for fresh air. There's a file box sitting by the door, surrounded by yellow maple leaves that have blown from the trees.

A folded note on top reads: Some light work. Get it done today.

Great. Today's almost over.

I sigh loudly and pick up the box, storming back inside. I grab a wine glass and pour myself a large cup, then settle onto the couch, opening the box on the coffee table. Another night with me, myself, and my inescapable math.

I sort through the files efficiently and begin cataloging the purchases in the ledger. After hours, and several glasses of wine, I finally enter each number into the calculator, adding and subtracting accordingly. The books balance perfectly. Too perfectly. Again.

Flipping through the bank statements a second time, my gaze falls on the times of the transactions. An odd purchase subtraction shortly after a deposit here and there creates continuity in the documentation. Everything appears legitimate, except that the odd purchase receipts have dates prior to the deposits that they balance.

My fingers fly across the keys as I check the numbers twice more. Perfect. Again, and again. Everything adds up. Except, something isn't right.

Olivia

Saturday, November 19th

E lle and I arrive at Annaliese's house thirty minutes before our first event. Sleep was close to impossible.

I would've considered asking Elle to drive herself today, except that I hadn't told her where I live, and it didn't seem like a great idea to reveal that information to her. Apparently, it was inevitable, because Annaliese just made some joke about how she loves refurbishing old furniture to get a break from her husband and son ... when she's not hanging with her neighbors ...

"You two are neighbors?" Elle asks, interest flashing in her eyes.

My stomach dips.

"Olivia's one of the best neighbors," Annaliese says. "Now, if only she'd fill her massive home with babies."

I suck in a breath, trying to still my jitters.

"I'd like to, someday," I answer honestly.

"Where would you like us to set up?" Elle asks, provoking the change in subject that I'm desperate for.

"Oh, just in the den over there." Annaliese points to a space down her hallway.

It's similar to my home, only smaller, and with more furniture.

We bring two folding tables inside, and I cover them with tan table-cloths and set vases with fake fall arrangements on them. I make a mental note to get new floral arrangements for our parties after Thanksgiving.

I bring in my totes full of food and begin to set things out on one of the tables. Annaliese was kind enough to host our first party, but since none of us knows how this'll go, I thought it fair that I bring all the party favors this time.

I set out a charcuterie board and instantly regret it. "Oh, I um—"

I turn to face Elle, who should be setting up the other table. Instead, she's sitting in the corner, watching me.

"Don't worry about me," she says. "Though, you should be worried about the bottom line."

My cheeks flush in embarrassment. I turn back to the bags and pull out some crackers.

"Do you need help bringing in your stuff?" I ask, trying to casually prompt her to get up.

She nods. "That would be great."

The cleaning machine is heavier than I expected it to be. I grunt more than I like as we carry it into the house. Elle must have the lighter end because she's not struggling at all.

We set it on the sturdy plastic table. "That was a workout," I huff.

"You'll get used to it," she says, wiping the front of her clothes with her palms.

"I'll go get those appraisal slips you had me print," I say, pulling myself away so I can find a place to catch my breath in private.

I become lightheaded and lean against a wall in the quiet hallway. This is going to happen.

The sooner I pay Jared back, the better. The too-perfect numbers make me nervous. I want out ASAP.

"Are you okay?" Elle asks, coming into the hall.

I push off the wall and nod.

"Great," I say, and lower my voice, "remember, today is just this."

"Of course," she says, smirking.

Elle

Saturday, November 19th

I've convinced Olivia that appraisals take complete concentration. Her job is to keep everyone away from me while I inspect the jewelry. Assess the metal, calculate carats, and grade the stones. It takes some focus, but it's second nature for me. Still, I'll fake anything to not have to socialize with these women. I don't care about their children, their terrible hair day, or the new outfit that they bought for this occasion. None of that bullshit is ever interesting.

"Rachel," I call in a sing-song tone over the growing volume of the crowd.

"Yes." A woman with great curves waves her hand.

She skips over, her confidence catching me off guard. I like it. I don't like that I like it.

I return her set of dangling earrings with tiny diamonds leading to teardrop rubies at the end. Attached is the glossy cardstock where I've written the appraisal out.

Olivia did a good job with these forms. Very professional.

"These are beautiful," I say to her.

She inspects them with a big grin. "They haven't been this clean since I bought them, thank you."

"The bracelet, though, it needs some work."

I pick up her second card, holding a gold cuff with a large ruby and multiple diamonds surrounding it.

"If you'd like, I can fix the mounts on these stones," I say, pointing to three of the diamonds.

Her brows furrow, and she nods. "That would be great, thanks."

Confidence fills my chest. I grab some of the cheap jewelry soap.

"This will help keep your pieces shining at home, between professional cleans," I say, lifting the container. "Would you like some?"

Eddy would be so proud right now.

"Oh, fantastic. I should get a container for my mother-in-law as well. She's always obsessing over her jewelry, ordering different cleaners off infomercials. I bet your stuff works way better than anything from TV."

Nope. That bullshit stuff probably works better.

"That's a great idea with the holidays coming up," I say, hating my own voice.

As she walks away, Olivia scoots over and leans on the table. I slide Emily's cuff to the side and away from Olivia's immediate scrutiny.

"How's it going?" she asks.

"Great." I flash a big smile and hide my urge to roll my eyes. "Five left."

Making a point to slide the next one in front of me, I hunch over my magnifying glass and begin poking at the stones.

"I'll let you get back to it," she says, patting the table.

As she walks away, I slip the cuff into the bag with two other pieces that I'm taking home today.

The second party Olivia has us slotted for brings a familiar face—Charlie.

Fucking Charlie. I watch from my perch behind the cleaning products as Olivia approaches her and hugs her like they've never been better. Clearly, she's chickened out, unable to stand up for herself. Charlie stands near her, chatting about her children, who have apparently reached new milestones, and asking Olivia for help with an upcoming gathering that she's having. She's using Olivia, and Olivia just lets her. These women are so fucking dysfunctional.

When Charlie brings her item to my table and fills out her information, I give her the most counterfeit smile. She doesn't get genuine from me. I'll take the genuine out of her tennis bracelet, too.

Olivia runs the show, making announcements and reminding everyone that we only take cash. For someone so nervous all the time, she commands attention with a professional air. The ladies mingle, eating, sipping punch, and milling about at the Glorious Kitchen table that the host has set up. Charlie makes her own rounds, talking up her cheap-ass jewelry business and getting some to commit to pre-orders. What a fucking mooch.

I keep my head down, resisting the urge to use her as my punching bag. I'll go to the gym later, and I'll outsell her. It's easy. I convince nearly every one of them to buy two tubs of watered-down soap on account of the holidays.

When I reach Charlie's tennis bracelet in the line of items, I scowl. This bracelet is as flashy as the woman wearing it.

And as fake.

I stand from my spot at the table and cross the floor to where Charlie's carrying on a conversation with a boisterous woman. She's cackling at every hushed statement that Charlie throws her way.

"Charlie, do you have a moment?" I say when the two ignore my presence. This bitch will not mess with me.

"Sure," she answers, stepping away from her comrade. "I could have come to the table like everyone else."

"How could you manage to notice me waving you over if you can't see me standing right in front of you?" I counter. She doesn't answer. I don't expect her to.

Since I'm running a scheme that relies on a professional business front, I lean in close. "Listen, I wanted to return this to you. We can't charge you for an appraisal when the item is worth less than the service." I hold it out to her. "It wouldn't be right."

Her jaw drops and her face turns a ghostly pale followed by a bright red.

"What do you mean?" she manages to ask.

"These aren't diamonds. They're crystals. They're not Swarovski or anything special, and the metal is only plated with sterling silver," I explain, then force myself to add, "I'm sorry."

She snatches it from my hand as she snaps her jaw shut, clenching it in frustration. Then she catches herself and relaxes, gently tucking hair behind her ear. Time for her to put on a show.

"I know what it is. I was testing you to see if you know what you're doing." She huffs and storms off. She's a fucking class act.

Next time, I won't be so chill.

She makes her way to Olivia's side. She whispers and points at me. I move my eyes to the next piece of jewelry and watch them out of my peripheral vision. Olivia comes to the table and grabs a bottle of the cleaner, then returns to Charlie's side, handing it to her. Charlie snatches it, says something under her breath, then grabs her coat and leaves.

Olivia comes around the table and kneels next to me. "She says it's real, and you're messing with her."

"It's as fake and cheap as her," I snap.

My body flushes out the anger, replacing it with warmth. I smile, realizing that Charlie's off to see why her husband—or someone else—is lying to her.

Elle

Sunday, November 20th

My car's engine hums as I wind through quiet neighborhoods in the darkness. The only disruption of what would be a peaceful drive is this phone call.

"Is it possible that you made a mistake," Olivia's cautious voice comes through my phone and grates on my nerves. "Charlie was adamant—"

"I didn't make a mistake," I hiss, "but I suppose it makes sense you'd defend a bitch like Charlie." They can be bitches together, for all I care.

"Well ... you're not exactly forthcoming—or trustworthy—either. You don't exactly *like* Charlie ..." Her voice is meek, hesitant, but she speaks her mind. Thank the fucking goddesses.

"What happened to trusting me? And, I don't like anyone." I stifle a laugh and pull in front of Olivia's home, killing my engine. "You want to come over tonight? Help me with a project?"

Her house is dark. The sounds on the other end of the call indicate that she isn't snuggled in bed.

"Camden and I are out with some friends. Sorry."

My lips pull up, calm settling through me. Both of them are out.

Her phone muffles, but through her palm, I hear a familiar woman's voice say, "Hey, you coming?"

"Sorry about that," Olivia says, returning to our call. "I should go."

"You're having dinner with Charlie?"

"And her husband. Sorry. I should go."

"Have a great time with fucking Charlie," I say, hanging up.

I have more important things to do.

My phone lights up. I glance down, expecting it to be Olivia calling back. It isn't. I flinch at the next vibration. The numbers are burned into my brain, but I can't stop staring. I won't hit ignore, either. It's the same New York area code calling again. It's called at least twice a day for the last fifteen days. The voicemails, when left, are heavy breathing—no words.

It's not a telemarketer, or a wrong number.

It's not a call that I'm willing to take.

It's the motivation that I need to get this the fuck over with.

I move my car down the road and leave it next to a large park built for the wealthy. My black leggings and black hoodie serve two purposes: to blend in with the night and to look like an exercise addict.

An evening jog through the brisk, almost winter air chills my hot skin that burns with anticipation. I loop around the far side of Olivia's cul-de-sac first, taking stock of the homes around me one more time. Then, I skim along the shrubs lining Olivia's property and pull myself up and over the fence.

I drop into her backyard with a light thud and peer up at the neighbor's windows. Their curtains are drawn. Perfect.

Now that I'm not jogging, my heartbeat pounds in my ears. My muscles tingle with warm blood coursing through my veins under my rapidly cooling skin. I move along the side of the house to the far corner and find what I was hoping for: a door leading to the back of their garage. I remove my lock pick set from my deep legging pocket and find the two picks that fit perfectly. It takes a couple of minutes—because I'm rusty as fuck—before there's an audible click. Tucking the tools back into the case and sliding it into my pocket, I turn the handle and step inside.

The garage is dark. But once I enter the house, there's some residual light from the streetlamps outside. It's enough to navigate without a flashlight, which is better. Who knows if they have cameras in here. I would.

There's no alarm system, though. No chirp upon entering. No obnoxious warning beeps. I take a breath and run my eyes over the doors of the long, wide hallway. Rich people even have halls that make normal corridors look bad.

The scratching of paws from the other end of the corridor tells me that there's a security system that Olivia hasn't mentioned. A gorgeous labradoodle sprints toward me, full of excitement. I squat down to greet the pup and let her lick my face.

I hug her neck and pat her back. My heart squeezes, longing for a dog of my own, but it's not in the cards. If I fall in love with a pet, let it get close to me, there's no telling how long it'll take until it gets hurt. If people who know me wind up dead, it's guaranteed to extend to a selfless, blindly loving dog. This dog has given me instant friendship despite me breaking into her guardians' home.

The last dog I called mine was taken to the animal shelter the day after my parents died. My selfishness destroyed the entire family.

I rise, scratching my new friend's head, and move down the expansive hallway.

A picture hanging in the vast space stops me in my tracks. I turn abruptly, my gaze fixed on the two people in the photo.

Stinging spreads from the base of my skull out along my arms.

Frantically, I search my other pocket for my light, flicking it on and pointing it at the picture just as a blaring erupts around me.

Olivia

Sunday, November 20th

The low volume of jazz in the background is welcoming, and the other patrons have quiet discussions at their tables. Along with the lighting that's just dim enough to create a soothing ambiance, I can imagine myself being quite relaxed here.

Unfortunately, I'm not.

It's still bright enough that I can see Charlie's face across the table and the slight twitching of her lip. It makes her smile look even less genuine than normal, though I'm probably the only one to notice this detail.

"It's so nice to get you two out with us," Charlie says, then takes a sip of her wine. "You never come out anymore."

She's loud enough to disrupt the tables to either side of us.

"We've been busy," I say, offering an apologetic smile to both Charlie and Billy.

Billy's a great guy. He cooks, cleans, and makes sure that his family is well taken care of. He dotes on Charlie so much that it makes me more envious than I'd ever confess. He has his arm over her shoulder, his hand rubbing the base of her neck.

I reach across the booth to Camden and place my hand on his knee. Charlie finds a way to make everything a competition, and no doubt, she'll use this night in her next gossip chain if Camden and I don't act affectionately.

She's worse than the tabloids.

"Well, *you've* been busy, anyway," Charlie says, shooting me a glance.

"Just helping out some friends," I say, hoping that she lets this go.

She leans into Billy's hand, clearly relishing his massage. I scoot closer to Camden and slide my hand up his calf. Camden gives me a questioning glance but doesn't say anything, he just picks up his bourbon on the rocks and takes a long sip.

"Yeah, helping your friends. More like helping yourself," she says, with a groan.

Anger rises from my belly to my cheeks. I silently plead for the men to take over the table conversation. They discuss cars, sports, and who knows what else, so seamlessly. They never fight. Meanwhile, I'm ready to launch across the table and tackle Charlie to the ground. If I did that, I wouldn't stop there, with my pent-up rage.

Tonight is about making amends. Not clearing the air—completely—but making it as breezy and bright as we can.

"Come on, Charlie, that's not true," I counter, letting my lips curl into a sweet smile. "I helped you a few weeks ago. Someone is always asking for help."

"One in particular," she says with disgust. Or is it jealousy?

She rolls her eyes and swats Billy's hand from her neck. I slide an inch closer to Camden. This is my time to take the lead in our competitive game.

"I spoke to her again. I wanted to make sure that there was no mistake. She reassured me that there wasn't," I say cautiously. Charlie's body stiffens. She reaches for her wine glass and makes a fist around the stem.

"Your tennis bracelet," I glance at her wrist still wrapped in it, "isn't made of diamonds. She says that she's sorry, but she'd be happy to look at something else for you free of charge."

Elle's going to be livid when she finds out that I've offered this. But I hate confrontation, especially with Charlie. Somehow, the thought of dealing with Elle later seems easier.

Charlie's lips pull together as she casts a quick glance at Camden, then back to her wine. I follow her gaze. Her knuckles are white.

"I'm really sorry," I say, feeling my anxiety spinning out. "I know Billy gave it to you as a gift. And—"

An odd cackle comes from the base of Charlie's throat. Her face is flushed.

"Olivia," she snaps, then shakes her shoulders out. "This thing ... is something I picked up at a knockoff jewelry store. Not a gift. Nothing special."

My face scrunches with confusion. She just gave me this big sob story thirty minutes ago. She said it was made from high-grade diamonds. It was a special gift from Billy, on a random Tuesday, because he loves her so much, and because he thinks she's an excellent mother who deserves more recognition. She insisted, again, that Elle was a liar and a cheat.

Elle is both those things, but Charlie doesn't know that. And it doesn't apply here. Not when it comes to jewelry. It's probably the only thing that Elle can be honest about—when she's not trying to steal from you. Even if I have little reason to believe Elle, I know for a fact that she'd rather steal diamonds from Charlie than lie and tell her a real thing is fake.

"But you just told me—"

"I was testing her," Charlie interrupts.

She takes a sip of her wine and chokes a bit. I've never seen Charlie uncomfortable like this. It sends a chill through my core and covers me in goosebumps. Something isn't right.

"Oh yeah," Billy says, taking her hand in his and tracing his finger along the bracelet. "She brought this home from the mall six months ago. She has been wearing it nonstop, but it's not from me. Don't worry, Olivia."

His eyes are reassuring, meeting mine with a steady glance, but they do nothing to settle the nerves lighting up my body.

I should defend myself and tell her that she's a bad friend for pulling a prank. I should call her out, corner her with the swarm of lies she's been bombarding me with, but I can't. This lie, the one she's telling to get her name cleared and out of this conversation, isn't one that I want to unpack.

Camden shifts in the booth as Billy picks up his menu, casually perusing the options. Charlie shoots daggers at Camden with her eyes.

I hold my own menu, pretending that I'm not seeing the silent exchange happening between Charlie and my husband. When Camden drapes his arm over my shoulder and pulls me to him, tilting his head down to whisper "I love you" in my ear, I know Charlie received the tennis bracelet as a gift. She absolutely thought it was real.

And it wasn't from Billy.

Before

A Place Worth Missing

This is my home, the one I bought for me and Travis. I can almost see him passed out on the couch after a late night of video games, his textbooks still open and spread out with his notes across the floor.

My throat tightens. I still can't believe he's gone and not coming back to find me. If he was still alive, he would have come back by now.

There's no point in putting this off. My train leaves for D.C. in a couple of hours. No more excuses. My bags are packed. Xander is waiting for me.

Travis isn't ... Not that it'll stop me from leaving him a note, just in case. It won't give my location or any other revealing information because who knows what lengths Sam will go to try and find me.

If Sam wasn't hunting me for vengeance on my brother, I'd question whether he was the one who came for Travis that night. With Sam and the rest of the people on his payroll convinced that Travis was the rat, that he's in witness protection somewhere after a *staged disappearance*, I know—without a doubt—this is one thing that Sam wasn't behind.

Travis didn't do shit. He'd never rat me out. He would have taken me with him to hide forever in some terrible place.

Travis and I used to write letters to one another, like a secret club for siblings. Before Mom and Dad died and we were split up, we used to hide notes for each other in our house. My favorite hiding spot was in the linen closet, tucked behind the towels and blankets. It's where I could put letters that detailed my annoyances with our parents because I knew they'd never find them in a closet that only the two of us used.

The dinky cupboard here that serves as my linen closet will work perfectly. Along with the photo that I keep hidden of Travis and me on our last vacation with our parents in a ridiculously picturesque downtown area.

Despite all the letters that I still write to Travis, this one is harder. I write to a dead person no problem, but I'm at a loss for words when it's a fictitious event in which he's alive.

On the sixth piece of paper, I scribble out:

If you're reading this, welcome home.

~ L

I fold it around the photo, then shove it into the closet before I can talk myself out of this childish notion that he's in a coma, ready to wake up, or is an amnesiac who will remember who he is—who I am—any moment now.

As I step back out into the tiny living space, I catch sight of the stains on the carpet. They don't look like blood stains anymore, but I know that the bleach spots mark where Travis' blood splattered. I picture the scene that I've settled on in my mind as a way of trying to understand. I imagine the assailant broke into our home—which apparently wasn't a challenge, because the police say the lock wasn't tampered with. They think that I left it unlocked, maybe even open, that night.

I'd like to think that he tried to fight back. In my mind, he was knocked unconscious so that they could ravage our home and steal our jewelry, including the cross around my neck. They took my mother's old jewelry box, the one with secrets I knew existed but hadn't yet uncovered.

The thieves probably dragged Travis out the front door. It's here that the story that I've created goes blurry. I try not to think about them pulling his lifeless body from the apartment to destroy the evidence of their murder, but that is what the cops think happened.

In the back of my mind, there's constant pecking, stabbing holes in their theory. It seems impossible that they'd get a dead body out of the building without being seen. He must have been alive. If they were after information, they knapped the wrong sibling. Travis only ever knew what was happening with our unethical ties *after* I told him. I was dating Sam. I was the one who eavesdropped on discussions of the drug ring breaking into something new—though I hadn't heard what. Travis had no clue because he wanted desperately to stay clean.

He ran away from his foster home and came to New York City because of me. He slept on the streets because of me. He sold pot because of me.

He wanted nothing to do with illegal schemes. He wanted to go to school and play video games. He wanted nothing more than to make sure his little sister was always happy and safe. He did everything because of me—for me. He would never compromise me. Destroy me. That was my job.

L,

With the way I've always followed you around, doing as you command, I wasn't sure that I could ever choose me over you. If it ever came down to it, I was certain I'd save you every time. Like, if one of your brilliant plans got us into more trouble, I'd confess your sins and let you escape.

I guess I was wrong. When asked if I'd choose my life or yours, it's super easy.

Mine. I choose my life.

Love you, Lizzie, just not more than I love me.

~ Travis

Elle

Sunday, November 20th

I don't believe in ghosts.

Yet, here I am, staring at a double-crossing, piece of shit, jewelry-thieving ghost.

It's a photo of him, anyway.

Dead people don't get married fifteen years postmortem, nor do they buy monstrosities called houses and live happily ever after.

"What the fuck?" I whisper through gritted teeth.

The unbearable screeching around me becomes clear now. An alarm. I triggered the alarm. The labradoodle at my side is whimpering.

Nausea wells deep in my belly. I resist the urge to pull the frame from the wall and chuck it at … a wall. Aa precious piece of furniture, or a window.

I have no idea how long I've been standing here, staring at the image, willing it to tell me a different story. But it's been too long. Way too long. The alarm blares all around me.

Move. Elle, fucking move.

Move.

I spin and bolt back into the garage, shutting the door before my furry friend can follow, then burst into the backyard. I turn back only to relock the door.

I cover my tracks. I don't reveal a thing. Even when I'm too shaken to think clearly, I must.

I sprint around to the side yard and scramble back over the fence and out onto the sidewalk. I don't slow down until I'm a block away, and sirens make faint sounds in the distance.

My throat dries up, and my eyes burn with confused rage. The stinging on my skin is slowly replaced by the twitching of my muscles as I stop my sprint and force a walk. My eyes burn. I won't shed a tear over a jackass who faked his own death just to get away from me.

The sirens fade. I keep a steady walk, doing my best to appear calm. A black and white could come through the neighborhood without lights and sirens. I don't want to seem suspicious.

I'd give anything to have the slightest uncertainty, a wavering of whether my memory serves me well.

I run the sleeve of my hoodie across my wet cheeks as I close my eyes, trapping tears behind my lids.

This is absolutely fucking perfect. I've started a business with my dead brother's wife. My sister-in-law. I have a fucking sister-in-law. We have a fucking family business.

Fuck. I didn't get my jewelry, never mind the jewelry box. I'm running out of time. This needed to be done tonight.

Fucking alarm. Fucking ghosts. Fucking fuck.

I bet she's thrown the box away in the trash. Hidden key be damned. She doesn't give a shit about family, but then, neither does her fucking husband.

The park comes into view on the left as I break into another jog. I climb into my SUV, slamming the door. As I pull onto the street, a sharp pain strikes my chest. I look down, expecting to find a bullet hole or a knife ... but there's no blood, no indication that anything is piercing my sternum.

He fucking left me high and dry. He set our shady ass drug gang up, including me, and left me to rot in juvie. He never tried to come back or contact me. He never gave a flying fuck.

As I come to a stop sign leaving Olivia's rich-ass neighborhood—my *brother's* neighborhood—the irony sends me into a fit of laughter. We came from a long line of jewelers, running generation after generation of family storefronts. I've inadvertently stumbled into the same family business. With the fucking ghost's wife.

I swing the SUV around the corner and punch the gas, flying down the road. I pull over when I hit a shoulder that's wide enough for my car, then I climb out, walk around to the ditch, and sit down, hitting my head against the side of my car.

Fuck, that hurt. I guess this isn't a dream.

I wish this were a fucking dream. Like all the other nightmares. I wish I could wake up screaming, drenched in sweat. I've never wanted anything more. I've never wanted to forget about Travis more than I do now.

And I've been cavorting with his wife. With her social circles. I've been running amuck in his hometown, without a fucking care in the fucking world. I've been flaunting my presence.

He can't know I'm here. He may have had the advantage the last twenty years, playing me like the mourning sister fiddle he thinks I am. He knew I refused to come back here, to this horrible place, after our parents died.

I have the advantage now. He didn't take into account that I'd marry someone who gives a shit about me. I'm going to get every last piece of revenge I deserve. Nobody gets to fuck with me and get away with it, and he's fucked with me way more than anyone else ever has, and more than anyone ever should.

Unfortunately, I don't know what to do yet. That's perhaps the most dangerous thing in this world: a vengeful sister like me, without a fucking clue what's next.

Olivia

Sunday, November 20th

I clutch my chest to still the shaking in my hands. A keen sense of awareness kept me searching the roads the entire drive home.

He drove his expensive sportscar too fast, like life is irrelevant. That would make sense, since he said we couldn't afford IVF, then he bought this car ...

"You think someone broke in?" I ask. I stare at our house through the windshield.

The house is serene, untouched.

"Stay here," Camden says, reaching over not to reassure me but to dig through the glove compartment. He extracts a flashlight and climbs out, leaving me to close the compartment door for him.

My knees bounce as I watch him slip through the front door without turning on any lights.

I've offered to put the alarm service on my bills before, so a company is contacted if it's triggered, but Camden has always refused. He refused again tonight when I tried to bring it up. He hushed me and set a timer for five minutes before disarming the alarm from his phone.

This isn't safe. Not having backup. Trusting the blare of an alarm to do the work of police. Who does he think he is right now, anyway? John McClane?

The longer he's in there, the tighter my muscles get. When he finally flicks on the front room light and steps onto the porch, my body is aching.

He gestures for me to come inside. It would have been nice if he'd come to get me so I'm not in the dark. Alone.

I take deep breaths in the security of the car, then step out. My eyes travel the edges of our property, searching through the bushes and trees along the fence line. As I race to the door, nothing jumps out to attack me. I'm alone.

So alone.

Right now, I can't decide if that's a good thing or a bad thing.

Once I'm over the threshold, I stop, daring to inch forward into the house that's supposed to be my safe place. This is one more reason that it isn't. Two—because dinner tonight was jarring.

"Not sure what tripped it," Camden calls from down the hall.

A door creaks, and his feet thud downstairs.

I gulp and pull my hands together, one finger finding the thumbnail of the other.

The basement.

Elle.

Her jewelry. If it's missing ... if someone stole it, I'll be out of business. She'll refuse to help me.

My body urges me not to follow, but I move forward down the hall. I descend the stairs with caution, and come around the corner, into the storage room.

Camden is kneeling by the black bins with the locked red lids, checking them for damage. My gaze flashes to the wall with old cardboard boxes.

It's still here and looks undisturbed, but I'll have to take a closer look later. I don't dare check with Camden here.

"Everything okay?" I ask timidly, a shiver coursing through me.

As he nods, my gaze drifts to the wall again. Do I remember the box correctly? I can't be sure. Did I leave the corner hanging off the shelf instead of tucking it against the back wall?

My vision blurs as I realize I shouldn't be fearing what Elle will do if the jewelry is stolen.

I should be concerned that she's the one who tried to steal it.

Could she be capable of breaking and entering? I don't really know her. I only know that she can forge jewelry and that she wants mine. Rather, she wants the jewelry that resides in my basement.

I step back, slipping out of the room to separate myself from the cardboard box.

It wasn't Elle. There's no reason—we have an agreement.

Camden stands, walking toward me. He stops inches from me, touching my cheek.

"You're trembling," he whispers.

"I'm scared."

"No need to be." A smile dances on his lips. "I'd never let anything happen to you."

His words smooth over my emotions but leave a slight question in their wake.

Camden brushes his lips across mine and pulls me against his body. He's hard. His hands slide down my waist, pressing my hips against him. I grab his neck, needing him closer, needing his lips against mine.

As our tongues lock, our breathing shallow, frantic, my throat constricts.

He's turned on by the potential intrusion, by the risk—the thrill—of being unsafe.

Charlie.

Charlie is that for him.

I push away, taking a breath. He tries to pull me back, but I place my hand on his chest.

"Can we check the house one more time?" It's a perfect excuse to collect my thoughts.

He grins and releases me.

"Sure," he says, then turns and climbs the stairs.

I follow him, waiting in the kitchen as he clears one room at a time, turning on the lights as he does.

When he returns, he laces his arms around my hips and lightly kisses me. I don't protest. I don't ask the thousands of questions running through my mind.

Instead, I let him hold me. I ask him to keep me safe. And I lead him to our bed.

Tonight, it just might be enough.

Elle

Sunday, November 20th

"Hey, are you okay?" Zane asks as I lurch forward and catch myself on the entry table.

"Umm, yeah. Sure."

I'm vaguely aware of Zane watching me as my autopilot fails and I trip over a suitcase. I drop my coat, not caring that it lands on the floor instead of the chair that I was aiming for, and head to the bedroom, where I fall onto the pristine bedding.

"What's wrong with you?" Zane says, quick on my heels.

"I think I have a migraine," I mumble into the comforter.

I don't get headaches, but Eddy's told me about his—the disorientation and out of body experience. It's fitting.

"Do you need me to take you to a doctor or something?" Zane's words are heavy with concern.

"No. I just need rest." And a shit ton of whiskey.

His footsteps move around the room and the blinds groan as he twists them closed.

"I was supposed to head out of town for a case that just came up in Louisiana, but I'm going to call and tell them to change my flight," he whispers.

I roll over and sit up. "No, I think I'll be fine after some water. Maybe some food. I'll be okay."

"And I'll stay and get those things for you." He's firm.

198

"No, Love. You should go. I'll be okay. I just need some rest."

Worry ripples through his eyes, overwhelming me. Tears brim and one falls onto my arm. I need to protect him from this. If he finds out about my brother, he could find out about everything else that I've kept from him. All the things I've lied about. I could lose him. It would crush me. I'll tell him about Travis, but I need more time—I need my inheritance.

I stand and cross the room until I'm close enough to wrap my arms around his waist and bury my head in his sweater.

"You don't seem okay," he says, rubbing my back.

"It hurts like hell, that's all. Do you have any of that Vicodin left over from your shoulder injury?" I ask, my words muffled.

"No. I took the extra back. Sorry."

Zane is too good for me. He keeps everything spotless, always tells the truth. Returns narcotics when he doesn't use them all.

"You better get going," I say, stepping back.

He runs a hand over my forehead, then leans forward to kiss it. "I'll call you before we take off, just to make sure you're okay. Maybe have Olivia check in on you?"

"Yeah, I'll ask her to come by."

If only he knew.

"I love you," I tell him as he grabs my hand and gives it a squeeze.

"I love you, too. Just say the word, and I'll be back here in a flash."

One last kiss, and he's gone. Just like always. Only this time, I need him to leave, but I'd kill to have him stay.

Elle

Thursday, November 24th

Days and nights are irrelevant. I sleep. I wake. I drink. I sleep. I turn the television on and listen to its drone with the covers over my head. I get angry and turn it off.

Showering is pointless. There's no running. No gemology work. No boxing. I may kill someone in the ring with the rage I have right now.

I don't eat. I only drink.

Losing my parents sent me into a spiral, but I couldn't express my grief.

Their deaths were my fault.

Before their bodies were in the ground, Travis and I were removed from the only home we'd ever known. We had no family to take us in. We were torn apart, separated into different foster homes. First, it was due to placement availability. Later, it was because I made poor decisions. I stole, I lied, and I picked fights. They tossed me from one home to another—a problem to be fixed by someone else.

I tried to mourn, hiding in whichever makeshift bed I was placed in, but it wasn't enough. The memory of our last vacation as a family, just weeks before their death, began playing on repeat in my mind. Dad talking about moving—making Leesburg our new home. Mom hushing him; nothing had been decided yet. Travis was eager to make a change. I demanded that we didn't. That was my first mistake of many. It led to the events of their death. The one catapulted by my selfish nature.

I urged Travis to run away with me to New York City. My dream. The only place I'd ever wanted to go, to move.

I begged him. Pushed him. Until he said yes. It didn't matter that we had to live on the streets, lie to get into school, and forge signatures of an aunt that never existed. I didn't care about any of that. I was an expert liar, even then, but my commitment to making our life better was strong. When I caught Sam's eye, I didn't turn and run like I should have. A twenty-seven-year-old drug dealer taking an interest in a fifteen-year-old wasn't normal, but it was an opportunity for me.

I practically yanked Travis into the scheme of selling drugs to high school kids for Sam. Ramp up business with the younger, more stable crowd.

Travis was such a great student. He worked hard to pull good grades despite living on the streets and selling marijuana to minors. He was going to be somebody.

His dedication to me pushed me further. I didn't attend school much. Instead, I worked harder and longer hours. I got us off the streets. Then, I started forging replicas of multiple pieces in our inheritance. Our dad had often said that I had the family gift. Travis wasn't interested in delving deeper into crime, but he loved coming with me to flea markets and secondhand stores to find the supplies I needed for the forgeries. It reminded him of weekends with our parents. It reminded us both of what it was to be carefree.

I earned enough to buy us an apartment. When Travis turned eighteen, I found the perfect place and bought it under his name since I was still a minor. The home would set us free from the constraints of our lives.

At the time, I thought it was enough. I thought that we could sever ties with the gang, walk away, start fresh. I was wrong.

Dead wrong.

I was a liar. A thief. A lowlife.

Then Travis disappeared. I went to juvie.

That should have been a clue.

Mourning—crying—in juvie, wasn't an option. Hope was the only thing that held me together. I was dead wrong about that, too.

Now, there's nothing—nobody—to prevent me from feeling. From mourning. It fucking sucks. It would have been far better if his lifeless, disintegrating body was found. At least then I'd have closure.

I can't kill him. I wouldn't get away with it since I wasn't convicted of his first death. Nobody was. Despite twenty years of anguish, feelings aren't convictions.

Instead of killing him, I stay in bed with my black out curtains drawn, buried under the comforter.

My cell vibrating somewhere in the sheets shocks me out of my trance. I pat my hand around, flailing my arm, until I find it. It's Zane so I click the green button. Otherwise, I'd throw the damn thing into the toilet.

"Hun, why is it dark?" Zane asks on the other end.

Shit, he must have called me on FaceTime.

"Under the covers," I say, my voice groggy.

"It's mid-day. What are you doing?"

"Napping."

"You've done nothing but sleep since I've left," he says with concern. "I'm worried about you."

"It's just a bug. It'll pass." My words are unconvincing.

"A bug," he repeats.

The statement lies silently between us.

"You have to get out of bed, my love," he says even gentler.

My stomach twists. God, this man is a fucking saint. If only he knew how much I wasn't.

"I know. I will."

"Have you eaten?"

"Yes," I lie.

That's me, just keep on lying to the one I love more than anything in the world, forcing a deeper wedge between myself and a true connection.

Tears warm my cheek, shocking me. I hold my breath, but instead, it comes out like a stifled choke.

"I'll be better tomorrow," I rush out the shaky words. "Call you later."

I hit the end button as my entire being rips apart. For the first time since Travis was presumed dead, I sob uncontrollably until I pass out. When my phone startles me awake sometime later, I don't search for it. Vulnerability doesn't look good on me, and there's nothing Zane can say to make me believe that it does.

Olivia

Thursday, November 24th

T hanksgiving is a time to spend with loved ones, with those who we are most grateful for.

With my mom and stepdad now living so far away, I wasn't thrilled for this day to arrive, especially with recent events.

Camden had a cure for the Thanksgiving blues because he surprised me with plans.

They involved his good friend Billy and the woman I'm certain that he's having an affair with. A cheap affair, though, since he's giving her pretend diamonds and expressing her worth with such gifts.

Their kids have been yelling and screaming all evening, which wouldn't bother me, typically. Today, I tense under the screeches, annoyed that they come from children birthed by the woman who pretends to be my best friend just to stab me in the back. Since I have no idea how long this fling has been going on—if I'm right, because I hope I'm wrong—I watch the children with a focused eye. A fresh perspective. Are they Billy's? Or are they Camden's?

Poor Billy. He's blissfully ignorant. He chases the children around, clears the table, refills drinks. He's too busy and too confident in his marriage to notice when Charlie and Camden slip away, leaving the little screamers and docile spouses on their own.

I try not to think about how long they're gone. Two minutes, five, ten. Instead, I force myself to think about the words coming from the Alexa, playing Christmas songs one after the other. Speeding us into the next season.

When it's not enough, I offer to help with the dishes. Billy agrees appreciatively.

"Where did Charlie go?" I ask nonchalantly, hoping to bring his attention to the two missing people.

"Probably refreshing herself. She worked hard all day, making the meal." He grins.

The turkey was dry, and the green beans, mashed potatoes, rolls, and pies were clearly from a catering company. The only reason she made the bird was to have it come from the oven piping hot, her gold star for a job well done.

Billy didn't notice because every Thanksgiving, she insists that he and Camden go golfing so she can order food and lie about it. She once described it to me more eloquently than that, insisting that I not be selfish with my husband's time. Camden deserves to have a good time golfing with Billy on occasion.

Ten minutes. Twelve. I wish I could dismiss time. Forget how it works.

I'm halfway through the pile of dirty dishes when Camden emerges from the darkness of the back hall. He comes around behind me and tucks his hip to my waist.

His phone rings inside his pocket. He pulls it out, the name *Libby* flashing across his screen.

Libby. The same person he told me that he was working on a gaming project with. He was so quick on his feet then, just like he was quick to dismiss the obvious tension the other night at the restaurant.

My chest tightens. Libby could be another woman. Maybe she's the one good enough to get actual diamonds.

The corner of his mouth twitches up as he reads his screen, unaware that I'm staring at it too. He silences the ring and shoves it back into his pocket.

"You ready to go?" he asks.

"Yes," I answer, setting the mostly-washed pot back in the dirty pile. Sorry, Billy.

Unfortunately, I'm too late to avoid Charlie.

She peeks out of the hall entryway, her hair smooth, her skin glowing. Are her cheeks flushed?

The wait for Camden to say goodbye to Billy takes forever, his bro unaware of the infidelity. I find the children and give them hugs. Maybe I didn't want to tolerate their screaming earlier, maybe I don't know who their father truly is, but I can't fault them. I'd much rather dote on them than pretend to like Charlie right now.

Camden slips his hand in mine as we walk through the chilly night air to his sportscar.

My body melts into the heated leather of the passenger seat, and I hate the thrill of the gears clicking as the car speeds away from Charlie's house. As the tires chirp on the pavement, it's unclear whether I secretly like the car or if I like the idea of ripping it away when IVF works.

"My boss called earlier. I need to go in to work tonight and pull an all-nighter. Get the night owls' perspectives on who'll be playing our game."

An ache crosses the car, slamming my chest. His boss? Or Libby? Or Charlie. Maybe "Libby" is code for Charlie.

"Okay." I don't protest. I can't be bothered. If he's no longer mine, there's no point in me trying to keep him.

"Yeah, if that's alright?" He drapes an arm over the back of my seat, but not me, as if the gesture and the question are enough to provide comfort.

The car lurches into the driveway, and he leans over, his face next to mine. He pecks my cheek, like he would a child. Or a friend.

I pull my coat tight, trying to hide my longing for the other night. His hands all over me, like there was nothing else in the world. Or anybody else.

"I'll see you sometime mid-morning?"

My throat constricts. He's dropping me off...to go into the dark house alone.

"Alright." I swallow.

I stand in the driveway, clutching my purse.

The rumble of his car pulling away from our house isn't as reassuring as it was leaving Charlie's. Whether he's stepping out on me to have an affair or play a game all night, it's wrong.

I don't do a thing about it.

I turn toward the house, its presence ominous. Last weekend stabbed away at my composure, bled my insecurities.

There's no way that I can go inside. I have no strength left. My eyes search the porch. A box sits by the door. A note is taped on top, flapping in the cold breeze.

The street is eerily quiet. A lone black car sits across the street a couple of houses up. No matter how hard I look, nothing welcomes me here.

When does a house become a home? I once thought that it would be when we had children. I was so naïve.

Elle

Thursday, November 24th

The banging at the front door does little to disturb me, and I refuse to get up when it doesn't stop. Give it up already, asshat. I'm not answering the phone. I'm not coming to the door. My patience wins out over the knocker's impatience, and finally, it grows quiet again.

The front door creaks open, and quiet footsteps enter. If I gave two shits, I'd get out of this bed, but whoever's coming for me can have me. They've been trying for too long. I no longer care. If Zane were here, it would be different, but he's not. I'm alone.

"Elle?" A light voice comes as a whisper through the house.

Well, I'm not dying today.

"Elle?"

I can't be bothered to move.

"Elle, are you already asleep? It's only seven."

I throw the covers back and stare at the darkened ceiling.

"You breaking into houses now, Olivia?" I groan.

"You have a key under the mat."

Fuck. If Zane knew I kept a key under the mat for when I go on runs, he'd lose his shit.

If my stalker knew, I'd be dead.

"Give me that," I say without reaching out a hand.

Olivia tosses it onto the bed.

"What are you doing here?" Maybe if I'm more direct, she'll get to the point.

"Honestly? I don't know." She slumps onto the foot of the bed, her back to me. "Camden decided to go pull an all-nighter at work, and I just ended up ... here."

Convenient. For her.

"You know I could have you arrested," I say grumpily.

"You know I could have *you* arrested," she repeats—but with an edge.

"The jewelry is mine. I'm not sure I can steal something that belongs to me."

"Then why is it in my basement?"

That's a fantastic question. One I wish I didn't have the answer to.

I sigh, deciding it's time that she knows something. "Someone stole the collection from me when I was sixteen. How you got it, I can't say. It's not like I've been stalking you."

She leans against the bed and peers in my direction.

"Haven't you?" she asks sarcastically.

"I was stalking my inheritance, not you. You're hardly interesting enough."

"Your inheritance," she repeats, processing. Her shoulders hunch. "I suppose you're right: I'm not interesting. Camden seems to agree with you, anyway."

Travis. Not Camden.

We used to agree on a lot, but I won't be categorized with him any longer.

"He's an ass," I mumble.

I stretch my legs, expanding the length of my spine along the mattress, then flip the comforter back over my face. "There's wine in the kitchen. You can open any bottle you want."

The mattress shifts as she stands, and her footsteps crossing the floor fade as she leaves the room.

I groan as I sort through my situation. With Olivia, I'm sort of free from pretending.

I could make her leave, but I don't hate her. Anyone who suggests we con a bunch of rich ladies has some inner demons who I'd like to know. Plus, we're family.

The click of her heels returns along with a quiet thud on the nightstand next to me. She walks around the bed and plops down on Zane's side.

I reach up and pull the covers down enough to peer out and spot a snifter next to me. Full of bourbon—not wine. Sliding up in bed, I bring my knees to my chest and then lift the glass to my lips, letting the warmth of the whiskey slip down my throat.

When I set it back down, I grab the remote and turn the television on. The screen flashes as I click through the channels, finally landing on a Saturday Night Live rerun.

"You know," I say, turning my head in her direction, "You aren't that bad."

She lifts her own glass to her lips and takes a couple of gulps of her red wine.

"Also, thank you for not making me drink that crap." I point to her glass.

She tilts her head, and in the television's glow, she looks devious.

"You lie about liking wine? Here I was offering you something stronger ... seems like you could use it right now."

"I always need it. Please don't tell Zane. He'd be crushed."

She twists her finger and thumb, which are pressed together by her pursed lips, sealing the secret.

"Not like it matters," I say, trying to bring light to my secret. "We all have a vice."

"Ice cream," Olivia says. "That's mine. I love milkshakes. Ben & Jerry's pints."

"Of course, it is," I grumble, but the corner of my lip twitches at her admission.

"At least your marriage is sound ... aside from the wine thing," Olivia mutters. "I'm pretty sure mine is crumbling, and Charlie's at the core. Or Libby. Who the fuck knows."

The man at the gym ... he was so close, and I dismissed it. I grab my glass and bring it to my lips, letting it hover there for my own comfort. I'm unable to pay attention to what's happening on the television. Yet, I manage to hear Tina Fey asking Betty White how many people live in her apartment. I unexpectedly laugh when Betty announces her name in a drawn-out "Blarfengar."

"When does Zane get home?" Olivia asks.

"Tomorrow sometime. He'll be glad to know that you were here."

"Really?" She turns her head, searching my face for something.

"Really." I chuckle. "He was worried about me and suggested I call you."

"You could have, you know," she says in a soothing tone.

I couldn't have, but she can't know that.

"Well, I'm glad he's coming home," Olivia says as the skit on TV ends. "Have you ever thought of getting a guard dog? In case your crimes catch up with you or someone other than me discovers your hidden key."

"Nah." I take another sip. "I'm going to adopt a homeless man like Betty White."

Olivia slouches further into the headboard and giggles into her wine glass. For once, the anxiety she carries releases from her.

"Someone tried to break into our house the other day," Olivia says.

The hand holding my glass begins to shake.

"Or someone did break in, but they didn't take anything. Maybe. I don't know. Camden thinks the wind tripped the alarm," she rambles.

"Maybe you need a guard dog," I suggest, forcing my words to come evenly.

Her cuddly dog didn't guard shit.

"Camden has one." Olivia rolls her eyes. "She didn't bark. She was lying by the garage door, whimpering, when we got home. She doesn't like the alarm. He's convinced it wasn't a break-in, because he thinks if it were, she would have attacked ... barked. Something."

Her knees start bouncing as a frown crosses her face. "But, he took her to a kennel for a few days just in case. God forbid his dog be home alone if a risk—the one he swears doesn't exist—shows up again." She takes a gulp from her glass and shakes her shoulders as if shedding something from her back. "When he dropped me off tonight, like a cheap date, I just couldn't go in. So, I got in my car and showed up here."

"He's a fucking asshole, Olivia!"

"He had to work ..."

Her gaze meets mine, and I know she doesn't believe a word she says.

"Fucking Charlie," I say, holding her gaze.

She shakes her head. "Fucking Charlie."

Olivia

Friday, November 25th

I park in the driveway then enter through the garage. Camden's flashy car is inside. I'm glad I won't be at the house alone, but I'm weighed down by the thought of seeing him.

"You were out early," Camden says as I set my purse down and hang my coat in the closet.

That's a problem when you were out all night? I want to ask, but I'm too relieved—and perplexed—that he didn't notice my clothes are unchanged.

"I was," I say, quieting the voice in my head that keeps growing louder.

He comes over and wraps his arms around me. He reeks of alcohol and gym clothes.

"Did you go to the gym this morning?" I ask, scrunching my nose and stepping back.

He twists his face to one side, his eyebrows rearranging like a question mark.

I clench, fearing I've stumbled into a situation I can't escape. Do I want to know?

"Your clothes," I say, pointing to his shorts and hoodie.

"Oh, yeah. I went early this morning, then went back to work. I didn't have a change of clothes, though, so ..."

"You couldn't just put your other clothes back on? Or did they smell of something worse than BO?" I ask.

Apparently, the voice inside won't be stifled any longer.

"What are you talking about?" he says with disdain. His shoulders expand.

My head buzzes in warning. I shrink reflexively.

No. I won't back down. I deserve better, or at least I deserve an explanation.

"Sex," I snap. "Your clothes. Do they smell like sex? Perfume maybe? Another woman?"

Regret seeps through my pores as his eyes darken and his jaw tightens.

"You really think that? That I have time for anyone else?"

But isn't it obvious?

"Yes," I say. The back of my eyes begin to burn, and my throat stings.

Don't cry. I'll lose all my power.

No urging stops the tears from revealing my weakness—I still love him. I'll always love him.

"Charlie's tennis bracelet, the one that she thought was real, it was from you, wasn't it?" I say, conviction strong through my wavering emotions.

His face strains as he steps toward me. I step back.

"It was." He sighs. "It's not what you think ..."

My stomach drops like a broken elevator. What does he mean? What other reason would Camden buy my supposed best friend jewelry? Fake or not, it's not normal. Not when it's kept secret from spouses.

"Then what, Camden? What should I think?"

The tears fall freely now. I sniff and wipe at my face, but it's no use; the tears flow too fast.

He steps toward me again, his hand outstretched like he's trying to reassure a frightened dog. I don't move.

I'm not sure if I should believe him, but I want so badly to trust everything that he says, to keep him as mine forever. I should have never started this.

He pulls me to his chest and hunches over, bringing his chin to my shoulder.

"I'd never cheat on you, Olivia," he whispers.

My heart pounds, and my throat constricts. A fresh wave of tears breaches my eyelids.

I'll believe him. I want nothing more than to truly believe. And his tone, his touch, they are so sincere.

"I love you, Olivia," he says, hugging me tighter and running his hand over my hair. "I love you. Only you."

Olivia

Thursday, December 1st

E lle slams a large bottle of dish soap on her Formica kitchen counter next to a couple of large mixing bowls.

"You brought the labels?" she asks.

"Yes, and more of the appraisal pamphlets," I say, setting my tote on a barstool so I can dig them out.

"Good," she says with a grunt as she lifts a big box onto the counter. "Put the stickers on these."

She removes a plastic jar with a cheap strainer inside, identical to those with the jewelry cleaners we sold out of during our trial run. My brain slowly clicks into gear.

"We aren't making it, are we?" I ask, already knowing the answer. "I thought we ordered professional cleaner."

"Yes, and no. Eddy made some for us last time, but I've been making this shit for years. I'm thinking, though, if we make enough this time, we could convince your friends to sell it for us like the pyramid schemes they already love so much. What do you think?"

I swallow. "I don't know, Elle."

"Yes, you do. You want to make money. You're game for stealing. This is another stream of revenue, only more legit. You need to learn how to do it so that you could continue this part on your own ... if I wasn't involved."

A chill passes through me.

"What do you mean?" I ask, studying her face. I know she hardly ever gives hints there.

"You just never know," she says. "Speaking of money ..."

She spins on her heels and heads through a door near the entrance of her home's narrow hall. She pokes her head back out of the room.

"Come on," she urges, then disappears inside.

I do as I'm told. There's a long desk against the wall with equipment and tools spread out. One is a bit like a microscope, but not quite.

Elle holds a small box out to me with three felt bags inside, each attached to an appraisal slip with familiar names.

"You'll need to return these repairs," Elle says as I consider the contents of the box in my hands.

"Just repairs?" I ask, not wanting to know the answer.

"Sure," she says, patting me on the shoulder and sliding back into the hall. "Let's get this cleaner made."

I follow her out of the room, set the box on the table, then return to the kitchen. Elle yanks a bottom drawer open and extracts a single apron, holding it up to me.

"Here," she says, jutting her chin at my chiffon sweater.

My cheeks warm as I slip the apron over my head and tie it behind my back.

"Good thing I called in sick," I grumble, even though it was my choice. I can't focus on work with too many other things in my head. There's so much possibility and uncertainty, especially today.

"If you hadn't, I would've had you over bright and early Saturday morning," Elle says, nudging me. "This concoction is mostly water—warm's best—and a non-abrasive dish soap, about a tablespoon to one cup of water. And a teaspoon of salt added to that ratio to preserve the water-based solution. That's the recipe for gold and fine stones. For silver, add a tablespoon of baking soda to the mix; same ratios. You got that?"

I nod rather unconvincingly.

She laughs. "I'll write it down."

I get to work, and the whisk in my hand is weighted down by a number of feelings that I can't seem to quantify. Soap and water—that's what all these women have been buying from us—and raving about it.

Elle takes over labeling and prepping the plastic jars. Most get a gold sticker on top, while some get a silver round dot.

"So, what's the plan with ... our other plan?" My words come out shaky.

She looks up at me, her hands still at work.

"What?" I ask, shifting my weight to the other hip.

"The plan is, I'll ask some of our guests if they'd like to leave their pieces with me for repair. When I'm done, you return the items to the women."

A weird relief settles over me at the same time the familiar anxious buzz kicks in.

I think I'm okay without any other details.

She starts removing the lids from the round containers. Her smooth, rhythmic movements seem bred not just from confidence but from repetition and from comfort.

I want to know how she does what she does and how she's so calm about it all, but instead of asking, I keep quiet and pour this cheap cleaner into the jars, preparing myself to sell it like I believe it's the best in the world. If I do, will Elle continue to stay in business with me?

Why would she stay once we get our needs met? When she has all her jewelry pieces—there's no guarantee she'll even stick around to get me to my financial goal.

The unrelenting thoughts keep me distracted during the day and awake at night. All the *what ifs* and *hows* of her collection landing in my basement.

I could ask Camden if her things came from one of Jared's lockers, but I don't want him to stop me from taking them. I definitely don't want to explain why I need them—how I owe Elle. I'm terrified to find out the truth behind the cross—the family heirloom—because knowing how he got the other pieces will inevitably reveal the lie behind a cherished connection he gave me.

Taking a break from the monotony of mixing, whisking, and pouring, I set a few jewelry pieces by Elle's bowl.

Her eyes twinkle.

"Thank you," she says.

"Can I ask you a favor?" My stomach pinches.

"Depends on the favor." Elle picks up a set of earrings to admire them.

"Can you replicate the cross?"

"The one you sold for a quick buck?" Her sarcasm grates at me. She knows which cross.

"It's just that, Camden ... he gave that piece to me after we got married. He said it was a family heirloom."

Her face darkens, and she bites her bottom lip.

"I know it's yours. I know. He obviously lied." I speak faster now, wishing that I didn't have to ask. And I'm hating that I'm once again protecting Camden, "But he gave it to me as a gift, and the other day, he asked why I haven't been wearing it. I just think it may be better if—"

Her hand flies up, her palm at the level of my face. I flinch at her sudden movement.

"I'll do it," she says, irritation embedded in her tone. "Just don't ask me to replicate any others, Olivia. I won't have the time with all the other work I'll be doing."

The guilt of asking her this favor mixes with the dread of the theft to come in our partnership. It makes me jittery, as if I drank too much coffee on top of a dose of Adderall.

It doesn't matter how many calendars I keep; I still double-book myself. It was likely the forty-five-minute variation in start times between my standing appointment with Dr. Marcellus and my first of many fertility appointments with Dr. Foltz.

I scurry into Dr. Marcellus' office because nobody's answering the phone. When I arrive, the admin isn't at the desk, but Dr. Marcellus pops out when I chime the bell.

"Olivia," she says, beaming. "Sorry, I'm between admins—"

"Dr. Marcellus, I can't stay," I say too frantically, and chide myself for interrupting. "Sorry, I didn't realize that I forgot to cancel our appointments for the rest of the year."

She takes a breath, exaggerating the movement. I join in the soothing action.

"Come inside for a moment," she says, opening the door for me.

I follow her in, but don't sit.

"Now, what's going on?" she asks.

"It's IVF," I say. "I have to take the appointments available ..."

She nods slowly, her jaw tensing.

"I've already paid through the end of the year. I don't expect any refunds. I'm sorry, but I need to do this." My throat dries. I'm going to miss the emotional support, but the rest is up to me, my uterus, and Dr. Foltz.

As I step out of my car and head for Dr. Foltz' office, an unnerving sensation travels along my spine and out to my arms, causing goosebumps that prick the inside of my coat.

"Olivia," a familiar voice rumbles, confirming my intuition.

I spin to face him, the dread seeping into my bones.

"Jared?"

The expression on his face is dark, his jaw is firmly set, and his eyes burn through me. I've never seen him like this, but I'd expected escalation ... imagined this anger. But my imagination didn't prepare me for this look that makes me feel like he's killing me.

I bring my hands together, stabbing my nails into my palms.

"What are you doing here?" I ask.

What I really want to know is how he found me here.

"The jig's up," he says. "Go upstairs and get me back my money."

How? How does he know? I haven't told anyone except Dr. Marcellus.

"I don't know what you're talking—"

"Don't you dare lie to me again," he barks.

I stiffen. "I can't get the money back."

If I could, I wouldn't.

My stomach drops, but I hold my ground, hoping he can't see right through me. Fumes radiate from him, his jaw and fists clenched.

I might puke.

"Give me until the end of the month. I'll get it all back, I promise."

My eyes plead with him, hoping that he can offer his nephew's wife more grace.

But right now, he doesn't feel like family. He feels like an enemy—a very real threat.

"How the fuck will you come up with thirty thousand dollars in a month?" He cackles.

"I'm working on an extra project. I'll get it. Trust me, Jared. We're family. That's what family does."

Shoving my nails harder into my palm, I let my words settle, hoping that he lightens up.

"Like Camden trusts you not to have debt?" he snaps, his fists at his sides clenching; unclenching.

"I'm late for my appointment," I say, sidestepping toward the entrance. "I have it under control, Jared."

He steps toward me, reaching for my wrist, but he lets go when a couple strolls up, their toddler in tow. As he composes himself, I scamper to the door and push my way in, stopping near the security stand to smooth my appearance.

Jared glares at me through the window, lifting his wrist to tap his watch. Then he storms off around the corner.

Elle

Saturday, December 3rd

Olivia insisted that we meet at a nail salon. It doesn't surprise me with the way she's been picking at hers incessantly. I watch the technician who is filing off her cracked and chipped nails. The smell of acetone and acrylic dust burns my nostrils.

"Do you think we will make sixty?" Olivia asks in a hushed tone.

"How long have you been doing this?" I ask, my face twisting in disgust.

The technician in front of me gestures at my hands again, and I reluctantly place them on the towel. A simple manicure. It's not my thing, but I'm here, so I might as well do this and look the part for our upcoming bullshit game.

"Since I was a teenager," Olivia says, her cheeks turning red.

"You could save money if you didn't."

A file meets my thumbnail, and I cringe.

Olivia's eyes widen. She shakes her head. "No, I couldn't give it up. My nails ..."

She won't finish. She'd never admit she destroys them with all her nervous energy.

"We'll hit sixty, depending on what business comes in this weekend and next," I answer her question finally. "We split it, though."

"You mean, sixty—"

"I said split."

She nods slowly as she processes the change in our terms.

"Do you think we could get more?" she whispers.

The two women working on our nails are having their own conversation. They don't care about what we're discussing. Olivia is so fucking paranoid. We aren't saying anything incriminating. She needs to lighten up. Her reaction to her fears will get us caught, not our discussion.

"Maybe, but I wouldn't count on it." I shrug.

"We could do more ... after Christmas."

"No. We couldn't. We had a deal. I get you to thirty. You give me my jewelry and whatever else is with it," I say, standing firm.

She better read between the lines here. I want my jewelry. All of it. But I desperately need that box. If Travis hasn't already found the key.

He didn't know about the key, though. Mom only told me. There'd have been no reason for him to inspect the box. I fucking hope he left it abandoned and forgotten with the rest of our inheritance in their basement.

Abandoned and forgotten. He didn't even notice that Olivia was wearing other pieces from the collection. He's either checked out of his marriage or inept at remembering his family. Or both.

"No, I know," she sighs. "But I was still hoping we could ..."

"Hmm," I grunt.

I could give her the predetermined and definitive answer, but it's better to keep her motivated. Hopeful.

On cue with my thoughts, my phone screen flashes to life on the table between us. My eyelid twitches in beat with the too-pleasant ringtone. I don't have to look.

"You need to get that?" Olivia asks as the technician pauses.

"Nah," I give a half smile. "It's just a telemarketer."

When my phone vibrates with a voicemail notification, my stomach does a somersault. I hate when the caller leaves a message. So far, they've been dead air and breathing, but I can't not listen to it. There could be an indication of who the caller is, a hint that it may not be Sam. Except, nobody else is this persistent.

I dread telling Zane. I'm not ready to leave Leesburg. I'll tell him ... as soon as I get my things back.

Something pulls at my chest. An odd sensation. I'd do anything to protect my one true love. I've done so much already. I've made sure he doesn't know the piece of me that would hurt him and take him from me. It's the same piece that would make him vulnerable to the shitshow that's my past, and my present.

I need my things. I need answers. I won't get them if we leave.

I shake it off. That's why the thought of moving bothers me so much.

"So, that woman's house this morning." I chuckle. "It's like Christmas threw up in there."

Olivia's face brightens. "Wasn't it amazing?"

"No." I laugh harder. "It was horrible. It made my skin crawl."

"Of course, it would," she says, bumping my shoulder, then apologizing to the woman who's working on her nails. "I love Christmas. It's full of magic and hope. The decorations are the best. And the sugar cookies Mindy made for her guests ... wow."

She's a full-blown fanatic.

"Zane loves Christmas," I say, cringing at the thought.

I decorate for him, but I only get through a third of his decorations before calling it quits with the promise of a better attempt the following year. If he wasn't gone so much, he'd do it. Some years, he does, and it's gross.

"He has good taste," she says wistfully. "Camden doesn't like Christmas. At all. I don't know why. It's ridiculous."

Gee, I wonder why. Perhaps because our parents died just before Christmas?

"Sorry, I mean, I know you don't like Christmas either, but come on. You can't hate it that much," she says, flashing her teeth in a playful grin.

"I do," I say.

The tech pats my hand, and I glance over to see if she wants me to put my fingers in a bowl of liquid.

"You just need someone to brighten your holidays; then you'll change your mind."

"Maybe you could—"

"Olivia," a gruff voice calls from the door.

My skin erupts in goosebumps as Olivia yanks her hands from the technician and stands.

"Jared," she says, her voice timid. "What are you—"

"You little sneak, running off like that the other day," he growls. He moves toward her, and Olivia stumbles back, bumping into her chair.

I nod to my nail technician with a friendly smile and mouth thanks as I extract my hands from the clear liquid and dab them onto the towel in front of me.

Rising slowly, I touch Olivia's arm.

"Who's this?" I ask casually. He's my new enemy, but I'd like to know his name. I won't be forgetting it.

"Jared," she says, her eyes darting between him and me as he takes another step forward. "Camden's uncle."

"Camden's uncle?" I ask, tilting my head.

My muscles tighten, a fist forming behind my back. The tension feels good, reminding me that I'm not imagining this. This is not a dream. None of it.

Travis doesn't have an uncle. Travis doesn't have any family.

Not anymore.

Except Olivia.

He's putting her in danger by lying to her about this motherfucker.

"The money, Olivia," he orders, trying to step around me to get to her.

I slide between them again, pulling my shoulders back.

"I told you that I have it under control, Jared," she says, staying behind me.

Good to know that she'd let her friend take a hit for her.

"Are you going to rob a bank or something?" He reaches around me, grasping at her wrist.

I grab his, twisting as I do.

"Now, why would she break the law for you?" I say with disdain. It's been too long since I've had a good fight.

"Who are you, anyway?" He glares down at me, posturing.

His eyes didn't flash with confusion, and he wouldn't acknowledge me until I stepped in. He knows something about me.

"The woman who has control of your wrist," I retort, giving it an extra twist with added friction.

He winces. It's hard to cover up some sorts of pain, especially from those that catch us by surprise.

"Do you need the cops?" the technician asks, waving a phone from behind her station.

I glance toward them. They've shrunk behind their plexiglass protectors, eyes wide. I give the woman with the phone a quick nod.

"I think the cops would be a great option." I smirk. "If Jared here doesn't leave."

He shakes his arm in defeat, willing me to let go. I comply, and he turns, moving toward the door.

He glances back as he pushes it open. "This isn't over, Olivia," he calls, pointing at her.

When he's gone, I turn to face her. She's collapsed back in her chair, her body shaking.

"I'm so sorry," she's pleading to the space around her, to me and to the two women who are also stunned by the intruder. "He's harmless, I swear. He's just upset. I'm so sorry."

The two nail technicians glance at each other then back at Olivia.

"Maybe you should go," one of them says apologetically.

"But you know me. This has never—"

"Sorry, Olivia," she says, shaking her head.

Her eyes are red when she stands, tears beginning their descent down her cheeks.

She scurries to the door but doesn't dare push it open alone. Instead, she peers through the glass, moving her head back and forth as she scopes out the sidewalk.

"Thank you for letting me handle it," I say, giving the women a final nod, and slip several twenties onto the station in front of me.

I move to Olivia's side and wrap my arm over her shoulder as I push the glass door open with my hip. Bells chime with the movement as we step onto the street.

"I've got your back, Olivia," I whisper.

She gulps and leans against me.

"You want a milkshake?" I ask. "While we find you another salon to finish your nails?"

"Okay." She hiccups.

It's exactly what she needs to pull herself together.

"Thank you," she adds.

"For what?"

"For back there," she says, peering at me, her eyes questioning. "I owe you."

Delightful.

"While I typically like holding IOUs over someone's head, I'm going to need to cash this one in ASAP. Take a day off this week; it's going to require some discretion."

It's almost midnight, which means that Zane is sound asleep, while I'm hunched over my desk determined to get a little more work done.

During our after-dinner chess game, Zane tried a new-ish strategy. My brain quickly mapped out how it would play out, but instead of using it to my advantage, I allowed him to defeat me. I needed to get back to my office, and he was due for a win.

My eyes are dry and lids itchy. I stare through the discomfort into the microscope, working on a green piece of glass that resembles an emerald. It's perfect for the cross that I've forged as a replica of mine. There are clear glass pieces to cut and metal to work for the party guests, but I'll use the machines for that, and they're too noisy.

Anger works its way through me, first at the back of my skull, then down through my chest, until it twitches in my fingers. Replicating this piece to fool an asshole is a waste of my fucking time.

I shouldn't expect any couth from him. His life is an indication of that. He lies to Olivia about an uncle, the cross, and God knows what else. His mere existence is a threat to her—the cons he runs heighten the stakes—and I don't like it.

The jewelry is mine, and soon, I'll have it all, but I'm invested now. I'll get revenge on Jared, the aggressive money shark posing as "Camden's" uncle.

I'll craft the perfect plan to take Travis down, too. He'll pay for every lie he's ever told, for every person he's ever slighted.

Framing him would be ideal, but too challenging without Olivia on board—which would be impossible, since she's somehow still head-over-heels for him.

"Hun?" Zane says groggily, rapping lightly on the door before pushing it open.

"Hey, Love," I say, the sight of him relieving me of my agitation.

"It's late. What are you still doing up?" His gaze roams over my workspace, and then he rubs his eyes.

"Just trying to get some repairs done. I have a lot to do." I smile at him.

"We should get you a new desk," he says, his gaze roaming the tattered desk the prior renter left behind.

"This one's fine."

"It's terrible." His nose scrunches. "It's falling apart."

I turn on my stool and glare at him.

"Who are you to judge whether it works?" I snap.

"I'm just saying, you could get a different one, if you'd like."

"Why does it suddenly matter so much? You dying to make this space mid-century modern, too?" My anger boils over at him, and I let it, even when I know it's irrational.

He sighs, indicating his lack of interest in a midnight fight. "What would you like, Elle?"

"I don't know!" I shout. He's always so fucking amenable. "Maybe a plant or a chair. A dog that you'll never agree to. I'd have better luck convincing you to adopt a homeless guy." His face scrunches and twists in his display of confusion. "Never mind," I grumble, standing. "We'll just be moving again in a few months anyway."

I step in front of him as my tantrum dissipates. Pulling his hips to mine, I press against him. He hums his pleasure as I slide my hand down his torso and into his briefs.

He lifts me, and I wrap my legs around his waist. He carries me to our room, where I'll hopefully find momentary distraction in his arms from the antagonizing, relentless thoughts.

Olivia

Sunday, December 4th

"Holy shit!" Elle bellows when she climbs into the passenger seat of my car. "That was something else."

Yeah, something else, alright. When Camille agreed to have a jewelry party alongside her fitness clothing popup, I never expected her to hold it at her church. After service, with all her friends from the congregation.

My grip cannot be tight enough on the steering wheel as I try to steady my hands from the twitches of fear. Nothing puts life into perspective like stealing from good-spirited, prayer-driven women in a house of God.

"Please tell me that we aren't going to replicate any of their things," I whisper.

"What are you talking about?" There's entirely too much thrill in her voice.

"The women are too good to have bad things happen to them," I say, doing my best to steady my tone and the wheel as I slowly pull through the lot, trying not to hit a speedbump too hard with the cleaning machine in the back.

"Most of them aren't that good, believe me," she grumbles. "They go to church to clean their consciences of all their daily sins. The sins that bought them expensive jewelry."

I pull the car onto the road and keep it under the speed limit. If we get caught, it won't be because of my driving.

"I'm not so sure about that. They all seemed ..."

"Righteous?" She scoffs. "That's because they were in their Sunday best, washed clean from their sins after confession. Besides, how is stealing precious gemstones different than swindling them out of their money? You convinced four of them to invest in cleaner bundles, charging them an obscene amount that you said was 'at cost.'"

In my periphery, I see her air quotes, but I keep my eyes on the road.

She's right. I stuck to the plan. I convinced them to buy bulk to start their own businesses and make extra holiday cash, then told them to only sell at our prices so they wouldn't devalue the product. This *excellent* cleaner. I need the money. I need to establish credibility and a long-term plan. I'll need extra cash when IVF works. If IVF works. Because I may not return to work full-time. Or at all. If Camden allows.

If Camden doesn't find out about this thing with Jared. About my debt. About the fact that I'm researching sperm donors.

Unease firmly planted in my gut, I try to think more logically and less out of guilt.

"Tell me about the pieces you took," I say, surprisingly confident.

She harumphs. "We talked about this. I decide."

"I've changed my mind."

To be fair, it was never an equal discussion. She told me how it would go, and I had no say. I'm tired of being the weak link in all my relationships.

"I have three. A simple necklace with one large diamond at the center, an emerald ring, and a diamond tennis bracelet, all of which are relatively new. I don't take pieces that are rooted in history."

From the corner of my eye, I see her shift and slide down in the seat a bit, resting her head back. Her eyelids flicker shut.

"Unless they're mine," I say, unable to stop myself.

"Unless they're *mine*," Elle corrects.

"This tennis bracelet is worth as much as a car, unlike Charlie's." Elle chuckles. "The owner won't miss a couple of diamonds from it, but she'd probably notice if the entire thing was replaced by cubic zirconium."

"Okay." I sigh. "And the others?"

I pull onto the street by Elle's house and jump at a branch running alongside the car.

Elle laughs. "Careful. Those branches will get you."

"Shut up," I grumble, but she's right. I'm too on edge.

"The other two are up to you. Both are valued at about three thousand. If I only repair them, we will make the one hundred we are charging. I guess it depends on how desperate you are for cash, and how desperate you are to pay Jared."

She pulls the latch and swings her door open, moving around to the back.

When the tailgate opens, I say, "Just repair them."

The money may be important, but the guilt is too much. It's hardly the fairytale story I want to tell my child one day about how I went out of my way to steal from people while at church just to pay back my IVF debt.

Despite how dangerous Jared is starting to appear, I doubt that he is, and I don't want to be like him, greedy and incapable of compassion.

"Your call," she says, grunting as she tries to drag the machine toward her. "You coming?"

I help her haul the machine onto the porch, then through the door and into her office.

Elle lowers onto her stool and looks at me.

"Why are you doing this?" she asks.

"Helping you bring your machine in?"

Her eyes bore into me.

"Jared, obviously," I answer, but I don't sound confident.

She shakes her head. "That's not enough. You're desperate. You took his money. Why?"

"I need the money for—"

The front door opens, announcing Zane's arrival.

My gaze meets hers, and in silent agreement, we drop it. I turn and step out of the office, Elle on my heels. She flings her arms around Zane's neck, and they kiss just long enough to make me feel like an awkward third wheel.

"I'm going to head out," I announce, heading toward the door.

"Yeah, okay," Elle says, not looking away from her husband. "Remember, you owe me."

Wednesday—because she couldn't pick a worse day for me to call in sick and make it believable. But, she did save me at the nail salon.

I'm back to my car in seconds. I shove the branch that startled me moments before away from my door, imagining Jared's face. When it snaps back too quickly, I grab it with both hands and break it. The action is cathartic.

When I get home, there are two boxes stacked at the door. The note says, "Get it done today."

Elle

Wednesday, December 7th

I prefer working in silence. Even with my noise-cancelling head-phones in, the Christmas music tears through the walls. Why the fuck Olivia thinks she *needs* to listen to it to decorate is beyond me.

The sound gets louder as the office door opens. I squeeze my eyes shut, trying to soothe the annoyance buzzing through me.

"Hot cocoa?" Olivia asks, then sets a mug down beside me.

The chocolate scent hits my nose, reminding me of my mother—the reason I'm doing this. Amidst the memories of caroling, ice skating, and snowball fights, I'm reminded of who I am.

I tilt my head and glare at her.

"Vegan." I point at my chest.

"Vegan." She points at the mug. "I'm not an idiot."

She turns to leave.

"Shut the door. Keep your music to yourself," I call after her, lifting the mug to my nose with a deep inhale.

"Scrooge," she grumbles as she shuts the door.

I finish my drink, then take the empty cup to the kitchen.

"The only thing missing is alcohol," I say over the music as I take in the sights of Olivia's work.

"Have to keep you sober so you don't mess things up," she explains.

Valid fucking point, Olivia. While she's busy digging through a box of ornaments, I splash some bourbon into my mug.

"Zane will like this," I note, twirling my finger in the air.

She turns to look at me, a perplexed expression crossing her face.

"How do you do it without your husband noticing."

I consider playing dumb, but I don't. Something's been on her mind all day—this must be it.

"I do my thing. He does his."

"You just lie?" She twists her face with the question.

I shrug. "Basically."

"But—"

"But what?" I chastise. "Like you aren't lying to ... Camden."

"That's different," she protests.

"How is it different?"

"Because ... he ... you ... you're so ..." she stammers.

I take a breath. "Why are you doing this, Olivia?"

Her jaw tightens, and her cheeks redden, but she doesn't answer.

"You don't have to tell me, but if you know the answer, you know it's possible. You're lying for your reasons, and I lie for mine."

She pulls tinsel from a bag and fiddles with it. I help her out by changing the subject.

"You have time to make some more cleaner before you leave?"

"I do have a life ..."

"Not anymore. Not until we're done with our rich mommy club heists. You're building a jewelry cleaner empire."

"*We're* building an empire. Not just me."

Not we. Her. She's going to need the footing if my douchey ex-brother leaves her high and dry. I nod to reassure her, then sip whiskey from my mug.

"Remember how we have four parties this coming weekend?"

"Tell me we get another church party." I chuckle.

"We will never have another church party." She wriggles like a dog shaking off water. "Our first host this weekend, Margo ... she wanted to hold her party at her winery."

"She works at a winery?" I ask, shocked any of these women would do shift work.

"She *owns* the winery," Olivia says. "She offered to let us hold all the events there this weekend. She sells wine, we do our thing, and we don't have to jump around from house to house. All our hostesses already agreed."

"Because women don't turn down wine," I tease.

"Except you," she retorts.

Except me. If I hadn't been force-fed wine all these years by an unknowing and overly-doting husband, maybe I wouldn't hate it so much. Instead, each glass is a solid reminder of every lie I've ever told him.

"Drunk customers are more trusting. They spend more. They'll be more open to new business ventures, too. You'll need to make more cleaner," I say tapping the recipe card on the counter.

Olivia

Saturday, December 11th

Elle and I set the cleaning machine on the table in the deserted event room. The large windows for walls make the space light and bright, and it's almost as if we are part of the rest of the space.

"Four parties today, two hours each. Like speed dating. Only much longer," I say, jittery.

"Exactly what I never wanted." Elle chuckles.

Fatigue from the birth control—necessary for a better response from the stimulation meds later in IVF—weighs me down. Along with my regular job, this new secret job ... and the heaps of receipts I've been sorting for Jared. Then re-sorting for myself. Something is off. I'm sure of it. His shifty behavior practically proves it, even if the numbers don't.

With my exhaustion reaching new heights, my brain runs rampant, and the only way to calm it is with so much coffee, and what little control I can take, hence my jitters and my uncontrollable chatter.

Elle turns to face me and casually plants a hand on her hip. "Listen, I think we need to go to New York next weekend to sell some things."

Despite our private space and her discreet words, it makes me uncomfortable.

"I don't know. The weekend?" I ask nervously.

"You're right. The weekend isn't great, but if we go Sunday night, we can catch the buyers at the jewelry stores on Monday morning while they're still fresh." She crosses her arms, a half-smile forming on her lips. "They'll need inventory just before Christmas. Men never shop in advance, and they hit up the jewelry stores because they think shiny things will bring them the most action."

My cheeks burn. She's so vulgar.

"Can't you go to New York on your own?" I shift awkwardly.

"No ... also," she says, pointing at me, "you need to stop being so trusting of others. You'll lose."

"What's that supposed to mean?" I demand, shoving my hands in my pockets so that she can't see the shaky, sweaty mess they've become.

"You know what it means." She turns toward the table and begins straightening things out. "Just be careful, okay?"

She's so odd. I can't tell from one moment to the next if she really cares about me. Is she trying to keep me safe? Or is she threatening to steal my portion if I don't come with her?

"I can't just go away for a night," I whisper.

"Two nights. Yes, you can. Tell ... your husband that you're going out of town for a pre-holiday business trip."

"Camden doesn't know I'm ... that we're—"

"In business together?" she asks, pausing her task of spreading the pamphlets on the massive rustic table made of large oak pieces.

"No." My voice quivers.

"What does he think you're doing today?"

"He thinks I'm doing what I always do. I help others with their events. As far as he knows, you're trying to get your business off the ground, and I've been helping you get organized."

Her eyes narrow, a question crossing her face, but she doesn't say anything.

"I wanted to do this on my own," I say, defensive.

"Do what on your own?"

"Pay back the money ..."

She shakes her head. "Whatever, Olivia. You're not going to tell me. You've made that clear. Which is smart since ... Camden won't believe you if you tell him that his 'uncle' is threatening you."

"Yes, he would," I choke.

The woman doth protest too much. Me, I'm the woman that Shakespeare spoke of.

She rolls her eyes. "Tell him that you're going out of town on a girls' trip."

Elle leaves the room, not bothering to wait for an answer. I dutifully follow to bring in the rest of the supplies. I'm still trailing her when we return to our event space.

"Thank you for setting up shop here today, ladies," Margo says.

I set my large box down and dust myself off before giving her a cordial hug.

"No, Margo, thank you for having us." My voice is high.

"I brought you ladies a bottle of our red blend. It's amazing, if I do say so myself." She smiles broadly, proud of a wine that she isn't involved in making.

"Thank you," I sing.

It doesn't matter who made it or who didn't, I'm not going to turn down a red.

I remove the cork from the bottle, already prepped by one of her team. As I pour wine into both the glasses that Margo brought in, my stomach flips at the oaky fruit scent that floats from the bottle. I breathe through my mouth, doing my best to keep my composure, and carry a full glass to Elle.

She shoots me a deadly glare before turning toward Margo. "Thank you," she says, lifting the glass in the air.

"You're welcome. I'll see you ladies in a bit." Margo spins and gracefully leaves the room.

I set my glass down, unable to stomach the thought of drinking it. Sucking in a breath to relieve the nausea has the opposite effect.

"Excuse me," I say, pushing past Elle and running into the bathroom at the back of the room.

I slam the door behind me and barely make it to the toilet before I vomit. When my retching gut calms, I lean back against the cool tiled wall.

Elle pushes the door open and leans against it when it closes, twisting the lock. Of course, I forgot to lock it. Not like I had time.

"You okay?" Elle asks, sounding genuine.

"I'm fine," I groan.

"You hung over or something?" she asks.

"No," I say curtly. "I'm on birth control."

"Birth control? But I thought—"

"It's the first step in IVF," I confess.

An understanding crosses Elle's face, and her eyes soften. She pumps a long strip of paper towel from the holder, then squats in front of me, handing over the bundle of thin material.

"Thank you," I say, wiping my face.

"That's what all this is about?" She waves her arms around as if the bathroom is the source of all our trouble. "That's why you took money from Jared?"

"Yeah, sort of," I moan, then bury my face into my knees.

"The things we do for love." Her words are melancholy.

"Having a child isn't about gaining Camden's love," I mumble into my jeans.

"I didn't say it was."

She doesn't have to say that she understands, and I don't know if I'd believe her if she did, but her presence is soothing, which is all I need right now.

"I'm going to need a toothbrush," I moan.

"You sure you don't need some wine?" she chides.

I lift my head from my knees and let my eyes go wide, holding up a hand in front of me. "Just a toothbrush, thanks. There's one in the center console of my car."

She tilts her head and scrunches her eyebrows. Her silent way of asking why I'm so weird.

She stands and heads toward the door.

"Please don't tell my husband."

"No way in hell I'm telling him anything," she says and leaves the room.

Elle

Saturday, December 11th

This gig is great. I meet women who have unimaginable amounts of money. They explain why they love whatever cult product they're pushing—as if they do it for any other reason than to prove that they can take more from others—and then I take their jewelry.

I evaluate the women and their pieces, collecting as many as possible without triggering red flags. Olivia's desperation isn't surprising. It wouldn't be my choice to take on risky debt for the potential of a child, but to each her own. The only problem is, I doubt that she realizes her sperm donor's shooting blanks. Travis had a vasectomy as soon as he turned eighteen. I don't know how he got a doctor to agree. Women aren't so lucky, especially now. I've never met a doctor who would agree to remove my uterus or tie my tubes simply because I asked.

Seeing Olivia get hurt by this extra information will be shitty as hell. She'd make a great mother—if she had a partner who could make her one.

Since I can't tell her that her husband is a lying sack of shit named Travis who died twenty years ago, I can't save her, but I can steal more gems from the rich. Robin Fucking Hood over here.

I can switch my half-empty wine glass with her full one, too, drinking the red crap for her. She saves face. I stay buzzed.

She escorts the last of the women from our third party out, reassuring those who are entrusting us with their repair that we will have them returned before Christmas. When everyone's gone, she collapses in the seat next to me.

"Twenty minutes until the next group," she huffs, pushing some hair from her face. "This last party is hosted by Charlie's sister."

Fucking great. I knew that I wanted to finish my night with a bang.

"Should I offer to replace some of her fake diamonds with the real thing?" I ask, tilting my head to feign concern.

She slaps me on the arm, her jaw tightening. "Don't you do anything. She earned those fake jewels."

Through laughter, I say, "I'm not going to lie if Charlie brings another knockoff in here for me to appraise."

"You lie about everything else," she says.

"I have no reason to lie to her." My confession rings true. Telling the truth will bring me more pleasure.

"Maybe she won't come," Olivia says, sliding down in her chair.

"Yeah, or she will." I nod in the direction of the window overlooking the parking lot.

Her gaze follows my cue, and her face darkens as she lays eyes on a candy-cane-dressed Charlie, her sunglasses glistening in the sunset.

"Shit," Olivia says. "If she has another fake, just lie, okay?"

God, it brightens my day when Olivia cusses.

"Is that the man she lies to about where she got her fake diamonds?" I say, pointing to the man who's holding the door open for Charlie.

"Yes. Don't say anything," she demands through gritted teeth.

They meander through the main room. I stand, walk over to meet them, and open the private space door.

"Welcome," I say with a grand swoop of my arm. "Charlie, I just wanted to say I was sorry about the other day. If you'd like me to take another—"

"Oh, no need to apologize," Charlie says, flashing a fake, full-toothed grin at me. "It was a mistake. I'd gotten a Swarovski mixed up with the real thing. Grabbed the wrong one in a frenzy of children throwing tantrums."

Nope, still wrong. Not Swarovski.

Just another exclusive Charlie story. Bitch.

Olivia inches up behind me and gingerly pulls Charlie into a hug.

"Good to see you, Billy. What are you doing here?" Olivia asks, shaking the man's hand.

"Oh, just dropping this beautiful lady off so I can be her D.D. later. I'm meeting up with Camden," he says, pointing to the parking lot. "We're going to catch a movie while we wait."

Olivia's face flushes. Mine drains as I see the flash of blonde curls atop a tall, muscular man, standing next to a fucking sportscar outside. I don't wait to see what happens next. Olivia's on her own with this one.

I haul ass to the bathroom and slam the door, locking it behind me. Doesn't matter how long I need to wait.

This isn't *my* confession place. I'm not giving away my secret to Olivia, no matter how hard it was for her to share hers with me.

Olivia

Saturday, December 11th

C amden runs his fingers through his hair as I approach.

"Hey, Babe. Billy said to come pick him up at your job," Camden says. "What's the job thing about?"

My insides knot. Charlie did this. I'm trying to protect her, and she's desperate to take me down.

"I told you that I've been helping a friend," I say. "Elle needed a hand getting her business up and running."

His shoulders tighten. "Like the letter L?"

My face scrunches as I try not to laugh. "No, like the name, Elle."

He stares at me, confused.

"Like Ella, but no A," I explain.

"Oh, right," he says, loosening his shoulders a bit as he peers through the windows of the wine bar.

I bury myself into his side and wait for him to wrap me in his arms. When it takes longer than I expect, my stomach riles—Charlie is watching. The walls are floor-to-ceiling windows.

He finally slides his hands over my back and kisses my head. My nerves settle, our audience still aware of our actions. He's mine. Why can't Charlie wipe that look off her face?

An urge washes over me. It's hormones, maybe, but mostly, it's a desire to crush her self-centered tush. I yank the collar of his shirt, and he reluctantly brings his lips to mine, then softens into me as the make-out session begins to turn him on.

He pulls away and puts his lips near my ear. "When will you be home tonight?"

"Around nine," I say, enjoying his attention.

"I can't wait." He pecks my cheek and then steps back.

"Hey, Olivia," a man's voice calls from behind Camden.

He stiffens again, and spins, putting his arm over my shoulder, revealing Zane.

"Oh, hi, Zane," I answer, grinning, mostly for Camden's renewed possessiveness. "This is my husband, Camden."

Zane hesitates, then extends his right arm.

"Hey, man. Nice to meet you," Camden says, shaking his hand.

"You look familiar," Zane says.

"Maybe you've seen me around."

"Maybe," Zane says, his eyes falling on me. "Is Elle inside?"

I nod, and he smiles at us. He starts to walk away, then stops, looking at Camden. "Good to meet you. We should have you both for dinner sometime soon."

When Zane's out of earshot, Camden pulls my chest to his. He slides a thumb over my cheek and stops on my bottom lip. My skin tingles from his touch. Warmth spreads through my pelvis. It must be hormones.

"Uncle Jared asked me to tell you he's looking forward to Christmas Eve dinner," he says, a hint of a question in his tone.

I stiffen, all my desire for Camden disintegrating.

"Did we have plans?" he asks, pushing the topic.

I step back, trying to shake off the impending doom wrapping around me like a noose.

"Yeah, sorry. I ran into him the other day," I say, my voice strained. "He asked what we were doing, and he seemed lonely, so I invited him."

"I didn't want people over for the holidays." His words are cold. "You know I don't *do* Christmas."

Bumps rise across my arms as a chill crosses my spine, but the rest of me heats up.

"He was looking forward to spending the holiday with you," I answer, hoping I project an innocent need to connect two family members. "I couldn't tell him no."

He takes my hand, nodding.

"I better get back inside and see if Elle needs anything." I give his hand a quick, reassuring squeeze and go back inside.

A few minutes later, when Camden and Billy rip out of the parking lot in Camden's Maserati, I return to my station inside, this time taking a swig of the wine. An instant regret, as my stomach turns in distaste.

I beeline for the bathroom, but the handle doesn't budge when I yank on it.

Frantically knocking, I call, "Hello?"

Obviously, someone's inside if the door is locked, but I need whoever it is to hurry it up.

"Yeah." A familiar voice answers.

"Elle, let me in. I'm going to be sick," I say frantically.

The lock clicks, and I fling the door open, rushing to the toilet. As I do, the nausea dissipates. Thank God. Still unable to trust my body, I remain bent over the toilet, my hands planted firmly on the floor.

"What are you doing in here?" I ask, sounding out of breath.

"Upset stomach," Elle answers.

I look up from the toilet bowl and stare at her. She's lying. I can smell everything right now.

"Okay, I just needed some time to myself," she confesses, reading me like a book.

"Zane's out there waiting for you."

She peeks over her shoulder at the door. "Zane?"

"Yeah. I saw him outside when I was talking to Camden."

I try my legs and stand upright, bracing myself for another round of nausea. Thankfully it doesn't come. The black sink mounted under the gray-veined white countertops calls me, and I move toward it, running my hands under the faucet. I consider splashing my face with the cool water, but remember my makeup and turn the water off.

Elle hasn't budged from her spot.

"Are you going to go see him?" I ask.

"In a minute. Is your husband still here?"

"Nope, you'll have to meet him another time," I grumble. "Zane thought we should all have dinner together."

Elle's laugh is sharp. I smile in response.

"Please tell me we don't have to do that," I say, relaxing my back against the counter. "I don't think I can keep all our stories straight."

"God, no. We're not fucking doing that." She flings the door open, and for the second time today, leaves me in peace in the slate tile bathroom.

Elle

Saturday, December 11th

It's a scramble to get the last round of appraisals done and to gather as many "repair" pieces as possible.

"Love, can you help me load this?" I ask, peeking my head through the glass door and peering at Zane, who has taken a spot on the other side, sipping water, and reading a book. He stopped in to say hello on his way home from a bookstore—I begged him to stay and take me home, because there's no way in hell I'm riding home with Olivia. I need to be gone before Travis returns.

"Sure," he says, only glancing from his page for a second. "I'm almost done with this chapter."

I squirm. Everything else is picked up, and Olivia keeps giving me death glares because she thinks I'm rushing the guests.

"Please, Love. I'm ready to be home."

I nudge Olivia to open the doors and unlock her car.

"Why are you in such a hurry?" she whispers through gritted teeth.

"It's been a long fucking day."

She shoots me another glare. I've been too loud, and now I wish that I was louder.

"You need to tell ...your husband that we are going out of town next Sunday for two nights, to a beach cottage near The Hamptons. Zane already booked us a place," I say, patting Olivia on the arm. "Your office is closed next week, right?"

She's already told me that it would be. It's the only time her wicked boss gives her official time off.

She squints at me, ready to ask questions. "But—"

"No buts. We deserve a quiet getaway. Our treat," I say. "Bring the machine over Monday after work."

I look over my shoulder at Zane, who smiles his sweet, genuine smile. My throat grows thick. God, I love him.

He takes my hand and leads me out of the building and to his car, opening the passenger door for me.

I slide an arm around his waist and yank him to me, giving him a peck on his lips before releasing him. He steps away, winking before he turns. I smack his ass, then slide inside.

"She doesn't want to go to the beach with you?" Zane asks, landing in his seat.

"She does; she's just being stubborn. Besides, it's the least I can do for her. She's had a tough time lately with fertility treatments. She's pushed me out of my comfort zone."

It feels good to tell someone's truth, even if it's not mine.

"Is it something you want to do though, Hun? You're in such a hurry to get out of here today," he says, turning in his seat to look at me dead on with no indication of leaving.

My heart races as a car's headlights shine on us, and I catch a glimpse of a sportscar pulling into the parking lot.

I grab Zane's thigh and slide my hand up his leg until I reach his crotch. He leans over to kiss me, moaning in pleasure.

I don't meet his lips, instead, I whisper, "Get me home."

As always, he obeys, pulling out of the drive. I relinquish my grip on him and slide into my seat, hiding my face from the window with my hand.

"Nice car," Zane says, pointing as we drive past Travis' flashy piece of shit.

"Meh." I shrug.

"Have you met him? Olivia's husband?" he asks, taking my hand and rubbing my thumb as we head down the road.

"No?" I make sure it sounds like a question.

"That was him. He looked familiar, but I don't know from where."

Zane has no idea how close our world is to shattering in the presence of that man and his fucking expensive car.

I take several breaths to settle my nerves. When it doesn't work, I focus on my hand in Zane's, and let his touch ground me.

"Not sure, Love," I say, calm as possible.

A deep sadness rises within me, tightening and restricting my breath.

"Pull over." I point to an abandoned parking lot ahead.

"What's—"

"Please, just do it," I demand.

He eases the car into a spot and gingerly puts it in park. I navigate the small space, climbing over the center console and hunching to sit on his lap. Grabbing the manual latch on his worn cloth seat, I lower the back until it stops. The buckle digs into my knee, and my back presses against the cool steering wheel.

"Hun, we can't. Not here," he says, but holds me close to him.

"I can't wait until we get home," I whisper.

If I wait, I'll fall apart. I can't do that. I need a release that I can control, an emotion—or feeling—I can dictate.

He slides his hands under my shirt and across my nipples. I sigh with pleasure.

"What if we get caught?" he asks, pushing his hips against me.

"Take a chance." I kiss his neck.

"Okay," he says.

That's all I needed to hear.

Elle

Sunday, December 18th

The slam of my SUV's tailgate echoes through the parking garage. Hitching my bag onto my shoulder, I turn to Olivia, who has been silent the entire drive.

Normally, she chatters too much. Today she's taken to listening to something through her headphones, which are still in her damn ears. I glare at her until she removes them.

"What's the deal?" I ask, not sure I care.

The quiet has been nice.

"I just don't get why I have to be here and why we had to lie about going to the beach."

It's official; she has turned into a moody teen.

I turn away without answering and lead her to an elevator bank on the opposite side of the garage. Her heels click, each echo sending aggravated bursts through my blood.

When the elevator opens, I hold the door until she's through, then follow, selecting the fourth floor.

Anger erupts inside me. "What the fuck do you have against New York?"

Her lips part in shock, and she shifts nervously.

"Nothing. I just—"

"You wanted to do this, Olivia. This," I say, waving my arms about, "is part of it. And don't you fucking degrade my home again."

The rage loosens its grasp. A subtle disappointment creeps in. I know better. I don't lose control of my emotions.

"I ... I didn't mean—"

"Just don't do it again," I interrupt before she can get under my skin and make me feel something else unsavory.

The elevator doors creek open, and I rush out of the metal box onto the faded green carpet of the hall. The beige walls with the fake board and batten close in on me.

She's ruining this place—my sanctuary.

I pull out my old key ring and unlock the deadbolt and handle, then swing the door open. The tiny entry that's no more than an old mat over tile greets me. My living room hugs me as I enter. I glance at my wine barrel tabletop and smile.

"This is where we're staying?" Olivia asks. There's no hiding her disgust.

"It's a little dusty. The housekeeper's unreliable." I smirk, knowing her biggest issue is that it's cramped and outdated.

"It's not that dusty," she answers unexpectedly. "Compared to the level you keep your house, though, I can see how you think that."

"What the hell?"

"Sorry," she says, defeated. "I just ... Camden's pissed about me being gone."

Bastard. Ruining my life beyond his grave.

"He's an ass," I say, irritated.

I try to relax.

I need a drink.

This time, my bourbon is right where I left it. "You want a glass?" I ask.

She waves her hand and scrunches up her nose. "I still can't. Where's the bathroom?"

Not many options here. I walk over to the door and fling it open, revealing the closet-sized space.

I sip from my bottle while she fiddles in the bathroom. When she steps out, she looks around.

"I'm guessing there's no food or anything here. Besides that," Olivia asks, pointing to the bourbon. "I could use some ice cream or something."

The woman has a problem.

"Nope. We'll have to get your ice cream from the market a few blocks up."

Carrying the bourbon with me, I return to the living room and hold the bottle out toward the couch.

"The sofa is comfortable to sleep on, and there's a bed in the other room. Sheets and blankets are in the closet in there."

Her face twists again.

"I'll let you decide which you prefer," I say, spinning around to open the bedroom door and pull the bedding from the shoebox closet.

"So generous of you," Olivia mumbles from behind me.

I slump onto the queen mattress, lying back to stare up at the ceiling.

The floor creaks as Olivia walks into the bedroom. I don't turn to look her way. She crosses the floor and lands on the bed next to me.

"So, what's with this place?" she asks with a sigh.

Laying the bottle next to me, I place my hands on my stomach and feel it rise and fall with my breath.

"It's my lost haven."

"What does that mean?"

"I don't know. It's just—mine."

"Your lost haven requires like ten locks on the front door?"

"Four, and yes. If you want something to stay lost, you've got to protect it."

She may be on to something. Ten locks would be much more reasonable.

Olivia

Sunday, December 18th

Elle has a secret apartment in New York City. This fact about her should surprise me.

"Why do you keep this place hidden from Zane?" I ask, unable to get up from the old mattress just yet.

The hormones have been messing with my body. It's been years since I've been on birth control, and it's making me bloated and moody. Later this week, I'll come off them and start Lupron, which will likely make things worse.

"Why do you keep IVF from Camden?" she retorts.

Nerves, like bees, sting my body.

"I'm not sure that Camden wants a child," I sigh. "He says he does, but he also says we can't afford IVF or to continue basic medicated cycles, then he goes out and buys a flashy, expensive car."

I drape my arm over my face, concealing my eyes from the light shining from the ceiling.

"He'd be pissed if he knew about the loan," I add.

"I take it that Jared didn't know what the loan was for either," Elle says.

"Jared wanted me to pay off my debt." I groan.

"Hmm ... but you used it for IVF." She sounds delighted. "You're something else, Olivia."

"You say that like it's a good thing. I assure you, it's not. It was impulsive. Dumb."

"Why would Jared loan you the money to pay off your debt anyway?" Elle asks.

"Camden can't have debt to his name. Or mine. He can lose out on contracts that are high risk if he looks like he's risky himself."

"He's in gaming tech?" she asks, thick with sarcasm.

I chuckle. "Yeah. I know. Weird."

"Weird as fuck."

A silence falls between us. I stare into the crevasse of my arm. The light from the room makes my skin appear red.

"Zane doesn't know that I own this apartment. He doesn't know a lot about me. I lied when we first met, and it just stuck."

I roll to my side and prop myself up on my elbow to watch her. She's breathing slowly, intentionally, her hands on her belly.

"Like the wine?" I ask.

"The wine barrel out there," she says, nudging toward the living space, "that's what started it all. I store things in the barrel. Sometimes you just have to lie."

"You two seem so happy and in love." I swoon.

"We are." She turns her head to look at me. "I don't know if he'd feel the same if he knew, though." Her face darkens. "He also can't know we're in New York. He doesn't think I'm safe here."

"Safe? Why wouldn't you be safe?"

Elle doesn't answer. Instead, she spins off the bed and stands, returning to the living room in one graceful swoop.

I try rolling out of the bed like she did, but I fail, stumbling a bit.

"Do you want the bed or the couch?" Elle asks.

"The couch, I think," I groan, straightening my back and placing my hands on my hips. "How far is this grocery store that you mentioned?"

"The market? It's not too far. Do you want to go?"

I nod. I need something to eat. I *need* ice cream.

"Where's the jewelry?" I ask, looking around the rutty place.

I hope that we didn't leave them in the car.

She turns to the duffle she dropped by the couch earlier and pulls out a teal bag, holding it up for me to see, then tosses it. I barely catch it. Pursing my lips in displeasure, I watch her as she digs through a drawer at the edge of the kitchen and extracts a hammer. With it, she methodically wrenches nails from her tabletop.

"What are you doing?" I ask.

Elle shakes her head and continues. When she's done, she sets the hammer down and moves the objects from the table to the kitchen counter.

She slides the surface of the table until it reveals just a sliver of the top of the wine barrel.

"Like I said, it's perfect for storing things," she says, the corner of her mouth quirking.

I reluctantly hand her the teal bag, and she drops it inside and then pulls the top back in place.

"Ready to go?" Elle asks, shoving her phone and cash into her front pocket.

Following Elle onto the streets, I wrap myself in my coat. The sun's already set, but the streetlights shine bright. She moves fast down the sidewalk, and I struggle to keep up.

"Do you think there will be any problems tomorrow selling the pieces?"

My nerves sting my insides as the cold nips at my skin.

"Not now, Olivia," she admonishes.

I guess we aren't discussing our sales in public anymore. Not in New York City, anyway.

She leads me into a little store a couple of blocks up. The shelves are disorganized.

Elle heads to the alcohol section. Not surprising.

She's getting her vice, and I'm getting mine. I walk down the refrigerated wall until I come to a small section of ice cream and grab a pint, then another for good measure.

"You ready?" I call to Elle, who's still contemplating the selection of alcohol.

"Yeah," she says, not moving.

I go to checkout and wait for her to meet me. She places the items from her hands and my basket onto the small counter and pays the cashier.

"Thank you, Gloria," Elle says, nodding to the lady behind the counter. I take a double look at the woman, curious whether Elle read her nametag or if she knows her.

I carry my bag out of the store but I turn when I realize that Elle isn't behind me. She's stopped inside, stiff and staring down an aisle at a hooded man.

"Elle?" I call, confused.

She startles and looks at me. For a minute, she seems disoriented, then she moves toward me, yanking my arm as she walks by.

"Let's get out of here," she says, moving faster than she did on the way here.

A wave of nausea washed over me as my anxiety heightens, but my desire for the frozen treat overwhelms me. By the time we hit the front door of the apartment, I'm desperate, wrenching the lid of a pint off.

Elle tosses her phone on the couch and heads to the kitchen.

"Spoon?" I say, licking the side of the pint before it drips.

She flings one at me, and I blissfully sink into the old couch cushions.

"So good," I hum to myself.

Her phone lights up beside me with a bell tone. I reach for it, sliding my thumb across the screen to answer.

"Hello," I say to the caller.

"Elle?" a man's voice says.

I take another bite of the ice cream. "Nope. Hold on."

Elle's standing in the space between the kitchen and living room, her body tense. I hold the phone out toward her. She swipes it from me.

My neck grows hot.

She holds the phone to her ear, her eyes narrowing. Whoever's on the other end is speaking, and she's listening intently.

"You don't know shit," she snaps and ends the call.

My chest tightens, concern bunching my face as I watch her take several gulps of her drink, emptying the glass. She slams it on the counter and refills it.

"Everything okay?" I ask, unsettled.

"Wrong number," she says, shrugging.

My skin crawls.

"But—"

She puts up her hand, stopping me, and pours more alcohol into her glass.

"Do me a favor," she says, her gaze flashing to me as she closes the blinds. "Don't answer my phone."

I nod, my throat too dry to respond.

She settles into the couch next to me, cracking her neck and rolling her shoulders.

"Cheers," she says, clicking her glass to my pint.

"Cheers," I croak.

"SNL?" she asks, her angst gone.

She clicks on the small tube TV in front of us, and the screen makes a zapping sound.

The scent of my peppermint ice cream fills my nostrils as I watch the show on the fuzzy screen. It almost feels like middle school again, the pure joy of a genuine friend and the promise of a night of giggles and decadent treats. When there was no care in the world, before my mother moved us to give me more opportunities and friendships started coming at a cost.

A pang of sadness strikes me, missing the simplicity of those times, but nothing ever stays the same. Nothing ever remains perfect.

Elle

Monday, December 19th

The chill in the air stings my eyes. I inhale the New York City cold, and it satisfies me in a disturbing way.

"Put your purse under your coat," I say, turning to point at the strappy black bag at Olivia's side.

"What?" she calls, jogging to catch up.

"We're in New York."

She unzips her coat, struggling to pull the purse inside while trying to keep up in her wedge heels.

"Would have been easier with different shoes." I point out, beginning the descent to the subway.

"Like yours?" she snaps back, her gaze darting to my kicks. "People like professional businesswomen."

"Then I guess you'll have to manage the sales."

"What's that smell?" she asks, catching up to me.

"That's the unmistakable smell of the NYC subway. You got a problem with urine and body odor?"

She giggles, twisting her face in disgust.

"Don't make me laugh," she chokes out.

While she's distracted, I glance over my shoulder, making sure we're alone.

As the train thuds to a stop in front of us, I yank her forward, navigating the crowd. She stands close to me, her gaze darting around the space, taking in the array of people.

A man shoves into us. The hair on my neck stands. My muscles engage.

"Watch out," he demands, giving my shoulder an extra bump before settling inches from me.

He faces me and Olivia, looking us both up and down. First, in dominance. Next, in desire. He closes the distance between us.

Olivia squishes into my side, clearly uncomfortable. The man takes it as an offering and with the movement of the crowd, shuffles until his crotch is resting on Olivia's hip. The unmistakable squeak of a woman afraid to take back her rights escapes Olivia—making my blood boil.

This asshat is fucking with the wrong woman.

The train lurches forward, and in the movement, I slip my hand into his pocket and extract his wallet. Smooth. Unnoticeable. With the flick of my wrist, I slide it up into the wide sleeve of my coat—the tweed design that Olivia insisted I wear may make me look like a rich bitch, but I'm just a basic bitch acting on anger and taking revenge.

When we shuffle off the subway fifteen minutes later, I pull Olivia up the steps and back into the fresh-ish air. I don't fucking care if this place reeks; it's the best place on earth.

"Want a coffee?" I turn to Olivia.

"Yes, that would be..." Her words trail as I extract the man's wallet from my coat and hand it to her.

"Courtesy of asshat on the subway," I say, flashing a wry grin.

"You didn't," she gasps, but her eyes twinkle with satisfaction.

I link our arms and match my stride to hers. Coffee or no coffee, I think I've stolen her heart with my thieving ways.

Olivia pulls her shoulders back and walks into the jewelry store, clearly taking my earlier remark to heart.

Fine. I'll stand back and see how well she does with her sales pitch.

She walks right up to the register with a grin plastered on her face.

"Good morning," she says cheerily. "Is your buying manager in?"

The woman behind the register crinkles her forehead. "Yes," she answers, dragging the word.

"Great," Olivia proclaims. "We'd like to meet with them." She gestures behind her back at me.

The woman reluctantly turns and retreats into the backroom. A couple of minutes later, a middle-aged man with thick, salt-and-pepper hair follows her out. He's fit under his suit, and I watch as Olivia takes him in. Liam.

The cashier points to Olivia. The man offers a warm smile.

"Hello," he says, nodding to Olivia. "How can I help you?"

"We would like to discuss the possibility of partnering with you to sell some one-of-a-kind pieces," Olivia says with all the confidence in the world.

As Liam extracts a velvet platform from beneath the counter, he makes eye contact with me. I place a finger to my lips and gesture toward Olivia.

His eyes return to her as I come to the counter. Her cheeks are bright red.

She bats her eyelashes at him and nudges me with her elbow.

"Elle is our designer. Her things are exquisite."

"Nice to meet you," I add, playing along.

I lay out a couple of our items on the black velvet pad as Olivia continues, "These are a few of our pieces, but we have more with us if you'd like to see them."

Liam picks up a ring, admiring the work he's familiar with.

"These are beautiful," he says, grinning.

"Would you like to see the rest?" Olivia asks.

"Yes, thank you."

Piece by piece, he picks them up and admires them.

"I think several of our high-end clients would be interested in this collection, assuming that the stones are high quality." He peers up at me. Our agreement is unspoken. He'll check, but he knows that they are.

I nod. "Go ahead."

His eyes twinkle as he picks up the velvet board full of our jewelry.

"We have some other buyers interested in many of these pieces already, but we thought we'd stop here first," Olivia adds, stepping up her selling game.

Liam glances at me. I shake my head just out of Olivia's periphery.

"I'm Liam, by the way." He reaches out a hand to her.

"Olivia," she says, placing her hand in his.

The two linger for a moment, enjoying each other's touch. Then, her cheeks brighter than ever, Olivia pulls away and tucks a brown strand of hair behind her ear.

"If we buy these, are you looking for cash or account deposit?" Liam asks.

"Oh, umm," Olivia glances at me, confused.

"Cash or check would be great," I answer. It's been a long time since I've opted for my own payment rather than depositing it into Ricardo's account.

Liam nods, smiling brightly at Olivia.

When her eye candy disappears behind the locked door, I turn to Olivia. Her face is ablaze.

"You dog," I say, chuckling.

"What?" she asks, her hands coming together as she rubs her thumb along her nails.

"You know what." I drape my arm over her shoulder and bump her hip with mine. "Good job, by the way. You know this business stuff, after all."

If I hadn't already gotten preliminary confirmation from Liam that he'd be our buyer, Olivia would have sealed the deal with her wily ways.

Olivia

Monday, December 19th

I can't believe that we sold everything. Everything. It's exhilarating.

"I have to hand it to you, Olivia; I did not expect that," Elle says, patting me on the back.

Liam's card gleams in the sun as I shift it in my fingers. My body tingles, warming my cheeks. I can't remember the last time that someone looked at me like he did; like a person, not a possession.

"You going to call him?" she asks.

"I'm married," I say sharply, and shove the card into my pocket. "It was just business."

"Okay. Whatever you say." She takes off ahead of me. "If it were just business, you wouldn't have managed to sell everything in one shot."

Guilt clenches my stomach, and I protest more. "You wouldn't do anything to jeopardize your marriage. Why would you insist that I do?!" I shout after her, then begin jogging to catch up.

"Zane is fucking amazing. You know that. I'd be the biggest idiot to fuck things up with him."

"And ...?" I demand her honesty.

"And ... your husband is a douche."

"He isn't." A feeble protest. Not like I'm kidding her, anyway.

She flashes a look that screams *whatever* and continues down the street.

"I love Camden. He loves me. I don't want anyone else."

"Keep telling yourself that," Elle says.

My brain defies me and a list of descriptions flashes through my mind. Donor F has a master's degree in social work and an impeccable jawline. Donor C has an artistic vision and can play several instruments. Donor M is tall, dark, and reportedly handsome.

Elle steps away from me, casually dropping some bills from her pocket into the cup of a teenager begging for money. Not missing a beat, she waves to the kid, then steps over to the curb, lifting her hand in the air, delicate yet demanding. She's a vision, hailing a Taxi as though in a movie.

"I thought we'd take a cab home," she says, opening the door and sliding inside.

I scurry over and bounce onto the seat.

She gives the driver her address and leans back in the worn vinyl seat.

Elle doesn't buckle, but I do, as the car pulls into traffic and begins weaving between slow-moving vehicles.

"Have you ever wondered," Elle whispers, sounding philosophical, "if perhaps it's not you who's causing all the problems?"

"What?" I ask, genuinely confused.

"Maybe you don't need IVF. Maybe—"

"That's none of your business," I snap, rage swelling in my belly.

On cue, my phone pings. My *father*. He wants his money, an increase to fifteen hundred. Disappointment ripples through me. My chest tightens. I'd forgotten about owing him on top of everything else.

I wonder if I could ever buy his silence permanently and cut him out of my life completely. I don't think there's a way to do that, aside from confessing all my sins to the world—to my mother and husband. I would risk Camden leaving because I catfished him into believing that I could give him a family. My mother would probably never speak to me again because she thought that she raised me differently—to believe an embryo's 'life' is more important than a woman's. I could never be so nonchalant about people's opinions or their approval.

"You're right," she says, putting up a hand in defeat.

"No." I frown. "No, I'm not sure I am."

Her gaze moves over my face, searching.

"I had an abortion when I was younger. There was a party. I was just starting grad school."

The memories flood my mind. With my throat constricting, I'm not sure how much I can share. Nobody knows this, except my father, and I'm desperate to free myself.

She slips her fingers between mine and gives my hand a comforting squeeze.

"Someone raped me. I don't really remember that night. My father loaned me the money I needed after I found out. My mom and stepdad don't know. My mother is so conservative that she'd think I failed, or worse, that she did. I never told Camden. I didn't want him to know that I was broken. They had to do a D&C to remove what was left—what the pills didn't—and during the procedure, they found a ton of endometriosis. They removed what they could, but they warned me that it could come back, especially with the scar tissue. When Camden and I talked about having a family early in our relationship, I couldn't bring myself to tell him, and now it's too late." I let out a heavy sigh. "I've only ever told my father about this, which was a massive mistake. And now, you."

I swipe away my tears and look into Elle's eyes. Her face is soft, comforting, yet there's a hint of confusion.

"My mom and stepdad don't know that my father came back into my life. I can't bear to tell them. It would crush them both. My stepdad's done so much for me. My mother, too. My mom ... she had been so heartbroken when he left."

Elle gives my hand another squeeze. "It's safe with me," is all she says.

"Thanks. I just have to ... my father, I have to pay him, so he keeps his mouth shut and he leaves them alone. I should have never—"

"You did what you had to do," Elle says sincerely.

I pull my hand away, wrapping my arms around my chest, and stare out the window.

"I'll help you deal with your father if you want."

I nod. I do want her help. I don't know what it will entail, but I'm not sure I care anymore. If I have a child—if IVF works—I want him out of my life. Forever.

Elle leans her head against the back of the seat. I cringe at the thought of doing the same. The bugs that might exist in this overpopulated space. The germs, too.

There are all sorts of invisible things that we don't know about, and yet, we all trust something that doesn't make sense. Elle trusts she won't get lice or bedbugs from a cab—I shift in my seat, muscles tightening as I think about the possibility. And I ... I don't know who, or what, I trust anymore.

But I do trust Elle. It doesn't make sense. It doesn't have to. I just do.

The cab drops us off near a building that's unfamiliar.

"Come on," Elle says.

I look around, then pick up my pace to keep up with her.

"Where are we going?" I ask, catching up to her.

"To see Ricardo and Eddy," she answers as if it's obvious.

She steps into a small doorframe and smiles at me before pushing it with her behind. The bell clatters at the top, alerting the owners to our presence.

"Eddy," Elle calls boisterously and takes long strides to the counter, holding her arms open.

He scowls, pushes the partition up, and slides through, leaning into her embrace with a comical reserve.

"You aren't supposed to be here," he says grumpily.

"You remember Olivia?" Elle asks, stepping back to point in my direction. Apparently ignoring his statement.

"Is that Elle?" I hear another man's voice call from somewhere in the back.

"Hi, Ricardo!" Elle shouts. "Olivia's here, too."

I stand in the tiny shop, admiring the jewelry in the cabinets, trying to ignore the feeling that I'm an outsider.

This store is far different than the one Liam works at. The lighting is florescent and bright, as opposed to a romantic, dimly lit space. The cabinets are in good shape but older. The register is something straight out of my childhood.

Despite their age, everything is clean. There's not a speck of dust. It's clear these men pride themselves on what they do.

"You two going back to Virginia?" Eddy asks, snapping my attention back to the conversation that I'm not actually a part of.

"Not until tomorrow," Elle answers. "I thought we'd take you out to dinner."

I envision a restaurant with black tablecloths and white napkins, faintly lit corners, and impeccable food. My stomach drops. We should go home, not stay another night. We completed our task early, and I could see Camden, if he's even home himself.

"Elle," Eddy grumbles. "You shouldn't be here."

Why does he keep saying that? Does he know about our supposed beach destination?

"We had to sell some jewelry. Sold a bunch of pieces to Liam at Diamonds Are Forever."

"Pieces?" Eddy asks with despondency, like the tone my parents used to have when they thought I wasn't telling the truth.

"Oh, that's great," Ricardo adds with delight.

I hold back a laugh. These two men either can't read each other or choose not to.

"Where did you get the material, Elle?" Eddy's pushing hard now.

That's my cue. I step beside Elle and say with as much confidence as I can muster, "I'm investing in her."

Doesn't matter that it's not financially, I hope.

"So, you two are really giving this business thing a go?" Eddy says, spirits lifting.

Elle peers at me and nods.

"You two should head home. I hear there's snow coming," Eddy suggests, his tone dropping again.

"That's not until later this week," Elle dismisses him.

Her smile is gone now, replaced by something dark.

"Dinner tonight. At Anthony's. See you at seven?" Elle says, turning and striding toward the door.

"See you tonight," Ricardo says, resting his arm on Eddy's stiff shoulders.

As I follow Elle, I stop in the door to say goodbye.

"It'll be alright," I hear Ricardo whisper to Eddy. It wasn't meant for my ears, but it makes me uneasy, nonetheless.

"Nice to see you." I offer a faltering smile and a halfhearted wave before rushing after Elle, yet again.

Elle

Monday, December 19th

This city is too perfect to sit inside my apartment all day while Olivia nervously twiddles her thumbs, so I drag her out.

"I hate New York," Olivia grumbles beside me.

I ignore her, looking at the bald trees that tower over the green grass. They line the paved path we're on. Ahead, there's a pond that's typically strewn with geese, but it's December. It's cold. The water wrinkles from god knows what, reminding the world of its depth.

This is the place where I memorialize Travis. This is where I come to be closer to him, and to remember.

Sinking onto a bench, I stare out over the water. The tall grass at its edge twitches in the breeze. My heart sinks, blanketing me with sadness. I miss Travis. Not who he's become, but who I thought he was, the brother who was my rock.

Then, he chose to crush me.

The cold grips me suddenly. My throat stings, so I clear it, regaining composure.

"I love New York," I tell Olivia. "This place reminds me of my brother."

She doesn't sit, only leans on the back of the bench to my right.

"He died when we were young. Sometimes, I imagine he's here, at this pond, sitting next to me."

The water ripples with the wind, and Olivia and I simultaneously shiver.

"Want to go back? Warm up?" I stand, pulling my coat tight.

"Please," she sighs.

"Don't act so disappointed," I say grumpily.

"How far is your place? We've been walking forever."

"A mile," I lie. It's closer to two.

By the time we get back to my place, it'll be dark. This city at night is amazing. I can't wait.

I veer to the sidewalk along the buildings. It's a faster route than the path through the park.

My heart aches with longing for when this city and I belonged together. Another chill settles through me. It's different, unnerving. With so many fucking people in this city, it feels like I'm being watched. Footsteps grow louder behind us, and Olivia instinctively slides closer to my side. I don't turn—acting invisible. It could be anything. Kids playing, teens goofing off—adults acting like children.

"Lizzie!" a man yells. It's too close for me to escape. He grabs my arm, spinning me to face him.

"Sorry, you have me confused—"

The back of his hand lands on my face, and he drags me, half by my shoulder, half by my hair, into a dark alleyway. He shoves me against a wall behind an overflowing dumpster. His lips graze my neck, slowly. Intentionally. My blood curdles, as I sense the prick of nerves along my spine.

"I knew you'd be coming around," Sam's raspy whisper drifts into my ear, and my muscles tighten in anger.

"Who the fuck told you I'd be *coming around*?" I snap.

How the fuck did he get my phone number?

"What makes you think someone told me?" he says in a raspy, eager tone that I'd wished I would never hear again.

"Come on, Sam. Everyone knows you aren't the brains of the operation you run," I taunt, adding an obnoxious wink.

He lets up slightly, then slams me into the wall harder, shrinking the space between us.

He presses his erection against my pelvis. He was aggressive when we dated. I was sixteen and an idiot. Now, I know better—two years in juvie, and fifteen years with a man who's nothing less than perfect teaches a girl some valuable lessons.

I'm also physically stronger, but I'll let him have his moment of glory. His rush from beating up a woman.

"Let her go," Olivia shrieks from somewhere behind him.

She better not get wrapped up in this. My eyes dart around the alley until I see her being held back by Sam's right-hand douchebag. Her normally kempt hair is displaced. Shit.

A protective air flows over me, anger bubbling under my skin.

"You heard her. You better let me go. As soon as she notices what your guy has done to her hair, she's going to be a fucking wild beast," I snicker.

"What are you doing in New York?" Sam spits out. "Running one of your cons?"

"Who wants to know? You aren't smart enough to find me, no matter where I am. If you were, you would have done it already."

"Nobody ever told me how to manage you, though, did they? That was all me." A shit-eating grin spreads across his face. "You'd forgotten your place. Tell me, did you ever learn to behave after I slipped you roofies?"

I stare at him, processing his confession. I want to demand that he tell me how many times, but that would make me look weak, and I am not.

He cackles and presses harder against me. "What are you doing here?"

He begins patting me down with one hand. He shoves his elbow under my throat with the other arm. I tuck my chin, but it's not enough. My air supply is scarce.

My energy rapidly depletes. Black spots swim in my vision. I've trained for this. Even before my parents died, Travis and I were taking defense classes, learning to box. Dad loved boxing. Mom hated it. I swore I'd never be caught off guard again, after Travis, after being arrested. All my hard work, never skipping out on workouts, remaining diligent—it wasn't enough.

I'm going to die. Sam is going to kill me.

His searching hand slides down my thigh, then up between my legs, lingering a moment before moving to one of my front pockets. He removes the wad of money, holds it up between us, sniffs it.

My vision grows darker. It's almost over for me. I look past Sam as he reaches into my other front pocket. Olivia's squirming, trying to get free. She's going to watch me die. What will happen to her? They won't just let her go, even if she promises to keep quiet.

Olivia. I let her in. I let Olivia see the real me. People who I care about—those I reveal my truths to—wind up dead. I never told her. I didn't warn her. I didn't think it was relevant.

Not again. I can't. Nothing can happen to her.

"Hiding any more?" Sam asks, running the second wad of cash across my cheek.

He shoves it in his pocket, then grabs my ass, pressing me against him. This time, I welcome his advance, because the shift allows me a quick breath. It's just enough to clear my vision slightly and relieve my screaming muscles.

In a quick motion—before the oxygen is gone—I lift my forearm and slam it into his bicep, barely catching the wince on his face before spinning from his grasp. When I'm free, I firmly plant my feet about a foot apart and pull my fists up in front of my face.

Keanu's voice fills my head. *I know kung-fu.* I don't, but oddly, it fits. Sam's eyes flicker with something. Shock. Confusion. Fear. Should be all of those things.

He's still stammering to get his bearings when my right fist meets his jaw, throwing him backward a couple of steps. I don't wait, delivering a killer left hook.

He falls to the ground, unable to keep his footing. I slam my knee to his stomach, then slide it down to his pelvis, stopping just before his cock, which isn't so erect anymore. It's no fun for him when I'm in control.

I resist cracking his nuts. I'm not mad enough to take everything from him. Not yet.

Olivia shrieks. I glance up to see that the douche has a knife to her neck. I glare at him.

My knee slides a little further down Sam's waist without taking my eyes off the man harming my sister-in-law. "Tell him to drop the knife, Sam."

When he doesn't say anything, I grab his neck, pressing on his jugular. His eyes bulge, and he finally figures it out. He's pushing the boundary between life and death.

"Let her go," he says, his words compressed by my chokehold.

The douche drops the knife.

"Kick it over here," I demand, riding high from my victory.

The knife slides across the pavement, stopping a few feet from me. Close enough.

I let up a bit from Sam's neck because he needs to be conscious to answer my questions.

"How the fuck did you find me, Sam?"

"Once a criminal, always a criminal," he grunts.

"Once a rapist, always a rapist!" My jaw tightens with overwhelming agitation. "Did you drug me the night Travis ..." I don't finish. Travis isn't dead. He ran off. He abandoned me. But I'm not telling this motherfucker any of that.

His pupils dilate, and his lips curl into a snarl.

"Now, that's what we'd call perfect timing. Maybe not for you, because you couldn't go with the snitch, but for them and for me. You know I like revenge. Even if I'd forgotten about your fine ass, you've always had admirers ... back in the day, I had to take a few out, but this is the first time that I've helped one. Revenge is served better with a bit of stalking, though. Wouldn't you agree?" The things he doesn't say boil under my skin, until I explode. I punch Sam's orbital bone. He goes limp under my grip.

I stand, and grab the knife as I head to Olivia's side.

"Let's go," I say, looking only at her, still in the douchebag's grasp.

When the man doesn't immediately let go, I lift the knife to his chin. "I can do a lot worse with your weapon than I can with only my hands."

He shoves her free, and I grab her arm.

"Roll him over," I gesture to Sam with my wrist.

The man doesn't budge. I step toward him, my movements too fast for him to skirt. The blade of his knife slices across his arm. It's just a surface wound, but it's enough to switch his alliance. He goes to Sam, grunts as he rolls him, then holds his arm with groans of pain.

I don't look away from Olivia's assailant while I reach into Sam's back pockets, taking my money back.

Not bothering to conceal it, I lock my arm with Olivia's and pull her away from the alley.

"We have to get out of here," I say, picking up my pace. "Now."

It's only after she starts to run that I follow suit. Nothing's happening to Olivia. Not tonight. Not ever. I'm breaking the cycle. Not everyone who knows the real me needs to wind up dead.

Olivia

Monday, December 19th

My lungs scream for rest despite the extra runs I've been getting on the treadmill lately. It's the catch in my throat, the tears stinging my eyes, and my racing thoughts that make breathing so hard, not to mention the night air that's getting colder by the second.

Sheer fear motivates me too.

But I run, speeding up whenever Elle urges me to.

She yanks me to an abrupt stop in front of a building. As I slam into her from the shift in momentum, I realize we're at her building.

She fumbles with her keys as she removes them from my purse. She insisted that I hold them so that she could protect some of our money. She swipes a plastic card attached to the keys, then yanks the door open.

She shoves me inside and looks over her shoulder before following.

"They aren't behind us," she gasps. "We need to be quick, though. I can't guarantee that they can't get in."

She moves toward the elevator and hits the up button repeatedly until the door gingerly slides open, revealing the small metal box. We step inside simultaneously. As the doors close, a feeling of safety hits, then gets snatched away as we lurch upward, and I have no way of predicting what's on the other side.

I hold my breath as the box stops and the doors open. I let it out when there's nobody waiting on the other side.

"Come on," she says, her composure—and breath—back. "Get your things."

She rushes me inside, then closes the door and engages all four locks.

The warmth of the room hits my wind-chilled skin, causing it to prick. The pins and needles progress as I move into the bedroom, opening the door to the small closet.

I stare inside, looking for answers.

Before I know what's come over me, I'm back in the bedroom entry, then the tiny living space.

Elle's taking a swig from her bourbon bottle.

"What the hell happened back there?" I demand.

She rolls her eyes.

"Don't be so dramatic." She puts the cap back on and shoves the bottle into the cupboard.

"You think I'm being dramatic?" I ask, my voice rising. "We were attacked. I was held at knifepoint."

"And I handled it."

She grabs nails from a drawer and sets them on her table. She props one up and aims the hammer, then pauses, looking at me.

"I thought..." I say, my voice cracking. "I thought that you were going to be raped, that they were going to skin us alive."

My stomach curdles. I had thought that the other man would rape Elle while the cool metal blade was pressed against my throat. The man held me too tightly; I couldn't escape, and I couldn't help her.

"Skin us alive? Nah. Not with that knife," she says too casually.

My body stiffens, tears rolling down my cheeks. She thinks this is a joke.

But her eyes are gentle, less intense than usual. "These men ... they're capable of anything, but I handled it. We do need to get moving, though."

She begins hammering. "Elle," I say sharply.

She peers up from her task, a large purple mark forming on her cheek. She pauses at the sight of me wringing my hands. I probably look pale. Sickly even. I think I might be sick.

"Who were they? How do you know them?" I ask, refusing to lose my courage.

"Sometimes," she begins, her eyes apologetic, "our past catches up with us."

"And the way you fought back? I'm guessing that wasn't just luck."

"Like I said, sometimes the past catches us. I was prepared."

She slams a nail into the table, then another.

"Olivia," she says without looking back at me. "You need to get your things. Now. Don't make me leave without you."

I head to the closet in the bedroom.

The linens swirl in my vision, twisting into the darkness of the cupboard. My stomach aches from hunger and exhaustion, anxiety, and something else.

I just stood up to Elle. I just survived a ... whatever it was.

"We need to go," Elle calls from the other room.

I pull myself out of my head, willing my body to move. I yank my bag from the shelf, and it drags a couple of sheets with it. They fall to the floor, along with a document.

I tuck the sheets back onto their shelf and grab the paper off the floor. There's a photo folded inside. Curiosity gets the best of me, and I open the top flap. The letter is short.

If you're reading this, welcome home.

~ L

I open the bottom flap, revealing the picture. I recognize a young Elle first. It's easy to suspect that it's her, despite the age. Her red hair gives her away, and her green eyes stare down at the photographer with an unmatched intensity. The young man next to her, with blond curls and beautiful blue eyes, is also familiar.

He's too familiar.

It's as if the wind gets knocked out of me.

No. It can't be.

My breath finally comes back, rapidly, and I begin to hyperventilate.

"Olivia, let's go!" Elle shouts, her footsteps approaching the door.

I fold the photo before she can see it and shove it into my back pocket.

"Coming," I say, just as she reaches the bedroom doorframe.

It's an out-of-body experience, running from an enemy that you didn't realize existed, riding in a car with a driver who's proving to be the same. An enemy. A stranger. A dangerous stranger.

I feel as though I'm floating above myself, watching through the sun-roof as I sit in the passenger seat, silently wringing my hands in my lap. I pluck all the nail polish from my acrylics. I urge myself to speak, but since I have no voice, either in the form floating above my body, or in my actual body, I'm silent.

I'm so confused.

When we're long out of the city, on the freeway headed for home, I once again connect with my body. The pain in my tense muscles is excruciating, making it impossible to relax.

Elle drives with one hand on the wheel, appearing as chill as ever, but I notice a carefully calculated alertness in her. She's perfectly poised and ready to pounce at a moment's notice.

She senses my eyes on her and glances over.

"I used to be mixed up with some bad people," she says.

"That's why you weren't supposed to be in New York?"

"Yes," she sighs.

I nod as if I understand, but I don't know what I don't know.

Is Elle on my side? There's no clear line between good and bad. Maybe it's all bad. Everyone. Elle included. And Camden ... he somehow plays a role.

I stare into the night, watching headlights pass in the opposite direction. Time is slow and fast, or not present at all.

At one point, Elle turns off the freeway, though I don't really process it. Not until she hands me a large cup of ice cream, and it triggers my senses back to work. Greasy hamburgers and fries saturate the air around me, and my stomach grumbles.

She pulls into a parking spot and fiddles with her phone before veering back out onto the road, then the freeway. I pick at the melting ice cream, thick with candy pieces, barely tasting the sweet comfort it's meant to provide.

"I cancelled our dinner plans," she announces.

What dinner plans? I mean to ask it out loud. But I don't have the energy.

I scoop at the bottom of my paper cup for several bites before realizing that I'm out of ice cream. Holding it to my lap, I focus on the vibrations of the wheels against the pavement—much like the anxiety buzzing through my body.

My eyelids shut, and exhaustion keeps them closed. I'm vaguely aware of my consciousness drifting in and out. Time and space are lost. Emotions gone.

Numbness. It's better here.

"Let's go," Elle says, startling me.

I open my eyes, trying to see through the blur of sleep. There are bright lights, a hotel.

"Where are we?" I ask.

"We can't go home tonight."

The familiar buzz of my nerves returns, but I still can't muster the energy to comprehend, let alone ask. So, I take the simplest route. I get out of the car, and once again, follow Elle.

Olivia

Tuesday, December 20th

I'm awakened by knocking. All at once, the memory of yesterday floods my mind, and my heart races, pumping blood at a rapid rate.

But I don't respond. I just lie there, hoping that the covers over my head will protect me and hide me like an invisibility cloak made of sheets and blankets.

The gentle padding of feet across the floor does little to reassure me, though it seems innocent, calm. It's only Elle, but Elle brings trouble. My heart pounds harder and faster.

"Breakfast," she says nonchalantly.

Cinnamon and warmed syrup pierce my nose, followed by an aromatic coffee, but I stay under the covers while Elle speaks quietly to the man who must be delivering the items.

The door shuts, and I'm jolted by a smack on my rear.

I groan, unwilling to move. Sleep hasn't come easily since I've met Elle.

Since before that, really.

Last night, though, I slept. I didn't think about anything. Not about being held in a choke hold. Not about the money Elle still has tucked in her purse and whether my share of it is enough. Not a thought about the man who bought the jewelry pieces from us, or how he made my insides ignite with pleasure when he looked at me. I didn't even think about the photo of young Elle and Camden, or what it means ... I've never known what would happen after crossing the threshold of too much stress and fear. Now, I know. Collapse. Loss of thought. Control gone. And sleep.

"Come on, get up." Elle tugs on my covers but doesn't yank them off, thankfully. "You know I'm not going to eat this food."

I pull the covers back from my eyes, and stare into the void of the bright room.

Groaning again, I sit up, flailing my arms and legs like a toddler being made to do something she doesn't want to do.

"Eat. You'll need it."

I look over at Elle now, who is sipping a cup of coffee. My stomach and my resistance betray me, grumbling at the sight of French toast and bacon.

The food couldn't go down fast enough. Unlike last night, I taste the rich flavor of every bite, and chase it with two cups of coffee.

"Thank you," I mumble, falling back into the sheets.

"Welcome," Elle responds, not looking up from the book that she holds inches from her face. "Your phone kept buzzing last night. A Larry called on repeat."

"My father," I say, my words short. "He wants his money."

"And Jared," she adds.

My stomach twists. "He wants his money, too."

"We don't have to leave yet, if you want more sleep." Her words are soothing.

I don't answer. I don't have to. My fatigue must be written all over me.

Elle

Tuesday, December 20th

Z ane better not be home when we get there. I need Olivia out of my hair before he can speak to her. I think she's lost it. Whatever was holding her together is gone. She's a vacant vessel, eating and sleeping and not giving a fuck about what comes next.

I've done that to her.

No. Not me.

Travis, or Camden, or whoever the fuck he is has done this to her.

He's the one who betrays her with every living breath. He's the one who betrayed *me*. He's the reason we ended up together. The reason we started our con.

Her absent, self-serving father—Larry. Camden's money-obsessed, fake uncle—Jared. They pushed her over the edge. She's a shell where Olivia once was, destroyed by the men she's stuck with.

Yet, I feel so fucking guilty. I have no idea how people live like this all the time. Like Olivia. Poor thing.

She's humming along to music in the passenger seat. She has been for hours. At least she's not talking incessantly, asking questions and demanding answers.

As we enter Leesburg, a black sedan is sitting in the dirt just before the welcome sign.

The car pulls out behind us.

Delight spills through me with a hint of concern. This asshole can come for me. I can handle it.

But I don't think Olivia can.

Cautiously, so as not to startle Olivia, I take a corner, then another, then punch through a yellow as it turns red. The car stays with us. Bastard.

At the next intersection, I turn again onto the road that will lead to my house. We go right, and the other car goes left.

My shoulders slump with disappointment, but my muscles relax. Olivia's safe, for now.

"What's with all the corners?" Olivia asks, aloof.

There's no need to reply. She's not here with me. Not really.

I keep my eyes on my mirrors, but the black sedan doesn't return.

Olivia follows me inside, setting her overnight bag on the porch. The house is eerily quiet. Zane must have gone for a run.

"Remember, we were at the beach," I say gently to her.

"What happened back there?" Olivia says as she moves from the open door to the dining room. She's more alert than she let on.

"In the car? I thought someone was following us."

"Following us," she says, her words wavering between statement and question. "Why would someone be following us?"

"I don't—"

"Yes, you do." Her gaze snaps up at me, her eyes narrowing. "Or do you have more past that we haven't met yet?"

Her harsh words seep through me. Normally, I would welcome an attack like this, but this is different.

"One set of enemies, that's it."

I place a hand on her shoulder. She recoils.

"That I know of." I shrug.

"What's that supposed to mean?" she demands, her voice shrill.

"It means, when you live on the edge, you risk people hating you." I draw an invisible line between us with my index finger. "You and me, we are living on the edge."

"So what? It's a coincidence that we were followed after we were attacked by your past in New York?!" Olivia's shouting now, a new level of rage behind her still-absent eyes. "Attacked. Almost raped. Could have been skinned alive. Lost all our money..."

Money. Her focus shifts. Her gaze darts frantically around the room.

I inch backward toward the still-open door. She's like a wounded animal that won't handle being startled, but the door needs to be shut.

"Olivia, I need you to listen to me. Zane can't know that we were in New York," I say, my desperate tone shocking me. Honesty. Truth. She needs me to tell her what nobody else knows so that she can trust me again. So that she won't destroy me.

"It's not just the wine that he doesn't know about. That call ... the one you answered ... that was Sam. The same man who attacked me. An ex ... boyfriend and drug lord. Zane's kept us on the move since before we were married. To protect me. But I've doubted there was any risk for years now, so I go to New York often. Sell jewelry ... to Liam. It's not dirty, but not exactly clean. And I thought this time we'd be safe, mostly. Even though, lately, I've felt like someone's been following me. Calling me ... I didn't know it was Sam until last night. It's weird ... that a dumb grudge from twenty years ago would still be festering. It doesn't make sense. We sold pot, for fuck's sake! I think there's more to—"

Her eyes dart over my shoulder, through the still open door.

"New York?" Zane asks from behind me.

My stomach knots. Shit. I spin to face him.

"Love, you're home," I sing, turning my lips upward.

"Were you in New York?" he asks, punctuating each syllable. "Jesus, your face—"

"Yeah, it was a blast!" Olivia shrieks, full of vengeance, not forgiveness. "Our trip was complete with offloading stolen items and being attacked by thugs."

My heart drops. I spilled my guts, and she throws me under the fucking bus.

Zane's eyes are sharp, staring right through my fake smile. Disappointment is dark on his face, betrayal stealing his expression. What I don't see is surprise.

He's *not* surprised.

My reserve crumbles. My lips quiver, and my hope disintegrates.

He never believed that I could change. He didn't trust me to be more. He always expected me to let him down like I've let down everyone else that I've cared about.

Olivia

Tuesday, December 20th

I hate it when people argue.

My father used to pick fights with my mom before he left. Constantly. He took pleasure in seeing her shrink from his harmful words. When that didn't work, he'd keep at it, finally throwing things, and harming her physically. He would do anything to make her small. To make her less. To control her.

The yelling. Their screaming. Mental abuse ... a constant onslaught.

My mom tried to defend herself, defend me. Tried to protect me. But she couldn't, not from everything. Not from anything.

The anger surrounding Elle and Zane is palpable. Their words are loud. It's an unloading of whatever has been building between them.

I can't grasp what's being said. I can't remember how their fight started.

I drift about unnoticed, floating in the sounds bouncing off the walls, and watching the blurred movements of frustration between them.

"I was perfectly fucking safe..." Elle snaps.

The pressure of my fingers pressing against my nails, plucking at the damaged acrylic, reminds me that I do exist, though I'm not sure how.

I glance at my nails. I've destroyed them. Embarrassment warms my cheeks as I shove my hands into my pockets. Something grazes my skin, prompting me to extract them.

"You could have been killed!" Zane shouts.

I lower onto a chair and place the item on the table, unfolding it.

Elle's green eyes stare back at me from her young, freckled face in the photo. Camden's arm around her shoulder—as if it's always been there—brings tears to my eyes.

I slide the edges of the image between my fingers, trying to grasp what it means, but I know there's only one possibility. They belonged together. The love between them is clear. I flip the picture over, searching for a date. Instead, I find words. Names.

Collecting myself until I recall how to read.

Travis & L Monroe.

L, not ELLE.

And there's only one last name...

Camden told me that he'd never been married before. That's true. Camden never had. But Travis, well, it appears Travis has been married. Maybe he still is.

I will the knot in my throat to dissolve into sobs, but it doesn't. I wait for my stomach to twist and tangle, but I don't get the urge to vomit. Instead, I'm numb.

Why would Camden have another name?

Why do the names before me seem so familiar?

Libby. He gets calls from Libby. The guy who attacked us in New York called Elle by a different name. I thought it was Lizzie, but maybe I misunderstood. Elle and Camden—Travis and Libby—they still talk. They still fit.

How could Elle use me like this? If they're still—whatever they are—then why would she need me to steal from him? It doesn't make sense.

My hands lift from the photo, and I hold them up in front of me, turning them over for my observation. My fingers speak to me. No, not my fingers, my thoughts.

Something's not right.

Leave. Go.

Get out.

And so, I do. It doesn't feel like I'm picking up my purse, moving myself to the door, or grabbing my duffle bag—but I do. Somehow, some way, I manage to get in my car, drive, and arrive at home.

It's not home. It hasn't been for a long time. It probably never was. A home would require a connection. A husband who I belong to, who belongs to me. This is not home. Not here. Not with Camden or whoever the hell he is.

Before

From Las Vegas, With Love

"Do you, Xander Crawford, take Elizabeth Monroe to be your lawfully wedded wife, to love, to honor, to cherish through the rollercoaster of life?" the officiant asks.

On cue, the rollercoaster of New York, New York, in Las Vegas roars overhead.

I chuckle as I gaze into his brown eyes, that sparkle in the January sun.

"Yes, I take you, Elle, as my wife."

"And do you, Elizabeth Monroe, take Xander Crawford ..."

Tears sting my cheeks. My chest is full of regret for the lies that I've told and my commitment to uphold them, because I will not lose him.

"Yes, I take Zane, as my forever husband," I say, my throat catching.

"Elle, I never thought I'd marry someone with a record." Zane laughs nervously and squeezes my hand. "But we both know you stole my heart, so what could I do?"

"You'd make a terrible comedian," I say, squeezing his hand back.

"I know our life will be full of struggles. There'll be some circumstantial guilt. We won't always agree on the terms of our sentence ..."

We both laugh uncontrollably.

"But," Zane says, composing himself. "I'll always love you. No matter how many times you mess up—"

"Because you're perfect." I roll my eyes at him.

"I am." He smirks. "But you're perfect for me. No matter what. I'd like to keep you forever if that's alright with you."

I prop up on my toes and kiss him, not caring that it breaks the rules. Structure is irrelevant in this love and this ceremony. We paid two random people to be our witnesses, and we did warn the officiant that we wouldn't be typical.

"Zane, you have me forever, whether you want me or not," I say, my words unsteady. "Even if you insist that we change our names to keep a low profile. Even if you keep us on the move for the rest of our lives. Even if we couldn't get married in the actual New York."

We both look around at the miniature rendition of NYC and the people stumbling by with large alcoholic slushies.

"The truth is ..." I say, with all sincerity. "Without you, I'd be lost. I'd go through every heartache, every tragedy, every challenge ... every crime, again and again, if they'd lead me back to you."

He runs the side of his hand across my face, his eyes filling with tears.

"I love you, Zane. I love that we are starting new, on this New Year's Day, and I also kinda like the new name thing."

Zane wraps me in his arms, lifting me until my face is just above him. I run my hands through his hair, then get lost in the last kiss we'll have before being pronounced man and wife.

Elle

Tuesday, December 20th

A lifetime of being misunderstood changes someone, especially a girl who has been held to high expectations all her life—be the girl that's:

Quiet and trustworthy.

Doesn't question others.

Does as she's told.

The friend everyone can rely on that never waivers.

A girlfriend that's a pretty picture. Only a picture. Not a vocalist.

The daughter that succeeds in everything and never falters or fails.

When she's this girl, this is when she gets good at pretending to be everything to everyone. If she doesn't, she'll fail miserably.

That's what I've come to understand.

That's what I've come to be. Perfect for everyone. Perfect, but never myself. The only security I've ever had is in the comfort of what I become.

And now I've lost the security of my lies.

Zane slams a box on the kitchen counter that he extracted from a hiding space below the floor of the office.

My foundation—our relationship—cracks.

"You found them?" I squeak.

My hands shake, exposing weakness.

"About a year ago," Zane says. "Before we moved here."

He breathes out slowly. His shoulders momentarily relax. Then his entire frame tightens again.

I can't breathe.

A year. An entire year. He's read reveal after reveal of confessions to my brother, who's supposed to be dead.

I never should have written those fucking letters.

"You read them?" I ask, like an idiot.

"Yes. I know about it all. Your hatred of wine. The knockoff jewelry you hid in the wine barrel; how you sold it as if it was real to buy that apartment. You owned that apartment," he says, his voice rising. "You weren't just a drug dealer caught up in a possessive relationship with your boss. You *chose* crime. You conned so many innocent people. You still do. You convince people at garage sales and flea markets that what they have is fake, and then you use them to make your own pieces ... good as new, or that's what you tell the jewelers, right?"

I open my mouth to answer, but he doesn't stop.

"It's also how I know you blame yourself. For your parents' car accident. For your brother's abduction and death. For everything bad that's ever happened to your family. It's why you have the nightmares. You have so much guilt. So much hate.

"But you talked about this place. The memory of Leesburg, and how you'd change everything starting with your visit here. That's why I brought you here. You were so complacent, so empty. Your nightmares were getting worse. I thought ... this place would help you. Bring you closer to the memory of your family—the memories that seemed good—so that you could be happy."

He has no fucking idea how much closer he brought me to them.

A sensation of confused emotions wraps around me, tight, squeezing life from me. He saw everything. He's known how much I've lied to him. He knows everything. And yet he brought me here because he was worried about my happiness. He was worried about me.

He shifts his weight, uncomfortable, impatient. If he expects a rapid-fire confession, he's mistaken. The truth has always been harder—and takes longer.

"I know it sucks for you sometimes, knowing they're all gone," he continues. "It's really shitty for you, especially since your brother was the only person you were ever honest with."

The last words are harsh, as they should be. The shaking from my hands spreads up my arms and into my torso, my whole body vibrating now.

I've destroyed him. I wanted to protect him, but my truth has ruined him.

Yet, he's hidden this from me for a year, dancing around the continued onslaught of perfectly crafted lies. Lies that I thought were airtight. Lies that were supposed to remain my truth forever—to keep his love.

"Travis isn't dead," I whisper.

"What do you mean he—"

"He's alive!" I shout, pounding my fist into my thigh. "Skin intact. Breathing great. Walking. Talking. Working. Married."

My arm instinctively lifts toward Olivia. This confession is for her, too. I twist my head, searching for her, but she's gone.

"You lied about that, too?" Zane's voice catches. "You lied about your brother dying?"

"No. *He* lied," I say frantically. "I only found out because Olivia has my jewelry ... my inheritance."

I'm somehow moving toward Zane, slowly inching closer. Though I can't recall my feet moving, and his haven't. He's too angry to be close to me.

He's ready to get a divorce. That's what this moment means. I'm sure of it.

A jarring of nerves sends electricity through my body. Divorce. I can't lose him. I won't survive it. I need him.

I take the remaining steps and wrap my arms around his waist, burying my face in his chest. I hold tight, staking my claim. Making it known that I'm not going anywhere.

"I found out just before you left for your last work trip. That's why I couldn't get out of bed," I mumble into his shirt.

He smells of cedarwood, the scent of him. I inhale deeply, trying to hold onto it before it's gone.

His hand rests on my back, rubbing it. We stay like this for a moment before he drops his hand to his side and steps back.

"I may have lied about the wine. About the barrel. About my criminal background. Eddy and Ricardo didn't teach me how to make jewelry, they just helped me to improve. And they tried to teach me the right path—the clean path. Eddy pushed me to say yes to your requests for a date. Said you'd be good for me..."

Zane stiffens, taking another step back.

"Obviously, not everything they tried to instill stuck," I say, shifting my weight, "But there's one thing I've never lied about. I've always loved you. It killed me a little at first because I thought I was strong enough to resist petty things like falling in love. I was wrong. Then I couldn't do anything but follow you and continue to lie so you wouldn't leave me or hate me. You're far better than I have ever been, and I knew that if you knew me—really knew me—you'd leave."

My cheeks are cold, wet from tears that I didn't know were falling.

He rests his palms on my shoulders, then slides them down my arms, taking my hands.

My entire being weakens at his touch.

"I don't care that you don't like wine," he says. "I kind of care that you're a thief, though I knew that when I chose to date you. It's not a big stretch from drug dealer to thief. I'd find emptied wallets in your dresser drawer. Men's wallets. That's not normal, Elle."

His lips betray him, twitching up for a split second.

"I wouldn't have drawn the line at clever con artist with a jewelry crafting skill. I was too in love. Besides, you were a teenager when you sold fake replicas."

My heart clenches.

"The flea market flips—"

He squeezes my hands gently. "It's shady, but it's not illegal." He rolls his eyes. "It's not like you're the only one playing for bargains at garage sales."

The ball of nerves in my gut grows larger. I try to swallow it down with my rising hope.

"What I do care about," he continues, "is that you *chose* to lie to me all this time. You didn't trust me. You wouldn't let me in."

I choke on my breath.

"No," I protest. "That's not it at all. I didn't trust me. And the person I am. The person I've been. Nobody has ever liked the real Elle. Or the real Lizzie. Nobody. Not even my parents. I thought that Travis did, and it turns out that he'd rather fake his own death than be around—"

He puts his hand up, stopping me. I stare at him wide-eyed. Scared shitless.

"You didn't think I'd love you, but you never gave me the chance to try. I've waited—hoped—you'd come clean. But you were never going to."

My insides twist harder. Sharp, like I'm simultaneously going to be squashed and explode into a million, tiny pieces.

He relinquishes the grip on my hands, letting them fall. When he turns, he doesn't look back. "I'm headed out of town tomorrow. I'm going to stay near the airport tonight."

My body doesn't move. I don't object. I only stare as he picks up a bag near the door—his regular work suitcase—and disappears, slamming the door behind him.

When his car engine is too far down the road for me to hear, I collapse onto the floor. My body rips apart, yet it's still somehow in one piece. My whole world is gone.

I have no idea how to lie my way out of this one.

Olivia

Wednesday, December 21st

A ction. That's the only solution that I could come up with. So, I acted.

I pretended to be asleep when Camden got home. I kept my eyes shut, unmoving, until he settled in bed. When he was sound asleep, I snuck into the closet, dressed in black joggers and a black sweatshirt, then slid back into bed, hiding with the covers pulled up to my chin. I stayed there, still, but awake, until he woke up to leave in the morning.

When I heard the front door, I climbed out of hiding. Channeling what I hoped to be my inner Elle, I stealthily rushed to my car and followed him.

Now, sitting here, staring at a warehouse building that's bright orange, I'm not sure how I've pulled off following him without being noticed. I'm suddenly very aware of my lack of experience in being stealthy. I glance down at my entirely black outfit. This won't keep me hidden.

Snow begins to fall, landing on my windshield. It's fogging with every breath.

I groan as dread fills me. Yeah, black was the wrong choice.

What will I do once I'm inside that warehouse?

I don't know if this is where Camden's been working on gaming technology, if that's really his job. For all I know, this is where Jared stores all his storage unit crap. It would make sense because his books tell me he's making a killing off buying storage lockers full of other people's things. If I walk in there and it is, I might as well be walking into a lion's den.

There's also the possibility that this is where he's coming to meet Elle. Or L. Or Libby. Whoever she is. The thought of confronting them both at once—of confirming my spiraling fears about the two of them—is terrifying. I don't know how I'd manage losing them both simultaneously.

This is absolute garbage. It's appalling that there are only two people in this world who I thought I could lean on. Camden hasn't been the person I married for so long, but losing him would kill me. Elle ... well, I let her in too much, and way too soon. That one's on me.

A month ago, no, two days ago, I would have believed that this mystery warehouse was full of large televisions, desks, and computers. I'd imagined his workspace with beanbags and weird floor gaming chairs. Now, I have doubts.

I shove my car door open and pull the handle as I close it, doing my best not to make a sound. Inching around the bright orange metal building, I stop at the corner and peer around. I snap my head back when I see a man coming out of the building carrying a black box with a red lid.

This is precisely why I went to business school and didn't bother exploring any career path that could have been remotely dangerous. I don't have the skill, or the ability to stay calm.

To prove my point, my heart bangs against my chest, probably loud enough for the stocky man, also in all black, to hear. At least I'd blend in with him ...

"Anything else, boss?" the man in black shouts, followed by the slam of a truck door.

"That's it for today, Ralf," the familiar voice of my husband says. "Straight to New York, you hear me? No pitstops this time."

"You got it, boss. No more titty bars." The man in black chuckles.

I tilt my head, my lips parting as disgust traces its signature across my face.

My skin pricks and twitches. I breathe in through my nose and let my eyes close to counteract it. I know Camden is here. I followed him.

But he's not anyone's boss.

Someone begins whistling near where Camden's voice originated, joined with footsteps. The footsteps are coming toward me.

My muscles are tense. I will my body to move through my fear, to run. Finally, it listens. I get back to my car and make as little noise as possible as I climb in. I turn it on, immediately throw it into drive, and take off in the opposite direction through the parking lot past a long strip of warehouses.

The trip back to the house is a constant loop of replays.

Boss is a terrible nickname. If the other man had called him by name, maybe I'd have a clue. Is he Travis to the man in black, or Camden?

My skin stings. I'm an idiot. His uncle calls him Camden. He has an uncle. He's clearly Camden.

So, what the hell is happening?

I pull into the driveway and turn off the ignition, then sit outside the house that I'm supposed to call home.

Another replay begins ... orange building. Burly man next to a truck, dressed in black. Camden's voice. The nickname. A box being loaded into the truck.

The black box with the red lid. I've seen it before. I've seen many like it in my basement.

Rage rips through my bloodstream as I sprint through the entry to the hall and down the stairs to our basement. I can't entirely trust my memory, especially not with how things have been going.

I fling the door open to the storage room, and my gaze falls on the black boxes with red lids. All locked.

None of them have a speck of dust on them. They stand out like sore thumbs in this place where things are forgotten.

The room begins to close around me. I slide down the door and onto the ground, staring at the boxes. I always expected them to stay here, full of tech, forever hidden from the world, just as Camden described.

I bury my face in my hands. Could I be overreacting? Coincidences happen all the time.

Like a photo of Elle and Camden together.

Like Jared knowing about my debt, and IVF, when nobody else does.

Like Elle's family inheritance locked away in my basement.

My gaze travels from the boxes to the shelf. The old cardboard carton with the jewelry box holding all of Elle's precious heirlooms. I need to get that crap out of my house.

The black spine of the baseball card binder catches my attention.

The letters ...

Everyone loves Elle. He probably did, too, more than he ever loved me. They were so young in the picture. Like babies.

I step toward the shelf, grabbing the binder. As I do so, I slam my toe. "Ouch!" I shout.

I set the binder down and reach for the culprit. It's a white container tucked under the bottom shelf. Removing the lid, I sink to the floor again.

Inside is the signature book from our wedding. Our marriage certificate is tucked in a pretty case, next to a photo of Camden and I staring into each other's eyes. Happy. In love.

Camden had big dreams for us. We had big dreams together. We used to talk about the names we'd choose for our future babies. Audrey for a girl, like Audrey Hepburn. James for a boy, after my late grandfather. My chest warms, and I realize that I'm smiling, but the constant ache doesn't dissipate.

This is everything that I needed to solidify the decisions I've already made. I knew what I must do on the day that he brought the Maserati home.

This next path will be my own. He never wanted a family, not with me.

Standing, I dust myself off. I grab the baseball binder and flip it open, revealing the letters. The letters that tell the story that I've been trying to unravel for days.

They are letters between Travis and L.

I drop the stack on top of a red-lidded black box, then carry the things upstairs. I set them on the floor in the den we never use, the empty one across the hall from the nursery that's full of hopeless dreams and baby things still in their original packages.

A sense of hope mixes with my need for resolution. I step into the hall and move through the house, looking for something—anything—that might work. A baseball bat should do it. I snatch the one from Camden's office and consider slamming it against one of his large screens, but decide not to. Not yet, anyway.

I carry the bat in my right hand, letting it skim the walls to the kitchen. I remove the cork from a wine bottle and take a swig. I guess alcohol's no longer bothering me.

With my hands full, I return to the vacant living room and slump down on the red lid of the black box. One curiosity wins out over the other. Plus, reading pairs better with a red blend.

I grab the letters, gulping alcohol and flipping through the stack. No amount of booze can bring me to focus on the words, though. Only the hearts next to the "L" at the bottom of each letter make an imprint on my mind.

Inside one, there's a small, unmistakable photo of the two of them. They are teenagers, with his arm over her shoulder, holding her close. They beam at the camera, emanating bliss. Another letter has an etching of a ring—this one's from L.

The pit burns in my stomach, twisting and tearing every bit of hope I have left until it's gone. If I could read the words through my distress, I wouldn't want to. Each word would take a piece of my life, killing me slowly. And for what? It's already clear—the thing I somehow missed all along.

My frustration reminds me that there's one other thing I need to crack. I stand, picking up the bat as I do. I pull the heavy wooden object into the air and let it hover above my shoulder, then crash it down. Swinging at the lock several times, I have little success with horrible aim. I give up and take my shot at the lid. With each hit, a release of endorphins escapes. Pieces of me—invisible and secret—that I've kept tucked neatly inside for so long.

The lid cracks. My aggression builds momentum until the lid breaks.

An uncontrollable laugh rips through my core, shaking my body until I'm in tearful hysterics. I collapse to the floor next to the box and stare inside. Its truths reflect back at me.

Elle

Wednesday, December 21st

The bathroom floor is cold. Hard. Cramped. Uncomfortable. But I don't budge.

The darkness of the room consumes me. I don't deserve light.

I tried calling Zane a dozen times. I sent twice as many texts. I tore through the box of letters he left out. If they held a clue for what to do next, I'd be grateful. They don't. They hold nothing.

After hours, minutes, or days—I can't be sure—of staring at the letters and my phone, waiting for something—anything—I gave up. Somehow, I ended up here. Alone.

Nothing makes the heartache better.

Time makes it worse.

So much worse.

I can't fucking breathe, then I hyperventilate. I can't speak, then I sob loudly—uncontrollably.

Olivia ignored the texts I sent her, too. She disappeared. She fucking walked out.

Fuck, I think that I need her more than she needs me.

Forcing myself from the floor takes almost all my strength.

I stumble into the kitchen and stop at the window to the backyard. I stare out, my eyes—my everything—fixed on the snow.

The bright sight makes my heart squeeze unbearably tight.

Zane loves snow, especially at Christmas.

A pounding on the door startles me. The aggressive banging continues despite my sluggish movements. I don't realize that I'm answering it until I do.

"Olivia," I gasp. My heart swells, then cracks again.

She stares at me, blank-faced, her foot tapping in impatience.

"I'm so glad you're—"

"I need my money." She's curt.

"I was worried about you," I say, shifting to allow her space to come in.

She doesn't budge from her spot on the porch.

"Were you now?" Her question rumbles through me.

I'm taken aback. She's never been mean. I didn't think she could be.

That's why she needs me. Or needed me.

Nobody really needs me anymore.

Olivia

Wednesday, December 21st

E lle turns from the door, and I demand my body to stay put outside, despite the growing cold.

Speak. I came here to say my piece. *Speak.*

Nothing comes out of my mouth.

She returns with two envelopes.

"Here you go," she says, handing me both.

Confusion washes over me. One has my name, and the other has hers.

"What game are you playing?" I demand.

"You're going to need it," she says, with so much effort that it sounds like it hurts.

Rage wells in every fiber of my being.

"Why? Are you and Camden —Travis—done running your game? Cutting me loose now? *This*," I shout, shaking the envelopes, "is my severance package?! How considerate!"

She stares at me blankly.

My hands shake, and tears well in my eyes.

"I found your letters," I say, yanking the stack from my bag and holding them out like they're a weapon.

Her eyes close as she breathes, creating a whiff of steam in the cold air surrounding me.

"Great, you too," she finally says. "Fucking letters."

Me too? My lips purse, and my eyes narrow.

Elle turns away, and I glare at her back, bewildered, as she moves slowly toward her table. She frantically swipes at the items on its surface, scooping them up in her arms.

She takes several steps towards me, then stops, defeat written all over her.

"You can have them all!" she screams. "Take every last fucking letter!"

She flings the paper at me. I watch as they flip and spin, slowly making their way to the ground.

My throat constricts. There are so many more.

She sinks to the floor, landing on her knees. She sits back on her heels. A sob escapes her lips, and she leans forward, burying her head into her arms.

Fine, she can cry. Fall apart. Act this out however she'd like. But I'm not done.

"How long were you married? Are you still married?" I demand.

"Zane isn't here," she groans.

"Not Zane. Travis," I correct.

Every vertebra of my spine is locked and ready.

Elle doesn't budge. "Married? Are you fucking high?"

I stare at the back of her head, unsure what to say. She's clearly two steps ahead of me, as always.

"No, I'm not high," I choke out.

Her sobs merge with a horrible cackling.

"Travis ... Travis? That's who you're talking about? Do you fucking pay attention to anything?"

Goosebumps prick my skin. Ringing fills my ears. I missed something. What was it?

"Travis is my *brother*!" Her yells are muffled against the floorboards. "*Was* my brother."

Her *brother* ... the one who she told me about at the pond in New York.

I pick up one of the fallen letters, then another. I catch sight of one with a rough variation in the handwriting, contrasted against the smooth handwriting of the others. "Even though you're dead ..."

Scrambling to grab the rest, to process what I'd missed, I search for clues in each. Again and again, I catch renditions of *death* and *dead*.

"You thought he was dead," I whisper, realizing that I'm on the floor now too.

She told me that he was, but these letters that hold her secrets confirm it.

Elle doesn't move from her coiled position. She's gasping and choking on each ragged breath she takes. Her body convulses with her sobs.

Warmth fills the cavity that's been forming in my core. She didn't betray me. She wasn't playing me alongside a lover *or* a brother. She was honest.

I set the letters down and crawl to her, grabbing her torso and pulling her up. Elle molds into me, moving with my steps, as I clumsily lead her to the couch.

Her skin is like ice.

"You're so cold," I say softly.

She sinks into the couch, and I lift her feet onto it. I go into her room and swipe the down comforter from her perfectly made bed and pile it on her.

Elle gathers the blanket in her grasp and pulls it over her head.

This looks familiar.

I close the front door and gather the rest of the letters, then go to the kitchen. I pour water into the coffee pot reservoir and locate the breakfast blend. As the beans grind, I take several deep breaths.

Elle doesn't stir. Perhaps she's fallen asleep. She looked exhausted, with dark circles under her bloodshot eyes.

My body is heavy with my own fatigue.

I don't start the coffee, instead, I climb onto the opposite end of the couch and listen to her rhythmic breathing. Slipping my boots off, I tuck my feet under the comforter and ease into the soft cushions. My eyelids close. Perhaps I'll sleep, too.

"I thought that you two were married," I say, handing Elle the picture and letter I stole from her apartment.

"I thought that I was going to have to commit you," she responds, taking the picture from me. "Not that that's a bad thing. Just that I could tell you weren't doing well and needed some help."

The coffee steams in front of me as I sniff at the roast with hints of caramel.

"Fair." I give her a faint smile. "I felt like I was floating above myself for a while, but I'm back now."

"I wish that I could say the same." Elle pulls the comforter up around her neck.

"You two will work it out. You belong."

My heart aches for her. They do fit together.

"What about you and ... Camden?"

My stomach drops.

"Is that what we're calling him, then?" I mean it to sound like a joke, but it's too soon. I can't even smile.

"Fuck if I know," she grumbles into her blanket.

"I don't know what to do. Where to begin. I thought he loved me, but now..."

I peer at her, searching her face for an answer. She doesn't give one.

"I go back to my OBGYN Friday morning before the long weekend. At that point, I'm supposed to give an answer about which sperm to use. I haven't even spoken with Camden about IVF, and I don't—"

Her eyebrows knit together, and it dawns on me that she doesn't know this part.

"It's either Camden's sperm, or a donor. But I—"

She groans, interrupting me again.

"What?" I ask. "Too much information?"

It *is* her brother. Maybe she doesn't want to imagine him watching porn and ejaculating into a cup. Honestly, neither do I.

"No," she moans, covering her face. When she retracts the comforter, her eyes are full of concern. "I have to tell you something."

My pulse quickens. What could she possibly have to say about *this*? I shift uncomfortably, leaning my side against the back of the couch.

"He had a vasectomy when he was eighteen."

I shiver, but I'm suddenly hot.

"No, that's not right. He had his sperm tested a year ago."

"Olivia, think about it," Elle says. "He faked his own death. Don't you think—"

"He's great at faking almost anything," I finish, glad I got to interrupt her. "It never crossed my mind. I never expected this."

I wait for my head to swim with doubt and confusion. I expect to slip back into a dissociated state, but it doesn't come.

"I'm sorry," Elle says quietly.

Tears slip down my cheeks as I nod in acceptance. I knew he wouldn't be the one to give me a child. My mind was made up. But there's no way I could have known it was made up for me long ago. Before I was even a part of the equation.

"The decision that I'm supposed to have an answer to isn't whether I use Camden's sperm ... I made the decision not to a while ago. I'm supposed to have a sperm donor selected," I say, my words catching on the dryness of my throat.

A sip of my coffee relieves it.

"Thank the fucking goddesses," Elle says, leaning her head on the back of the couch.

"Elle?" I say, watching her eyes close.

"Hmm?"

"How did you know I was married to Ca—Travis?"

I hold my breath as she opens her eyes, looking me over.

"You're going to be pissed," Elle answers.

My left index finger twists around my mug until it finds the polish on the nails of my right hand.

"I'm the one who broke into your house."

My gaze fixes on her, and I'm unable to look away.

"You didn't trust me to bring you the jewelry," I say flatly.

"I don't trust anyone," she sighs. "I knew that I was being followed, and I knew that as soon as Zane found out, he'd have us move. I needed my inheritance."

I nod as my throat constricts.

"Olivia," she says softly. "I *still* need my inheritance. "I need you to get it for me. I can't go back there."

Her eyes are big—pleading. She didn't trust me before, but she didn't take them.

She's trusting me now, and I trust her.

Taking a breath, I change the subject.

"Regarding Camden ..." I clench my jaw to hold myself together. "What should I do, Elle?"

"What should *we* do?" Elle interjects. "We're in this together."

"Okay, then," I say, nodding. "There's one more thing ... Camden has diamonds. Lots of diamonds."

Elle

Thursday, December 22nd

I dial Zane's number for the umpteenth time. This time, he doesn't send me straight to voicemail. It rings instead.

A flutter in my stomach, like a fucking schoolgirl, fogs my brain. He didn't automatically dismiss my call. He's wearing down. Considering my side.

The ramblings of his voicemail box bring back the heartache. He doesn't have his phone on him. He's not wavering.

I need to hear his actual voice, not the same recording stuck on repeat in my head.

There's a beep. My turn.

"Olivia," I start off because I need him to listen. "This is about Olivia, not me. We—she—needs your help. Your expertise. Her husband, Camden ... Umm ...Travis. I think I already told you that. We—she—thinks he's doing something illegal. He says he creates games, but I think it's a front. She's hoping ... and I'm hoping ... you could look into it. Hack his accounts. Zane, please come home for Christmas. I can leave. I will leave. You should be here for your favorite holiday. Just please, come home. I love you."

I let the phone fall from my ear. Olivia is watching me, waiting for another breakdown. I can't promise that another won't come, but I can't quite figure out when it'll strike.

"Are you okay?" she asks, in her motherly tone.

I put up my hand and shake my head.

"You're sure you that you found an identical box and lock?" I repeat. It's the same question I've asked multiple times since she's come back and we hid her car in my garage.

She puts her hand up, mocking me. "Elle, please."

I shake my head. "It needs to go perfectly. You can't get caught."

"*We* can't get caught." She rolls her eyes, leaning against the counter. "It's all taken care of. All his diamonds look untouched in the new tote. He thinks I'm going to see my parents for Christmas. I paid Jared back. Everything's in order."

I cringe, thinking about how she dropped nearly thirty thousand dollars in a locked mailbox. Jared legitimately had her make a drop—like a criminal.

"You're sure you're good staying here?" I sound like an insecure ass-hole.

"If I don't, who will drive me to my appointment today?" A smile dances on her lips. "And if I don't, who will get the brunt of my Lupron moodiness?"

"What are sisters for?" I laugh—hard.

She stares at me, willing me to stop.

"Too soon?" I choke out between uncontrolled fits.

She chuckles, slapping a hand over her mouth.

"Stop," she shrieks.

My phone vibrates to life on the counter. My body stiffens and my pulse quickens as I reach for it.

"Hello?" I say breathless, wiping away the tears of laughter from my cheeks.

"You really think he's breaking the law," Zane says, a statement instead of a question.

"Yes," I whisper, soaking in the seconds with him on the line, even if his tone is curt and lacking the hints of love that I'm desperate for.

"Is she safe?" This time, it's a question.

"Yes, at our house. He thinks she's out of town," I say, keeping it short. I don't want to lose him or muddy the waters with my urge to declare my love for him.

"I'll be home tomorrow," he says. Blunt.

"Thank you, Zane."

His heavy sigh echoes through the phone.

He thinks I'm lying. But this time, I'm not. I'll never lie to him again.

"I love you," I blurt, knowing that I need to say it before this call ends and I'm left without him.

"Tomorrow," he says, and the call ends.

Olivia's watchful eye catches the shift before I do. She's around the counter and holding me in her arms before I sink to the floor.

Elle

Saturday, December 24th

Zane arrives with a knock at the front door. Each knock is a bullet to my chest.

This is his house. He is allowed in; no permission needed.

I try not to be too eager as I open the door, but I smile meekly at the love of my life. Better to have loved, they say. Fucking fools. Their loss didn't feel like this.

"Hi," I gasp. A single syllable sounding desperate.

"Hi," he says, and for a second, the world stands still.

He tilts his head and peers up at the ceiling, waiting for me to get out of the way. I scamper to the side and hold my breath as his body passes mine—so close, so very far.

"Tell me what you know," he says to Olivia and gestures to the table.

"Alright," Olivia answers, her eyes drifting to me for confirmation.

I nod and grab my coat, slipping it on. I grab the duffle I've packed and pull the strap over my shoulder.

Zane turns to look at me. His deep brown eyes search mine for understanding. My heart cracks further—as if that's possible.

"I love you," I mouth, unable to get out even a whisper.

As I reach for the door handle, an overwhelming urge takes over, and I spin back around.

"Zane, there's something that you need to know."

Olivia shakes her head, eyes widening. She knows exactly what I'm about to do. We discussed telling him about our crimes. She thought it best we kept quiet.

She can't stop me. I won't lie anymore. Not completely—my confession doesn't have to be hers.

Zane's impatience radiates through the room. He expects more begging. More attestations. All things that serve no purpose here.

"When Olivia and I were doing the appraisal parties," I begin. Olivia waves her hands frantically in the air behind Zane. "I stole things. I took gems off some of the items I said I'd repair, replacing them with fakes like cubic zirconium. I dragged Olivia to New York so I could offload them. She had no idea. It was my con, not hers. Unfortunately, she figured it out. Hence, her outburst when we got back."

He takes in every word I say, his face contorting.

"The truth is," I continue, "I had no reason. I wanted to—for fun. My life has been so disconnected from reality because of the lies I created. I was stuck. I needed disruption. So, I disrupted the lives of others."

I let the words settle over me. I don't know why I do anything anymore.

I tilt my head to Olivia, her secret safe with me. "Thank you for listening," I say, collecting myself, this time leaving as promised.

"Thank you for seeing me on such short notice," I say.

I didn't expect any offices to be open over the holidays. In a late night search a couple of days back, I discovered that mental health support is in high demand this time of year. I'm grateful I got in.

"It's no trouble, Mrs. Crawford. Please take a seat." Dr. Armstrong says, gesturing to the couch.

My heart leaps at my formal name. Zane's name.

As I sink into the stiff sofa, my stomach clenches.

This is how normal people feel when coming to see a therapist.

"Your forms say you were seeing Dr. Marcellus not that long ago," the middle-aged woman says.

Her black curls are woven with silver. Her clothes are tailored. Her office radiates with natural light. Plants line the large windows. The room is impeccably cleaned, the furniture well maintained.

I nod. "Yes, for a short period."

"Why did you leave?" she asks professionally.

"I'm working on honesty, so bear with me," I say, clearing my throat.

She's incredibly patient while I dig through my bag and pull a bottle of water out. I take several gulps. Then several deep breaths.

"I wasn't completely honest with Dr. Marcellus," I begin. "Actually, I wasn't honest at all."

It's uncanny, hearing my voice deliver the shortened version of why I sought out therapy before. How I followed Olivia and became a patient so I could get close to her.

"Olivia knows," I finish. "I've reconciled things with her."

I don't include the part where we stole from other women. It's not my story to tell. My forms show my past criminal record. My present is unnecessary—it'll implicate Olivia, and I won't break her trust.

"Is it accurate to say you're looking for a fresh start?" she asks as she bends over to look through files in a desk drawer.

"That's accurate," I answer. "Though, in keeping with honesty, I would have reconciled with her. Given her a chance to help me, but ..." I take another gulp of water. This part should be easy for me. I get to destroy someone. So why doesn't it feel good? "Dr. Marcellus has a camera in her office. She records sessions. She recorded mine, anyway. I never gave permission. I don't feel safe being myself there."

Dr. Armstrong scribbles a note, then rises from her desk.

"I can assure you, there will be no recorded sessions here." She hands me a pamphlet. "This is regarding our patient confidentiality practices. I take them quite seriously."

"Thank you," I say, taking it.

"And this is a behavioral contract. I'll need it signed before our next session," Dr. Armstrong says, holding out a stapled packet. "Take it home, read through all of it, and when you bring it back, we can discuss any questions you have."

I look at her quizzically.

"Essentially, the document outlines the expectations of our sessions. You'll be forthcoming and honest with me. There will be no manipulation. No games. I'm here to help, but I'll revoke our time together if you don't respect the clear boundaries set within the contract."

I set the papers next to me and shove my hands between my knees. I can respect her wishes. If I were her, I'd give me rules too. Hell, I'd refuse to see me. Screw a contract allowing me a chance.

She takes a seat behind her desk, settling against the back of her chair. "Shall we begin?" she asks.

My face puckers.

"We can discuss whatever you'd like," she explains. "Only you know where you think your story begins."

I swallow, preparing myself for the reveal of some deeply rooted shit.

"It starts with my childhood," I say.

She smiles, nodding with understanding. "All the hardest stories do."

Olivia

Saturday, December 24th

I pour Zane a cup of coffee and rejoin him at the table.

"It's uncomfortable being here," I say, handing him the mug.

He nods and takes a sip.

"I get it," I reassure him. I get it more than he knows.

He does his best to conceal a pained face. It's just like sitting here with Elle. Both try to hide so much from the people who care about them the most. They're meant for each other. I just hope that's enough to bring them back together.

"I'm sorry that she used you like that," he says, staring into his steaming cup.

I gulp some of my water, stamping back the anxiety bubbling to the surface.

"She didn't use me, Zane," I say with indignation. "I was part of it."

"Sure," he scoffs. Clearly, he knows this part of his wife.

"No. It was my idea. I kind of ... blackmailed her."

His eyes shift up to me now. "You don't have to take the fall for her, Olivia."

"I'm not. She didn't tell this part of the story because we swore not to say anything to anyone. She kept her word."

He watches me. Curiosity pulls his eyebrows up.

"I'm not a liar," I tell him, but the truth settles in my bones—I've been lying far too long. Clearing my throat, I add, "I'm not lying about this."

His fingers drum on the surface of his mug. "Why?"

"I have debts. I took a loan from the wrong person to pay it off, but ... I needed money for IVF. I've been trying to get pregnant for a long time," I sigh.

"You're married to Travis?" he asks, seeking confirmation.

"I didn't know that he couldn't have kids. He's as good at lying as Elle." I chuckle nervously. "Better, actually."

His clenched jaw relaxes.

"You've been duped too," he says.

We are comrades.

"The difference is, I don't think Camden—Travis—ever did it for love." I pause, processing. "Elle did it *all* for love."

His lips turn up, faintly acknowledging me. His hurt isn't for nothing. He didn't waste years of marriage; he had years of marriage saturated in love. That's more than I can say.

Elle

Saturday, December 24th

Stepping out of Dr. Armstrong's office, I'm hit by a refreshing chill. That hour kicked my ass worse than any hard day at the gym.

I take my cell out and wait while it powers on. The last thing I needed during my session with Dr. Armstrong was a distraction. I need to make progress with her. With myself. Fast.

Notifications populate across the screen. Olivia's called several times. No voicemail. Only a single text:

Come back to the house. We have information.

"We" can only mean her and Zane. My heart thuds.

As I rush along the sidewalk to my car, a window display stops me in my tracks. I turn to face it. It's an intricately crafted mahogany board that rests on a prop. It's perfect.

Olivia answers my front door and ushers me in.

"You have to see what Zane's found," she says excitedly.

I take her in, confused. "Is Camden not…"

I don't know how to ask if he's not the criminal we think. We don't know what he is. All my childish delusions could be reality.

"Not what?" Olivia asks.

"Not ... bad?" It comes out like a fucking question.

"Oh, he's definitely shady," she answers.

This is an alternate universe. She's happy that her asshole husband is the bad guy, while I'm hoping he's innocent.

"Come on." She waves me in eagerly.

"He's buying and selling stolen diamonds through gaming channels under the name sadrabbit2001," Zane says, less enthused than Olivia. He's bending over his laptop at the counter. His gaze flashes in my direction, unwillingly, before returning to his computer screen.

"It doesn't look like he's working alone," Olivia adds. "From what Zane can tell, he's not in charge. He does the negotiations, but there are pauses that indicate he's running it by someone else. Someone who doesn't have..."

"An electronic footprint," Zane explains. "There's a lot more to unravel here, though. I'm going to have to open a formal investigation."

He straightens, looking at Olivia. "The only problem is, it'll potentially incriminate you."

She nods, unsurprised by this.

"No," I say, grabbing their attention. "You didn't do anything."

"But we have ..." she says, her eyes too reassuring.

Fuck that.

"No, what I've done is different," I protest.

No. It's not so different.

"What we've done," Olivia adds.

God, she's persistent. I glare at her, willing her silence.

"I told Zane." She crosses her arms, definitively taking her stance.

My stomach drops. I shoot her a look, then tentatively move my gaze to Zane. He's watching me. I look away.

Omitting the truth isn't the same as blatantly lying, but to him, there's little difference.

Reflexively, I run my hands through my hair, a nervous habit I once had in childhood. Hair falls as I comb through the tangles with my fingers. The strands land on the floor. "Sorry," I mumble.

I stand, retrieving the broom and begin sweeping the house. It does nothing to soothe the lump in my throat.

"Elle, it's okay," Zane says in a comforting tone.

"No, it isn't," I answer angrily.

There's movement around me, but I keep my eyes focused on my task. I won't cry. I won't crumble. Not now.

Warm arms scoop me up from behind, wrapping me in a tight hug. My body tenses in regret and warms with hope. I spin around and bury my face in his chest.

Zane strokes my hair as I sob, soaking his tee shirt with my tears.

"You put someone above yourself," he whispers between my whimpers.

"Sweeping?" My question muffles against him.

"The con. It wasn't even your idea..." he says, his words trailing off.

I pull back and peer up at him, my vision fogged with tears.

"I ... well ... my inheritance—she had it, and I wanted it." My confession comes out fragmented, chaotic.

"Olivia told me about that, too." He places his hands on my shoulders and slides them down my arms, clasping my hands.

"I'm not a good person." My body shakes with the words.

"You have your moments." He smiles genuinely.

"I've lied so much. I'm working on it, working through it, to be different, but..."

"But what?" He tilts his head, releasing my hands.

"What if you don't like who I really am? Who I *really* am?"

He takes a step forward, cupping my chin in his palm, tilting it upward. Our eyes meet, and we stay like this, silently speaking to one another.

"A thing you should know about me," I say, breaking the silence with my shaky voice, "is that for a long time, I've held myself to three constants—three things I'd always believed I needed to remember if I wanted to continue to exist."

I hold up one finger. "The first thing I know to be true is that people are blinded by love."

He opens his mouth to protest, but I keep going before I lose my nerve, holding up a second finger. "The second thing I know to be true: I'm one hell of a pretender."

"The third thing I know to be true," I say, holding up the third finger, "Is that people who know the real me wind up dead. I thought they did. It's why I never told you the truth. I'm so scared that letting down the walls of lies will put you more at risk than I already—"

He lowers his head, grazing his lips against mine. It sends a tingling through my cheeks and into my body.

Kiss me, please.

My lips part, and he presses his mouth to mine. Unable to contain my joy, I smile, breaking the kiss.

"I love you," I mutter into his cheek as he pulls me closer into a loving hug.

"Get a room," Olivia teases.

This can't be easy on her. Her world is collapsing. It's not going to come back together as neatly.

Neither will mine. This is only a moment. Only the beginning. I'm not sure that I'll succeed, either, but today I did well.

"A room it is," Zane says, pulling away from my grasp. He takes my hand and tugs me to our bedroom.

This is only a moment, but I'm going to make it memorable.

Olivia

Sunday, December 25th

C hristmas is only a day. That is what I keep telling myself. It's only a moment—a blip in time.

The needle inserts into my hip, and I wince with the sting of pain. This, too, is only a moment. It's temporary. It's a task, another day, leading to something greater that's worth more than anything else.

"Sorry," Elle says. The sting from the needle turns into the burn of medication.

She extracts it and hands the syringe to me, the needle uncapped. I slide the lock in place and shove it into the durable plastic container that the pharmacy gave me.

I hold a cotton ball over the injection site, keeping my face as relaxed as possible.

"Thanks," I say to her. "I'll be out in a second."

She leaves, shutting the bathroom door behind her.

Silence fills the tiny space. I lean against the gray counter. I've imagined this moment so many times, but never this way, under these circumstances, without Camden.

Still, I'm full of hope.

Next Christmas, no matter how exhausted and overworked I am, I'll be in front of a decorated tree with a beautiful baby, counting all my blessings.

Next Christmas...

My phone vibrates, and I jump, my nerves pricking under my skin. It's my father.

"What, Larry?" I say as I answer, annoyed.

"Merry Christmas, Darling." His tone is always the same: condescending and self-righteous.

"Merry Christmas," I mumble.

"Do you think that you could come see your old man today?" he asks, as if he wants to see me on a holiday—enjoy a family meal.

"Umm..."

"It would be great if you could," he says. "Let bygones be..."

"Be what? Let bygones be a money-delivering daughter ... or you'll tell everyone my dirty little secret?"

My heart thuds. I think of the manilla envelope Elle left under my pillow last night. It held her entire split, thirty-two thousand dollars. I could bring Larry his money ...

I spent years trying to fill the void he left, and even more years trying to rebuild a relationship with him. Buy his silence. Buy his love.

The only thing that I gained was his greed.

"I was going to let you pass with fifteen hundred, even though you know how this works. More time, more interest. With that attitude, I'm feeling the holiday spirit less."

My mouth falls open. Still the same father.

"Double or nothing," he says with a cackle. "Three thousand, or we bust your secrets wide open."

My free hand forms a fist. I close my eyes and take a slow, steady breath.

"Double or nothing, huh? That sounds good to me," I say, my voice steady and methodical. "How much money have I given you over the years? Fifty grand? One hundred grand?"

"Oh, I don't know." His voice is full of delight. He thinks I'm going to try to pay him off permanently.

Thanks to Elle, I know that's not the only option.

"What would you say that you've invested that money in, Larry? Stocks? Bonds?"

He laughs. "Hardly."

"Hmm ... hardly. Yeah, that's what I thought."

"What are you getting at?" he asks, growing weary.

"I'll take double or nothing. Let's say you write me a check for, what?" I shrug at my reflection. "Let's make it one-fifty. That seems fair. Though I'd be happy to get the bank statements out and do the math if you'd prefer."

"Or what?" he snarls into the phone.

"Or, I suppose I could have a conversation with the police. I'm sure they'd be thrilled to find out about your scams. Your tax evasion. The years of alimony and child support you skipped out on. The thing is, when they know where to find you, they can come after you."

I watch myself in the mirror as my lips twitch up into a grin.

"I don't want to have to do this," he says, wavering in his voice, "but I'll have to pay your mom a visit, and stop by your house, tell Camden about—"

"Go ahead, Larry. Tell whoever you want. I'm done playing games. I'm done trying to hide from the person I've always wanted to be."

There's a stammering on the other end of the phone. He's fresh out of ideas for how to corner me.

"Larry." My voice is stern.

"Yes?" he asks in a strained tone.

"Don't fucking call me again."

I slam the phone down, then pick it back up and turn it off. Taking several deep, slow, breaths, the red on my cheeks dissipates.

With some reluctance, I compose myself and join the lovebirds in the living room. It's amazing how they've been married for over a decade, and yet they look at each other in a way that I've never seen—so in love, so unwavering despite everything.

They don't have any presents under the tree, only a wooden chessboard. None of that seems to matter to them.

Elle stands, grabbing an envelope from the side table. She hands it to me. The bulk is heavy.

"A gift," she says.

My hands shake, making the envelope quiver.

She taps the envelope, then sinks back into the couch next to Zane.

Sliding my finger under the flap of the envelope, I slowly open it. The object inside is tightly wrapped in tissue paper. It unravels with some effort, revealing a necklace. The gold cross with an emerald in the center.

Perplexed, I lower onto the couch.

"Oh, I don't need this any—"

"It's the real one," Elle says.

My heart pounds.

"But—"

"That necklace means a lot to me. My mother gave it to me when I was twelve. It was a reminder that she'd always be with me, no matter what. I think she gave it to me when I told her how cruel the girls at school were. It ended up carrying me through far worse times. Now it's yours. To pull you through yours."

I search her eyes. Guilt wraps its tentacles around me.

"It's your family heirloom," I protest, unable to come up with another rejection.

"And you *are* family. Our family," she says with finality. "Just don't go out and sell it. Again..."

"Thank you," I squeak. "I ... I have something for you, too."

I clasp the chain around my neck, then stand and scurry to their guest room. The closet door slides back under my light touch, and I untuck the large jewelry box from underneath a blanket.

Returning to the living room, I hold it out to Elle. She slips out from under Zane's arm, her eyes wide.

I hope it's everything that I owe her.

She hesitates before finally taking it from me. Elle opens it and dumps the contents onto the coffee table in front of her. A bracelet falls on the floor, and I snatch it up, setting it gently on the tabletop.

"What are you doing?" Zane asks her, touching her arm with concern etched on his face.

Elle holds a finger up. Her gaze doesn't leave the box. She runs her hand along the inside. There's a rip as she separates the velvet fabric from the interior.

"Elle," I snap. "Why are you destroying..."

Her eyes widen as she extracts a key taped to a tiny note. She springs from her seat, and in one swift motion, she has her arms wrapped around me, squeezing me tight.

"Thank you," she whispers. "For everything."

Olivia

Wednesday, January 4th

"See you in an hour?" Elle asks as I climb out of her car.

"An hour." I shut the door, pulling my large hood over my head.

These days, I can never be too careful. I never know who's lurking, who's watching, following.

Dr. Foltz' office isn't busy today. Still, time crawls as I wait in the lobby, then as I wait in the cool room that the medical assistant places me in. The thin cloth gown does nothing to help, my arms pulled tight across my chest.

"Hello, Olivia," Dr. Foltz sings as she enters the room. "Ready to get started on more fertility meds?"

Her positivity is contagious. I smile broadly, my feet tapping with excitement.

"I am," I answer, straightening my spine.

"Sandra, my assistant, says you'd like to use donor sperm?"

I swallow the nerves that are rising.

"That's right," I say with the most confidence I can muster. "Donor J-335. I wrote it on a form..."

She thumbs through my chart. "Ah yes, here it is. Well, let's get an ultrasound, and then we'll begin stimulation." She claps her hands together, smiling. "You ready?"

"So ready," I respond.

She slips gloves on and preps the ultrasound. I watch the screen eagerly, just as I have so many times in the past, only this time there are no follicles to see yet. One more step, then trigger and egg retrieval.

When she's all done, she helps me sit up, beaming.

"New year, new adventures," Dr. Foltz says cheerily.

I chuckle. She has no idea how right she is.

When I leave the office, hood pulled over my head, I take a left out the building and push through the doors of my bank, then deposit thirty thousand dollars.

I tried to return this gift to Elle, but she insisted. She swore that she and Zane didn't need it. She said I would, and she's right.

It's also a framing in progress.

Jared did loan me money ... technically, I should have deposited it. Now, I have. It'll be trackable. Jared will inevitably check to see if I've completed my side of the bargain. I've paid him back. Soon, he'll see I've paid off my credit card debt, the accounts pending closure.

On paper, I'm a good wife to Camden. I've obeyed my "uncle-in-law."

That's how it'll look when the authorities track my private account as well. A payment received *after* completing the accounting for Jared. Just as he asked. Not a loan. A transaction with strings because he was doing me a favor, giving me a job so I could eliminate the debt bogging me and Camden down. I didn't know the implications of our arrangement until I found documents that didn't add up—or rather, did. I couldn't return the money to Jared when I discovered he was having me cook the books. That would cause Jared to become suspicious—so I kept it, and paid off my credit cards as he expected. That's what I'll say when I speak to the police.

Reporting Jared will be too easy. Camden, on the other hand ... Elle will take care of that.

As I step back onto the snow-covered sidewalk, I search my phone for Sarah's contact and listen while it rings.

"Hello?" Sarah answers, having to pick up her own calls while I'm out.

"Hi Sarah," I say, my words bright. "How are things there?"

I need to be cordial, because I need this job more than ever now, unfortunately.

"When are you coming back?" She's straight to the point.

My chest tightens.

"I'll be back tomorrow. Thank you for letting me have this time off."

"It's not like I had a choice," she mumbles. "You had the vacation time."

I had an excessive amount of PTO accumulated, but I appreciate her approving it.

"I needed to check in with you before the end of the pay cycle. I need to switch to paper checks for now," I explain. "We're—I'm—switching banks."

Camden and I have been using a *joint* account since we've gotten together. It's only in my name, and now I know why.

"Is that all?" she asks, irritation ringing in her voice.

"No," I say, sucking in a courageous breath. "We can talk about this tomorrow, but I wanted to give you a warning that I'll be asking for a raise. It's long overdue. We both know it. I wanted to give you the time to think about how much you'd like to offer."

Elle insisted I do it this way. She coached me through it.

The silence on the line sets my nerves ablaze. I second-guess this move and start thinking of a way to retract my request when there's a deep sigh on the other end.

"Alright," Sarah says calmly. "See you tomorrow."

The expanse in my chest is delightful. Hope. For a baby. For a future. For a final con.

Elle

Wednesday, January 4th

"It's quiet around here," Zane says, handing me a snifter of bourbon.

"Olivia said she needed to go *home* and resume life as usual," I say, then hold the glass to my lips and inhale the hints of smoke, tobacco, and oak.

I've imagined this moment too many times, often with gritted teeth, as Zane handed me wine.

"Somebody's bitter." Zane sits facing me on the couch and squeezes my shoulder.

"I'd hardly call that hell a home, but to each their own, and she's right; we need her to pretend all is normal."

I lift my glass.

"What are we toasting?" He chuckles.

"Here's to the quiet, to worrying about grown-ass women ... and to a decade of marriage."

"Cheers to that." He clinks his glass with mine.

We both take a sip.

"Now that it's just us," Zane says, kicking his feet up, "tell me about New York."

I've known this was coming, but I put it off under the guise of protecting Olivia in her fragile state. I take a long pull of bourbon and clear my throat.

"My ex came after us. He attacked me. I'm pretty sure that he wanted to kill me."

He clenches and unclenches his jaw. His knuckles pale as he grasps his glass tight.

My ribs constrict my lungs. He could stand up right now and walk out.

"Sam," he says in a low rumble.

His is a name that haunts him more than it does me—keeps him moving us annually.

"There's more." I bite my lip. "He was calling me. Daily. For weeks beforehand."

Zane's eyes cut through me. I close my eyes so that I can get through the rest.

"I didn't know it that was him. Not officially. Until I was in New York."

"What did he want?" he asks, trying to be chill, but his shoulders give his tension away.

It's an excellent question that we both are asking, and both know the answer to: revenge.

"He wanted to know what I was doing in New York."

"That's something that he and I have in common," Zane says curtly.

Fuck. I walked right into that one.

"He admitted that someone gave me up, but he didn't say who," I confess, my gaze falling. "I won't go back."

It stings, because this time I mean it. This next piece will sting more.

"The apartment that I told you I rented—"

"The apartment that you actually owned," he shoots back.

I gulp.

"I still own it," I say, wincing. "I won't go back, but that means you'll have to sell it."

The stricture on my ribcage tightens. My breaths shallow.

My home is here, with Zane. Zane *is* my home.

My apartment—the place that was always mine—isn't. I've missed reality all along, but letting go of the thing that I held onto so tightly—fearing that I wouldn't survive without it —will be really hard.

Zane sets his drink down on the end table and awkwardly crawls across the couch until there are only inches between us. He takes my face in his hands, forcing me to meet his gaze.

"We can keep it, if you want to," he says, kissing me gently, "but it's got to be worth a fortune."

I let out raw laughter filled with discomfort and acknowledgment. It really is like sitting on a winning lottery ticket.

"Get your new chessboard. I'll play you for it," I say, standing and crossing to the chess table, already knowing that I'll let him win.

Olivia

Friday, January 13th

Being back at the house with Camden is no different than when I left. When I first got back, he asked about my trip, but he didn't even listen to my lie about how busy it was visiting my parents.

Now, he moves about just as he always did, but he occasionally pauses to run his fingers along my back and gaze at me with those piercing blue eyes.

Whenever he's out of the house, I sort through my things. Today, I stumble across the Citizen watch I bought for him—the gift that may have started all of this. I slip it on my wrist, then tuck essentials into my luggage, because I'm not exactly sure what comes next and whether I'll need to leave.

This part is hard. I loved—love—him so much.

It's incredible to be so enamored with someone—to long for them—and yet, know that they're taking advantage of you. I'll never know how much, or how little, he loves me. I may never know if he ever loved me at all.

It doesn't matter. Not really. None of it does. I can't erase the lies. They're too large—too many. They weren't ever to protect me.

His lies are to protect him.

And yet, a familiar ache—a longing to be near him is still etched onto every fiber of my being.

Tomorrow, I'll give myself a trigger injection. The ultrasound showed follicles that are nearly ready. All I need to do is force ovulation with the synthetic hCG hormone. Tomorrow, at 9 p.m., I'll insert the final needle into my hip. Monday morning, my eggs will be retrieved and will be inoculated with donor sperm.

That's tomorrow.

Tonight, I pour a glass of wine to soothe my nerves and relieve the hormonal mood swings. I've made dinner, and I've begged Camden to sit with me to eat, and he's agreed.

Tonight, I'll love my husband. As he was. Because come Monday, all bets are off.

"How's work?" I ask nervously across our large farmhouse table.

The food on my plate appears touched by my incessant pushing and twirling, but I've only taken a few tiny bites.

He shrugs and takes a swig of his beer, then rambles about his job that doesn't exist.

Tonight, I pretend everything that he says is the truth because more than anything, I wish it were.

"You've been so busy lately. I miss you," I say.

My stomach clenches as the last words echo in my mind. I do miss him.

His bright blue eyes reflect the desire that I have for him.

"I've missed you, too."

The words stick to me, allowing me a moment to believe that he does love me.

I sip slowly from the crystal wine glass, letting the remainder of the red trickle over my tongue. The taste of berries and spices plays with my senses.

When it's gone, I stand and walk around the table, keeping eye contact with Camden, and slide onto his lap. I push my sweater up my arm, unclasp the watch that was hiding under it, then place it on Camden's wrist.

"What's this for?" he asks, a smile tugging at his lips.

"It's a gift—a thank you, for all the time you've given me," I whisper into his ear.

He nuzzles his lips into the curve of my neck, and a tingling erupts in my belly, spreading through my abdomen and stopping between my legs. I slide my fingers along the waist of his jeans, letting my touch skim lightly along his skin. His breath changes, more controlled, shallow.

He takes my hand, pulling it gently until I stand. He gets up, runs his thumb across my cheek, then leads me to our suite and eases me onto our bed.

It's dark here. He won't be able to see the bruises from my injections, or the extra cellulite around my hips, but the darkness isn't only a blessing for hiding my secrets. In the dark, every touch, every kiss, will feel more like a promise and less like the reality it is.

Tonight, we are together as we used to be.

Dear Elle and Travis,

If you're reading this, your father and I are dead. It seems silly to write it down, but it gives me the peace needed to admit all of this, and to do right by you two.

I'm sorry. I hoped it wouldn't come down to this, but some things we can't anticipate, no matter how obvious it becomes later on.

We only wanted what was best for you two. And when we had to choose between our lives, or a better future for our children, we knew right away—we'd choose you. We're giving you a different opportunity now. A life without regret, corruption, and crime.

This isn't much, but it should be enough to get you on your feet. Start something real. Something successful and stable. It's what we'd hoped to do as a family before we realized what we'd gotten into.

And when you're ready, this should be all you'll need to take down the man who had us killed.

Love, Mom

Elle

Saturday, January 14th

The letter from my mother feels insignificant between my fingers. Zane's hand resting on the small of my back is a relative thing. Distant. Like it's all a dream.

It's not.

Mom and Dad knew they were going to die. It wasn't my fault. They didn't get hit by a drunk driver on the way to meet my demands.

It didn't matter what they were doing, or where they were driving. It was going to happen.

And I have the threats. The bookkeeping. The recorder, tape still intact, that one of them secretly used to incriminate one man.

Camden's Uncle Jared.

"Elle," Zane whispers, pulling me close. "Are you okay?"

He's been by my side for the last half hour while I read the note on repeat. Here in the bank's private room, the pieces of my parents' past surrounding me.

If I could go back in time, what could I have done? My parents helped run an illegal scheme with this man. They lost—he capitalized.

"I'm okay, Love." He rubs my back. "I *will* be okay," I add, knowing that we both need to hear it.

My nerves poke and prod to remind me of my existence. Every breath is intentional, calculated, otherwise, I might hyperventilate.

"This will says that you own a building in Leesburg, and a quarter of a million dollars."

I peel my eyes from the letter and look at the document in his hands.

"It says what?"

"She did say that she was going to set you up for success..."

I let out a guttural sob that spirals into laughter.

"Elle," Zane says again, concerned.

I can't put it into words even if I wanted to.

There were so many things that I didn't have to do, and ways that I didn't have to live. The lies I've told myself all these years, and the lies I've told others to keep from hurting them.

"It could have all been erased if I'd been able to come here ..." My words catch. "if I could have seen these things first, if Travis hadn't played dead ..."

Through the blur of tears, I see Zane's face shift.

I place my hand on his cheek. "I'd do it all again, for you."

He leans down and kisses me gently. Zane isn't the only thing that I would have missed out on. With this information, I would have never discovered New York, or Eddy and Ricardo's undying love for a daughter that they never knew they wanted ... I would have never met Olivia—my sister.

"Holy fuck," I say, squeezing Zane's arm. "I own a storefront in Leesburg."

My skin tingles as it gains goosebumps. This is what I've been searching for.

"Zane," I say, pulling back to look him in the eyes. "I don't want to leave Leesburg. Please, can we stop running?"

He laces his fingers with mine and drops his gaze, taking in our intertwined hands.

Suddenly, I'm so fucking thirsty, but I don't dare move, because what if I ruin the moment and make him think I'm less invested? The only thing I know is that I'm allowing myself to be uncertain for the first time in forever.

He returns his gaze to mine. "I'd like that," he says, sucking in a breath. "But, on so many conditions. There's still the matter of Sam, and Travis ... and whatever the hell is going on."

I nod. "I'll take a maybe. Also, I think I may have an idea who tipped off Sam ... It all makes sense, the timing of the gang falling under new leadership just before Travis' disappearance. Sam slipping me a roofie the night it all went down ..."

"Jared," Zane says.

"A master puppeteer all along."

He smiles and begins collecting items from the counter.

"I need something else, Love," I say, helping him collect the documents. "I need you to anonymously turn in this evidence."

In all the unspoken things between us—the fear, the uncertainty, the hope—we lean on one another, sealing our fate with love.

Elle

Friday, January 20th

E verybody has something that they excel at. Olivia's extraordinary with details. Her documentation of our business from day one has been ironclad.

And I'm an excellent liar.

> The egg transfer is complete.

Olivia's text sends a thrill through me. She's getting what she wants; now it's my turn.

I push through the glass door, skirting around a stumbling man in handcuffs being guided by a police officer. His messy, graying hair and bloodshot eyes droop as the officer buzzes through a door and leads him inside.

When it's my turn, I step up to the window and say, "I'd like to file a complaint."

The officer behind the window doesn't look up from her computer. "What about, ma'am?"

I ignore her disdain—for her job, for me, or both—and continue, "I don't know what type of crime it is exactly."

A felony, Class C.

She sighs. "How about you start with what happened."

I pucker my cheeks, feigning concern. "I think my business partner's husband stole from our clients. Diamonds, mostly. We do appraisals and repairs, and I caught variations in some items before returning them."

She tilts her head, looking at me. She isn't convinced yet, but she will be.

"How much do you think was stolen?" she asks, monotone.

"I don't know how many pieces were compromised exactly, but I think there were at least ten items, maybe as many as twenty," I say, tapping my index finger to my chin as I pretend to think. "Depending on how many diamonds were stolen and the quality of each, the value could span from fifteen thousand to one hundred and fifty thousand."

"Alright, I'll need you to fill out this form, please." She hands me a clipboard.

I take a seat on a metal chair among a couple of other people weary and waiting for something—none of which is my business nor interests me in the slightest.

The form is daunting. For the potential loss that we're claiming, this won't take off right away. At best, if I report the right things, they'll be compelled to investigate sooner.

At worst, this form will help us file insurance claims for our wronged customers, to clear Olivia's conscience and our names. At best, two assholes will go down.

To get the ball rolling, Olivia filed an anonymous complaint from the public library to the Better Business Bureau a couple of days ago. She reported oddities regarding Jared's storage unit purchases that could have been observed by his competition. It isn't much, but it's something.

I double-check the form as I get back in line. When the same officer's window opens, I hand my clipboard back to her. She skims over it, making sure that I have filled it out correctly, but something catches her eye, and she stops.

"Camden Bradley?" she asks, keeping her head tilted down but pulling her gaze up to me.

"That's correct. My business partner's name is Olivia Bradley."

We've talked about having to be forthcoming with our names and our business. Still, it's an uncomfortable confession.

"Hmm," she says, grabbing a card from beside her keyboard. She scribbles on the small piece of cardstock.

My body lightens. That hum sounded promising.

"Here's the case number. If you don't hear from someone within twenty-four hours, please call the number on the card and check-in."

"Thank you," I say humbly and turn to go.

I'm pulling onto the street when my phone rings.

"Mrs. Crawford?" a man asks on the other end.

"Yes?" I answer.

"I'm Detective Carlos Sanchez. Can we talk? I can come to you."

"Are you ready?" I ask Olivia, squeezing her arm.

"I think so," she says, breathless.

Detective Sanchez agreed to speak to us at the same time. Since we're business partners, and Olivia is as innocent as I am. She's also scared, in need of emotional support and a safe place to speak.

She's prepared for further questioning. She's married to Camden Bradley—who isn't my brother. I've never even met the guy. Naturally, I play only a small part in this.

The detective at the door can't be older than thirty. His dark hair and olive skin are shiny. His eyes are tired. He steps inside and takes each of our hands in turn as we introduce ourselves.

As I close the door, a prickling sensation crawls up my spine. He drives a black sedan.

Olivia gives her best fake smile, like the one she gives her friends. She's physically present, but there's an absence in her eyes.

"Can I get you something to drink?" I ask, crossing the floor to the kitchen.

"No, that's alright," Detective Sanchez says in a gruff voice.

I pour a glass of water and set it casually in front of him. "Just in case."

He nods his appreciation, and I settle in across from him in the spot next to Olivia.

"Nice home you have here," he says.

Giving my warmest smile, I say, "Thank you ... We can skip the formalities if you'd like."

He releases a breath, his shoulders loosening.

"So, you two have a jewelry appraisal and repair business?" the detective asks.

We nod simultaneously.

"My friends are big on home shopping parties where the products come to them, so we thought it would be a great way to bring them the services we offer," Olivia says, animating with her hands.

She's nervous.

"We have been storing pieces at Olivia's house after I repair them," I say. "That way, things don't get piled up here. Olivia's house is more secure, with a great alarm system, and she typically does the returns. Recently, I tagged along and noticed that some of the gems I'd already cleaned and appraised looked different."

He tilts his head and removes a pen and paper from his pocket, making a note of something.

"I thought it was my eyes playing tricks on me, reflecting through the silicon bags," I continue, "but then, I sent one of my own pieces to

Olivia's house with some of the items so that she could pack it with our display things and several stones were removed from it."

Extracting a bracelet from my pocket, I set it on the table in front of him.

"See these," I say, pointing to four stones in a bracelet I made last week. "These were diamonds, but now they're cubic zirconia."

"They look the same," he says, puzzled.

"Yes, they do, but they aren't."

Detective Sanchez peers at Olivia. "What did you say your husband does?"

I hate the question. She never said what Camden does, and he's never asked.

"He's a gaming engineer. He helps create different video games. Other times, he's a tester."

The detective's eyes light up, presumably from an interest in gaming, but there's something else there. It's a different type of intrigue.

"What kind of games?" he asks.

"Console systems and online games, mostly," Olivia answers.

A grin crosses his face. He covers it with one of his hands, scrunching his lips between his pointer finger and thumb.

"Do you know who your husband works for?" He positions his pen, ready to write.

"He gets different contracts. He works for himself, but then he collaborates, and he's hired for different jobs."

The detective twists his lips and drums the pen against the table, thinking.

"Have you ever heard the name Jared Libby?" he asks, his pen beating faster.

A new recognition crosses Olivia's face. My chest tightens. I didn't tell her about the evidence in the lockbox. My mom's records revealed

Jared's last name: Libby, not Bradley. While a coincidence would have been nice—a common first name, and a good old mix-up—I doubted it. Especially with the diamonds in Olivia's basement.

She takes a breath, her cheeks reddening. "He gets a call from a Libby sometimes. I'd always assumed ..."

"He has an uncle named Jared, though. Jared Bradley. Same last name as my husband."

Detective Sanchez leans back in the chair across from us, then rethinks his position and leans forward, laying his arms in front of him on the table. The dark circles under his eyes are more prominent in the glow of the dining room light.

"We believe that your husband works for Jared Libby, a prominent counterfeit jewelry dealer we've been following. In our investigations, we've noted the presence of your husband, Camden Bradley."

"You think Jared Bradley is Jared Libby? My husband is lying to me about an uncle?" Olivia's shaky.

"That's the other thing, Mrs. Bradley ... I don't think that the Bradleys exist at all."

Silence blankets the room. Detective Sanchez and Olivia stare at one another.

"What do you mean the Bradleys don't exist?" I say, feigning confusion. "Olivia is a Bradley. She married one. How is that possible?"

His eyes don't leave Olivia.

"Is there a chance that you know what his real name is?"

"I ... I married Camden Bradley ..."

"Detective, please," I demand, "We came to you. What do you need from us to—"

"He doesn't have a bank account," Olivia says. "He buys things in cash. I file my tax returns—as Olivia Bradley—on my own. Camden bought our house ... with cash. But all the utilities are in my name. I assure you, I exist. But my husband ... I'm not so sure." She leans her face into her hands, shaking her head. "I've been confused for a while. I've been unsure about who he is. I never suspected that he'd make up an identity."

She looks up, her eyes red, her makeup smudged. I wrap my arm around her and pull her to my side.

The detective opens a manila folder, revealing photos. On top, there's one of Olivia. I stand, walking into the kitchen. I cannot see photos of Camden. I can't admit that he's my dead brother. Not today.

"Is this Camden?" Detective Sanchez asks Olivia.

"That's him," she whispers. "Have you been *following* us?"

I glance toward them. He's nodding his head.

"For some time," he says. "This is bigger than a few diamonds missing from your friends' bracelets."

He pulls out another photo. Her eyes widen.

"That's him, and that box ... we have several in the basement of our house."

"Thank you." He slips the photos back into the folder and stacks his things neatly.

I make myself look busy, cleaning.

Detective Sanchez rises, gathering his things. He sets his briefcase on his chair and reaches for the glass of water I left for him. He chugs it.

"Thank you, ladies," he says, sliding the strap of his briefcase on his shoulder. "Olivia, do you think that you could show me those boxes?"

She nods vigorously and gets up to grab her coat. I can't imagine her not complying with the authorities.

He turns, holding out his business card.

"Thank you," I say, taking the card. I glance toward Olivia, then lower my voice. "Have you been here too? Watching my house?"

His brows wrinkle as he shakes his head.

"No. We haven't been following Mrs. Bradley. There's been no indication. There would be no reason to watch you."

I nod appreciatively. No need for him to have further concerns. I know who's been watching me.

They leave together in his black sedan. The aching—an urge to protect her—is strong, but she needs to do this on her own, and I have to trust that she will get it right. I hope Travis isn't there when they arrive. As I turn around to head back inside, my phone pings.

Can I stay there tonight?

Olivia.

"Yes." I answer. I can't help it if our raggedy guest mattress is more comfortable than her premium king-sized bed.

Dear Travis,

It's time. I'm coming for you.

~ Elle, January 2023

Olivia

Wednesday, February 1st

I'm officially, maybe, pregnant. I've been nauseated all morning with painful pelvic cramps that aren't like those that accompany each period. And not like the times I've simply imagined it. They aren't the barbed wire pain of endometriosis, either.

My hopes aren't up. I won't let them be. And I can't test. Not yet. Two more days. My doctor is more confident than I am that the embryo transfer will lead to a successful pregnancy. After all this time, it's hard to believe.

"Coffee?" Sarah asks, setting a mug down in front of me.

She's been kind lately. I guess taking time off and getting a raise comes with more respect.

My stomach flips at the first hint of arabica, and I put my hand to my mouth and dash down the hall to the restroom. This time, it's not just nausea. As I vomit in the office toilet, my chest warms. It's not a burn from the acid, but the first allowance of hope—the very hope I've refused myself. I run a toothbrush and minty paste through my mouth, thankful I'm "so weird," as Elle puts it, and keep supplies on hand.

Lately, I've spent my evenings at Elle's house, returning to mine at night. Detective Sanchez suggested my safety first, but also encouraged life as normal, to reduce suspicion.

Camden's fallen back into his normal routine of ignoring me to focus on his "work." I don't protest. I know what's coming, so I take it in stride, grateful for the distance from him—for my heart.

Elle says revenge is sweet, but so far, it's only bitter.

"Two more days," I say, letting myself into Elle's house.

"Until what?" Elle asks, peering over her book.

"I threw up at the smell of coffee today," I announce proudly.

She doesn't offer a follow-up, and there's no question in her expression. She asks questions out loud at times. I think for show. I'm not sure if Elle ever asks questions, though. She always just ... knows.

She sets her book down and gestures to the opposite end of the couch. She clicks on the television, letting Saturday Night Live spring to life on the screen.

"Two more days," she says.

One of the comedians on screen is reading a letter to the audience.

"Can I ask you something?" I ask, leaning my chin into the pillow I've pulled to my lap.

"Shoot," Elle says, turning the volume down.

"Why did you sign your letters with an L?" I draw the letter in the air between us.

"Oh, that." Elle chuckles. "My parents named me Elizabeth, which became Lizzie. Travis always called me L."

Her smile is warm as she recalls moments of happiness with a brother who no longer exists.

"When Zane and I got married, I was technically Elizabeth, and he was Xander. We both changed our first names when I changed my last. Zane did everything he could think of to protect me."

I laugh. She hardly needs protection.

"The names fit. I'd often called him Zane, and because I was 'L,'" she says, making air quotes, "it just made sense to be Elle ... plus, t was a way to commit to each other beyond our vows. Some people get tattoos. We changed our names."

They're the perfect love story.

"Elle," I say, my body alive with anticipation. "Zane and I have been scheming. When everything is complete, my dog—Camden's dog—will need a home. Zane thinks you would be the perfect person to adopt Bella."

She squeaks and covers her mouth. If I'd ever thought I'd seen Elle surprised, I know that I haven't until this moment.

"You're not serious," Elle says, her eyes shimmering with tears.

"I know it's weird since Bella is Camden's, and that's well ..." I wave my arms since there are no words for this. "You can say no, if you don't think—"

"No! I mean, yes. I do want her," she says, her voice shaky. "Thank you."

She vibrates next to me, her excitement palpable, as she turns to face the TV.

I return my gaze to the television, but Elle doesn't turn it back up.

"My news is small, in comparison, but I was thinking," Elle says, ignoring the commentary on the T.V. "Maybe we could start an actual business. This time, in a storefront. I could use a business manager. Or, a partner, if you're up to it."

A jewelry store. I chew on the idea for a moment.

"Do you think we'd be any good?" I ask.

"With me making jewelry, it's impossible not to be great, as long as there is someone around to keep me in line. And if that person also has mad business skills ..."

Pride flutters through my core.

It would be great. We both know it.

"Also, I may have recently come into an inheritance," Elle says, grinning.

My muscles twitch. "You aren't selling your family heirlooms?"

"God, no." She chuckles deviously. "Remember the key from the jewelry box? It was magic. It's given me a storefront deed and a quarter of a million dollars."

Olivia

Friday, February 3rd

"It's so good to see you," Charlie trills, as she makes her way through the coffee shop crowd with her large paper cup.

I hold my own tightly, the peppermint tea wafting to my nose and soothing my nausea.

"Good to see you, too," I say with a matched vibrato.

"We haven't done this in so long." Charlie pulls her face into a pout.

"We should do it more often." I can give false sentiments, too.

She flops into the seat across from me and leans in. "So, how are you?"

"I'm great, actually," I answer. "Camden and I have been working on our marriage lately, and it feels good. It's like I have the old Camden back, you know?"

She gives me a knowing nod.

She has no idea. No *fucking* idea, Elle would say.

"Part of the steps we've been taking is reconciling things with each other, and ourselves," I explain.

Her face darkens. "He told you ..."

I nod. My mouth dries. He hasn't told me anything.

"It was a long time ago, before you two got together ..."

I tilt my head. The truth. Give me the truth.

"Really?" I ask, questioning her honesty.

"I swear," she says, shifting uncomfortably.

I pat her hand, pretending I believe her.

"I have news," I say, beaming.

"News? Please share." She's delighted I'm changing the subject.

I take a breath, simultaneously rejoicing and preparing myself.

"I'm pregnant. Camden and I are having a baby," I say, my voice squeaking.

Her eyes grow wide. Her breaths are short—frequent.

"He said that he couldn't ..."

My chest tightens. Revenge is bittersweet, isn't it?

I knit my eyebrows together, acting confused.

"He couldn't what? What are you talking about?" I ask her, my voice full of concern.

She's notably struggling to breathe now, having a full-blown panic attack. She waves her hand in front of her face and leans over her knees.

"Charlie? Are you okay?" I bite my lip to suppress a smile.

"He said that he couldn't have kids," she gasps. "He said that he couldn't. Asked me not to do a genetic test. Gave me a ..."

A bracelet. He gave her a bracelet that she thought was real.

I put my hand over my mouth, concealing my grin. Pretending to be horrified.

"You said that it was a long time ago," I say with so much judgment.

"I'm so sorry," she chokes out, beginning to sob.

"You slept with my husband," I say loudly.

Her eyes dart around the room, wild with fear.

"Please," she whispers. "Please don't tell Billy. Camden reassured me that we didn't need a genetic test. He basically refused. He said that he couldn't ... My kids are Billy's ... they have to be."

I don't conceal my lips as they quirk up this time.

"Camden said that he couldn't. Did you ever think that he told you that because he didn't want any with you?" I snap, rising from my chair.

Billy will be crushed when she pushes for DNA tests, absolutely destroyed. I'd worry about this part if there was a possibility the kids were Camden's. But Billy's a good man. A great man. He deserves the truth so that he can find someone who will love him like he loves—with his whole heart.

I leave her frozen in her chair, her mouth agape. I have someplace to be.

Elle

Friday, February 3rd

There aren't many people in the boxing gym today. That saves me some trouble.

I warm up on the bags, kicking and punching to stretch out and activate my muscles. My punching bag is close to the ring, where two men are dancing around each other.

Men do that. Dancing is their specialty, for instance, creating pyramid schemes and calling them MLMs so that they can prey on women's insecurities—placing the wealthy housewives at the top of their *teams* to entice the desperate—making rich men even richer under the ruse of female-run businesses.

Or, in this instance, setting up multiple fake LLCs to funnel money overseas, then buying and selling stolen diamonds that "accidently" fell off freight liners between ports.

One of the men on the platform is an expert at dancing. When he knocks the other down, counting to his not-so-peaceful victory, I make my way to the ring.

I shove the bite guard into my mouth, between the slits in my helmet, and climb onto the platform.

"I'm not done," a familiar voice says.

"I'm not asking you to leave," I say, my mouthguard slurring my words and making me spit. "You and me." I nod my head, pulling my gloves on.

"You're a girl," he chides.

"Then you might have a chance." Smack talk was always a trigger when we were kids, and it seems to be working now, too.

A bell chimes, and he begins his bouncing and sashaying around the ring. I waste no time. I take a swing, connecting my glove with the side of his helmet.

Today, I don't give a fuck about rules. This first strike is for Olivia—all the lies he told her, and the hell he put her through.

He stumbles backward, regaining his footing. He's not fast enough. I strike again—for the years of unsuccessful fertility treatments that he put Olivia through.

"What the fuck?" he mumbles, straightening himself again.

"You spend too much time sidestepping," I tell him, taking another swing.

This time, when he stumbles, I spin, my foot connecting with his body. He loses his footing and hits the ground.

For stealing my shit.

I back off, allowing him to stand again.

As soon as his gloves are in front of his jawline, he tries to swing at me, but I duck and spin through the move, striking him again.

For faking your own death and leaving me all alone.

When he lands on the ground, he gasps for air, not scrambling up like the time before.

I move slowly, stepping over him and squatting down. I slam my glove into the mat, counting down to his defeat.

"Where did you learn to fight like that?" he gasps.

Locking my eyes with his, I yank my gloves off and remove the mouthguard before slipping off my helmet. His eyes widen with fear, and he tries to get up, but I shove his shoulder down.

"From you." I make my words like ice so they'll chill as they sink in.

Leaning over him, I bring my face within inches of his.

"Tell me, where'd you learn to sell counterfeit jewelry?" I ask in a low rumble.

"From you," he spits back, a cackle rising from his chest.

"Really?" I let a purposeful grin cross my face. "I heard you're too cowardly to work for yourself. Instead, you let someone else boss you around."

He stirs underneath me, a fresh rage boiling from his core.

"Libby made me a great deal. It's the same one he made our parents. The difference is, I was smart enough to take it."

Anger pulsates through me. I shove him into the mat, pressing against his throat.

His face turns red as his oxygen supply drops.

"I tried ... to protect ... you." His raspy tone is colder than my blood, pleading for redemption.

"No, you protected yourself and took everything—leaving me for dead. It didn't work, did it?"

He can't speak now; I'm pressing too hard.

"Elle," a calm voice calls from behind me. It's my reminder.

I give one final shove, then release him, standing and backing away. He gasps and chokes on air, his hand to his throat.

"Olivia?" he finally manages to say as I climb out of the ring.

She tosses a white stick at him.

"Let's go," she whispers, steering me toward the door.

I stare over my shoulder at him, unable to walk away with the confidence that she has. As the officers pass us, running to the ring where Travis is lying on his side, I finally pull my eyes from him.

"You're pregnant?!" he shouts after us.

Olivia lifts her arm and waves, a man's watch shifting on her wrist as she does.

"Why do you have my watch?" Camden says with exasperation.

She turns back toward him, her eyes locking with his.

"For all the time you stole from me," she says, then spins around and links her arm with mine. "Ready to get home? There's a pup waiting for you."

My chest is full as I settle into an existence that's focused on neither lies nor revenge.

"But first, there's a little shop down the road..." I say with excitement. "It's full of baby things. Maybe you know it. I'd like to take you there."

She squeezes my arm. "Yes, please."

To my future child,

You may not ever know all the things I've been through, but don't fret that I've kept them from you. It's all to protect you. I don't want you to think that you come from a faulty foundation. There is nothing faulty about you. For me, it was always you. I always chose you. And I will forever choose you.
Please know, no matter what challenges we may face, we'll conquer them together.
If I could give you only one thing, it would be this wisdom: know your worth. Speak your mind. Be yourself. Don't ever let anyone hold you back.
I will always love you. I will always protect you. You are my world, the love of my life.

~ Love, Mom, May 2023

Elle

Saturday, May 13th

My light catches something white in the duct of Camden's office. Camden, because here, he's never been Travis.

Tingling travels up my spine. Shit. I hate when I'm right.

"Olivia, do you have a screwdriver?!" I shout down the hall.

"Umm ... what for?" she calls back.

"Ask Zane to grab one from the car, would you," I ask, squinting into the dark space.

The house is packed up. This is a final comb-through to make sure that we haven't missed anything. It's no longer Olivia's. It never really was. It was in Jared's name since Camden doesn't exist, same as his asinine car.

Turns out what's his was not hers, and vice versa. He can't touch her accounts. Not that he'd have use for money in prison.

"Here you go," she huffs, waddling into the room.

She's holding the bottom of her belly, rubbing it. It's been a long day.

"Thanks," I say, reaching from the ladder to take it from her.

I jam it into the first screw holding the grate in place on the ceiling.

"What is it?" Olivia asks, out of breath.

"Not sure," I say, handing her the screw.

I remove one more from the same side and pull down gently until a large white envelope falls along the metal. Retrieving it, I return the grate and trade Olivia the envelope for the screws.

She grunts behind me, and I glance back to see her lowering onto the floor.

"They're letters," she says.

"No shit," I laugh, tightening the screws in place. "Who are they to?"

"Me. And you."

My stomach drops as unwanted anticipation travels through me. I've already come to terms with who my brother is, but the idea of finding out something new is unnerving, especially if it fucks with Olivia's mind.

I lower myself down the ladder and fold it up, leaning it against the wall.

"Good thing you thought to leave the ladder. Otherwise—"

"Otherwise, you wouldn't have started snooping around."

"Yeah," I answer, and plop onto the floor next to her, bumping her shoulder with mine.

I guess this old habit refused to die for him too. "Why didn't the police find these?" she whispers.

I take one from her, addressed to me. "Because they weren't looking for...I don't even know what this is. An apology?"

She sits in silence, reading one of the letters from her stack.

"This one's more like a hate letter," she says, her lip quivering. "He ... he wasn't in love with me."

I take the stack from her and begin thumbing through it. She sits next to me, defeated, choking back a sob.

"According to this one, he did," I tell her, patting her knee.

I turn to her and take in her blotchy face.

"You know what this looks like to me?" I ask, wrapping my arm around her.

She tilts her head, resting it against my shoulder.

"What?" she sobs.

"This—my lovely sister—is closure."

Elle

Tuesday, July 11th

The gray concrete building sends chills up my spine. It's a reminder of a past that I'd rather forget.

"Mrs. Crawford," a guard calls.

My turn.

The heavy security door buzzes, then clicks, and she waves me back to a room with a table and two chairs. The air is musty with hints of bleach, making my nose scrunch involuntarily.

I sit on the cool metal chair and drum my foot on the ground. Not a fucking soul visited me in juvie, aside from the state-appointed lawyer that showed up twice in three years.

The guards bring a balding man with an expanding stomach into the room. They sit him down, locking his cuffs to the table between us. The skin on his face, once tight, is now hanging loose, and gray stubble runs across his jaw and onto his neck. The orange jumpsuit and fluorescent lights sallow his skin.

But his eyes ... they're the same dark orbs I saw from the alley and again at the nail salon. They are the same eyes that I recall from my childhood—now placed in a memory of the man from our trip to Leesburg who propositioned my parents with a business opportunity.

"Lizzie Monroe. The one who put me here." He rubs his hands together,

"I'd say that you did that on your own."

"Ah, but you were sour that I stole your brother, so you played a petty game of revenge." He sneers.

I thread my fingers together between my knees, stabbing a thumb into the palm of the other hand. The pain reminds me why I'm here.

"You took more than my brother." My voice is low and methodical. "But I'd love clarity on that. Were you always into the drug game? Or did you have a special attraction for the pot business Sam was running."

"Sam," he cackles, slouching in his metal chair. "That idiot was barely running that gang. Seemed to me an itty-bitty teenage queen was the one who made it successful. So successful, in fact, that the gang stopped flying under the radar. The police needed a bit more to nail them all to the ground than some measly marijuana. A touch of heroin, a scoop of cocaine ... a dash of Rohypnol, and a dead rat made the recipe sing."

I clench my jaw, preventing a more appropriate reaction from surfacing.

"Sam was an idiot," he continues, "but not a complete idiot. He knew that you were too good for him, that you'd leave, or worse, take over. Sam is driven by power, and he didn't want you taking it from him. It was so simple; I just needed to plant the seed and the product. Run a new business without you in the know and sedate you when you tried buying your way out. I imagine that he finally got to show you the man he'd always dreamed of being that night. Of course, Travis was at the center of it all, introducing me, convincing Sam to partner with me, and suggesting new products for bigger paydays. I hadn't been convinced that I was coercing the right sibling until then."

My fists clench under the table, my nails digging into my palms. I breathe through my nose so that I don't choke on my disgust.

"Travis was a natural, planting evidence, feeding valuable information to the police, appearing absorbed in school so that you'd think his head was down. He covered his tracks and then learned to fly. Can you believe he thought of the vasectomy on his own? Brilliant! The night that you went to pay off Sam, he gave him a heads up—told him that you were onto the gang's expansion and thought you were leveraging to take over. He even seeded Sam's inferiority complex and encouraged him to get you under control. Then Travis slipped away with the cops convinced that their informant was exposed and murdered. When they presumed Travis was dead, I told Sam my *concerns*. You know the rest."

"I do," I say through gritted teeth as the weight of the truth crashes down on me.

"Travis didn't know that he could shine until I shoved him out of your shadow. He only lost his touch a short time ago when he met Olivia ... what a nuisance that was. Dr. Marcellus was all too willing to help with that."

My vision tunnels as I stare at the chipped tooth that protrudes through his smug grin. My mind is jarred by all the scenarios I'd conjured over time as they merge with a clear reality.

For so many years, I was convinced that I'd caused Travis' death—I'd involved him in the gang, I'd made poor choices and befriended enemies, I'd risked his safety by naïvely thinking that I could buy our way out of the trap I'd gotten us into. I'd decided to be *myself* and disregarded him.

Discovering that he was alive sent me into a different, yet familiar, tailspin. I'd driven him away with my bullshit—who would want someone like me in their life?

It took me coming here, sitting in this uncomfortable chair, across from this fucking slimebag, to realize that it hadn't been me. Travis was his own person all along. He could have exposed Jared. He could have changed the outcome. He chose this path for himself.

And maybe, just maybe, the person that I'd suppressed all these years once made stupid decisions, but she did so out of hope, desire, and love.

I blink, clearing my vision, then lean on the table, ready to address one final thing.

"Tell me," I say, my voice strong. "What could you have possibly wanted with two hard-working, honest people?"

"Ah," he breathes. "You're not here to find a remnant of hope for your brother." A frown replaces the sneer that seemed permanent. "You came here because of your parents," he jests. "Your dead, dead, dead parents."

I splay my fingers on the table. He won't get me to react. I won't be removed from the room until I get what I came for.

"Nailed it," I say flatly.

He nods, acknowledging my willpower.

"Your parents refused to follow through on our deal. I helped their business grow, and they should have done the same for me. We'd agreed that I'd loan them money, and they'd pay me back with interest," he says, tapping his index finger on the tabletop. "They thought that paying me double the cash they owed would suffice."

I stay frozen, my feet grounded, my palms flat on the table. My breaths barely move my lungs.

His lips curl. "That's simply not the way it works. Once a partner, always a partner. They couldn't even see the money-making opportunity that it could have been."

He pauses, and I wonder if he'll finish his confession or if I'll have to speculate forever. I don't say anything, for fear that the encouragement wouldn't work in my favor.

"You could have gone to any colleges that you wanted, you and your brother both," he finally continues. "I could have given you that. And your parents could have purchased a home four times the size of their existing house—if it were in Leesburg—my homebase. Hell, they could have retired early if they'd agreed to move forward as planned. I could have given them everything they ever wanted. I could have let them *live*."

My anger rises to a boil as his words trail off in self-satisfaction.

Zane had warned me not to come here. He had been right—this won't turn back time, but I needed his confessions.

"So, what, you recruited Travis to pay back a debt? Killing my parents wasn't enough?"

"You know the answer to that. If it wasn't him, it would have been you. In hindsight, that might have been better—I wouldn't be in these." He lifts his arms, the chains clanking on the table. "Travis was loyal. I doubt you'd have been satisfied as my compliant pawn.

"Now, if you'd been eliminated as I'd asked after you started your little play business with Olivia—threatening my livelihood—then you'd be dead and I'd be carrying on as always. But Sam fucked that plan up. He was always a weak son of a bitch."

Well, he topped that off nicely. I hadn't expected this confession ... we had already known that he was the mastermind puppeteer.

I let my silence do the talking.

The metal chair legs scrape across the concrete floor as I stand. I bang twice on the bulletproof window in the center of the door. The guard opens it, letting me out.

When the door slams behind me, it locks, securing me from the motherfucker who stole my family.

"Did you get the confession?" I ask the detective waiting in the hall for me.

She nods. "The way he gave it all up, he probably knows."

"Knows?" I ask.

"He probably figures he's dying in here anyway. With an increased sentence, he gets added benefits and a clean conscience."

I grit my teeth and move briskly down the long hall to the exit, then wait for the guard to let me back into the sterile waiting room.

The air is stale, suffocating. Rushing, I shove through the main doors and out into the hot sun.

He may have thrown the game by moving his king into a vulnerable spot on the board, allowing my queen to clear his conscience, but I've still won.

Olivia

Thursday, July 27th

"Welcome to the third trimester," Dr. Reese, my OB-GYN, says in her singsong voice as I waddle from the ultrasound room to a small exam room.

"Someone should have warned me how uncomfortable it would be to be pregnant in the summer. Perhaps I would have postponed," I say, lowering into the cloth chair with weathered wooden armrests.

She laughs. "Would you have listened?"

"No," I respond, smiling and resting a hand on my growing belly.

This simple action is extraordinary. I'd often dreamed of rubbing my belly, feeling the kicks and flips underneath. It's so much more than I imagined. So much more.

"It'll all be worth it, I promise."

The air conditioning kicks on, and the draft of cold air is refreshing. I sigh with pleasure.

It's a reprieve from my stuffy second-floor walkup in downtown Leesburg, the apartment that came with Elle's newfound inheritance. Despite the stifling heat, it's perfect now that Elle, Zane, and I have brought it into this century. The front window overlooks the shops lining the street, creating my own movie scene to peer out at. I can't wait until Christmas when the street is lined with decorations and people rush around in their ugly sweaters and colorful scarves. The second bedroom is tight, but it's a perfect nursery, already painted gray with cloud decals on the walls.

"I trust that you're taking it easy," Dr. Reese says, checking my blood pressure. The first two checks today by the medical assistant clearly weren't enough.

"I'm trying," I say, breathless. "I've been helping my parents shop for a condo."

My mom and stepdad are so excited to become grandparents that they decided to move back.

Elle and I have been prepping to open our jewelry store. I've been putting together proposals and whisking her away to meetings with banks. Her new handyman, Herald, put in tons of hours at the shop. Elle met him almost a year ago when she started following me. She said she'd stop and visit him and his support dog and was determined to get him off the streets. When she told me last Thanksgiving that she wanted to be like Betty White, she wasn't kidding. It turns out that she and Zane are pretty good at giving people a leg up.

"I'm off to New York this weekend, though," I add, catching the concern in her eyes. "My boyfriend is taking me to see a new play on Broadway."

Liam is persistent and charming beyond belief. You'd think my round belly would be a deal breaker, but apparently, it's not. It helps that Elle has allowed me to use her apartment as much as I'd like, and I use it far too often because the butterflies never cease when I'm around Liam.

For a while, I thought I'd never date again. There were too many unanswered questions. How do you simply accept that something is over? Maybe Camden always knew I'd need closure in the end. Maybe that's why he wrote all those letters. As heart-wrenching as they are, they've brought me peace.

Dr. Reese helps me to my feet, and gives me instructions to stay well hydrated, ushering me out the door just in time.

"You ready?" Elle calls when I step out into the hot sun.

"I am," I say, grinning.

She takes my arm, and we walk slowly to the courthouse.

"We'll still be sisters, right?" I ask Elle as she opens the glass door above the tiled steps.

"As long as you'll have me," she says, giving me a side hug.

Legally, we were never sisters. Turns out that Jared had a hand in our forged marriage certificate, too. Camden Bradley is a ghost. Travis Monroe has taken his place, back from the dead.

I hand my papers to the clerk. "I'd like to change my name."

"My husband lied to me," I blurt an explanation.

She grunts in affirmation as she hands me a confirmation receipt.

I take the paper and breathe in new life.

After

The clip, clop, clip of a uniformed guard's boots echo off the concrete walls. He pays no mind to the sound that's become so familiar. Rounds of guards pass through all day long.

He lies back on his thin pillow, pushing it together with his hands to fluff it up, but it only puffs slightly because there's not much filling inside to work with. The onslaught of disappointment in his accommodations sends him into a shiver. Cold space. Crappy pillow. Thin linens.

The guard's footsteps come to a halt outside his cell.

"Mail," the guard's gruff voice announces, straight to the point.

Shocked that something's arrived for him, he stands and strides to the bars, casually reaching out to take the envelope. The guard's cologne reminds him of a sandalwood scent he used to wear, back when he was free, when he had a large house and a wife who loved him.

He returns to his narrow bunk and sits on the edge, taking in the envelope with a familiar print across the front. It's already been opened and searched for contents that could be used with malicious intent. Even the pleasure of opening his own mail is a thing of the past.

He turns it over, and removes the folded letter. He sets the envelope on the bed next to him, and eagerly unfolds the paper. Nobody comes to see him here. Nobody ever writes. Perhaps she's forgiven him. Maybe he still has a family, after all.

A photo rests inside. There in the colorful image is a brunette—the woman who once loved him—holding the hand of a little girl with curly dark brown hair and a large pink bow atop her head. She's barely tall enough to reach her mother's hand. On the other side, a redhead smiles through the picture at him. Her green eyes are piercing and all-knowing. There's a vibrance around the trio standing there on a sunny sidewalk. Behind them, the building reads B.L.A.R. and, underneath, in a beautiful cursive print, there's a single word: Love.

What are the initials for? He thinks as he savors the image frozen in time, reminding him of all he's lost. When his heart can't take it anymore, he holds up the letter, anticipating it's an extra piece of them of which he can hold on tight. He'll have hope again. It's there he reads:

Dear Travis,
There's only one thing that can be found between lies and revenge.
Love.
We do everything despicable for love.
~ L

Author's Note

Infertility is a difficult subject. The experience we have as individuals tattoos us, marking us forever, but the ink is invisible to others. Please note: every fertility journey is unique, as they are created for individuals with the guidance and recommendations of their providers. For this story, I compiled my own experiences with those of accounts from others, then laced in my experience as a nurse. What this work of fiction captures is not all-inclusive and should not be considered as such.

Likewise, stalking is not normal and is a crime. If you or someone you know is a victim of stalking, or if you'd like to learn more about how you can help prevent and un-normalize stalking, please visit unfollowme.com.

Acknowledgements

In an odd twist, I'd like to start with MLMs—the companies that prey on women and their desires for community, comradery, financial freedom, and hope. Their greed and lack of compassion brought me to a place in my life that was equal parts amazing and terrible. It was in this cultish world that I found an overwhelming need to show my support of others by shopping, spending, and giving all my time. It taught me to use credit cards, kit knap, and hide purchases from my husband. It also introduced me to the most wonderful, caring women—the MLM boss babes—who I'll never forget and never stop supporting. It was here that I found friendships before the #writingcommunity.

To Alexandria, Kayla, and Abby, who encouraged me to chase all my writing dreams and funnel my energy into this—writing—rather than whatever direct sales company had my current attention with all its shimmering false promises. You ladies gave me permission to follow my path and step away. Thank you.

To Kate, who taught me that not all MLM tribes are yucky. You have always been a powerful being that won't conform, instead, creating community for us outliers. You're a goddess, always and forever. Thank you for being you and teaching me to accept me for me, and reminding all of us that our inner Bish deserves to shine.

To my #writingcommunity, I would be lost without you! Bianca, thank you for creating a podcast worth cussing about, then inviting Carly and CeCe to join you. The #TSNOTYAW community you ladies have created means so much, not only to me, but to many writers. Also, you brought me two very important people: Kat and Heather. For that, I'm eternally grateful.

To Kat, you are the meow! You're one of the strongest people I know. Despite your eternal lack of sleep, you keep growing stronger every day. You are incredible and selfless. I'm so glad that I get to know you, and I'm honored you call me your writing bestie.

To Heather, I simply don't know how I thought my world was complete before you. You are a light in my life and a brilliant writer! Thank you for trusting me to read your work when you didn't know me. And thank you for loving me and accepting me, idiosyncrasies, and all.

To Jodi, I'm incredibly thankful for everything you have done, still do, and will continue to do for me. My writing is better because of you. You ask me the tough questions, then make sure I do the near-impossible work of answering them. More so, you accepted the part of me that was struggling, disorganized, and utter chaos, then taught me to own it. And I cannot wait to see Elizabeth in the world (the OG—I'm incredibly honored Elle gets to be her namesake).

To CeCe, thank you for pushing me to dig deeper, think harder, and create better stories. Thank you for making me see that spies are not the answer (not now, not ever). This story and my MCs are indebted to you for this. Elle and Olivia would be very different women without your intervention.

To my writing group, you ladies bring me joy with your stories, our discussions, and lasting friendships. You pulled me out of my hermit shell and onto Zooms, which I cherish!

Thank you, Lindsay, Megan, Bonnie, and the dynamic duo (Amanda and Lisa Marie), for all your wisdom and encouragement.

To all my beta readers (for this story and others), you helped bring this book and my writing to life, and I'm so very thankful for the time and thoughtful feedback you gave me. Jen, my P2P peep, I'm honored to know you. Keep sending me your romances to read and brighten my days. Haley, keep dreaming and discovering yourself. You are re-markable, and your stories are magical. To the entire #TSNOTYAW community, thank you for your encouraging, funny, and supportive existence. Huck, you're a positive glimmer in this writing world, and I'm so grateful for you. Kiersten, thank you for sharing your realities with me, and reminding me I'm not alone and sacrifices are acceptable (our children will appreciate us, and our pillows will last longer than their counterparts). Nidhi, you've taught me what strength and positivity really look like, infused with comic relief in tough times. Elaine, thank you for always smiling and asking the best, well-thought-out, and engaging questions—if I ever need to speak publicly, I hope you're in the audience.

To Saida, thank you for always encouraging me and checking in on me. Thank you, friend, for always being in my corner. To Bre, thank you for always making time in life for me, and for allowing our friendship to never falter even when you don't hear from me for extended periods of time. To my co-workers, Donna and Kristina, thank you for encouraging me to follow my dreams and find a semblance of work-life balance. To the countless people who checked in, encouraged, and motivated me, thank you.

To Alex and Tina, thank you for giving me a chance and helping me turn a story I love into something worth sharing with the world. Alex, thank you for believing in me and always being in my corner. Tina, I thought I knew what a challenging edit was, but then you showed me otherwise. Your edits, bred from honesty, morphed this book into what it is, and I'm eternally grateful for that. And both of you, thank you for being flexible, for understanding each writer is unique, and for adapting and adjusting to allow this book to change far beyond what any of us originally thought it would. Then, when I thought it couldn't improve, you sent me a request for a "surprise" edit—and a surprise it is! You believed in me enough that you'd suggest one more round of revisions, and for that, I'm grateful. Add in the incredible Bonnie (who I'm eternally indebted to and thankful for) with her brilliance and selflessness in helping me brainstorm and restructure, and voila! This book is born. Thank you for giving me this chance and investing in me!

My family... I saved you for last because I knew I'd feel all the big emotions.

Mom, thank you for the many times you have helped (and no doubt will help) us with the kids, and for giving them the grace that, often, I cannot. Thank you for showing me that life isn't all the hard things, but what we learn from those things, and how we recreate ourselves when we pick ourselves up from the rubble.

Dad and Jane, thank you for making me practice my spelling words a million times (no, I still can't pronounce or spell some of them). Thank you for teaching me I need to pay the bills and find the balance between reality and dreams while also being on my side and believing in me. Jane, thank you for teaching me not to suppress my inner perfectionist but to, instead, use it for good. Dad, thank you for teaching me that it's good to have a passion, that hyperfocusing on it is normal, and that it's okay when new passions come along.

To my siblings:

Ashley, I love you. You deserve the world. In this story, Bella dog gets an alternate happy ending that I hope you'll love.

To my brothers, all the buttons you've pushed have given me personality, dark inner dialogue, and a twisted sense of humor.

Tay, you and Sarah helped me create Elle, who is no doubt a little like you (Tay), in more than one way.

Austin, keep smiling, because it brightens the room.

Cam, you're an incredible powerhouse and a human who sees everyone for who they are—accepting them and teaching the rest of us to be a little more open.

Kolton, thank you for flinging shit at me and allowing me to poorly attempt to sling it back (and Shawna, thank you for putting up with his ass).

Matty, you are stronger than you will ever know; please remember that, and that we love you so very much.

To my in-laws, Tracy, Kevin, Brittany, and Brett, thank you for believing in me, and understanding our chaotic life.

And to all the grandparents (mine and Mat's), thank you for encouraging me and understanding the same of our always busy existence.

To my children, you three are everything wonderful and aggravating in this world. I needed each one of you, and I will continue to need you every moment of every day for the rest of my life. I'm so incredibly grateful I get to be your mom. I'd also be forever thankful if you allb would stay in bed at bedtime and not wake me up in the middle of the night. Love you!

To my husband, Mat. You are my biggest fan, and that's everything to me. You encourage me, push me, and believe in me when nobody else in this world does. You make me do the hard stuff, and you encourage me to balance life. You never get upset when I hyperfocus—you just understand. You love me beyond words, which is an immense privilege. Thank you for always believing in me. I'm so lucky to have you as my partner. Loves!

About the Author

Hannah D Sharpe is an American suspense author. She is a member of WFWA and SinC. Hannah is a nurse who historically specialized in emergency medicine and nursing education, and is now thankful for alternative career options as she navigates motherhood with three young kids ... while working from home as an appeals and grievances nurse. She's also very grateful her husband gets home from work at 2 p.m. In her (not so) free time, Hannah listens to and reviews lots of audiobooks. She lives in Marysville, Washington with two sons, a middle daughter, a supportive husband, and a moody cat, where they constantly juggle time and coordinate extracurricular activities. *Between Lies and Revenge* is her first novel.